PLAYED BY THE EARL

BOOK FIVE IN THE LORDS OF DISCIPLINE
SERIES

ALYSON CHASE

Cover image by Dar Albert.

Visit the author website: http://www.alysonchase.com

ISBN-13: 978-1-944802-09-7
ISBN-10: 1-944802-09-6

A Note from Alyson

This book is a work of fiction. Even with the wonder of the internet as a research tool (or maybe because of it), I will make mistakes in some of my historical facts. My focus was in crafting a fun and toe-curling story. There *was* a man named Sir Raffles who was accused of financial misconduct in one of his posts. After he cleared his name, he went on to become Lieutenant-Governor of Bencoolen and played a part in the founding of modern Singapore. It is also true that the British, even while expanding their empire, were pivotal in the elimination of the global slave trade. If you do see any inaccuracies in my book, I'll always appreciate an email letting me know. Readers in this genre are impressively knowledgeable and I tip my hat to you.

Also, I feel the need to insert a word of caution. The characters in the book get up to some kinky good times. John likes to, in today's parlance, mind-f*ck with his partners. There are some predicaments in this book that are decidedly not safe unless the practitioner is experienced. Don't use this book as any sort of reference. Please, have sex responsibly.

Chapter One

London, 1818

The pendulum of the metronome swayed to and fro, its unceasing ticking as irritating as a small pick digging into his brain. The device had been adjusted to pulse every one and a half seconds. The unfulfilled expectation was its own form of torture. The mind wanted the regular, once-per-second beat of a clock, and the difference between expectation and reality had John Chaucer, Earl of Summerset, digging his fingertips into his thighs. His hand itched to hurl the infernal contraption against the wall.

He could only imagine how the naked and blindfolded lady-bird standing on tip-toe upon the small wooden chair with a noose around her neck felt about it.

She knew it was a game. She knew John's punishments culminated in pleasure. Yet still she quivered, aswirl in anticipation...and trepidation.

The mind was a funny thing.

John pulled out his pocket watch to check the time. Still two minutes remaining. He blew out a silent breath.

Cyrus, the man who had set up this predicament play, leaned against the opposite wall. They were in the Amethyst Room of The Black Rose, the Venus club that catered to more unusual inclinations. The American banker had become a friend of sorts during their acquaintanceship at the club. Enough so where John had been hard-pressed to think of a reason to refuse him when the man had asked for his assistance to set up a game for one of the club's women.

What John couldn't figure out was why he'd wanted to refuse. He usually adored scenes such as these. When the woman was willing, it gave him a rush like no other to manipulate her mind, make her question reality until need and fear made her body shake with the thrill of it.

He glanced at Suzy, and yes, right on schedule, a tremor rippled through her luscious body, her small breasts jiggling, her dark nipples hard as buttons.

John leaned his head against the wall and adjusted himself. Such a beautiful sight before him and still only half-hard. Perhaps he truly was getting old as his friends had joked last week.

Cyrus dragged his gaze off of Suzy. He looked expectantly at John.

Time to get this charade over with. John straightened and approached the woman. "I'm pleased you've learned to hold your tongue as you wait. Are you ready for your punishment?"

"Yes, my lord. My apologies once more for spilling my wine on you." Suzy's voice was high and breathy. She turned her head, following his footsteps through sound alone.

John stopped next to Cyrus and took the end of the rope from his hand. The rope travelled over a beam in the ceiling before coiling around Suzy's throat. Cyrus had kept just enough pressure on it to make the woman believe it was tied fast to the beam.

"I know you're sorry, but still one must pay for one's mistakes." John leaned against the wall and adjusted his grip on the rope. If Suzy fell, it would slide harmlessly through his fingers, causing no injury to the girl. "Wouldn't you agree?"

She flexed her shoulders. By this point, her arms tied behind her back must be burning with the need to adjust their position. "Yes, my lord. And I know how much you like your finery."

John twisted his lips. The burgundy stain on his peach-colored waistcoat was a necessary evil of this scene. His valet would be most seriously displeased. He supposed that was why Cyrus had asked him for his participation. It was most believable that John would be upset over the ruination of an article of clothing.

Too bad Suzy didn't know that Cyrus had intentionally jostled her, causing the spill.

"You still have the option to make amends by cleaning the garment." John tugged at the hem of the apple-green waistcoat he'd had the foresight to bring with him that night as a replacement. "It will only take you several hours of scrubbing."

She wrinkled her nose. "No, thank you, my lord. I'd rather have my punishment over and done with." She swallowed and angled her neck, her skin scraping against the rope. "I think."

Cyrus circled the woman, running his finger along her waist.

Suzy jolted but remained silent. She and John had played in the past but the last several months she had seemed uninterested in his touch. John had a sneaking suspicion as to why. Would she object, thinking it was him stroking her skin?

Cyrus came around and stood next to him. He looked at John and raised his eyebrows.

John nodded. "Your punishment is almost at an end."

Cyrus struck a bit of flint against steel, sending sparks cascading to the rough wooden floor.

Suzy squeaked and edged away.

John made the rope pull tighter about her neck, keeping his eyes trained on her. The mind truly was a curious thing. She must know that if he wanted a flame he would merely pick up one of the candles about the room as Cyrus was now doing. He would have no need to strike a flame anew. But the sound effects were an integral part of the manipulation. Hearing them helped to circumnavigate the rational part of the brain, making her uneasy as to what would come next.

John took the candle Cyrus handed him and released the end of the rope, making sure there was nothing it could catch on.

The American waded silently into the sea of pillows lain about the chair and stood in front of Suzy.

"This punishment shouldn't be too harsh." John stepped closer and raised the candle so the light flickered across her bare arse. "I remember how much you used to enjoy playing with Sutton after all." A blatant lie. She was the one girl who had outright refused to work with the Baron of Sutton, John's close friend and owner of The Black Rose. The baron enjoyed bringing fire play into his bed sport. His flame and wax were now reserved solely for his wife, but when he used to play at the club, Suzy would make sure she was occupied doing anything, or anyone, else.

John moved the candle closer, letting her feel the heat from the flame.

She screamed and flung herself forwards, unheeding of the noose. The rope slid easily over the beam and Suzy tumbled, right into Cyrus's waiting arms. He staggered back and they both fell to the cushioned floor.

Suzy rubbed her flushed face against Cyrus's chest, dislodging the blindfold. She glared up at him from her one exposed eye. "You! I should have known you were behind this."

Cyrus chuckled and untied her wrists. He chaffed her arms. "And you shouldn't have told me your dream about a rope around your neck if you didn't want this to happen." He nuzzled her throat.

John blew out the candle. Another successful mind game. Some sort of thrill should have passed through him.

Suzy smacked Cyrus's shoulder, but there was no heat behind it. "You know I hate fire."

"But you love being scared," he replied.

"I adore that you know me so well." She dug her fingers

into the back of Cyrus's head and pulled him to her.

John blew out his cheeks. Another nauseatingly happy couple. Why couldn't people merely enjoy fucking anymore? Everyone had to have *feelings* nowadays. develop a tendre before tupping. It was all dreadfully dull.

He turned to leave, but Cyrus's words stopped him at the door. "You're going? I'm certain Suzy and I can think of an inventive way to thank you."

John turned. Suzy was draped over Cyrus, her lithe body a delicious inducement. Her eyes glittered, the excitement from the game still evident in her smile.

He should accept the invitation. It didn't look as though he'd be able to play with the woman much longer, and she had been one of his favorites. But Cyrus's looks were becoming much too proprietary and Suzy gazed at the American as though he placed the stars in the sky just for her. No, those two would stop playing with others and belong only to each other soon enough.

Another pairing. John forced his upper lip to remain uncurled. "Thank you, no. It's time I returned home."

Cyrus squeezed Suzy's hip. "All right. You celebrated your birthday last week, did you not? I guess old men need their sleep."

"Oh!" Suzy nodded at John while tracing a pattern on Cyrus's shirt. "Much joy. Was it your fortieth?"

"I have just attained five and thirty," he said through gritted teeth. Yanking open the door, he stepped through, slamming it shut on Suzy's, "I could have sworn someone said he was forty."

John stomped down the hall to the main room. At this time of morning, it was nearly empty and he could see at a glance that Sutton wasn't among the men. Although his friend managed the club with his wife, he was rarely in attendance. He was probably snuggled up tight to his bride, snoring away in domesticated boredom, slinking into decrepitude with every breath.

John accepted his greatcoat and hat from the footman

and plucked up his walking stick. He smacked the head into his palm. The sting on his skin from the thirty-six rubies encrusted into the nob only served to increase his irritation.

"Your carriage is being brought around, my lord," the footman said.

John nodded and strode outside. The brisk early morning air hit him like a slap to the face. The sky was a sooty grey, the color that foretold when sunrise was only minutes away. The time when all good men of sense were winding up for their next round of debauchery.

A muted roar of laughter at the corner of the cross street caught his attention. He walked to the end of the short drive and looked down the street. A group of five young bucks swayed together as they sang a lusty song.

John rubbed his breastbone. Not too long ago that had been him and his friends. Perhaps they had never sung, badly or otherwise, but the five of them had ripped through London with the same *joie de vivre*. They hadn't turned for home and bed at the first signs of morning light.

John's shoulders rounded. He'd just come from a club that catered to his every desire. Been offered an invitation to indulge in wicked pleasures. He should have felt as those boys did. Exuberant. Invincible. As though he straddled the world.

Instead, exhaustion weighted him down. Ever since the prime minister had told him his services were no longer desired, an insufferable malaise had slowed his step. No matter how many hell houses or clubs he patronized, he couldn't escape the boredom of an early retirement. And the hell of it was, he couldn't even blame Liverpool. The prime minister had no choice but to let him go. His identity as a spy was fast becoming the worst-kept secret in London, at least among the roughs and criminals he targeted.

John had, in point of fact, become useless.

Another shout went up, and John glared at the men. Insufferable pups. They had the world by the ballocks and didn't even know it.

The club's footman hurried to his side. "Your carriage is here, my lord."

"Thank you." John looked to his coach. Wilberforce sat on the driver's bench, even though John had told him not to wait up. He gave his stick a twirl. Perhaps Wil would be up for a drink at Simon's before retiring for the night.

With one last glance down the street, John turned for his carriage. And paused. He narrowed his eyes, tracking the small shape that brushed past the group of bucks. The boy's gait was exceedingly casual as he bumped into one of the men. Too casual. And unfortunately for him, the man he targeted wasn't nearly as inebriated as his friends.

"You buggering bounder!" The man grabbed the back of the boy's collar and yanked him to the ground. "Give it back!"

John removed his hat and gave it to the footman.

"My lord?" he asked.

"Give me a moment." John stole down the pavement towards the fracas, not that stealth was needed. No one was taking any account of him.

The boy crab-crawled away, and the loud-mouth grabbed him by the boot and dragged him back.

"Please, sir," the boy cried. "I didn't do nobody no 'arm."

"You stole my watch." The man roughly went through the boy's pockets, came up triumphantly with a gold pocket watch. "You're a thief. A pickpocket."

"Well, no 'arm's done. Everything's back proper." The boy got his feet under him and made to stand.

The larger man planted his boot into the boy's shoulder and kicked him back down.

"Come on, Alfie," one of the man's friends said. "Let it be. You have your watch back."

"I don't take kindly to someone stealing from me." Alfie drew his lips back and grabbed the lad by the collar. "This sneak deserves to be taught a lesson." He shook the boy roughly.

A soft 'eep' reached John's ears.

John sighed. This was not the excitement he had been looking for. "All right, that's enough." He stepped into the light of the gas lamp. Truly, he enjoyed knocking about a thief as much as the next man, but only when the odds were more evenly matched. The thief in question was short in stature and round in belly, hardly the fiercest opponent. And if he had achieved three and ten years of age, John would be surprised. "You have your watch back. You won't beat a child over it."

Alfie tossed the boy to the ground and swung around to face John. "Is that right? And who the hell are you?"

"The Earl of Summerset," he said mildly. Sometimes a title was a lovely tool to drop into a conversation. It put the right sort of person in his place.

Unfortunately, Alfie wasn't the right sort of person. "And I'm Viscount Devlin. The Marquess of Havenbridge is my father. As I see it, I'm doing a public service. If every right-minded person kicks the gutter rats hard enough, perhaps they won't show their filthy heads anymore."

The gutter rat in question rose to his feet. He held himself with a quiet prepossession, and John raised the estimate on his age. Such things were difficult to determine, however, with dirt streaked across half of the boy's face.

Summerset pulled his silk handkerchief from his pocket, simultaneously sliding his two-inch dagger from his sleeve to his hand. He palmed the blade, using the handkerchief to hide the metal's sheen. "You can kick up your heels all you want, but do it somewhere else." He fluttered the bit of lavender fabric at the man. "Now run along home to daddy. I'd hate for the marquess to receive a bill from a surgeon to patch up his son. I hear his finances aren't what they used to be."

A low blow to be sure. Havenbridge was in debt to half the ton but it was poor form to publicly acknowledge such a thing.

Summerset cared sod all for being polite to arseholes.

Alfie's face went blotchy with anger. He stepped forwards, hands clenched at his sides. "Lord or not, I'll have your head. I'll—"

A throat was gently cleared behind Summerset. From the way Alfie fell back a step, Summerset could only assume that his driver and right-hand man, Wilberforce, was pointing his trusty blunderbuss at the lot of them. An antiquated and unwieldy weapon, but effective in shutting men up just the same.

Wilberforce moved closer to John, his distinctive tread, one heavy step followed by a slight drag of his left foot, as welcome a sound as any to his ears.

"Perhaps it's time for you and your friends to run along home," Summerset said. "I believe you've had sufficient entertainment for the night." He crooked his fingers, beckoning the street urchin to stand behind him.

The lad didn't need to be told twice. He darted forward, putting John's body between himself and Alfie.

"Come on." One of the friends slapped Alfie on the back. "We've time for one last drink at The Pidgeon Hole if we hurry."

Alfie looked from John to Wilberforce and back again, his nostrils flaring. "Fine," he bit out. "The smell of trash is making me sick anyhow." And with one last glare, he stomped away, his friends trying to cajole him back into good humor.

John snaked out a hand and grabbed the boy by the back of his collar as he tried to sneak off. "Not so fast. Isn't it late for you to be out and about? Where's your home?"

The boy ran the back of his wrist under his nose, inhaling a phlegmy breath.

John winced.

"Iffen the night's good enough for yer lot to be out and about, it's good 'nuff fer the likes of me." The disdain dripped as thick as treacle from his reedy voice. He jutted up his grimy chin, and the light from the gas lamps fell on his face.

John's breath hitched. There was a softness, a roundness, to the child's face that spoke of youth, but the eyes staring impertinently back at him held no such immaturity. They were striking, a blue so clear that they seemed to glow above the dirty cheeks. Or were they purple? Regardless, intelligence glimmered behind them. Intelligence, and a shrewdness one could only develop through harsh experience.

Wilberforce grunted behind him, his version of a laugh, and John tore his gaze from the boy.

John twisted the tip of his walking stick into the ground. "I would expect gratitude over attitude, but I've always said manners were wasted on the young. Now, I'm not going to let you roam about getting into ever more trouble." The boy might think he was the predator, skimming coin from drunken lackwits, but he was but a guppy compared to the sharks that swam through the London streets at night. "I'll take you home. Just tell my man where to."

The boy remained stubbornly silent.

John rolled his head, feeling his neck pop. He could have been home abed by now if he'd left from the club straight off. Saving grubby little street thieves wasn't in the job description of a spy.

His gut hardened. Nothing was in his job description any longer. His status as spy was on permanent hiatus.

"Sir?" Wilberforce shifted. The concern in that one word was obvious, but then Wilberforce always did have a soft spot when it came to strays. If John were to wash his hands of the boy, he would most likely be out of the services of a driver for the next hour or so. The blasted man would follow the child home to ensure a safe arrival.

John blew out a breath. He ran a hand up the back of his head, ruffling his locks into a state of charming disarray. He'd practiced the motion so often in his youth it had become second-nature. "Are you hungry?" he asked the boy. He eyed the rounded belly. The answer was likely a safe bet. The lad must be more successful in his thieving than John thought if it kept him so well-fed. "I'm going to Pierre's to break my fast. You're welcome to join me. His plum cake is quite exquisite."

The boy narrowed his eyes. "Wot's yer game?"

"No game. A free meal, some conversation, and then you can go on your way." When it would be full dawn and Wilberforce wouldn't feel compelled to watch over the boy like a mother hen. "The coffeehouse is only a couple of blocks away. We'll walk."

"And you don't want nothing in return?"

John's chest tightened. No, the child wasn't so innocent after all. Someone had taught him a harsh lesson or two. "Nothing. You have my word."

The boy cocked his head and squinted, examining John like a bug under a microscope before nodding. "All right. I'll let you buy me some 'o that cake. But no funny business."

John refrained from looking heavenward. Like the child was doing *him* a favor. He held out his hand, and was glad of the leather gloves he wore when the filthy hand slipped into his to shake. "Summerset."

"Ned Pickle."

They turned and headed down the block.

"Are you really an earl?" The boy looked sideways at him.

"Of course. Why do you ask?"

"No reason. Didn't think aristos truly wore 'eels that 'igh." He pointed at John's boots, a magnificent pair made of ivory kid-leather with mother-of-pearl buttons. "My da told me yer lot were all fops and dandies, but I didn't believe 'im. Till now."

Another muffled chuckle from behind had John swinging around to glare at Wil. *This is your fault*, he mouthed. Only to save his friend and servant from tiring himself out following the boy had John made such a generous offer. One he was beginning to severely regret.

He adjusted his cravat. "I prefer the term coxcomb myself."

The boy snorted. "*Cox*-comb. You reckon they meant—"

"No." John ground his back teeth. It was only one breakfast. Half an hour at the most of irritating company, and he would have done his good deed for the year.

"Oy, I don't s'pose a cuppa chocolate comes with this cake?"

John closed his eyes. Thirty minutes had never seemed so endless.

Chapter Two

Netta looked at the ruby winking at her from the depths of the man's snowy white cravat. At the server bustling about taking orders from the early morning crowd at the coffeehouse. Anywhere but at the glove of the man who sat across from her—and the two loose threads at the cuff that used to hold pearl buttons. If she didn't look at it, neither would this Summerset fellow.

A bloody earl. She sure knew how to pick them.

He. He knew how to pick them. She was Ned now, and had to remember that. A performance was always more believable when the actor immersed herself in the character.

She pressed her palm to the pocket hidden in her shirt. The two small bulges the pearls made sent a dark thrill through her body. She shouldn't have taken the fop's buttons when they'd shaken hands. It had been risky. Too risky. But she couldn't end the night on a failure. She had been caught by a drunken sop named *Alfie*, and she'd needed to redeem herself.

Pride demanded nothing less.

"Now," Summerset crossed one leanly-muscled leg over the other and flicked a bit of lint from his tight pantaloons. "What's a nice boy like you doing out on a night like this?" An equal measure of boredom and derision coated his words.

Netta tilted her head. What was the man's game? He'd rescued her from a thrashing, of that there was no doubt. But he didn't seem the charitable sort. She'd encountered more than her share of would-be Good Samaritans, eager to save her soul, to know the type.

The server arrived with their plum cakes and drinks, coffee for the earl and a steaming cup of chocolate for her.

"Well?" Summerset tapped his thumb on the rim of his mug. "Aren't you going to entertain me with your tale of woe?"

Netta snorted. "Don't got one," she lied in her false voice. She had at least thirty sorrowful tales, trotting them out when the occasion called, but something told her this man wouldn't believe a one of them.

"You will if you don't choose another profession." He brought the mug to his nose and inhaled. His eyes watched her from over the rim. They were a lovely shade of blue, darker than the afternoon sky yet brighter than sapphires. His blond hair was trimmed to short curls, with two locks on either side of his forehead artfully coiling up towards his crown. His nose was long and straight; his cheekbones high and graceful. It was one of the most symmetrical and beautiful faces Netta had seen. A face she surely would have engaged in a bit of flirting with had she met him at her theatre.

But she had dirt streaked across her face and was pretending to be a boy. Life just wasn't fair.

His penetrating gaze seemed to see beneath her disguise. She itched to adjust her wig, but she knew better than to break character. "Profession? Wot's that?"

"Your profession. Career. In your case, a pickpocket." He cut a precise wedge off the small round cake and delicately placed it in his mouth. He leaned back as he chewed and swallowed. "You're not very skilled at it."

Netta narrowed her eyes. "I'm better than you think." And then, because she could, she picked up the cake whole and shoved it in her mouth, biting off a full half of the pastry. She chewed noisily, enjoying the faint look of horror on the man's features. She was trained to elicit emotional responses, and this man was an easy mark.

He flicked his gaze from her mouth, to the hand holding the cake, down to her wrist.

She tugged at her cuff, pulling it over the bump that protruded below her thumb. The break had healed, but the bone hadn't knitted back together in a flat line.

"Be that as it may, it isn't a profession with any longevity." Summerset pointed at the man who'd shadowed them to the coffeehouse. He looked of similar age to the earl, and next to Summerset, the man's plain clothes looked as drab as a laborer's. "You see Wilberforce there? He has an especial concern for wayward children. I'm afraid if you don't make a good show of at least attempting reform, he'll follow you home like a puppy. He won't leave you be until he knows you're safe." He twisted his lips. "I should know."

The man saw them looking at him and stood from his table. He limped over. "Did you need something?"

"No, Wilberforce, I was merely using you as a cautionary tale on the consequences of a wayward life."

"Yes, sir." Wilberforce returned to his seat. He picked up a newspaper and flicked it open.

Netta opened her mouth, snapped it shut. Her character wouldn't know that the servant had used the incorrect form of address. She shoved the rest of the cake in her mouth and slouched in her chair.

"Sit up straight." The earl pulled a gold lorgnette attached to a chain from his waistcoat pocket and examined her through the lenses. "If I'm to do my good deed for the year by attempting to reform you, the least you could do in return is sit with proper posture when we dine together. Otherwise, it's like eating with a hunched monkey."

She snorted. If that was his biggest problem in life, he had no right to complain. She looked at her empty plate, looked at the door. Pierre's did have lovely pastries, but she didn't think any more would be forthcoming. No need to remain.

"If you don't like eating with me, then I'll leave." Netta slid from her chair, the stretched fabric of her borrowed shirt catching on a splinter on the table. She tugged it free but before she could stand, that damnably quick hand of the earl's snuck out again and grabbed her arm.

'Before you go, I'll have my buttons back." Summerset raised his other hand out and held it in front of her, palm up. "My valet will be in quite a temper if I don't return with those."

Netta blinked. "How long 'ave you known?"

"From the instant you pocketed them." The earl shook his head. "As I said, your talents don't appear to lie in larceny."

The absolute gall of the man. Fuming, Netta pulled the pearl buttons from their hiding place and slapped them on the earl's hand. She had many talents. The bounder had just gotten lucky. And, she was tired. It had been a long night. Her performance would naturally suffer.

He slid the buttons into his waistcoat pocket beside his lorgnette, a smug smile hovering about his lips.

Netta wanted to wipe it right off. For three nights she'd successfully palmed small trinkets and coin from the well-heeled toffs with no one the wiser. Not only did the petty thieving help her get into the mind of her character, but, well, the extra blunt didn't hurt. Her theatre paid very little and she needed to save.

"Do you want another?" he asked.

She looked down at the flaky crumbs, all that remained on her plate. Of course, she wanted another plum cake. It had been laden with butter and sugar and was one of the best things she'd ever put in her mouth. But she should leave before the man called the magistrate. Getting caught twice in one night was fate's way of telling her to quit.

He arched a perfectly curved eyebrow, the self-satisfied condescension extending from his smile to encompass his entire face.

Pride overcame common sense. He thought he had her figured out. That he was one step ahead of her. Her body warmed. She'd make him regret his arrogance. She could be an excellent thief when she put her mind to it. Besides, it was morning. A new day. Her bad luck was in the past.

Sticking around might not be smart, but most of the things she enjoyed weren't.

She sat back down. "Too right I want another."

The earl waved a lazy finger in the air and the server hurried over.

Netta eyed Summerset as he ordered. He had the air of a man who always got what he wanted, which should have made him just like every other toff. But something about Summerset was different, and she couldn't quite put her finger on what.

Well, his clothes, those were certainly different. Even among the preening peacocks of the Quality, lavender silk jackets and pantaloons paired with bright green waistcoats were uncommon. The large jewels on his cravat pin and walking stick were certainly more flamboyant than most men sported. Even his lorgnette had been studded with diamonds.

She shifted in her seat. Now that would be a plum prize. The chain might be a bit tricky but—

"Mr. Pickle?"

Netta jerked her head up. The earl stared at her, his gaze as intense as lightning.

Her lungs stalled. "Wot?" That was what made him different. It wasn't his uncommon good looks or his ostentatious adornments. It was the whip-sharp canniness in his gaze. This earl made it clear he wasn't a man with whom to trifle.

She bit her lower lip. She couldn't lie to herself. His self-possession made her want to trifle.

"I asked if you wanted another cup of chocolate, as well?"

"Too right." Netta covered her wince. Had she already used that line? She hated when a playwright was redundant.

Summerset waved the server off and turned back to her. "Now, what say we...." He snapped his mouth shut, his jaws grinding together.

Netta turned, trying to find what had distracted the earl. She was surprised anything, or anyone, had the power to still the fop's tongue.

A man with a hat pulled low and the tips of his collar poking into his cheeks strode through the door. After a moment's hesitation, he angled his body through the patrons and towards their table. He stopped by the earl's side.

"I must speak with you," the man said.

"Is that so?" Summerset directed a barely perceptible shake of his head behind Netta.

She twisted, and caught Wilberforce settling back into his chair, a worried look on his face.

"It's urgent." The man raised his head to glare at the earl.

Netta sucked in a quick breath. The side of his face, from his jaw to right below his eye, was scarred with ridges of smooth and shiny flesh. His left eye was a faded periwinkle, a striking contrast to the cobalt blue of his right.

She looked at Summerset, saw a flash of the same deep blue in his eyes as he stared up at the man.

Relatives then.

"All right. Speak." Summerset stretched out his legs, crossing them at the ankles, the picture of elegant ease. But his shoulders remained tense.

The man shifted his weight. "In private. It's the least you can do. *Brother.*"

"If this is about more gambling debts, I don't care who hears," Summerset said. "I'm done cleaning up your mistakes. I told you this before, Robert."

The man, Robert, barked out a bitter laugh. "Why would I expect any less? You couldn't even clean up your own."

Fascinating as this show of unbrotherly love was, Netta sensed her opportunity. "Oy, well it don't seem proper me being 'ere for this and I 'ave to get meself 'ome in any case."

She stood as the server approached and snaked out her hand to grab the cake off his tray. If she pressed down on the tray with a little too much force before freeing the pastry, no one was the wiser but her.

As if the waiter were moving through syrup, his tray slowly wobbled, the pot of chocolate sliding to one side. The man tried to counterbalance, but his feet *somehow* tangled around Netta's own, and the tray toppled over along with the server.

Netta squawked, wind-milled her arms in an exaggerated fashion, and landed bum-first on the earl's lap.

He wrapped a strong arm about her waist, steadying her. His gaze dropped to his chest...and the cake crushed into his snowy silk cravat.

"I'm right sorry, I am." Netta brushed at the sticky crumbs. She stuck what remained of the cake between her lips and swiped at the mess with both hands. "Eet 'ill 'ash rit as 'ain."

Summerset gritted his teeth and grabbed her hips. He lifted her off of him as though she weighed no more than a child and examined his cravat. Then he looked back up at her, exasperation wrought in every line of his face. Reaching out, he grabbed the end of the cake and tugged it from her mouth. He sighed. "What was it you were saying?"

She shoved her hands in her pockets and hung her head, trying her best to look like a sulky youth. "It'll wash out, right as rain." When he remained silent, she added, "At least the chocolate pot didn't get you." No, that misfortune had landed on the poor bloke at the next table, who's hair dripped with the sweet, brown liquid.

Summerset twisted his mouth. "As you say. Now—"

"I'll jus' leave you with your brother." Netta backed away. "Thanks fer the breakfast." And without waiting for a reply, she scooted out of the coffeehouse and hurried down the street.

She turned a corner and patted her hidden pocket. The slim leather case she'd lifted from the earl's jacket met her hand, and she couldn't help but grin. Not skilled, was she? She wished she could see his face when he discovered his banknotes were missing, when the pieces came together and he realized the scamp he'd condescended to had finagled him, after all.

She crossed the street, heading in the direction of The Burns Theatre. Cerise was going to scold her for this adventure, she knew. Although her friend would have no compunction over the actual theft, she wouldn't be pleased that Netta had succumbed to the temptation. Again. She could just about hear her friend's lecture on keeping one's emotions in check, on the need for a carefully thought-out plan before taking action.

Netta snorted. Logic was all well and good, but there was something to be said for acting on instinct. For—

A hand grabbed her from behind and yanked her into an alley.

A shock of fear ripped through her body. She struggled against the hold, against the man who dragged her deeper into the shadowed lane.

He pushed her into the wall of a building, and her chin struck the bricks. Ignoring the sting, she spun around, pressing her back against the wall and holding her hands up in front of her.

The man who'd caught her stealing his pocket watch, Alfie, loomed over her. Without his drunken friends around him, he looked even less friendly than he had earlier. And that hadn't been friendly at all.

"What do you want, mister?"

Casually, as though she were nothing more than a fly he was swatting, Alfie raised his arm and struck her with the back of his hand.

She stumbled, landing on a pile of empty crates, and pressed her palm to her burning cheek.

"It's Lord Devlin to you." He straightened the cuff of his jacket. "And what I want is to make it clear that no one, least of all trash like you, steals from me." Grabbing the front of her shirt, he hauled her to her feet.

She didn't see it coming. Just off her triumph over the earl and a tasty breakfast, her internal warning system was too slow. A sharp pain arced into her abdomen, and she gasped.

"Filthy scum." Alfie lowered his face to whisper in her ear. "You're not even worth the time it would take to fetch a magistrate." He pulled his arm back and stabbed her again.

A roar filled Netta's ears. The pounding of her blood, a commotion from the street, it didn't matter. When Alfie pushed her away and the back of her head hit the brick wall, the roar faded away.

She slid down the side of the building, holding her hand to her abdomen. She tilted sideways, her vision closing in on itself. The last things she saw were the heels of Alfie's pumps as they skittered from view.

Chapter Three

"Why?" John craned his neck, trying to keep the thief in sight. He glared at Wilberforce. "Why is it you feel the need to save every stray, sad-luck case you encounter?"

He would have thought that after thirty years of seeing the realities of human nature, Wil would have shed himself of his savior complex. But no, the runaway sneak had piqued his servant's protective instincts and when the boy had slipped away, Wilberforce had followed.

Leaving John no choice but to do the same. It was either trail after Wil or have a discussion he didn't want with his brother. The decision had been easy. And when he'd finally noticed the emptiness of his pocket, his step had quickened until he'd caught up to Wil.

Damned sneaky child. After he retrieved his blunt and gave the boy a good scare, he wasn't quite sure what to do with him. Such inventiveness, distracting John by tripping the waiter, should be rewarded. If it hadn't been his money that had been lifted, John would have been tempted to congratulate the imp.

They waited for a carriage to pass then crossed the street after Pickle. John hesitated. The boy had disappeared. He pointed to the mouth of an alley. "There. He must have gone that way."

Wilberforce nodded and they strode to the mouth of the alley side-by-side.

"Not everyone can be saved," John reminded him. "The boy is most likely...."

Getting the piss beat out of him.

The arsehole from earlier, Devlin, held Pickle by his collar. Silver flashed, and before John could shout a warning, Devlin had plunged the blade into Pickle's round belly.

Heat flared through John's body. With a roar, he leapt forwards.

Devlin tossed the boy against the wall and took off running.

Indecision stalled John a moment. He longed to tear after Devlin, mete out his own form of justice. No one should hurt a child. But he merely glared at the man's retreating back and dropped next to the boy. He'd handle Devlin later.

"Pickle?" He tapped the boy's smooth cheek, but the lad didn't respond. "Ned?"

"How bad is he hurt?" Wilberforce squatted next to him, an angry red flush darkening his face.

"I don't know." John moved his hands to the boy's torso and frowned. "What the hell?" He pressed again, and instead of pudgy flesh, a soft bed of feathers met his fingers. He ripped open the shirt and gaped down at the pillow tied around a girl's abdomen.

No, judging by the ripeness of the breasts the padding had hidden, the *woman's* abdomen. Not only was Ned not a boy, she wasn't a child, either.

Two cuts sliced through the pillow, and red streaks stained the fabric. John slid his own knife from his boot and cut the strings holding the pillow in place. He raised the woman's chemise above her trousers, exposing her wounds.

"The cuts don't appear life-threatening." John cursed. "The damned pillow saved her life, preventing the knife from going deep."

The woman mumbled, her eyelids flickering before settling back down.

John skimmed his fingertips over her hair. He pulled off the wig before examining her scalp. "She's got quite the lump."

Wilberforce picked up the wig and pillow. "She'll need a quiet place to rest after the sawbones sees her."

John rolled his gaze in Wil's direction. "You are all that is subtle." He gathered the woman in his arms, her padding-free frame still feeling soft and plush against his body. "Go hail a hackney." He stood, a slight twinge in his knee telling him he'd done so too quickly. Bloody birthdays. "We have a new stray for you to protect."

* * *

Netta swam through the swirling fog. The back of her head throbbed, and memories of the alley twisted through her brain.

She blinked awake. A satyr danced above her, his frolics on the ceiling joined in by three women in Greek gowns that barely covered their abundant curves.

What the....?

She turned her head and shrieked. A face was planted on the bed not two inches from her own.

The girl jerked back. "You're awake. Good. I thought perhaps you'd never wake, and that I wouldn't ever get a chance to serve as a lady's maid. If you'd died, my plans for advancement would have been severely thwarted."

Netta scooted away until her back was against the headboard, ignoring the dizziness that threatened. She searched the strange bedchambers she was in, the salacious fresco on the ceiling, but no explanation appeared. "What? Who are you? Where am I? What is going on?"

The girl, or young woman as Netta now saw, stood and dropped a quick curtsy. "I'm Mags and we're in the Earl of Summerset's home. The one in London, not his country estate. Either of them. Nor his castle in the south of France. Cor, how I'd love to see that." Mags clasped her hands to her bosom and sighed. "As to what's going on, I have no earthly idea. No one tells me anything. Just to watch you and make sure you're all right and serve as your abigail if you woke."

"If?" Netta raised an arm to feel her aching head, and pain sliced through her side as the skin stretched.

"When." Mags skipped to a pitcher on a side table and poured a glass of water. "I'm sure I said when."

"I'm sure you said no such thing." Summerset glided through the open door. "What have I told you about lying, Mags?"

"To only do it when it will improve my situation and there's no chance of being caught." Mags handed Netta the glass. "I don't think she would have caught me out." The girl turned wide brown eyes on Netta. "Would you?"

Netta looked at the maid, looked at the earl, and took a large swallow of water. Truly, her head must have suffered quite a blow.

A fat orange-haired cat trotted into the room and twined around Summerset's ankles. The earl toed it aside and stepped to the bed. "You'd best be wary of this one, Mags." Summerset ran his eyes up and down her body.

Netta followed his gaze. An unfamiliar night rail, one made with a great deal of semi-transparent lace and without much substance, sloped off one of her shoulders. She hiked it back into place and pulled the coverlet up to cover her bosom.

"Our guest makes her living at deception," the earl continued. "*She* is quite an expert at it."

Netta frowned. The judgment in his voice was rich. Her foray into petty theft was recent. Besides, nothing she had done could compare with the deceit baked into the Beau Monde. Her first teachers had been from men of his station.

"I'm an...." She trailed off. It wouldn't do to tell the man her profession. What he deemed deception, she knew to be protection. The less he knew about her, the easier it would be to escape him, should escape become necessary.

She wrapped herself back into her character. The sex might have changed, but the identity of street urchin remained. "So, I'm a girl." She sniffed. "Wot's it to you?"

The coverlet slid to the side, and she grabbed for it. When she righted it, an orange head popped over the edge of the bed and the cat crawled next to her, butting her with its head. She set her glass on the side table and let the animal sniff her hand.

Summerset leaned his shoulder against the bottom post of the bed and crossed one ankle over the other. His pantaloons, lime-green today, stretched snugly over leanly-muscled thighs. And other things.

She glanced away, heat rising to her face, and stroked the cat's back.

"Your deceit is nothing to me," he said. "Nothing but a curiosity. Why pretend to be a boy?"

"It's safer." And that was the truth. Walking around London at night as a woman was fraught with trouble. She loved the nights she and Cerise would don trousers and wigs and stroll the city streets after dusk. The freedom a costume gave her was immeasurable. A man such as the earl could never understand.

"Mags, I believe I hear my brother at the door, and you know how he likes to tromp mud in." Summerset crossed his arms. "Will you go tell him to wipe his feet before dirtying the carpet in my drawing room?"

"Of course, my lord."

"And take this, will you?" Summerset picked up the cat and handed it to the maid, but not before giving it a small scratch to the chin.

Mags took the animal and skipped from the room.

Netta stared at Summerset.

He stared back at her.

The silence grew thick, uncomfortable.

She tucked the coverlet firmly about her waist. "You stopped that git from beating me? I s'pose I owe you one."

"Ah, you recognize debts, do you? I wasn't sure someone in your situation would."

"Wot's that s'pposed to mean?" Netta rolled to her knees and planted her hands on her hips. Nausea slid through her stomach and her head spun, but she ignored it. "You lot think jus' because I'm poor I don't know right from wrong?"

"You did steal from me. Twice." He patted his jacket pocket. "Luckily for you my banknotes are back in their rightful place."

"Only because that other man stopped me." She shuffled forwards on her knees and stabbed the air with her index finger. "I got you good."

Summerset's lips twitched. "But you were caught nonetheless. And by someone not as kindly as I am." His expression hardened. "Perhaps if you were a better student of right from wrong, you wouldn't have been stabbed."

"Stabbed?" She slid her hand to her abdomen. Her fingers brushed the bandage under her night rail, and she winced. "I'd forgotten." She sank back on her heels. What an odd thing to forget. "It felt like he 'it me."

The earl pushed off the bedpost. "You were fortunate with your padding. The blade barely entered you. Now, as I can no longer call you Mr. Pickle, thank all that is holy, tell me your true name."

"Netta." She didn't see the harm in him knowing that much. But she flashed him a wide smile when she said, "Miss Netta Pickle."

He winced. "It had to still be Pickle."

"Nothing wrong with me name." Cerise said she was always getting herself into one pickle or another. She thought it suited.

"Well, Miss Pickle, how do you fare? The doctor believes you will make a full recovery."

Considering she'd been stabbed and knocked about, she was feeling remarkably well. "Right as rain. If you'll jus' point me to my clothes, I'll be on me way." She hopped to the ground, and black dots swam before her eyes. She swayed on her feet, the earl's hands on her elbows the only thing keeping her upright.

Remarkably well might have been a stretch. "Just a bit

light-headed." She blinked, but there were still two devilishly good-looking earls frowning down at her.

"I brought you to my home to heal." He guided her back into the bed and pulled the coverlet over her form. "I won't have you insulting my hospitality by leaving too early."

"If you put it that way," she murmured. She sensed no threat from him. No reason why she had to leave the soft sheets and fine attentions of a grand house. Not yet in any case. "If it makes you 'appy, me lord, I s'pose the least I could do is stay a bit longer."

"Your condescension knows no bounds." He brushed a strand of her hair off her cheek.

The caress was gentle, one a parent might give to a beloved child, and unbidden tears burned her eyes.

She turned her head so he wouldn't see them.

He was a stranger, one showing a bit of kindness. That shouldn't be something that made her want to weep.

She rolled onto her shoulder, giving Summerset her back. It had been a trying day. A couple hours sleep and she'd be back in her usual spirits.

The door eased closed behind her, and Netta let herself relax into blessed sleep.

Chapter Four

John stopped at the bottom of the stairs, looking back in the direction of Netta's room. "Did you find him?" he asked the man lurking in the shadows.

"Yes." Wilberforce separated from the wall and shuffled towards him.

"Has the message been sent?"

Wil nodded. "Lord Devlin won't be hurting children any time soon." His gaze flicked up the stairs. "Or at least what he believes to be children. He'll be limping as badly as me for the next few months until he recovers."

"Who did you take with you?" Over his years as a spy, John had developed a network of men who were willing to dirty their hands for the right amount of blunt. Or if the fancy took them. And delivering a punishment to a man who would stab a woman or child would strike many of their fancies.

John tapped the balustrade. He wished he could have joined them. Hearing Devlin squeal like the pig he was would have been gratifying.

"I took no one. I handled him on my own."

"Wil." John pressed his lips together. He'd known the man since they were both children. Such foolishness shouldn't have surprised him.

Wil neatly changed the subject, nodding to the drawing room. "Your brother seems in high dudgeon. Or more so than usual. Go talk with him."

"And now you give me orders in my own house." John arched an eyebrow. "We truly need to discuss the finer points of the terms 'master' and 'servant'."

Wil snorted. "Go on. And don't be too hard on him. Brothers shouldn't fight so."

John flipped his hand at Wil in a dismissive gesture and turned for his drawing room. He wasn't the brother that needed the lecture.

Robert sat in the seat below the window, his elbows propped on his knees, his face buried in his hands. He lifted his head when John shut the door.

"I've bungled it up." His brother's eyes were rimmed red. His scars seemed to stand more to attention against the pallor of his skin.

"Of course you have." John circled behind his desk and dropped in his chair. His brother could never pay him a call to say he'd invented a new method to improve their harvest, or found employment, or even found a woman. No, the only time John saw him was when Robert needed his help. "What have you done this time?"

Robert laced his fingers together, his knuckles going white. "I lost the deed to Crowhaven."

John's heart stopped. "Repeat that."

"Crowhaven. It's gone." Robert shot to his feet and paced the room. "I should have won. The dice were going my way all night."

John pressed his palms flat to his desk, the wood cool beneath his heated skin. Slowly, he pushed himself to standing. "Do you mean to tell me that you gambled your estate away in a game of hazard?" His chest heaved with his rapid breaths. His mouth went bone dry. "Your home that was left to you from our father's mother? The property that contains England's only known supply of chromite? That's what you lost?"

Robert clenched his hands in front of his chest. "I had him, John. He threw a main of nine. The odds were in my favor. He bid twenty thousand pounds, and all I had was—"

"Everything." John's legs crumpled and his arse hit the chair hard. "Crowhaven was everything to the Summerset estate. The source of all our wealth." Dark circles danced in his vision, and he blinked. "We're ruined."

"I'll win it back." Robert started pacing again. "No man can be that lucky every night. I'll challenge him to another game."

"You'll do no such thing." John turned his chair to stare out the window. He could fix this. He had vowed the House of Summerset would never be impoverished again, and he would stand by that oath.

A watery reflection stared back at him in the glass. Instead of a man, a small boy. Instead of a silk jacket, a torn and dirty rag clothed the image.

His hand trembled, and he balled it into a fist. "Who holds the deed?"

"Sudworth. Harlow Sudworth."

John tried to picture the man. They had only met once or twice, but his story was known well in London. Born to a family of little means, Sudworth had sailed for India as a young man. He'd returned wealthy. Wealthy enough that he was allowed entrée into the higher echelons of a society that respected birth above all else.

And now he held everything that John had worked for his entire life.

"I can beat him." Robert gripped the back of a chair and leaned forwards. "I just need one more game."

John steepled his fingers and blew out a breath. "You're a fool, just like father." He ignored the way his brother blanched. He couldn't understand it. They had seen the horrors of unchecked gambling, watched as their father bankrupted their estate. How could his brother have fallen into the same trap?

His mind whirled. He wouldn't accept the loss. He had spent his life figuring his way out of sticky situations. All he needed was a plan.

"Go home," he told Robert. "Until I recover your deed, I don't want to see your face." John stood and went to the brass urn in the corner of the room. He plucked an ebony walking stick from the pile and buffed the round nob against his sleeve. And without sparing another glance at his brother, he strode from the room and out of his townhouse.

His regular driver took him to Sudworth's home. When John gave the butler his card, it was only a moment before he was shown into the man's study.

"Lord Summerset." The smile Sudworth gave him was pleasant, but he remained seated behind his desk, and John recognized the insult. "What a surprise this visit is. How might I be of service?"

Without waiting for an invitation, John took the seat across from the desk. He draped his left leg over the armrest and lounged back. "Let's not play games, Sudworth. My visit can hardly be a surprise. You know you have something of mine."

Sudworth pulled a thick cigar from a wooden box on his desk. He drew the cylinder under his nose, inhaling deeply. "Do I? I know I recently acquired a lovely little estate in Shropshire, but I do believe that belonged to your brother." He pulled a candle from the corner of his desk and lit the cigar, his cheeks hollowing. "You're not going to try to claim it was part of your entail, are you?"

Wouldn't that have been lovely. How much more profitable would his metallurgy business be if he'd had control over all the resources? All the times he'd overpaid his brother for the raw ore out of a sense of fraternal duty had been poorly compensated.

"I make no such claims," John said. "I am here to discuss terms. I'd like to purchase the property."

A cat, pure white excepting one golden patch over its eye, meowed loudly from the door and trotted into the room, heading for the desk. It jumped onto Sudworth's lap and butted its head into his hand.

Sudworth scratched the animal's chin. "I'm certain you would. The mining operation on the property is quite valuable."

"Only to me." John pointed his toe, letting the emeralds

on his boot catch the light. "I am the only person in England who uses chromite because I hold letters patent on my process of steel manufacture. The mine is useless to you."

The cat batted at the cigar, and Sudworth teased the animal with it, bringing it into reach then pulling it away from its paw. "You are an interesting man, Summerset. I've heard much about you these past months."

John's foot paused a moment before continuing its swing. "I personally leave the *on dit* to women, but to each his own." He curled his lip as the cat stretched out on Sudworth's abdomen, and the man cooed softly to it. "I didn't take you for an animal lover."

"It takes a cold man not to appreciate the intelligence of cats." Sudworth kicked his legs up on his desk, making a flatter bed for the animal. "Delilah here has had me wrapped around her paw since I found her hunting mice in a back alley." He looked up. "You wouldn't be in the market for a kitten? I have eight I'm trying to find homes for. Good homes, mind you. You don't have a dog, do you?"

John blinked. He looked over his shoulder. No one stood there laughing at the joke. He swung back around. Sudworth was serious.

"No dog, and I don't want a cat." Well, not another one.

Sudworth shrugged. "Your loss." He smirked. "That seems to be the theme of the day. How badly do you want the deed back?"

"I'll give you twenty thousand pounds." It was worth ten times that, but he knew to start low when bidding.

Sudworth chuckled. "That's sweet." There was a scratch at the door, and Sudworth bellowed, "Come."

A girl in a starched and pressed maid's uniform crept in, holding a tray of tea. "Cook said you'd want this, sir."

He nodded to his desk, and the girl skittered forwards, depositing her burden.

"Pour for me." His voice was hard, mocking, and John

remembered something else he'd heard about Sudworth. They were both members of The Black Rose, and Sudworth's tastes ran towards younger women. If John recalled correctly, Sudworth's predilection was in humiliating proper misses.

At The Black Rose, it was a game that the doxies played along with.

The maid's hand shook, and a splash of tea hit the desk.

But perhaps it was a game Sudworth took too far.

The man waved the girl from the room and took a large swallow of tea. When the door clicked shut, he focused back on John.

"I don't want money," he said. "I'll ask again. How badly do you want the deed?"

John gritted his teeth. "What *do* you want?"

Sudworth tipped a bit of tea into the saucer and held it out for the cat to lap up. "There's a job. One I think you are peculiarly qualified to perform."

John hesitated. "As an earl, you mean?"

"No, as someone who has performed delicate tasks for the Crown." Sudworth put the cat on the floor and dropped his feet, sitting up straight. "You and your friends have done admirable work. Your career need not be over."

John dug his nails into the wood of the armrest. "I'm an earl. I have no career." Perhaps the man was digging. Perhaps he wasn't certain of John's past.

Sudworth chuckled. "Come now. There shall be no pretense between us. You were one of the Crown's top spies. I'm sure you miss the adventure. I know I would."

John's eye twitched. "And I'm to work for you now, is it? In exchange for the deed?" Bloody hell, had Sudworth engineered Robert's loss at hazard in order to get Summerset into this spot? His estimation of the man rose along with his ire.

"Do you know Stamford Raffles?" Sudworth asked.

John nodded. "I know of him. Prinny made him a Knight Bachelor just last year."

"Correct. He also got away with a bit of embezzlement when he was lieutenant-governor of Java. Managed to shift the blame to a chap in the East India Company." Sudworth pursed his plump lips and blew a neat circle of smoke. "I'd like to see him get his comeuppance."

"How?" John tired of the misdirection. As someone who excelled at gaining other people's confidences under false circumstance, he could recognize the talent in others. So far, Sudworth's story stank as badly as a pile of shit.

Plugging his mouth with the cigar, the man reached for a leather folio and removed a folded document. He slid it across the desk towards John. "This letter was never entered into evidence. There was no formal trial, of course, but I know the Home Office maintained a file on him, with witness statements and ledgers."

John picked up the paper. It bore a wax seal, broken, and held the faintest traces of age. He flipped it open and quickly read the letter. "This is his signature?"

Sudworth nodded. "If the Home Office had that letter during the inquiry, he would have faced trial. I want them to see it now."

John tossed the paper on the desk. "Send it to Liverpool. Hell, a low-level magistrate will do."

"The letter came into my hands through...unusual methods. I can't deliver it without exposing myself to scrutiny."

"Which you'd rather not do." John folded his hands across his abdomen.

"Which I'd rather not do," he agreed. "I want you to place this letter in Raffle's file at the Home Office, with no one the wiser."

"The case has been closed. No one will see it."

Sudworth stubbed his cigar out. "It will be reopened. That I can see to. Will you do it?"

John tapped his thumb against his stomach. "I add a letter to a file and you give me my brother's deed?"

Sudworth chuckled. "Give away a hundred-thousand-pound investment for such a trifling? I hardly think so. That is just the first job. But your next task will be as simple. And you are helping bring a criminal to justice. What say you?"

"The property isn't worth such a sum of money to you." Only John's smelts could use the ore to such a profitable purpose.

"No, but it is to you."

And that was the hell of it. Sudworth had him by the ballocks, and the man knew it. He picked up the letter again. "Just add this to the evidence file?"

Sudworth stood, smiling. "As simple as that." He plucked a walking stick from the wall by the door and tucked it under his arm. The nob was ivory, carved in the shape of an elephant's head. Large sapphires formed the eyes, and John had to admit to a tug of cane-envy.

"It is past time for my afternoon stroll," Sudworth said. "Do I have your agreement?"

John rose, sliding the letter into his pocket. "I'll see what I can do."

Placing the letter into the file would be child's play. Finding out what Sudworth was up to would be more of a challenge. But discover it he would.

He rolled to the balls of his feet. Finally, a job worthy of his skills. And when he learned Sudworth's scheme, he'd have leverage over the man. Enough so to reclaim the deed, he hoped.

And if that didn't work, he'd resort to less honorable means. He kept the smile from his face as he brushed past Sudworth and out of his house. The first inklings of an idea were forming in his mind.

Sudworth liked to gamble, and for once, John was eager to indulge the vice.

Chapter Five

Netta peered around the corner, the morning pastry hot in her hand. The hallway remained empty. On the balls of her feet, she stole down the corridor.

What a strange household this was. A longcase clock she'd passed had told her it was twenty past nine in the morning. Not an hour she usually liked to see, but the pangs in her stomach had driven her from bed.

She took a bite of the iced bun. But aside from the cook, who'd been easy enough to sneak past to retrieve her breakfast, no one else seemed to have risen. She could well imagine the earl sleeping until past noon, but were even his servants allowed to luxuriate in their beds? If she—

"There you are," came a voice from directly behind her.

"Gah!" She jumped, and a wedge of the roll clogged her throat. Bending at the waist, she coughed, a spray of crumbs misting from her mouth with each heave.

A strong hand smacked between her shoulder blades. "Good Lord, must you be putting food in your mouth at all turns?"

She rolled her gaze up to glare, her wheezing slowing. She straightened and wiped her mouth with the back of her hand. "Must you be slinking about at all times? With the size of those 'eels, you'd think you might make more of a sound."

Summerset lifted his foot to examine his boot. "They're only an inch high today."

And the earl still stood a foot above her. Netta was only a mite over five feet, to be sure, a fact most annoying, especially as her younger sister had already grown taller, but she didn't appreciate how she had to crane her neck to look at the man.

"Come." He cupped her elbow and waved her through to his study. "At least sit whilst you break your fast."

Lifting her chin and the hem of her wrapper, she marched into his private room. She found the seat which looked altogether the most comfortable, the one behind his desk, and sank into it.

Summerset pressed his lips flat and shook his head.

She took another bite of breakfast. "Where are me clothes? Fine as this night dress is, I should be on me way."

"I didn't bring you into my home just to throw you out at the first chance." He cocked a hip on the side of his desk and examined her. "How do you feel? Does your head still ail you?"

"Nup." Swallowing, she wiped her hands on the sleeves of the wrapper, earning a frown from the earl. She bit the inside of her cheek. It was too easy ruffling the man's feathers. "I feel fine."

"I'll call the doctor back to look at your side, at least."

Her pulse kicked up a beat. "Where are my clothes?" His eagerness to keep her in his house put her nerves on edge. Yes, he seemed harmless and kind, in his own strange way, but he was a man. She should have been more on guard.

He leaned forwards and placed his finger under her chin. He raised it and turned her face one way then the other. "Without all that muck on your face, you are passably attractive. I wonder...."

She jerked her head back. She knew it. All men were the same. "A large coat will do. I don't mind walking 'ome in a night rail."

"Dramatic as that would be, it's hardly necessary," he said. "Your clothes, such as they are, were laundered. You can leave whenever you wish. However, I have a proposition for you."

The muscles of her back pulled tight. Of course. She should have expected it. Even for a woman who was only *passably attractive*, men like him would see an opportunity to take advantage.

At least he proposed it as a question. In the position she was in, he could just have easily assumed he could take what he wanted without asking.

"No, thank'ee. I'll take me clothes and be gone."

He drew his eyebrows together. The small wrinkle on his brow was the only flaw on his otherwise perfect face. A more handsome man Netta had never seen, but his heart was as corrupt as the rest of them.

"You haven't heard my proposition. How can you refuse it when you don't know what it is?"

She snorted. "I know your type. Your *propositions* are all the same."

His eyes flew wide. "Ah. You misunderstand. My proposal is not of an amorous nature."

"No?"

He chuckled. "Certainly not."

She should have been relieved, but her shoulder blades drew back even tighter. "Why not? Wot's wrong with me?"

He sighed. "If you are going to become vexed when men both make improper suggestions and *don't* make improper suggestions, you must spend most of your life in a state of offense. You also make it most difficult to hold a conversation. Could we perhaps proceed without reproofs for roughly five minutes? I believe you'll find my proposition most profitable."

Well, profit was a word she definitely did not take offense to. "I'm listening."

"Good." The earl pressed his palm flat on the desk and leaned his weight upon it. "I might have need of someone like you in the future. A woman with loose enough morals to engage in a deception and an adequate talent to make it believable."

There he went again. "Adequate?" she gritted out

between her teeth.

"Of course, I'd prefer someone more skilled." He drummed his long, tapered fingers on the desk, a thick bank of gold wrapped around his thumb clinking dully against the wood. "But beggars can't be choosers. How old are you, Netta?"

"Old enough."

He tilted his head, those devilish eyes raking her form.

A slight shiver hardened her nipples.

"When you dressed as poor Ned, you appeared quite young." He angled forwards, and the scent of oranges overlaid with something darker, spicier, teased her nose.

She shifted on her seat. Didn't matter how good a man smelled. This was business. She wouldn't allow for distractions. "Face paint and dirt. Given me height and round face, appearing younger is easy."

She turned the tables and examined him. It was no hardship. His form was long and lean. The tailoring of his jacket was exquisite, molding to his wide shoulders and nipping down to emphasize his trim waist. But it was the quality of the materials that caught her eye. Mostly. She wasn't dead, after all, and a handsome man sitting mere feet away was wont to pique her interest like any other woman's. But money beat out handsome every day of the week.

"Wot's your racket?" Was that how he'd earned his wealth? Through dishonest activities? She couldn't deny that a small nip of disappointment stung her breast. She might engage in a bit of larceny now and then, but it was necessary.

She pressed her lips tight. She couldn't develop qualms now. If she was to succeed in her dream of taking her sister and herself to America, she should encourage disreputable behavior on Summerset's part if it increased the profit on hers.

He pressed a hand to his chest. "You wound me. Do I look like a knave?"

"Yes. Absolutely."

He smirked. "I do like you, Netta Pickle. I believe we'll work rather well together."

"If we work together." She drew her knees up to her chin, hooking her heels on the edge of the chair. "Wots. The. Racket?"

"I might have need of a distraction." Standing, he plucked up a carved mahogany paperweight. He tossed it up and down. "There's a man."

She snorted. "There always is."

Summerset continued on as though she hadn't interrupted. "He has a weakness for proper, young misses. And most men I know are easily distracted by a pair of lovely violet eyes." He tossed the wooden ball to her, and she snatched if from the air. "Truly, I don't believe I've ever seen eyes such an extraordinary color as yours. They are sure to lure in any man." He rolled his shoulders and stretched. "The impressive set of breasts will also help."

Netta looked down. She didn't know if she would call them impressive. They were rounder than the fashion, but then so was the rest of her body. She liked her sweets too much. But the men of her acquaintance had never had any complaints.

"Truly, how old are you, Netta? I can't involve a child in my games."

"Three and twenty." For once, honesty served her well. "And you still 'aven't told me the game. Or me payment."

"The details aren't important." One edge of his full lips curled up. "Namely because I don't know them as yet. As to your fee, what would you say to four thousand pounds?" He threw out the number like it was an invitation to tea. Casually. As though such a sum were nothing.

Netta blinked. And blinked again. It was an incredible amount of money. More than she could hope to see in twenty years, even had she intended to include petty theft to her acting wages on a permanent basis.

He stood. "You're a clever little thing, but are you trainable? You will only earn your fee if you work hard and do as I say."

"'Ard at wot?" She wrapped her arms around her shins. She wanted that money. Needed it. Such a sum would solve *everything*. No more delays. No more nights tossing and turning worrying about her sister.

But even after all these years, after all the disappointments and degradations she'd faced, even she had her limits. There were some things she wouldn't do for money, not even for an obscene amount of it.

Leaning forwards, he picked up the end of one of her ash-blonde curls, pulling it out straight.

She slapped his hand away and the ringlet bounced back to her shoulder.

He grinned. "Miss Netta Pickle, in order to earn your fee, you will have to become the embodiment of feminine virtue. The pinnacle of everything that is lovely and charming."

He hooked his thumbs into his waistcoat pockets and rocked back on his heels. "In short, my dear, I am going to turn you into a lady."

Chapter Six

John closed his eyes. "Not that one," he said for the fourth time. Truly, he was beginning to worry about the mental faculties of little Netta Pickle. For someone who had seemed clever enough to employ a stratagem at the coffeehouse, her lack of understanding of the basic functions of the dinner fork was concerning. "It's the third fork from the right that you use for the main course, not the first. You persist in using the same utensil for each plate."

Netta clanged the fork in question against the china, and John snapped his eyes open. The set had been a gift from the Princess of Prussia. Perhaps until he had Netta better trained he should use the servants' dishes.

"I don't see why it matters." She flicked her hand over the row of silverware, knocking several to the carpet. She huffed and bent over. "As long as the food gets in me mouth, any fork should do."

She was dexterous. John had to give her that. The spoon she'd slipped into her bodice before she straightened and replaced two forks on the table made barely a whisper as it slid past the satin of her borrowed gown.

He sighed. One would think with the promise of four thousand pounds that a woman would constrain her felonious impulses. But not Netta Pickle. Really, he didn't know what he was going to do with her.

Wilberforce was, if not happy, content that the ragamuffin they'd saved was safe and secure in John's home. Robert was less sulky now that John had agreed to help him out of yet another jumble. And Netta looked as excited as a pig in a puddle of mud as she scoped out all of John's finery that she could steal.

It was only John who remained gloomy. He sighed again, more deeply. The things he suffered for his family and friends.

He slouched back in his chair, a niggle of shame sliding through him. Except it wasn't just John who suffered. Robert had done his share, too, and at John's hand. It had been foolish to believe that he could leave his brother to fend for himself. John owed him more than he could ever repay.

And Robert takes advantage of my guilt every chance he can.

John pushed the uncharitable thought from his mind. Perhaps if Robert was returned the responsibility of managing one of the family smelts. Or the gunpowder mill. Perhaps this time the work would turn him into someone useful and productive.

He cleared his throat, and the butter knife that had been inching its way towards Netta's sleeve popped back into its place.

"Do we ever get to actually eat with these forks, or am I to starve while staying at your house?" she asked. "I'm 'ungry."

"*H*ungry. Say it with the *H*. You can do it." Please let her be able to do it. He should have chosen one of the women he knew from The Black Rose. They were always eager for coin, and had the quality to pull off pretending to be a lady. But it had seemed such a tidy solution. He needed a pretty, young woman with easy morals. One had dropped into his lap. And besides, Netta had needed the blunt. Wilberforce would stop giving him that look, the one that implored him to make every situation right. A tidy solution all around.

If only she was teachable.

"'Ungry."

"Hungry. It truly isn't difficult." The girl was being

intentionally willful. She had to be. "You aren't getting dinner until you use the eighth letter in our alphabet. And I believe it's a lovely roast duck tonight."

She bounced angrily in her seat, and his gaze flicked to the flesh jiggling above the low neckline of her gown. And to think he'd once believed her to be a young boy. After a good scrubbing and a change of clothes, she'd turned out to be a pretty little thing. Lush even. With the kind of curves a man liked to bury himself in. With clear skin, surprising for one living on the streets, winsome curls that sprung from her head a lustrous chestnut brown but tapered into a pale blond by the ends, and entrancing eyes that made his breath stall every time he became trapped in their gaze, Netta Pickle had the potential to distract every man in the room.

John crossed his leg over his cock, which was becoming a mite too interested in the woman across the table. She would make a tempting prize to a man such as Sudworth. John would be wise to keep this endeavor purely platonic if he didn't want her to distract him, as well.

"Pleeease." She pressed her hands to her abdomen. "Me belly is rumbling so."

"And all you have to say is one word, properly, to feed it."

She narrowed those lovely eyes and glared at him. "*Hhh*ungry."

That one word was growled in an octave lower than her normal tones, and John felt it deep in his gut. The pressure against his pantaloons increased.

Wisdom wasn't always his strong suit.

He cleared his throat. "How delightful. You can be trained." He flicked his finger to the door, and the footman standing guard slipped out to tell the cook they were ready to eat. As he left, another visitor slid inside and made straight for John's ankles.

John picked up the cat and plopped it on the chair next to him before she could destroy his boots.

"Now, on to other matters." He tilted his head. "I can't

introduce you as Miss Pickle. That name just won't do. We'll have to come up with another."

"Wot's the cat's name?" Netta jerked her chin at the orange fluff-ball.

"Judith."

Netta's mouth widened into a perfect 'O'.

John's cock throbbed. She had a delightful mouth. Wide and plush and just the right size to wrap around his—

"You named your cat Judith?" she asked. "Wot a *hhh*orrible name for a cat."

"She's not my cat." The animal in question batted the air and hissed at him, apparently not liking the disdainful tone of his voice. John modulated it. "Wilberforce found her in the yard, bloody after a fight, and took her in." He gave Netta a pointed look. "The man is wont to do such foolishness."

The woman had the gall to stick her tongue out at him. He blinked, his shock somewhat lessoned by images of her using that clever tongue in imaginative ways. Would she lick a man's cock like a cream ice or would she dive right in and—

"Well, I'm not letting you name me. Not if you thought Judith was a good name for a cat." She plunked her elbows on the table and rested her chin on her clasped hands. "'Ow about...ooh, I've always wanted to be a Miss Moulin."

John blew out a breath and focused his thoughts. Netta was fully-clothed, and she would remain that way. He needed to restrain his imagination. "Too showy."

"'Ow about Miss Pa-pi-llon. Me mam told me that meant dove."

"Butterfly. And no."

"Fontaine?"

He shook his head.

"Labelle?"

Jesus, it was like she knew the name of every French whore in London.

Two footmen stepped through, each carrying a platter.

One laid a plate before John, and removed the lid, refilling his wine glass before stepping back. The other didn't get a chance to place his plate down. Netta jerked it from his hand and dug into it as though she hadn't eaten in a month.

John cut off a small bit of meat and fed it to the cat. "That's not the right fork."

She didn't respond, only squinted her eyes over the table at him, her cheeks bulging like a squirrel's gorging on nuts, and continued shoveling food into her mouth with the salad fork.

"We'll stick with calling you Netta for now, shall we?" There was nothing delicate or proper about this woman. He still refused to call her, to call anyone, Pickle, but Netta would do well enough. "We'll hold elocution classes in the morning, deportment in the afternoons, and lessons in dining etiquette at dinner."

She took a large swallow of wine. "Wot's et-cut?"

"To begin with, it means not eating with one's elbows planted on the table." He stabbed his knife in the direction of her elbows and was gratified when she slid them off the wood to her sides. "Next, instead of shoving the entire breast in your mouth, cut off a piece small enough where you need chew only three times before swallowing."

She cut a wedge and stuck it in her mouth. She bobbed her head with each gnash of her teeth. Counting in her head, no doubt. "Three times?" She spoke with her mouth half full. "I'm already at ten and that was a small bite."

"Cut a smaller piece. And don't"—he dropped his chin and gave her the sternest look he owned—"speak when there is food in your mouth. I want you to prove a distraction, but not of the appalling kind."

She made a show of swallowing and wiped her mouth with the back of her hand.

John winced. The lovely lace cuff on her gown would never survive. "And—"

"No. No more rules." She slapped her palm on the table. "Do this, don't do that. That's all I've 'eard."

John opened his mouth, and she rolled her eyes.

"*Hhh*eard," she corrected. "It's too much. Can't I jus' eat me dinner in peace?"

He pushed his chair back and stood. He circled the table and squatted next to her. The light citrus scent from his soaps drifted off her body, along with a hint of licorice that surprised him even as it made his mouth water. He cupped her forearm and squeezed. "We don't have much time to mold you into a lady. If I push, it is only because I believe you are capable of transformation."

"Truly?" She bit her lower lip, and glanced at him from lowered eyes. He knew it was a coy act, even down to that delectable waver in her voice, but knowing it didn't stop his body from reacting.

Oh, she was good.

He snapped her napkin from her lap and dabbed at the grease on her chin. "Even dogs can be trained to have good manners. Why not you?"

She snatched the napkin from him and tossed it on the table. "I'm done eating." She pushed her plate away and stood.

John followed her up. The aroma from her skin drew him in like a lure. He needed to change out the expensive French soaps in her toilette to something unscented.

"Of course," he said, and took a healthy step back. "It has been a long day. Tomorrow we will begin your speech lessons, so rest well."

Without a by-your-leave, she turned on her heel and scurried for the door.

"Netta?"

She paused, her back turned.

John padded up behind her. His hand on her shoulder made her start. "Is there anyone I should notify? Anyone who should know you're safe and staying with me?"

The muscles under his fingers hardened. "No. There's no one."

As he thought. If someone had cared about this woman,

he wouldn't have let her run about the London streets at night. "Well," he said, injecting levity into his voice. "That makes it easier for me. I won't have to worry about a disgruntled father or beau calling me out for having you under my roof."

She snorted, something else he'd have to train out of her. A pity; she made the indelicate noise almost sound charming.

"You toffs are a funny lot." Her curls scraped against the back of her gown as she shook her head. "You don't care if something is wrong, only if you'll be caught out."

"I'd say that gives us something in common with the rest of the world, instead of setting us apart."

"I suppose." She sniffed. "Goodnight, then."

He let her take a step. "Oh, and Netta?"

She stopped again, sighing. "Wot now?"

Grasping her shoulders, he turned her to face him. He held up his hand, palm up. "I'll take that spoon."

She rounded her mouth. Her elbows perfectly communicated shocked outrage as she planted her fists on her hips. "Well, really."

John fought his grin. "Indeed, really. You are not so sly as you believe yourself to be. Now, hand it over."

She crossed her arms over her bosom. "You've got a screw loose, you have. If you think...eek!"

With a finger hooked in the top of her bodice, he reeled her towards him.

She slapped at his hands but there was no heat in it. "Oy. Take your 'ands off me."

"Last chance." Her skin was silky smooth against his finger, and he couldn't help but slide it up and down in the cleft of her bosom. "Hand over your ill-gotten gains or face the consequences." A lick of excitement flicked behind his breast. He almost hoped she maintained the pretense. It had been so long since he'd felt any sort of excitement. Whatever else Netta might be, at least she was diverting.

She raised her chin, and the small dimple in the center

caught the light. "I don't know wot you're on about."

He tutted. "You disappoint me." He lied. She stimulated him. Before she could take her next breath, he spun her around and pressed her back against his front. He eased his hand into her bodice, splaying his fingers under her breast as he searched.

Her heart fluttered beneath his palm. Her arse snuggled nicely right up under his groin. It was with regret that he slid the spoon free.

He held the piece of silver in front of her face.

"Huh." She adjusted her bodice, plumping up her breasts with the motion. "'Ow'd that get there?"

"It's a mystery," he said dryly.

She turned, her breasts brushing his chest. She raised her face, her mouth only inches from his. "Is there any other part of me body you want to search, or am I free to go to bed?"

The base of his spine tingled. There were many places he'd love to search. Alas, he'd learned that mixing business with pleasure was rarely a good idea.

He took a step back, his body cooling.

A frown turned her lips down, the expression so fleeting John wasn't certain he'd read it correctly.

"That will be all." He slapped the spoon into his palm. "Good night, Netta."

She dipped an absurd curtsy, the deepness of it obviously intended to mock. She wobbled and threw her hands out wide to catch her balance, and John bit back a smile.

"My lord," she said. Lifting her skirts, she flipped her hair and strode from the room.

John watched the swaying of her wide hips as she disappeared down the hall. He adjusted his cock and returned to his seat. He tossed back the remains of his wine.

Judith leapt onto his lap, her purring body a poor substitute for what he wanted.

His brother had better show some damn gratitude.

He scratched the cat under the chin.

Working with Netta without touching her was going to be one hell of a sacrifice.

* * *

Netta sank onto the lambskin rug before the fireplace in her bedroom and toed off her slippers. She curled her feet under her.

That had been foolish. Flirting with an earl? She blew out her cheeks. Nothing good could come from that. It made no matter that he was wickedly handsome and had manners as smooth as melted butter over a scone. His very position made him a threat. No, it was best to ignore the attraction. This was business.

Four thousand pounds. She dug her fingers in the soft wool of the rug. It was enough for a new life, on a new continent for her and her sister. She had to play this right. Taking that spoon had been a calculated risk. Summerset would expect someone like Netta Pickle to be unable to control her impulses, so she'd given him a good show. And the results had been...unexpected.

She pressed her palm to her breastbone, her own hand a poor substitute for the pressure and heat of the earl's. Only a blackguard would molest a woman so. She trailed her fingers over her breast, but there was no echoing tingle like when Summerset had touched her. She sighed. He had been retrieving his property. His impropriety had a cause.

Netta nibbled on her bottom lip. If she stuck something up her skirts, would the earl—

No. Business. That's what she needed to concentrate on.

Would the earl stand by his word? It sounded as though he hadn't even figured out all the details to his scheme. What if he didn't need her assistance? What if he asked of her something she couldn't give?

Netta stood. Well, she couldn't lose a sure income, miniscule as it may be, for merely the potential of a windfall. She shoved her feet back in the slippers. She hated leaving the luxury and warmth of the earl's townhouse, but she'd missed one performance already. She couldn't miss another.

She shrugged into a long coat she'd borrowed from a servant's closet. Pretending to be a proper young miss would be the easiest job in the world. Aside from youth, something face paint would rectify, she had all the qualifications, even if the earl didn't know it. Summerset said he wouldn't ask her to do anything unseemly, but could she trust him? How far would he want her to go to distract a man?

How far was she willing to go for four thousand pounds?

A shiver coursed her body, and she pulled the belt of the coat tight.

She didn't *think* the earl was lying. She couldn't imagine him forcing a woman to do something she wasn't comfortable with, but she'd been wrong about men before. With four thousand pounds inducement, she might not be seeing the man as clearly as she ought.

She slid the window open and leaned her head out. She frowned. There was no convenient trellis below, nothing to give her a solid handhold. Closing the window, she went about her room extinguishing all the lights. In the dark, she pressed her cheek against her door.

Only silence greeted her. With a stealth borne of experience, she cracked open the door and slipped out. Making her way unseen down the back staircase was child's play. She escaped out the side door, tip-toed through the gardens, and exited onto the street.

Flipping up the collar of the coat, she hurried to the cross street, keeping an eye out for hackneys.

For now, she would trust Summerset. Trust that he'd keep his word. But she'd move forwards as though the four thousand pounds were merely speculative. She would continue her real employment at night, and during the day she'd allow Summerset to believe he was gradually improving her. A sensible compromise even Cerise would condone.

And no matter how charming the earl was, she would keep both eyes open for any tricks on his part. Eyes open and legs closed.

She'd pretend to learn to be a lady, sleep in his satin sheets, eat his fine food, and after she collected her fee, she'd shake the man's hand and bid him farewell.

It was a neat plan.

Pretending to learn the manners she'd had instilled from birth. Living in the lap of luxury until she was called upon to wink and shimmy as a distraction. If everything went as planned, it would be the easiest money she'd ever made.

Chapter Seven

Netta yawned so widely her jaws cracked.

Summerset winced, and belatedly she covered her mouth with her hand. She shifted on the parlor's settee, a niggle of unease slipping through her. That breach in etiquette hadn't been intentional. She'd never settled into a character so thoroughly, and while she enjoyed playing guttersnipe-Netta, she needed to remember it was only a role. A means to an end.

He paced in front of her, annoyance tightening every muscle in his lithe body.

Her belly fluttered as she watched him prowl. He was like a large cat, ready to take down his prey. Perhaps if she provoked him a bit more, he would turn his wolfish attentions on her and—

No. *He* was only a means to an end, and she couldn't let her mind wander down that path, no matter how delightful her imaginings. Besides, she was mixing up her animals now. He couldn't be both a cat and a wolf.

Summerset paused by the empty fireplace and rested one jeweled boot on the brick ledge. He wore breeches today, a lovely Pomona green silk, and nearly as tight as his pantaloons. The fabric gripped the firm muscles of his thighs, and molded to the long bulge trapped behind his falls.

She swallowed and averted her gaze.

He ran a hand up the back of his head, his hair getting a delightfully rumpled look. "Is there a reason for your fatigue? Is your bed not to your liking?"

She stifled another yawn. "The bed is fine."

"Is my company not engaging?"

"Cor, what are you on about now?" She slouched back on the settee. She could pretend many things, but acting wide awake wasn't one of them. Not after sneaking out of the earl's house for the past three nights for each of her shows. The promise of four thousand pounds was heady, but the reality of three pounds a show was not to be dismissed.

Besides, she enjoyed acting. She hadn't thought she would. She'd been raised knowing the theatre was where disreputable women went to make their livings. But when she'd been alone, hurting, and with nowhere to sleep, the people at The Burns had invited her into their family. And putting on a costume each night, having the freedom of a disguise, was a thrill unlike any other.

Except, perhaps, putting one over on pompous earls. She eyed him carefully, trying to measure just how far his patience would stretch. A perverse part of her enjoyed needling him, relished when those full, sensual lips of his pressed flat into a hard line. And when those deep-blue eyes went all squinty, she got a decided tingle in parts of her that hadn't tingled for quite some time.

But this was business, she reminded herself for the thousandth time, and she couldn't risk him throwing her out. "You're fine, the bed is fine. It's jus' being in a new place. I'll sleep better tonight."

"Just."

She pushed through the fog in her brain. "Wot?"

"Just, not jus'." He pushed away from the fireplace and stood before her. "What, not wot. Are you even trying?"

She decided to show him a little progress. Slowly, and overly enunciating each word, she said, "My lodgings here are most delightful. I *just* need to become accustomed to sliding all over those satin sheets of yours. I almost slipped right out of the bed last night."

He hooked his thumb in his waistcoat pocket, his eyes

going hooded.

"What?" she asked, shoving that *H* in there hard. "Was my diction not correct?"

"It was fine," he said gruffly, "but now I can't get the image of you slipping about in my bed out of my mind."

Netta stilled. He stood several feet from her, yet she swore she could feel the heat rolling from his body. Or maybe that was her own body acting like a furnace.

Summerset was so perfectly put-together. His cravats were always knotted just so. His stockings matched his waistcoat. There was never a crease or a wrinkle anywhere on his person.

Her fingers itched to disorder his perfection. To put some well-earned wrinkles in those breeches.

He turned his head aside, and the connection pulsing between them broke. "I have an idea to help you with your elocution." He strode to a sideboard and pulled a jar from the bottom shelf. Glass marbles rattled inside, glinting in the sunlight. He returned and sat beside her. "Have you ever heard of Demosthenes?"

Her father had a library full of Greek classics, but she couldn't admit to that. She shook her head.

"He was an orator who lived two thousand years ago." Summerset rested one arm along the back of the settee, his thumb just brushing the shoulder of her gown. "Legend has it that as a child he was a very poor speaker. In order to improve, he put pebbles in his mouth. If he could learn to speak clearly and understandably around the pebbles, then his speech when his mouth was free would be exemplary." He raised the jar, and the sea-green marbles clinked against each other. "I quite forget why he felt so compelled to improve his speech. Something about a lawsuit, I believe, and he had to act as his own attorney."

He exhaled, his nostrils flaring. "It always comes down to money."

She glanced around the parlor. The sheer curtains appeared to have spun gold threaded through them. The chairs and side tables were all made from the finest rosewood. Gems glittered on Summerset's cravat pin, the buttons to his jacket, the ring he wore on the thumb of his right hand.

Money didn't seem to be a problem. But if it was.... "You will have the four thousand pounds you promised me, won't you? I don't want to go through this performance only to have you claim poverty."

"Have no worries, my money isn't the issue." He cocked his head. "That sounded quite good, Netta. You didn't drop one *H*. Perhaps there's hope for you yet."

Drat. She'd forgotten herself. She gave him a cheeky grin. "You toffs always give my kind too little credit. Wot's the use of 'anging around you lot to lift a bauble now and then if I can't mirror 'ow you talk?"

"Right." He sighed. "Marbles it is. Open up." He plucked a round ball from the jar and held it in front of her mouth.

"I don't think—"

He pressed the marble between her open lips and dug out another.

"Oy!" The glass clicked against her teeth and she shifted it to her cheek. "That's right—"

He popped another one in. "Don't worry, they've been washed. Now, repeat after me. *The grey fox found himself a bit of fun and hardly had a happier time in his life.*"

She pinched her mouth shut and glared at him.

"No?" He lifted a lock of her hair and twirled it about his finger. "How about *the headstrong hen hated when the furtive fox fired up her fury.*" He tugged on her curl, and her scalp tingled. "I dare you to say that three times in a row."

"Yur da fox an' mm da 'en, I s'pose?"

His lips stretched into a wide grin, the edges of his eyes crinkling.

Her lungs stalled.

It was the first true smile she'd seen from him. The first

one spawned from sincere amusement instead of affectation.

It was beautiful.

How much of himself did Summerset hide away? How much of his insouciance was pretense?

She was all too familiar with disguises. She should have recognized he wore one sooner.

A door banged shut, and footsteps pounded down the hallway.

The earl's shoulders tightened and he swiveled his face to the parlor door, the happiness evaporating from his expression.

The earl's brother stopped in the doorway. As before, he wore a suit of drab brown. The high, starched collar covered the sides of his chin, but couldn't hide his scars.

"Here he is." He tossed his hat to the footman who came rushing up. "I told you I could find him on my own."

The distressed servant looked from his master to the intruder, clearly uncertain of what action to take.

Summerset nodded to the man. "It's all right. Tell cook to send some refreshments up. My brother appears uncommonly rapacious today."

The servant bobbed his head and retreated. Summerset's brother sauntered into the room, giving Netta a disinterested glance.

As discreetly as possible, she turned her head and spat the marbles into her hand.

"Was there something else you wanted, Robert?" Summerset lounged back and crossed one leg over the other, the picture of nonchalance. "I thought I'd told you I'd contact you when our business had concluded."

"You did." Robert strolled about the room, poking at the small figurines on the mantel, leaning in to peer at the life-sized painting depicting the birth of Venus that spanned one wall. "But as I suspected, our business seems to have slipped your mind." He turned and shot her an insincere smile, the puckered skin on his left cheek pulling tight.

"Charming as your lady friend appears, I don't think you'll find my lost deed between her legs."

Summerset shot to his feet. "Watch your mouth. Fraternal affection won't stop me from darkening your daylights."

"Why, John," Robert said, his tone mocking, "attempting to protect a woman's sensibilities? Whatever has the world come to?"

John. His given name was John. It was the first time she'd heard it, and the name rolled around her brain. She wasn't sure such a common name suited the flamboyant peacock. It was too dependable when the earl seemed eager to forbear responsibility.

Although he was helping his brother. Whatever this scheme was that he'd involved her in, she was certain it stemmed from the brother's problem.

And the earl had stepped in to prevent her from receiving a beating. She wasn't his responsibility, but he'd placed her under his protection.

Perhaps he had hidden depths. The desire to peel away all the man's layers spread like an itch beneath her skin, one that she really, really wanted to scratch.

John turned and extended his hand. "My dear, will you excuse my brother and me? Perhaps it is a good time for a nap."

She frowned. A nap? Now, when the house was becoming interesting? It had been three dull days of pretending to be a guttersnipe practicing to be a genteel miss. Three days of monotonous speaking exercises and dining lessons. A glimpse into the earl's jumbled life was the first bit of entertainment she'd had.

He crooked his fingers, indicating she should rise, and she blew out a breath.

She rolled the marbles into her other hand and placed her left into his right. The slight moue of disgust when her sticky palm met his lifted her spirits. "Am I free until this evening?" she asked, exaggerating her enunciation for

John's approval.

Apparently, she didn't merit it. He shook his head. "We still have more to work on. I'll find you in a couple of hours."

Her shoulders slumped. "Fine." And with a nod to the men, she trudged from the room.

John pulled the doors shut behind her.

A door opened down the hall, and Netta slipped into an alcove as a footman walked past her holding a tray of cold meats and rolls. He scratched at the door and walked in when John called out. She waited for the servant to exit, pulling the doors shut again, and disappear down the hall before abandoning her hiding place. On tiptoe, she crept toward his study, adjacent to the parlor, and slipped inside.

The lingering scents of orange and spice told her John spent much of his time in this room. She wandered past the rows of books arranged on shelves lining the walls, pausing as one of the titles caught her eye. *De re metallica*. On the nature of metals. She ran her finger along the spine. A very serious work for such a flippant coxcomb. Another crack in his mask.

She tapped the bookcase and turned back to her object, the window facing the small garden behind the townhouse. It's sister in the parlor had been open when she'd left that room, and she hoped in the warm air sound would carry.

She tugged at the window pane, and winced at the creak of wood sliding against wood. Cocking her hip on the sill, Netta swung her foot as she listened to the soft murmurs. Did Summerset say 'marriage'? That wouldn't make any sense. Carriage, perhaps? Why couldn't the brothers be shouting at each other? This dulcet conversation didn't help her at all.

She leaned forwards, her upper body hanging outside the window.

And jerked back in surprise when the window next to hers was slammed shut. Her head hit the top of the frame and she rubbed the ache.

Perfect. Another lump. And no intelligence gained because of it.

She sniffed and hopped down from her perch. A nap didn't sound like a bad idea, after all.

* * *

John pressed his palms on the windowsill and shook his head. The little street urchin was going to get into a bind one day that she couldn't get out of. Not everyone was as indulgent as he was.

"Why did you close the window? It's warm in here." Robert paced across the room, tugging at his cravat.

"This is a private conversation." John turned and leaned back against the sill. He crossed his arms over his chest. "I want to prevent little ears from listening in."

"What?"

"Never mind." John cocked his head, watching his brother. Something about the way he moved was off. Stiff, especially when he turned. "What's happened?"

Robert shot him a dark look. He pinched his lips together and narrowed his eyes and looked so much as their mother had when she'd caught John doing something he oughtn't, that John's chest squeezed.

It had been twenty-six years since her death, but the wound didn't seem to heal. If she hadn't died giving birth to their youngest brother, how different their lives might have been. Their father wouldn't have begun his descent into drink and gambling, and he would never have passed that particular vice down to Robert.

Or so John imagined.

If Robert's gambling wasn't inherited from their father, then the blame lay squarely on John.

It had been his experiment, his arrogance, that had scarred Robert, turning his sweet-tempered brother bitter.

"Can't a man visit his loving family?" Robert asked.

John ignored the sarcasm. "You're walking stiffly. You're agitated, or more so than usual. And this is your second call to my house in less than a week. Cut the horse shit. What's happened?"

Robert paused, breathing heavily. "Fine." He unbuttoned his waistcoat and pulled his shirt from his trousers. "You wish to see what's happened? Sudworth has added another scar to my collection."

Hiking his shirt up over his ribs, he turned, exposing the left side of his torso to the light.

John stared at the fresh wound, keeping his expression level, but inside he was seething. It wasn't a scar, not yet. But the red and blistered flesh that formed a neat 'X' would become one.

"A poker?" Jesus, sometimes the indifference in his voice chilled even him. But John prided himself on maintaining a dispassionate demeanor. Showing the world he cared only gave people a tool to cudgel him.

His brother dropped his shirt and shoved it back into his trousers. "Yes."

"Why?" John needed to have another talk with Sudworth. This one wouldn't be as friendly.

His inquiries into Sudworth had yet to yield anything of import. He might have to plant the letter in Raffles' file as Sudworth wanted in order to discover his game. His list of action items was growing. Retrieve his brother's deed. Stop whatever scheme Sudworth was up to. And exact revenge for his brother's injury.

Robert busied himself rebuttoning his waistcoat. "I couldn't pay," he mumbled.

John pushed off the window. His body was taut with need. The need to hurt someone, to pound out his frustrations. Sadly, only his brother was available. "Why did you have to pay? You already lost your home." But a sinking feeling in his gut told him what he didn't want to hear.

"I tried to win it back, didn't I?" Robert started pacing again. "I didn't want to leave it up to you. I thought I could win it back. I should have won it back. I don't know how he rolled that five. The chances against it were colossal."

"How much?" John's jaw ached from clenching it. Of all the asinine, impetuous, imbecilic things to do.

"Five thousand. Not too much."

Blood pulsed behind John's eyes. Not too much? He clenched his hand, willing it to remain by his side and not plant itself in his brother's face. No, John could pay five thousand pounds. He'd already paid twenty times that saving Robert from his scrapes. His businesses had been lucrative through the years, and none more so than the gunpowder mill during the war. He could pay the debt.

But it burned his insides to do so.

"Is there a reason for the *X*, or merely artistic license?"

Robert flushed. "It's a cross. He said if I didn't pay, you might not find my body to bury properly. Marking me with it was a favor to my eternal soul."

Right. Revenge had just moved to the top of his list. This had to be an attempt to intimidate not only Robert but John, as well. A warning to heed his instructions.

John hated acts of intimidation unless he was the one committing them. "You are going to Stonesworth House," he told Robert. "Alan Hampson has been in need of a new assistant manager for the smelts there, and you will take that role. We have three months' worth of chromite ore stored on site, and I don't want production to be interrupted whilst I resolve our Sudworth problem."

Robert gaped. "You wish me to work *under* Hampson? Under your servant? I am the second son of Summerset. If I decide to dirty my hands in business, it will at least be as the man-in-charge."

John chuckled, although there was no humor behind it. "You truly are an insufferable prat. You think birth gives you any claim to importance? I trust Hampson. He is a smart man who has proved himself time and again. You have done nothing but fail. If you want me to pay off this last debt and recover your estate, you will do what I say. You've gone too far this time."

"You would know all about going too far."

They glared at each other, the room becoming thick with memories.

"I will say this for the last time," John said quietly. "I am sorry for the hurt I caused you. If I could take it back, if I could be the one to have mixed those chemicals and suffered the explosion, I would. But what is done cannot be undone. And having scars on your face doesn't give you leave to act an arsehole."

John dug his fingertips into his hips. He'd been so sure of his calculations. Certain the mixture would be stable. He hadn't thought twice about directing his younger brother, his assistant, to concoct the new mixture of gunpowder.

The dreadful irony of it sucked the breath from John's lungs. The British government had bought barrel after barrel of his new gunpowder because of its stability. The soldiers in the field had a better chance of avoiding misfires because of the new formula he'd developed.

And because of one dropped decimal point, that extremely stable gunpowder had exploded in his brother's face.

It should have been John with the scars. John with the months of agonizing pain. But he couldn't let that excuse his brother's behavior, not any longer. "You've thrown away not only your future, but mine and all the future heirs of Summerset." He shook his head. "How dare you."

Robert dropped his chin to his chest. "I should have won. I'm a better player than he is."

"Hazard is a game of chance. There are no better players."

"There is skill in calculating the odds of the roll."

John kept his gaze level on his brother, not trusting himself to respond to that drivel.

Robert cleared his throat. "Do you think you can get the deed back? Our brother has inquired about visiting me at Crowhaven. He will be disappointed if he finds out it's gone."

Their youngest brother would be disappointed Robert was gambling. Kevin was studying to be a clergyman, and detested that sin more so than John. He had much love and charity in his heart, an amazing feat considering the family he'd been raised in, but even that charity would have its limits. Watching Robert devolve into the same profligacy as their father would break his heart.

John turned to stare out the window. "I will get it back. I promise you."

Robert gathered some of his old haughtiness about him. "Of course. My brother not only is the genius who saved the earldom from financial ruin, but he is also a great spy. No trial is too great for you."

"A fact for which you should be grateful." John rubbed his eyes. His anger was spent and fatigue tugged at him. That nap he'd recommended for Netta would serve him well also.

Christ, he *was* getting old. First sending Netta to bed and now himself.

He pursed his lips. Although, taking a nap *with* Netta sounded like a fine idea. Her plump little body nestled tight against his. Her mess of curls tickling his chin.

Such a nap wouldn't garner him much rest, but it would be delightful.

"Go," he told his brother. It was time to tuck his brother away. At Stonesworth, not only would he remain safe, but he wouldn't be able to cause too many new problems. "Go pack. My driver will pick you up tomorrow morning. And you will stay at the estate until I tell you otherwise."

Robert sketched a deep bow. "Of course, my lord. Your word is my command."

It hadn't been in the past, but it damn well would be now. No more coddling. It was time his brother stopped using an injury as an excuse to ruin the rest of his life. "You jest, but let this be a reminder. The consequence of birth seems to hold import to you. Since that is the case, remember you are a second son."

John stalked forward until they stood eye to eye, chest to chest, and pounded the point home. "You have nothing but what I give you."

Chapter Eight

Netta peeled off the wax nose. She loved wearing a costume, but she couldn't deny the relief when she washed off the heavy makeup of the theatre.

"What happened to you zis evening?" Cerise floated into their changing room, her long, frothy gown billowing out around her ankles, making it look as though she walked on air. The remnants of her French heritage lingered in her words. "You missed one of your lines."

Netta blew out her cheeks and stared at herself in the mirror. "I know. The audience didn't notice, did they?"

"Harold covered it well." Cerise pulled off her wig of long blond hair and turned her back to Netta. "Help me from zis, would you?"

Netta stood and worked at the gown's buttons. "I'm tired of this play. Do you think Jarvis will produce a new one soon? It isn't as though we're packing the house with *The Merry Wives.*" The Burns Theatre was several blocks off The Strand, where the fashionable playhouses were. It catered to the lower middle class, delivering solid entertainment to those who couldn't afford Covent Garden prices. Netta never had to worry about someone from her past coming to one of her shows, though that didn't stop her from only taking roles that required heavy face-paint.

Cerise stepped out of the gown, her tawny skin glowing in the lamplight. "He is talking of bringing back *Henry V,* foolish man. The fees he must pay to perform Shakespeare are cutting into his profits. We should turn to those musical productions like they show at the *Sans Pareil.*"

Netta ignored her friend's familiar lament. "A different play but I could still play Bardolph." Netta pulled on her bottom lip. "And he has a death scene in that one. That would be diverting."

Her friend pulled on a silk wrapper and knotted the belt. "You have never been restless before. What has changed? And where have you been zis past week? I went around to your apartments twice. I even brought those Pomfret cakes you like so much to have with tea."

"Pomfret cakes?" Netta sighed. She did love those confections. "Well, it couldn't be helped. I have a new job."

"At another theatre?"

Netta found her boots and bent to pull them on. "It is an acting job, but not at a theatre." She contemplated how much to tell her friend. She could already hear the lecture. There were too many variables, too many unknowns to be safe, Cerise would say. Unless she knew every point to the earl's plan, Cerise would never want her to participate.

And Netta didn't want to be talked out of it. She had four thousand reasons not to.

She also enjoyed her time toying with the earl. Received a thrill each time he believed her little deceptions.

Liked when his eyes went hooded when she stood just a little too close.

The tips of her breasts tingled. Summerset dressed better than her, styled his hair with more care. He even smelled better. His expensive *eau de Cologne* was a scent she looked forward to more than her morning's chocolate. It was light and peppery and blended so well with the bergamot scent of his soaps that it made her mouth water.

He had the power to give her everything she needed, and an ego to match. He wasn't the sort of man she should be attracted to, but her body paid no heed to her sensibilities.

Cerise narrowed her eyes. "You gamble too much with your safety, *ma cherie*. I worry for you."

Netta kissed both of her friend's cheeks. "Don't.

Everything is finally going my way." She slid on her coat and picked up her reticule. "I'll be by for tea as soon as I can. And save some of the Pomfret cakes for me," she shouted as she skipped out the door.

On the street, she hailed one of the waiting hackneys. "The corner of Wimpole and Marybone streets, please."

The driver, a regular for the after-theatre crowd, nodded and set the buggy into motion.

Netta settled back with a contented sigh. She loved this time of night, when she was still basking from her performance and the streets were full of gaiety and evening revelers. She felt like part of the crowd yet still completely anonymous.

She couldn't say she was glad for her flight from her family, but she never would have experienced the freedom she had now if she still lived under her father's roof. Being the daughter of a viscount was a stifling affair.

"We're 'ere, miss." The driver pulled the buggy to a stop and turned to look back at her. "Shall I wait for you again?"

"Yes, thank you." Netta raised her skirts and hopped down. The porch lamp on the third house down Marybone Street remained lit, but the rest of the home was dark. She turned her back on it and strode down Wimpole. Finding the path behind one of the houses that she knew so well, Netta slipped into the yard and made her way to the rear of her own. She and her sister had long ago discovered the small break in the fence, and she crawled under it now.

Shaking out her skirts, she stared at the back of her former home. Even in the moonlight she could see her father still hadn't painted the rear of the house. The front façade he meticulously maintained, but the back was left to peel and rot.

She hiked her reticule high up her arm and applied herself to the ivy-covered trellis by the back porch. The ropey green vines gave her make-shift ladder a strength the thin wood did not, and in no time she was scuttling onto the roof of the porch and crawling towards one of the windows. She slid up the pane and slithered inside.

The small figure in the bed shifted but otherwise made no sound.

Netta smiled. She always was a heavy-sleeper. Tiptoeing to her sister, she lay next to her and brushed a hank of hair from the girl's face. "Eleanor," she whispered. "Wake up, sleepyhead."

Eleanor swatted at her face and wiggled her nose, but her eyes remained stubbornly closed.

Netta picked up one of her sister's curls, only a few shades darker than her own, and teased her sister's nose with it. "Oh my Lord," she whispered. "What a huge spider!"

Eleanor shot straight up, and Netta pressed a hand over the girl's mouth as silent laughter shook her body. "It was only a jest, you goose. But, oh, you should have seen your face."

Eleanor narrowed her eyes and pulled Netta's hand off her mouth. "It wasn't amusing."

"It was to me." Netta rolled back and stared up at her sister. She tried to visit a couple times a month, but every time she saw her now, a new change appeared. Eleanor was at that precarious stage in life, no longer a girl but not quite a woman. Her face seemed thinner than it had Netta's last visit, and she mourned the loss of the child her sister had been.

"Stop growing," she told Eleanor. "Or soon our ruse won't work."

Eleanor lay on her side, her hands pressed together under her cheek. "You forget. As I grow older, so do you." She smirked. "You'll always look old enough to be my mother."

Netta pinched her sister's side. Netta was not quite ten years her elder, hardly a dotard. But ever since they'd decided to flee England as mother and daughter, Eleanor had teased her about her age mercilessly.

"It is only through my extensive knowledge of face paint that any one will believe it." Netta rolled to face her sister and propped her head in her hand. "And even so, people will still remark how unfortunate it is that such a homely child was borne to such a beautiful, entrancing young woman."

Eleanor's snort was cut off by a wide yawn. "We only"—she yawned again—"let you believe you're the handsome sister. We didn't want to suffer your lamentations if you realized the truth."

Netta rolled her eyes. "Go back to sleep, goose. You're dreaming in any case." She kissed her forehead. "I'll come back soon."

Eleanor nodded and soon was puffing out small, even breaths.

Netta watched her several minutes more. They had been speaking in jest, but Eleanor wasn't wrong. Her sister was developing into a beautiful woman. She swallowed, the back of her throat burning. And fine looks were a currency their father traded upon.

She pressed a kiss to her sister's forehead then rolled from the bed. Soon it would be just her and Eleanor. They'd have the rest of their days to tease and share confidences. But now she needed to return to her job, the one that would make all of their dreams come true.

She closed the window behind her and crouched down on the porch roof, scouring for a pebble of appropriate size. Her fingers closed upon one and she stood and took aim. She winced at the slight *plink* as the stone hit the window above Eleanor's and then sounded again as it plopped back down to the porch roof.

A figure came to the third-story window and nodded before disappearing.

Netta scrambled down the lattice and met Dollie in the darkest part of the yard.

The older woman grasped her shoulders. "How are you, child?"

Netta pressed her lips into a rueful smile. Dollie would always see her as a child, no matter how old she became. The woman had been both her and Eleanor's nursemaid before transitioning into their lady's maid. She'd kissed all of their scraped knees and bruised elbows. Cooed over them when they'd learned a lesson well. Doted over them as a mother would.

"I'm well." Netta squeezed the woman's arm. "Better than well. I have new employment." She reached into her reticule and pulled a small pouch from its depths. She pressed it into Dollie's hands. "Take it. Put it with the rest of your savings."

Dollie pulled open the drawstring, a coarse, grey strand of hair escaping her cap. "Lawks alive. Wherever did you get this, child?"

Along with the coin she could spare, Netta had included something else for Dollie, and the woman pulled out a platinum cravat pin. The diamonds encrusted on it shimmered in the moonlight.

A twinge of shame pinched her heart, but Netta ignored it. "I lifted it from a man who can well afford another. He has at least three more, just as gawdy." She hadn't been able to resist the temptation when she'd found his silk cravat, pin stuck through the fabric, abandoned in his study. Did he tug off the restraining garment late at night as he read by the fire? Did the frills he loved so much start to choke even him?

"You'll need it more than its previous owner," Netta said firmly. "When I take Eleanor, you'll be out of a position. I want to be sure you're provided for."

Dollie nodded and replaced the pin in the pouch. "When do you think that will be? Soon, I hope."

"Why?" Netta darted a look at her sister's window. It remained dark, her room unmolested by any visitors, but a chill rolled down her spine. "What's happened?"

"Nothing that I know for certain." A breeze rose, and she chaffed her arm with her free hand. "But I've heard your mother and father arguing again. About Eleanor. I think..."

Netta clenched her hand. She remembered those arguments. Arguments where Netta had prayed her mother would prevail.

She never had. "Think what?"

Dollie shifted on her feet. "He's had that man back for dinner. You know his wife passed two years ago. I think he's looking for another."

A vise clamped around Netta's lungs. Black spots danced before her eyes. "But she's only fourteen," she rasped out.

No. Not him. She'd known her father would want to marry Eleanor off to a man of means, but she hadn't thought it would be to *him*. Not after how things had ended the last time. And not now. Netta had thought she had at least two more years before she and Eleanor needed to flee the country.

"Women have been married younger."

Netta shook her head, not wanting it to be true. Yes, women had been married younger, but not anymore. Not in this modern age.

The peeling paint on the house mocked her. The rotted wood on the back porch making her face the horrifying truth.

Her father needed money. Eleanor was the only asset he had left to sell.

"It will be soon." Netta took several deep breaths before setting her shoulders. She had a plan in place, and the means to implement it would soon be in her possession. Everything was under control. "I'm staying at Lord Summerset's home on Grosvenor Street. If an engagement should be announced, send me a note at once."

Dollie nodded. "Take care, child. I have faith everything will turn out right in the end."

Netta embraced the woman then turned and slipped out of her family's yard. She made her way back to the street, a pit of dread opening in her stomach. This job of John's was now the only thing to stand between her and disaster. And the job remained too uncertain to bring any comfort.

She skirted a house and popped out on Wimpole Street. She looked left and right but the carriage was nowhere in sight. The blasted driver must have accepted another fare.

She blew out a breath. Well, it wasn't overlong of a walk. Head down, she set her boots to the ground and hurried for the earl's home.

She didn't see the man peel out of the shadows at the next cross street, only heard his footfall a moment before he grabbed her arm.

"Wot's your rush there, lovely?" He stood several inches above her, his lank hair scraping his dirty collar. He leered. "How about you and I become better acquainted?"

"No, I thank you." She tugged her arm free. "That idea holds no appeal." She should have kept her Bardolph costume on. No man would want to molest her in that. But it was easier sneaking back into the earl's home as herself. There would be less explanations required if she were caught.

"Oy, so proper you are." He stepped closer. "Makes no mind to me if yer friendly or not. I'll just take your bag and be done with it." He reached for her reticule.

Fury swelled within her, making her chest grow tight. Another man trying to take what he wanted from her. "You want my bag? You can have it." And with all her strength, she swung the reticule between his legs.

He gargled, clutched his hands to his groin, and dropped to his knees.

Another form melted from the shadows, and she jumped back, arm aloft, ready to swing again.

"Nice shot, miss," Wilberforce said. He toed the man's shoulder, a smile crossing his face when the man crumpled to his side and curled into a tight ball. "What do you keep in that satchel?"

The tension between her shoulders eased and she lowered her arm. "A stocking full of ha'pennies." She shook her reticule, the clinking of the heavy coins loud in the night air. "I find it makes a most efficient deterrent."

"I'd have to agree."

The man on the ground sputtered, coughing up something foul, and she turned her back and strode away.

Wilberforce was only a step behind her, his footfalls uneven, his soft tread distinctive with his limp.

"Did he ask you to follow me?" she asked.

"No, miss."

"So you did so on your own initiative. Why?" Was he looking for a bribe to keep quiet? She didn't know if she could take another impediment to her new life.

"I didn't think a woman should walk about at night unattended. It isn't safe."

No, nothing in life was safe. Not walking about London at night, nor conversing in a sitting room with the wrong man. She pressed her fingertips to the protrusion at her wrist. Safety was but an illusion. "As you see, I've learned to take care of myself."

"Yes, miss."

She whirled on him. "What are you going to tell your master, and how much do I need to pay to keep you silent?"

"No one is my master," he said with quiet dignity.

She couldn't argue that. Having her own taste of freedom these past years, she knew she could never subjugate herself to society's hierarchy ever again.

"Summerset. Will you tell him where I go?" Had he already done so? The earl did like to toy with her. It would be just like him to keep such knowledge to himself until he could use it against her with most effect.

Wilberforce looked away, down the street. They were only a block from the earl's home. A newly-installed gas lamp made his black hair appear almost midnight-blue. "When I was young, he helped me out of a bad situation."

His words were quiet but hung as heavy as mist. "I don't want anyone to face the trouble I did. So I'll walk you home if I'm able." He stared down at his feet. "I don't know which house you visit if that's your worry, and it's not my business. I only want to make sure you make it home safe."

"And you won't tell Summerset?" she repeated. It was a rare person who wasn't looking for an advantage at every turn. He sounded sincere, but she'd been fooled before.

He lifted his shoulders. "I don't think he needs to know right now."

Netta chewed her lip. That hadn't been the whole-hearted agreement she'd hoped for, but it would have to be enough. She nodded and turned once more for Summerset's house. At his neighbor's yard, she paused. "You understand I'm going to keep going in using the servants' entrance?" It was supposed to be locked at night, but one of the first things she'd lifted had been the housekeeper's key.

He yawned, covering his mouth with his palm. "As you like. Your mode of entrance doesn't matter; only that you're back safe." He even led the way, extracting his own key when they approached the back door. "Goodnight, miss." He nodded and turned for the kitchens, his duty apparently satisfied for the night.

What a strange man. Netta smothered her own yawn. But as long as he kept his mouth shut, his mannerisms weren't her concern.

She crept to the staircase and made her way upstairs to her room. Her eyes drooped as she changed into her night rail. As she settled under the covers one thought kept her awake longer than it ought.

What had the earl done to help Wilberforce out of trouble? For a man who cultivated an appearance of indifference, Summerset certainly seemed to be in the habit of rescuing those in need.

Even with all the roles she played, she couldn't help but think that John Chaucer, Earl of Summerset might be the most practiced actor of them all.

* * *

The fourth step on his staircase squeaked, and John glanced towards his study's door. Netta was home. Finally. Her excursion tonight had been longer than most.

Not that he was keeping an eye on her. As long as she learned her part, she could do whatever she wanted. Visit whomever she wished.

He slouched in his chair. Was she sneaking out to visit a lover? What kind of man would let his woman wander about at night getting into trouble?

What kind of man would be skilled enough to control her? Netta was quite the handful.

"Summerset?"

Should *he* learn where she went? After all, she was an investment. Any intrigues of hers could interfere with his scheme. It was his duty to investigate who might be handling his asset.

Handling her assets.

"John?!"

"What?"

The Baron of Sutton blinked in surprise at the edge in John's voice. He sat across from John, a snifter of brandy in his hand and a concerned expression on his face.

John modulated his tone, removing all signs of frustration. After all, why should he be irritated? Netta's affairs were none of his own. "Apologies. What did you say?"

"I only asked when you wanted to leave. The Home Office won't get any quieter." Sutton placed his glass down and scratched his chin through his bushy, black beard. "If you want to take a more direct approach, I'd understand. Sudworth deserves a thrashing for what he did to your brother. I'd be more than happy to use my fists tonight rather than sneak about adding bits and bobs to a file."

John smiled. Yes, his friends were always ready to get in

a mill or two on his behalf, and he was lucky for it. He, Sutton, Montague, Rothchild, and Dunkeld had been in their fair share of fights working for the Crown as spies, but he'd never felt in any true danger. He had the best of men fighting alongside him.

His eyelids went hot, and he buried his face in his own drink. It wasn't the fault of his friends' that their time together was now so infrequent. They were married, some with families, all having given up espionage. John had a standing invitation to each and every one of their homes, but he rarely accepted. He was the odd man out as his friends turned into fathers and rusticated in their domestic lives.

But if he was ever in need, he knew who to call. Sutton was the only other one of them in London at present, but if John sent a request for assistance to his friends in the country, they'd be upon him just as fast as their horses could carry them.

"A physical response to the assault on Robert is very appealing, I admit." One he'd had to talk himself out of several times. John tossed the last of his whisky down his throat. "But it won't recover my ore mines. Sudworth's beating can wait until after the deed is back in my brother's hands."

Sutton grumbled. "I hate waiting." He tapped the toe of his boot on the floor. "I say, is your cat dead?"

John looked at Judith laying on the hearth before the crackling fire. The animal was stretched out as though she were on an invisible rack, her paws stretched up above her head.

John frowned. Sudworth's cat most likely never lounged with such indelicacy. "No. She likes to sleep that way." It was damned annoying when the cat took up half his bed with that position. And she was mean when he attempted to prod her back to her side.

John rose and stretched his hands to the ceiling. His back popped. "There is also the matter of what Sudworth is up to. I don't buy his claims of seeking justice against Raffles one bit. There is some gain to him in ruining the man. I want to discover what it is before giving him a thrashing." He patted his breast pocket, the letter folded within crinkling. John had written it before his friend had arrived, copying from the original word for word.

If what Sudworth had given him was the original. There was a strong chance it also was a forgery, one meant to implicate Raffles. Regardless, John had mimicked the handwriting to a decent degree, keeping it close enough to not arouse immediate suspicion but distinctive enough that its falsity would be uncovered under stricter scrutiny.

He hoped to walk the fine line between giving Sudworth what he wanted while not sabotaging Raffles with his actions. The subterfuge soothed his conscience but added to the difficulty of his task. He needed to discover the plot before his forgery was brought to light.

Sutton pushed to his feet. "What does Liverpool have to say about the matter?"

"Nothing." John lifted his foot to the seat of his chair and brushed a bit of ash from his white leather boots.

"You have informed him." Sutton crossed his arms and squinted. "He does know we're breaking into the Home Office tonight."

John sniffed. "The prime minister has shown a decided lack of interest in our skills. As such, I have no interest in seeking his approval of our endeavors."

"John."

"Hmm? Yes?"

Sutton merely arched an eyebrow.

John blew out a breath. "I want to learn more first. As of now, I would only have the barest suspicions to tell Liverpool. My inquiries have turned up no connection between the man and Raffles." He rubbed the back of his head. "After I learn something of substance, then I will go to the prime minister." Perhaps. It could be satisfying to lay a fully-foiled plot at the man's feet. Show Liverpool just what he was missing by not utilizing John's talents.

"And if we are caught tonight?" Sutton asked.

John tutted. "When have we ever been caught?"

"Well, there was that time in—"

"Hardly ever," John interrupted. "Truly, you have gone soft since your retirement."

Sutton pinched his lips together. "Robert isn't the only Chaucer brother who likes to gamble."

John's stomach tensed as though punched. His friend was wrong. John never risked what he couldn't afford to lose. And he knew his limits. Breaking into a file room wasn't even close to them.

He turned on his heel and strode for the front door, Sutton following behind. They slid into their coats. The footman held the door, and John and Sutton stood on the front steps while his carriage was brought around.

"I wonder how long it will take to get around security," Sutton said.

John arched an eyebrow.

"Not that I'm not happy to spend the evening with you, of course," Sutton hastily added.

"Of course." John shook his head. He couldn't blame his friends. Having a fine woman at home did tend to change a man's priorities. But where was the excitement? The thrill of a good intrigue? How did his friends not knock their heads against the wall in abject boredom ever since they'd left the service of the Crown?

"Don't worry." John tapped his thumb against his thigh, trying in vain to squash the foolish feeling of abandonment that dug its claws into his skin. "You'll be home abed before the hour strikes three."

"Truly," Sutton said, "a night getting into trouble with you is just the thing. It will be like old times."

Old. Yes. Everything was starting to feel old. If he—John swallowed—was truly retired from the spy game, what on earth would he do with himself? He'd once dreamed of spending his life developing new metals. The chromium steel he'd created had yielded more profit and pleasure than he could have dreamed. If it hadn't been for the accident...if it hadn't been for his mistake, he might never have taken up working for the Crown. His small laboratory had fulfilled his needs.

Since the explosion, he only ever entered it to whip up some concoction that would assist in one of his clandestine assignments.

And now, not even for that.

These days, he woke up, read the papers and his correspondence, ensured production from his mills was running smoothly, and went to bed. Even with shopping jaunts and routs and races, it made for a dull life.

Only Robert's trouble had roused him of late.

His brother's trouble, and Netta.

He glanced back at his house. "Yes. Old times," he murmured. In times of old, he wouldn't have hesitated to liven up his job with an affair between the sheets.

His carriage pulled to a stop before them, and the driver hopped down to open the door. John followed his friend inside.

Perhaps if he didn't want to feel so bloody old, he should stop acting it. Life was short. No need for it to be made miserable with self-denial.

He settled back against the seat as they pulled into motion.

His charm, though legendary, had little effect on the woman, unless one considered an increased degree of insolence on her part a show of success. His generosity of spirit and forbearance as he showed her how to be a lady she only repaid with cheek and scorn.

His lips curved upwards. He did appreciate a saucy woman.

As they rolled through London's streets, he wondered: what would it take to seduce Netta Pickle? And how big of a mistake would it be?

Chapter Nine

"That's absurd." Netta slouched back in her chair and crossed her arms. The man was mad. Even in her days as the accomplished and learned daughter of Viscount Darby, she had never, not once, been instructed to walk with a book atop her head.

"A woman must glide when she enters a room." Summerset placed the thick tome on the crown of his head and provided her with an example. "She must exude a lightness of foot and a grace of motion."

Netta scowled. Damn him if he didn't appear to float across the parlor. The heels of his lavender suede boots made nary a sound as he made his way from one end of the room to the other. His hips remained motionless as his elegant legs stretched, one after the other, in an easy saunter. When he stood before her, he bowed deeply, catching the book as it tumbled from its perch and sweeping it as flamboyantly through the air as though it were a feathered hat.

He straightened and dropped the book in her lap. "And that is how a lady walks."

She looked at the size of the book, examined the size of his head, and sighed. It was no use. Nothing could deflate his ego, not even a sound thumping.

"This isn't difficult." He tugged at the billowing lace cuff of his shirt. "A lady should be polite, witty, and composed at all times. And when she enters a room, she must—"

"Bloody glide. I know, I know." She rolled to her feet. "But turning me into a blasted bookshelf won't do nothing to help me glide. I'm not a swan, you know."

"Won't do anything to help you glide." He shook his head. "I do believe for every double negative you use, I'll tell cook to serve you one less of those puddings you so enjoy."

She gasped, and caught the book as it tumbled from her head. "You wouldn't dare."

He merely quirked an eyebrow.

Yes, of course he would. He was the sodding Earl of Summerset, and if ever a man dared, it was he.

All right. She balanced the book back on her head. Time to start rapidly improving her speech. Those puddings were delicious. Far better than the offerings from the little bakeshop around the corner from her apartments.

She took a wobbling step forward. Perhaps she should start a bakeshop when she and Eleanor arrived in America. She'd never made anything before in her life, but she could learn. She was—

"Drat!" She swiped the book from the Persian rug. "I hope this book holds little importance to you," she said, overenunciating her words. "For it is sure to be bent and ragged by the end of this silly lesson."

"It's not silly, and I have two more copies of that particular edition." He tipped his head to the side and narrowed his eyes. "What are you doing with your hips? A woman's hips shouldn't thrust and bobble in that manner."

She gritted her teeth. No man had ever complained about her bobbling hips before. She muttered something rude under her breath, which, of course, he heard.

"I would have made a marvelous woman," he replied. "Perhaps in my next life I'll be so fortunate. But as we are stuck for the moment in this life"—he moved behind her and placed his hands at her waist—"be so good as to move just so." He fitted his front to her back and urged her forwards.

Netta sucked in a breath. He was warm and hard in all the right places. He wrapped an arm around her middle, his palm splayed beneath her breasts, and a delicious shiver danced down her spine. She wasn't as free with her affections as some of her friends in the theatre, but she also wasn't some untried girl. She knew when a man moved well, and how that would translate into his bed sport.

And the earl moved *very* well. With a casual press of his hand there, a nudge of his thigh there, he glided her about the room.

He bent his head, his breath hot on her ear. "How does that feel?"

"Quite nice." She swallowed, trying to bring moisture back to her mouth.

They came to a standstill, his hand still pressed indecently to her belly, his thumb just grazing the underside of her bosom. He was folded around her like a luxurious velvet coat. She could feel the steady beat of his heart against her back...and when it kicked up its pace.

He was as affected as she.

"Do you think—"

A scratch at the open door ended her question, and it was probably for the best. Nothing good could come from what she was about to suggest.

Nothing except good, sweaty tupping, she thought with regret.

John straightened, dropping his hands from her body. "Yes?' he asked the footman.

"Lady Mary Cavindish is here to see you, my lord. Shall I show her in?"

"Straight away. And send up refreshments, as well."

Missing his heat, Netta turned.

John rocked up on his toes, his eyes crinkling at the corners, looking much too happy to see this visitor.

All of her remaining warmth seeped away. "Who is Lady Mary Cavindish?" If her voice was waspish, it couldn't be helped. She plucked the book from her head.

"A very dear friend," he said, "and someone who I thought could help you with your lessons in deportment."

She tapped the book against her thigh. A female friend who had the grace, elegance, and intelligence to assist her in becoming a lady? Netta narrowed her eyes. She couldn't wait to meet such a friend. To have earned the earl's approval, the woman must be something special.

She probably had a bosom up to her chin.

An older woman with ivory hair peeking from her lace cap and spectacles perched on her nose toddled into the room.

Or not.

"Auntie May!" John swooped down on her. "How lovely to see you again. You are looking as beautiful as a dew-flecked rose."

She raised her cheek for his kiss. "I won ten pounds off you at whist just last week. Such an effusive greeting is hardly necessary. Neither is such flattery appropriate."

He patted her hand. "Where you are concerned, flattery is always appropriate."

The older woman shook her head, but the soft skin of her cheeks was decidedly pink. "Tosh. Now, what am I doing here? Are you finally going to call in your loan on my club?"

He pressed a hand to his heart. "You wound me. I would never do anything so boorish." He winked at the woman. "Or so unprofitable." Tucking her hand into the crook of his arm, he led her across the room to Netta.

"May I present Miss Netta Dudley."

Dudley? Netta wrinkled her nose.

"Miss Reed?"

Netta tapped her finger against her lips before shaking her head. Her character really didn't feel like a Reed.

He sighed. "We're still working on the name. Meet Netta. Netta, this is Lady Mary, or Auntie May to those of us who used to run through her gardens chasing Sheba, her long-haired cat."

Lady Mary hooted. "How my cat hated you and Marcus. I'd forgotten all about that." She peered about the floor.

"Speaking of cats, where's yours? This is a new dress. I don't want your beast ruining it."

"She's outside in the gardens." John settled Lady Mary on a velvet chair. "Your skirts are safe."

Remembering her act, Netta dropped into an inelegant curtsy. "Good afternoon, Lady Mary. *Hh*ow wonderful to make your acquaintance." She looked to John and frowned when he wobbled his hand from side to side. That enunciation had been just shy of perfect.

Lady Mary cocked her head. "What are you up to, Johnnie?"

Johnnie? Netta swished her skirts back and took the seat opposite the woman. "Yes, Johnnie. What are your plans?"

He draped himself on the settee, his coquelicot-colored jacket a perfect match for the stitching running through the gold damask sofa. He stabbed a finger in Netta's direction. "If my instruction has taught you anything, it is that you do not get to call me by my given name."

"But you call me Netta." She widened her eyes, trying and failing at looking innocent. She gave up the attempt and smirked. "Surely it is only fair that I use your Christian name, as well."

"I like this one." Lady Mary jabbed a finger at Netta. "She's not like those beef-witted women who usually hang off of you."

"Yes." Summerset pressed his lips together. "But she still maintains all the sauce even without the meat. She has yet to learn that a little impudence goes a long way." He inclined his head, like the king to a subject. "You may call me John when we are within these walls."

"How kind of you." Netta gritted her teeth. Truly, the man was too much. If one could measure impudence, his would exceed that of anyone in England.

"Now, Auntie May, I have a project for Netta and I need her to appear as refined a lady as a princess."

Lady Mary huffed. "With Princess Caroline as an example, no refinement is necessary. The daughter of a butcher could show more quality than her."

John pursed his lips. "Fine. To appear as a gently born woman of tender years if you prefer. I've been training her but I'd like to start the testing process. That's where you come in."

"Am I to understand that she is not of the upper class?" she asked.

"That is correct."

Netta bit the inside of her cheek to keep from smiling. How easily he was fooled. That small victory was enough to take the sting out of being discussed as though she weren't in the room.

"And what is it you'd have me do?" A servant entered carrying a tea tray, and Lady Mary pointed to the low table in front of her. She picked a sweetmeat from a bowl. "Take her about to teas and afternoon calls? Make sure she blends in?"

"Correct again. You are so wonderfully clever, Auntie May."

The woman shot John a look. "If you wish to give her the appearance of propriety, then why, pray tell, would you send her about with me? You know I'm a square peg in the ton's round hole."

John smiled. "And that's why I adore you. But while you might be seen as...eccentric, you still have the credentials our kind cares about. I can't think of anyone more suited."

Lady Mary poured cups of tea, handing one to Netta and John before taking her own. "My nephew's wife refused you."

"Marcus and Elizabeth are in Bath." John at least had the grace to look abashed.

"And the wives of your other friends?"

"Why bother wondering about what might have been when I have succeeded in obtaining the use of your unparalleled services." John rested his elbow on the armrest and propped his chin on his fist. "Do I have your services, Auntie May? It would be ever so helpful to me."

"Of course." She narrowed her eyes and smiled. "For another quarter point knocked off my interest rate. I want my club turning a profit in two-months' time."

"Done." He sat forwards, resting his arms on his knees. "Where will be your first stop?"

"I don't know." Lady Mary frowned. "I've avoided making calls for a good two months now. My reappearance with a new companion on my arm will raise eyebrows. She is supposed to be acting as a lady's companion?"

"I think I'll make her the daughter of an old friend of mine. A young lady I selflessly agreed to show around London." John ran his gaze up and down her body. "I won't mind if she raises a few eyebrows. I want people to wonder about her. Just not for the wrong reasons."

Netta stared back. So he wanted her to cause a minor stir. Why? He still hadn't condescended to inform her of his plan. "Wha—"

"She's a little old to be an innocent debutante." Lady Mary pulled a small flask from her reticule and poured a splash of its contents into her tea.

Netta plucked up the sugar nippers and dropped three lumps into her own cup with a bit more force than necessary. Tea splashed onto the saucer. She was not yet four and twenty. She sniffed. Hardly on the shelf.

"She'll be new and shiny." John fluttered his hand through the air. "I want her to be a little mysterious, making people want more of her. Making men want more from her."

Netta paused, the cup half way to her mouth. Proper, refined, retiring, alluring, and mysterious? That was a tall order, even for an actress as skilled as she. "I don't—"

"She certainly has the attributes to catch the eye," Lady Mary said.

Netta followed the woman's glance down to her bosom. Her décolletage was rather striking, if she did say so herself. It made up for the softness of her stomach.

The older woman nodded. "I'll do what I can, but most

of the effort will be up to her." Lady Mary turned in her chair to face Netta. "What do you think, child? Shall we make some trouble? What say I pick you up tomorrow afternoon?"

Netta raised her eyebrows. "Oh, I get to speak now?"

"When," John drawled, "have you ever had an issue getting a word in edgewise?"

Only around John and Lady Mary. It was highly irritating. She could understand a little better now why her mother had chided her as a child to hold her tongue and let other people speak.

"In that case, *John,* I must decline." She set her cup onto the table and leaned back. She cocked her elbow on the back of her chair and crossed one leg over the other. "Going about the ton acting like your trained monkey isn't part of the terms of our arrangement. You wanted me for one distraction. One. A singular event."

"I disagree on your understanding of our terms." He tilted his head, and the afternoon sunlight gilded his blond crown of hair. He looked like he wore a halo, but Netta knew better. "In return for payment, a very large payment I might add, you agreed to assist me in unspecified ways. I am now specifying."

Yes, and specifying something Netta wasn't able to do. Agreeing to bait a man was one thing. Even if John's target was a member of the ton, the chances were great she wouldn't know him. Her father rarely had friends visit.

Women were another story. She'd joined her mother in receiving her friends' calls. She'd escaped from Society for a reason. It wouldn't do to waltz back in now with naught but a false name as protection.

She scraped her teeth against her lower lip. But could a new name protect her? She'd run away before coming out. And she'd changed much from the awkward girl she'd been. There weren't many aside from family and close friends who would recognize her.

She turned to Lady Mary. "Who do you propose," she

said, stretching out each word as though each syllable posed a hardship, "to pay a visit to on the morrow?"

"I haven't called on Caroline Brennan for ages."

"Isn't she a member of your club?" John interrupted. "You must see her frequently."

"But I haven't *called* on her for a good while." Lady Mary adjusted her spectacles and peered over the rims at the earl. "There's a difference."

Netta tapped her thumb on her cup. Should she ask about this club they kept going on about? She wasn't certain Netta Pickle would care.

"I also owe a visit to that wretchedly dull woman, Lady St. John." Lady Mary pursed her lips. "Oh, and the Dowager Marchioness of Mallen, I would think."

John jerked from his elegant sprawl. "No." His voice was hard, flinty, his expression more so. "You will not visit that woman."

Lady Mary gave him a pitying look. "My dear boy, do you think because you refuse to acknowledge her presence that others do, as well? Tosh. The dowager marchioness might be completely lacking in finer feelings, but she has a good head on her shoulders. And if you want Netta to practice her polish, no other woman in Society would do so well. A trial by fire, if you please."

"I do not please," he gritted out. "That woman is malicious and vile, and I don't want her within fifty feet of anything of mine, including Netta."

Netta ignored the absurd possessive in John's comment. She scooted to the edge of her seat. "Who is the Dowager Marchioness of Mallen?" The name was familiar. The current marquess was reputed to be something of a rake, or at least that had been his reputation six years ago. In her new life, Netta was no longer privy to the ton's *on dit.*

"No one of import," John said.

"His grandmother." Lady Mary tutted. "I like holding a grudge as much as the next person, but you take your resentment to extremes. When is the last time you talked to her?"

John clenched then relaxed his hand. "It's only been six and twenty years since last we spoke."

A burst of laughter slipped past Netta's lips, and John glared at her. She turned it into a gentle cough.

"People change," Lady Mary said.

He looked away. "She hasn't."

A breeze shifted the gauze curtains at the open window, the rustling fabric sounding loud in the sudden silence.

"Well, it was only an idea." Lady Mary gathered up her reticule. "We need not bother the dowager tomorrow. Two calls will be sufficient. Shall I pick you up at three?" she asked Netta.

She'd be more eager to agree if the Lady Mallen were still on the itinerary. What could a grandmother have done to her grandson to garner nearly three decades of neglect? If any man seemed least likely to hold a grudge, it was John with his nonchalance and careless disdain. She dearly wanted to meet the person who could incite such violent emotions in the earl.

But this was business, not her entertainment. Visiting with two women she didn't know was a risk she was willing to take for four thousand pounds. Her heart beat a bit faster as she nodded. "I'll be ready."

John stood with Lady Mary. "She'll be properly dressed and on time. Whether she will be ready remains to be seen."

Irritation chased away her nerves. His lack of faith in her skills was most unjust. She was putting on the performance of a lifetime here and no one appreciated it. The fact that John didn't know he was witnessing a dramatic interpretation of a street urchin becoming a lady was proof as to its excellence.

Four thousand pounds. Four thousand pounds. It was more than enough to repay a bruised ego. She brought the street back to her voice. "I'll be ready. I'll be the most right proper miss your lot has ever seen."

He sighed. "Sometimes I despair of you."

She smirked. Poor fool. His exasperation was almost enough to compensate for a lack of accolades on her performance. Almost. "Have no fears, kind sir," she said her voice airy. "My behavior will be nothing but a credit to you and your teachings. Good day, Lady Mary." She lowered into a curtsy fine enough to present to the king.

She looked up to gauge the audience reaction, and John hastily shifted his gaze from the spot where her bodice met her flesh.

Cheeks warm, she rose.

Lady Mary clapped the earl on the back. "This just might prove to be a superior form of entertainment. I can't wait to see how it plays out." She adjusted her cap and strode for the door. She waggled her fingers in farewell and disappeared.

John circled Netta, his spirals growing ever tighter. Ever closer.

"Shouldn't you accompany your guest to the door?" Netta turned with him, keeping him in sight. She knew better than to turn her back on a predator. "Or do I now have to teach the instructor about manners?"

"Auntie May is family." His shoulder brushed her own, and a shiver tickled her spine. "We don't stand on formality with each other."

"So your friend's aunt is family but your own grandmother is taboo." His citrus and pepper scent filled her senses. Her endless turning made her head go light. She inhaled deeply, letting the essence of him sink deep into her lungs. "How interesting."

He stopped, his chest inches from hers. Lifting a strand of her hair from her shoulder, he slid his fingers down the lock. "Always looking for an angle, aren't you? Trying to find the profit in every utterance."

She lifted one shoulder. "It would be foolish not to in my position. And I'm nobody's fool."

"Is that so?"

She raised her chin. "You look at me and see a simple thief. But I'm clever. You'd best remember it." It was as much of a warning as she could give him. Her deception was beginning to curdle in her stomach like day-old milk. He most likely didn't deserve her trickery. But her future was too tenuous to trust to the earl's discretion. He could use the knowledge of her birth against her interests.

He could put her in danger even while believing he was doing the right thing.

He twirled his finger, wrapping her hair about it, and tugged. "You greatly misunderstand what I see when I look upon you. Perhaps it's time we changed that."

He was close, so close if she rocked up on her toes they could kiss. His gaze was unblinking, and she couldn't look away. His breath caressed her cheek. The cool silk of his cravat soothed the heated skin above her bodice. "How do we change it?" she whispered.

His smile was slow to unfurl, but when it reached its full extent, her core clenched. And for the first time, Netta recognized how dangerous this man was. If even his smile could cloud her mind, what could he do to her when he used his whole body.

He leaned closer, nudged her temple with his nose and inhaled deeply. "How would you like to play a game?"

Chapter Ten

Christ, he'd never smelled anything so good as the woman before him. He'd chosen the soaps from Paris for their subtle bergamot odor. But mixed with the hint of licorice that wafted off Netta whenever she moved, her scent was intoxicating. And if she smelled like a treat, he couldn't wait to taste her.

And taste her he would. He'd been playing the good earl for too long. No assignments from Liverpool with their promise of legally-sanctioned mischief to enliven his days. Getting his brother out of trouble. Again. Truly, he deserved some reward for his trials.

And Netta was one enticing reward.

Her alluring gaze narrowed, a small divot puckering the skin between her brows. He had never seen the equal to her eyes. The same striking violet color as his favorite waistcoat at the edges of her irises, darkening as they went inward to make her pupils look as deep as the midnight sky.

She was saucy one moment, a hard-nosed negotiator the next. Always watchful. He spared a fleeting thought to what in her past could have made her so wary. But such dull thoughts weren't to be borne at a moment like this. Not when he could lean forward the barest inch and brush his chest over her puckered nipples. Not when she flicked her tongue over her bottom lip in a teasing invitation.

"I've been known to enjoy a game or two," she said slowly. "What did you have in mind?"

He circled behind her, enjoying the tension in her shoulders. He liked putting this woman's barricades up.

Would make it that much more satisfying to knock them down. She seemed so sure-footed, and he wanted nothing more than to knock her off balance. She would be most diverting to toy with, but the knot of tension in his chest told him he did have some standards. "Netta, have you ever lain with a man?"

She pressed a hand to her bosom and looked over her shoulder. "What a shocking suggestion," she said, enunciating each vowel and consonant. "What kind of woman do you take me for?"

She was the kind of woman he wanted to take, period. But he had to know. He wouldn't be the man to lead an innocent astray. There was a tease in her voice which made him believe she was anything but innocent, but he'd read this woman wrong before.

He prowled in front of her and trailed the knuckle of his finger down her neck. Down until it rested in the hollow between her full breasts. His cock thickened. Fuck, he wanted those dugs. To suck them, bite them, slide his Thomas between their silky depths.

But not if she was untouched. Virgins were a pain in the arse he swore he'd never bother with again.

"You don't strike me as an innocent miss, but you've been known to overplay your hand." Her skin was so damn soft. He wanted more of it exposed to his fingers, his tongue. "If ever there was a time to be truthful, this is it. Do you wish to go on with our business arrangement as before and forget this conversation? Or do you want to play?"

His heart beat faster. It was silly to be so on edge over a woman's response. If she turned him down, there were other women to distract himself with. Other games.

But her reply mattered.

She walked her fingers up his chest, the tips tangling in the elaborate knot of his cravat. "What are the rules to this game, pray tell? And what is the reward for winning?"

John all but rubbed his hands together in anticipation. Oh, how he enjoyed this part. Devising an amusement to thrill and titillate a partner was almost as satisfying as sliding inside the woman when the game had ended. Almost.

Usually he liked time to plan, but he was willing to make do. His mind spun. What predicament could he put little Netta Pickle in? He couldn't do anything with a hint of danger. Those games did require time to plot, and he wouldn't subject Netta to even the slightest threat of harm. But something that would frustrate her. Make her press her lips together and give him that squinty-eyed look of annoyance he was becoming so fond of.

He'd set it up so she'd fail, of course. He did like to win. But her punishment for losing would be satisfying to both parties.

He picked up the book she'd grumbled so about. "I think this should do it. I want you to make an entire circle about the room without this falling from your head. And no hands," he added sternly. Netta would be the type of woman who would use any loophole in the rules to her advantage.

She plucked the book from him and plopped it on her head. "Child's play."

"I haven't finished." He stroked his chin. "At each corner of the room, you will have to remove one article of clothing. If you can do that, without touching the book or letting it fall, you will have your reward."

"Which is?" The book wavered, and she steadied it with a frown. "The game hasn't started yet," she reminded him.

He smothered his grin. Her confidence was endearing. And cock-hardening. Which was a novel combination of reactions for John. "Your reward..." He paused, thinking. He could offer her money; he knew she needed it. But he didn't want their game to be sullied by commerce. His mind whirred with all that he'd learned of her since her stay. Her sweet tooth had no equal that he'd yet met. "Your reward shall be one of Pierre's plum cakes delivered here for you every morning." He bent his head and nudged her cheek with his nose. "Hot from the oven," he whispered.

"And if I fail?" Her breath tickled his neck.

"If you fail, I get a kiss."

She pulled back. "That's it?"

Was that disappointment in her eyes? John hoped so.

"Just a kiss. Your virtue will remain intact." For now. It pained him to wait. Certain parts of him ached more so than others. But the anticipation always increased the pleasure.

She nodded, and blew out her cheeks as she righted the book. "Starting now?"

He waited until she removed her hands and held them out to her sides. One side of his mouth curled up. There was no chance in hell she'd win. "Starting now."

She eased her way to the first corner of the room, deftly avoiding an arm chair. John couldn't help but be impressed. Her step had definite notes of a glide now. She paused and slid her fichu from around her neck. She let it float to the floor.

John found a chair with a good view and settled in. This was damnably good entertainment. If he did lose his ore mines, he could probably recover his fortune by charging men to watch women slowly remove their clothes. He should suggest it to Sutton as a special room in The Black Rose. "The fichu was easy," he called out. "But what will you choose next?"

The book wobbled, and Netta drew up short, holding her breath.

If there was a next corner.

The book stayed in place, and John didn't know if he was disappointed or relieved that the show would go on.

At the next corner, she toed off one of her slippers, kicking it in his direction, and continued on her way.

John harrumphed. He'd forgotten about her slippers. Those were easy.

"You don't have to look so disappointed." She reached the next corner and turned with a military precision. She wiggled her slipper to the end of her toes and took aim.

The slipper flew straight at him, and John snagged it from the air before it could clock his head. "When I decide to do something, I do it to win."

Damn it, she only had one more corner to turn. He twisted on his seat to watch as she sauntered behind him. "Has anyone told you before that you're too cock-sure? You've divested yourself of the easy gets. This next one will be the true test."

She stood in the final corner and considered. Sinking into a low curtsy, she raised her gown, revealing inch after inch of tantalizing calf.

His breath stalled when her skirts raised over her knee. Her thighs were plump and shapely.

She raised her dress another inch, and his mouth went dry. Her skin looked like the softest silk, and the urge to flip her to her back, press open those creamy thighs, and slide his hands over every inch was almost overwhelming.

She tried unlacing the knot that held her stocking up. The book wobbled and she stilled. Biting down on her lower lip, she next attempted to tug the stocking down underneath the garter. The book slipped, and she tilted her head to keep it centered. Carefully, she straightened.

"Not so easy now, is it."

She glared at him from the corner of her eye. Reaching around her neck, she worked off the top buttons to her gown.

John leaned forwards, pressing his elbows into his knees. She wouldn't take off her entire gown, would she?

She lowered her hands to her mid-back, and the shoulders of her gown sagged, the bodice slipping low over her bosom.

She would. John raised his eyebrows. She did have a competitive streak a mile wide. Well, so did he. Her tease could be turned back upon her.

"Do you have someone at home to help you dress, Netta?"

She opened her mouth, swiveling her gaze to him. And

froze.

John stroked the toe of her slipper along the ridge of his hard length.

"Uh..." She licked her bottom lip, her eyes following the slipper's path. "What was the question again?"

He straightened his leg and thanked his tight pantaloons. They gave Netta a nearly unimpeded view of just what she did to him. Of how much was in store for her. "Do you have someone who takes care of you at home? Someone to peel you from your gown at night? To soap your back, get you clean in all the places you don't touch." He exchanged the slipper for his hand, squeezing his aching cock. The image of Netta being attended to by a lady's maid, in every way a woman should be, just about had him spending in his pants.

Her chest rose and fell, her breath quick. "I have no one to assist me. You know I can't afford the expense."

"The row of buttons along your back can't be easy to undo on your own." He widened his legs. "Living without a lady's maid must have made you...flexible."

She lifted her gaze to meet his. "You have no idea." And with a little shimmy, her gown dropped to her hips. She pulled one arm free from its sleeve, and the dress lowered another inch.

He muffled a groan. He was going to lose. Lose to this minx. And although a part of him wanted to see how far she could disrobe in his sitting room with that blasted book on her head, a stronger part of him needed to put his mouth on those breasts that heaved with every breath she took.

He needed to fight fire with fire.

He flicked open one of the buttons of his falls.

Netta froze, her eyes swiveling to track his hands.

Lazily, as though he weren't dying with need, he thumbed another button free from its hole. His smallclothes, and the pulsing cock beneath, tented the remaining fabric.

She yanked at her other sleeve, pushing the gown down

her thighs. The book slid again, but she tilted her head further and stopped its descent.

John reached under the front placket and gripped his Thomas. The chemise she wore ended mid-thigh. Her curvy legs were on full display, the dimples above her knees just begging for his tongue to trace them.

Netta swallowed. The skin above her stays was flushed pink. The tips of her nipples pressed against the cotton. Even with her head cocked at an unnatural angle, she looked provocative. Sensuous. Ripe to be ravished.

Closing her eyes, she took a deep breath. She lifted one foot out of her gown and stepped clear. She raised her other foot, but the gown caught on her toes. She shook it, swirled her ankle in a circle, to no avail.

John was moments away from losing, but he couldn't help but appreciate how her body jiggled delightfully with each movement.

She brought her knee to her abdomen and reached down, trying to unknot the gown from her foot.

The book slid. Netta corrected, tilting her whole body to try to keep it on her head, and with a shriek, she crashed to the floor.

"Hell!" John leapt to his feet and rushed to her side.

She rolled over onto one elbow and shoved her hair from her face. A very dirty word left her pretty mouth.

John's shoulders sagged. No one could be truly hurt and look that angry.

He grinned. And, her spill meant he won.

"I'll take that kiss now."

She kicked out, but the gown was wrapped around her ankle like a snake and didn't budge. "Right this moment? With me laying on the ground trussed up like a Christmas goose?" She flailed her leg with no success.

She was half-dressed, breathing heavily, and her eyes glittered with irritation.

His mouth watered. He loved when she was irritated. "Right now." He pressed on her shoulder, rolling her to her back and rested on his hip beside her.

She shifted her thighs, her chemise settling in the cradle of her quim. A pulse fluttered in her throat. And her breasts...

He trailed the pad of his finger over the lush mounds. Her breasts threatened to spill over the top of her chemise and stays with every breath she took.

She wasn't a sore loser; he'd give her that. She eagerly accepted the consequences to her loss. Netta parted her mouth and tilted her chin up, ready for her kiss.

John lowered his head. He paused, his mouth hovering inches from hers.

Her eyebrows drew together. "Your kiss?"

He nudged her nose with his own. "Don't worry. I'll take my kiss. But I didn't specify where." He loosened the strings of her stays with one hand, keeping his eyes fixed on her face. He loved the way she tracked his every movement, looking like she couldn't wait to see what he'd do next. Loved the way she sucked her lower lip into her mouth when he pushed her stays aside. Adored the slight catch in her breath when he filled his hand with her breast.

He slid down her body, and encircled one stiff nipple with his lips.

He drew on the bud. The chemise between them was a crime. He could only imagine the softness of her skin against his lips, her taste, her heat. But it was necessary. If he was going to stop at just a kiss, he needed every barrier available.

She arched, pressing closer, and he couldn't restrain his groan. A man could blissfully suffocate between this woman's breasts. If the last thing he had to touch, to taste, to smell, was Netta, he would die a happy man.

She threaded her fingers in his hair. "Oh, John." Her whisper was the sweetest music.

He spent more time than he'd intended, but less than he needed at her breast, laving the skin through the wet fabric, learning every contour and curve. He stayed until he knew her reaction to every caress. Found the pressure she liked. Discovered how she couldn't keep but moan when he scraped his teeth across her hard nipple. He stayed until his weeping cock demanded he either take it further, or let her go.

With a sigh of regret, he pulled back and refastened his pantaloons.

"Wait." She pressed her palm to her chest. "You're stopping?"

"Indeed." Delayed gratification was another game he liked to play at, but for the life of him he couldn't remember why. He rolled to his feet and reached for her. "That was the terms of our wager."

She grabbed his hand and let him pull her to her feet. "But I won't mind if we extend the terms to something more...agreeable to both parties."

His cock twitched. Yes, it liked that idea very much. But then the game would be truly over. He and Netta would have satisfied their urges. Maybe fall into bed a couple more times and then tire of each other.

He wanted to drag out his anticipation for as long as possible. Enjoy every drawn-out moment before the inevitable boredom set in. John straightened the knot of his cravat. "I won. I set the terms."

She shrugged, but he didn't buy her act. There was no way a woman could be desperate for it one moment and indifferent the next, but he appreciated her efforts. Bending, she swept up her gown and tossed it over her shoulder. The move was decidedly unfeminine yet absolutely beguiling.

"You think I lost?" She sauntered to the door, her hips swaying with each step. She glanced over her shoulder and dropped her gaze to his groin.

His wayward cock strained for her, not listening when he told it to stand down.

"From where I'm standing, I won that round." She floated from the room, with nary a concern that she wore only a chemise and one stocking. John waited to hear a scandalized shriek from a servant but none came. After all, who would dare shout at a queen.

John staggered to a chair and dropped onto it. Buggering hell, she was right. If this was what winning felt like, he didn't want to imagine losing to the woman.

It took him several minutes to clear his head. He didn't want to admit it, but the suspicion wouldn't go away.

He just might have met his match in Netta Pickle.

Chapter Eleven

John leaned closer to his floor-to-ceiling mirror and frowned. He ripped out the Ballroom knot in his cravat. "Wil!" He glared at the open door to his dressing room. "Wil! Bloody hell, where did he go?"

"I'm right here." Wilberforce strolled into the bedroom, holding a turquoise-colored waistcoat. "If you hadn't released yet another valet from service, we wouldn't be running late." He draped the waistcoat over one arm and brushed John's hands aside. "Let me."

John raised his chin, his shoulder muscles easing. If Wilberforce wouldn't have quit on the spot, John would have made him his valet long ago. No one tied cravats quite like the man.

"I'd like to arrive at Sudworth's before he leaves for his evening's entertainment." Which was a lie. He'd rather he didn't go to the man's home at all, but it needed to be done.

John hadn't seen Netta yet that day, and he missed her devious smile. She'd stayed in her room for breakfast, no doubt for the sole purpose of provoking him, thinking that her absence would only further stoke his lust.

He sniffed. It wouldn't work. He was the one who toyed and teased, and he wouldn't relinquish that role easily. "Has Netta left with Lady Mary yet?"

"Not five minutes ago." Wilberforce's jaw hardened, and the next tug at the cravat was a shade firmer than usual.

"Something on your mind?" John asked.

"Just wondering what your intentions are to the girl." Wilberforce gave one last adjustment to the elaborate knot and stepped back. "She's not your usual bored widow or experienced mistress. She could get hurt."

"Netta?" John's voice dripped with disbelief. "Hurt? If ever there was a woman who knew how to take care of herself, Netta is she." He hadn't even tupped the woman yet, and still he received the censure for it. Wasn't that just the way of life?

Wilberforce held up the waistcoat. "She's not like the others," he said quietly.

John slid his arms into the garment and considered. No, she kept him on his toes more than any other woman had. And the more he knew her the less he believed her street urchin act, but he'd let her maintain that deception for a while longer. But he didn't lie when he said she could take care of herself. She wasn't a woman to trifle with, and whatever pleasure John was able to take with her was only what she allowed. "You don't take her measure well."

Wilberforce button him up and reached for the jacket lying on the bed. "I know she's had a rough beginning to life. I know she's vulnerable. I don't want to see her hurt."

"And you think I'm in the business of hurting women?" John turned his back on his friend and smoothed the edges of his cream jacket, examining the image he made in the mirror. He didn't know if he should be offended by Wil's question or not.

Yes, he decided. Yes, he should. Wil had known him too long to insinuate such an unjust accusation. And he was offended on Netta's behalf, too. She was no thin-shelled egg, easily broken.

"Don't get your smallclothes in a twist." Wilberforce pulled a small silver brush from his pocket and swept the shoulders of John's jacket. "I, more than anyone, know you have a good heart. I just think you should be careful."

And now Wil was accusing him of having a good heart. "I can't believe we've known each other for thirty years." He turned at the scratch to the door and waved the footman inside. "It's like you don't know me at all."

He ignored Wil's huff of displeasure and flipped open the missive the footman handed him. Nausea roiled in his stomach as he read.

"What's wrong?" Wil asked.

"Nothing." He tossed the letter on his bureau and looked at his reflection once more. "Alan Hampson only writes me news of my brother's actions." He licked his finger and brushed his eyebrow into place. "Or should I say inactions. Robert has taken to napping in the mill's office in the afternoon."

"You've asked Hampson to spy on Robert?" Wilberforce slapped the brush into his palm. "That won't end well for either of you."

"I won't sit back and let my dissolute brother ruin the Summerset fortunes." He clenched his fist. "I've worked too hard to restore them."

Wilberforce rested a hand on his shoulder and squeezed. He caught John's eye in the mirror's reflection. "His actions don't reflect on you."

John snorted. Of course not. Society was most prudent about only implicating the individual with his or her own behavior. They never scorned anyone for the transgressions of his family. He shook his head. What a fine fantasy to live in.

Wilberforce turned and picked up a cherry wood case from the bureau. "Do you remember what you said to me when you found me those years ago?"

John had to strain to hear the man, he spoke so low. "Something about getting your lazy arse moving, if I recall." He infused his voice with a lightness he didn't feel. Anything to counteract those dark memories. Bile still rose up his throat when he remembered how callously his father had sent the small boy away to pay for his debts. Wil had been the orphaned son of Summerset's stablemaster, and had been pressed into service cleaning their chimneys and mucking out the stalls.

It hadn't been enough for John's father. The boy was

worth more as an asset to pay off his debt than as a laborer, especially considering it would be one less mouth to feed if he sold the boy.

Wilberforce lifted the lid and ran his fingers over the handles of the daggers that lay within. "You told me it wasn't my shame. That his actions were not my own."

John swallowed, the back of his throat burning. Even now, the words sounded hollow. But he'd just been a child himself, not five and ten years of age when he'd tracked down the man who'd bought the small child who liked to follow John and his brothers about with curious eyes and few words.

What did a person say to a child found locked in a closet, the evidence of man's capacity for evil marking his innocent body?

There were no words. Only actions. He and Montague, friends even from that young age, had made the man pay and taken the boy home, hiding him from his father's eyes while letting him heal.

And John had been stuck with the bounder ever since. Wil had followed him about like a lost puppy as a child and now he thought he could tell John his own business. It was like having one's mother shadowing every move.

"What are you talking about?" John tugged on the hem of his jacket and turned from the mirror. "The situations don't compare in the least."

Wilberforce dipped his chin to his chest. "Seems we all carry a lot of unearned shame is all I meant."

Wil was right. Robert's actions should only reflect on himself. Every man was responsible for his own behavior. But knowing that in his head and feeling it in his heart were two different things altogether. What would his brother have become if he hadn't been scarred by John's experiment?

Not knowing what else to do, he changed the subject. Holding his arms out wide, he spun in a circle. "Well? How do I look? Anything missing?"

"Only your hardware, sir." Wilberforce brought the wood case to him and held it up.

John picked out the shortest blade and held it to the light. "They've been sharpened?"

"They'll cut off an ear without any effort."

John arched an eyebrow as he slid the dagger into his wrist holster. "Your bloodthirstiness sometimes worries even me." He deposited another knife into his boot. He strode to the large Chinese vase by his armoire and fingered through his walking sticks. He picked out a fine malacca one with an ivory handle.

Wilberforce shook his head. "No, sir. You want the one with the panther's head."

"But this matches my jacket." John frowned and held it to his sleeve. The cream-colored nob disappeared against the fabric.

Wilberforce reached past him and plucked out the one he named. He gave it a twirl before pressing it into John's hand. "And the turquoise eyes on the panther match your waistcoat. Trust me."

John grumbled. Blast and damn, the man was right. He shoved the malacca stick back in the vase and turned on his heel.

"Is Sutton meeting you there?"

John paused at the door. "That would be surprising as I didn't tell him I was going today." Sutton was happier puttering around in his orangery, or managing The Black Rose with his wife. He'd slid into retirement like it was a warm bath.

John pushed that irritating thought away. "Why?"

"I don't like you going into his house alone." Wil rubbed his jaw. "I'll drive you. I'll have to wait outside, but if you shout, I can be with you in moments."

"It's an afternoon visit. I'll be giving the man a large sum of money." And a warning. He didn't care how much Sudworth held over his head. No one hurt his family. "The man will welcome me with open arms. No shouting will be required." He saluted Wil with his walking stick and strode towards the door. "Ta. Don't wait up."

His carriage pulled up to Sudworth's house fifteen minutes later. He hopped out and knocked at the door with the heavy panther's head of his stick. A footman guided him into a sitting room. Where he sat. And waited. And waited even more. Until the insult could hardly be borne.

He snapped the cover to his pocket watch closed and shoved it back in his waistcoat. It had to be intentional. Sudworth wanting to establish dominance over him by making him cool his heels.

Finally, the door opened and Sudworth ambled in. "Summerset. How good of you to come."

John twirled his walking stick between his fingers. "Yes, I thought so." He removed a small leather case and tossed it onto the low table before him. "There's a banknote. Robert's debt is paid in full."

Sudworth left the money on the table and sat across from John. "Cleaning up after your brother again? You make me wish I wasn't an only child."

"Family is important," he agreed. He twirled the stick in the opposite direction and when it rolled through all his fingers he tossed it up and caught it with a snap. "In fact, I consider an insult on any member of my family as an insult to me."

Sudworth chuckled. "You aren't here to complain about the little mark I left your brother, are you? I would think you'd appreciate such a reminder. It might keep him from losing any more of your property."

John gritted his teeth. He couldn't wait to inflict the same curtesy on Sudworth. "Beware you don't push too far. There's a point where other concerns will override my desire for my ore mines."

"Yes, but we're not there yet." Sudworth stretched out his legs and laced his fingers over his belly. "You and I are not so dissimilar. Neither of us passively accepted our lot in life. You inherited a name, but little else. We both of us had to make ourselves who we are today. We had to take what we wanted."

John shifted. "Everyone wants more from life. It's the methods we employ which differentiate us."

"Do you believe that your hands are clean?" Sudworth stared at him, unblinking. "How interesting."

John gripped the shaft of the walking stick until his knuckles went white. "Are we done here?"

Sudworth circled his thumbs around each other. "I heard a letter was found at the Home Office. Nicely done."

John inclined his head.

"How do you feel about a visit to the Dutch embassy?" Sudworth asked.

John kept his expression impassive. It could be no coincidence that Raffles was attempting to secure a British presence in what was an acknowledged Dutch hegemony. If he needed any further proof that the letter had nothing to do with bringing Raffles to justice, this was it.

"It hasn't endeared itself to me." John prodded the tip of his walking stick into the carpet. "The last time I was there the ambassador called me a dandy. I hate that word."

"Well, here's your chance to repay the man. I need a document from his office."

John inhaled sharply. "What type of document?"

"One signed by King William of the Netherlands himself. It will have a map attached."

"And if I recover this document for you, then you will return my deed?"

Sudworth lifted a shoulder. "Perhaps."

John's eye twitched. "Let's not play games. You intend to hold this deed over my head permanently, don't you?"

Sudworth smiled. "Not permanently. But for a good long while. I quite like having a former spy doing my bidding."

All of his muscles hardened. Even when he uncovered whatever scheme Sudworth was involved in, there was no guarantee that he would be able to recover the deed.

"You like to gamble; I'll play you for it." A slight chill settled in his bones. He'd sworn he'd never follow in his father's path, but it seemed the only answer.

He bit back a snort. If only his brother could hear him now, how he would laugh. Was that not Robert's reasoning, as well?

Sudworth leaned forwards and picked up the leather sleeve holding the banknote. He slid it into his pocket. "You have nothing I want well enough to risk the deed."

Netta's image invaded John's mind, and he knew. All his vague ideas of perhaps using her as a distraction coalesced into one overriding purpose. The pit in his gut told him that he had been heading in this direction all the time.

Sudworth had a weakness, and John had the means to exploit it.

Netta wouldn't appreciate being used as a stake.

But it's not as though John intended to lose. He stood. If the dice weren't rolling in his favor, he'd cheat. And against a man such as Sudworth, he wouldn't lose one wink of sleep over it.

He turned to leave, ignoring the warning bell sounding an alarm in his head. Netta would be able to pique the man's interest. She would do her job and John would reclaim his mines. There was nothing to worry about. All he need do was set the ball into motion.

At the door, he turned.

Sudworth remained seated, the first hints of overindulgence making themselves known in the stretch of his waistcoat, a softness about the jaw. He might have worked hard to attain his wealth, but he now enjoyed the excesses. He was self-satisfied. Smug.

He wouldn't know what hit him. "Think on it. There just might be something of mine you'll want to play for."

And with a swirl of his stick, he turned his back on Sudworth and began to plot.

Chapter Twelve

Netta sucked on the comfit and tried to look interested in the conversation. That amount of acting skill was almost beyond her reach. Did all society woman only talk of such nonsense as the latest cross-stitching technique? It had been twenty minutes of this tedium.

She idly rubbed her breastbone. In another world, another life, this would have been her. No worries about whether she could pay rent that week. No concerns except the latest fashions.

No intrigues with devilishly exciting men.

She didn't know if it was regret or relief she felt over her changed circumstances. Most likely a bit of both.

"...don't you think, Miss Courtney?"

Netta sucked away all the sugar until all that was left was the caraway seed. At least there were treats in the little crystal dish on the table. The visit wasn't a complete waste.

A sharp elbow poked into her side. "Miss Courtney," Lady Mary said pointedly, "what say you on this new trend of rouging one's cheeks."

Drat. She'd forgotten she was supposed to be Miss Courtney. It wasn't her favorite pseudonymous name, but it was the best compromise she and John could arrive at. "Rouge? Is that what the Countess of Avignon is wearing now?" She hoped they were still speaking of the French émigré. Lord, how she wanted to shock these women. Tell them how she'd employed all types of face paint to great success. But that wouldn't be in character with a little society miss. "I believe rouge to be the outward sign of inner moral decay. It's frightful that any woman would use it."

Their hostess, Caroline Brennan, nodded stoutly. "Very true."

Lady Mary snorted. "When you get old enough to show signs of outward decay, perhaps you'll be more understanding of those who wish to distract from it. A bit of rouge never hurt anyone."

Mrs. Brennan gasped. "You've never worn anything so scandalous." She shot a look at the empty doorway of the sitting room and leaned forwards. "Have you?"

"My cheeks don't get this hint of pink from walking," Lady Mary said.

"Well..." Mrs. Brennan sat back and lined her fingers together, circling her thumbs around each other. "Perhaps a tiny bit now and then never hurt anyone. A dab here and there to put one's best face forward. Wouldn't you agree just a dab is tolerable, Miss Courtney?"

Netta looked at the mantel clock. Would John be home when she returned? Would he have any new games for them tonight?

With memories of yesterday's kiss swirling through her mind, she did the unforgiveable. She broke character. "When I want to impress it's not my face I put forward. I find a tight French corset to be the most inspiring. When I wear it, I can assure you that no one is looking at my face."

There was a moment of silence, a sharp inhale from their hostess, then Lady Mary burst out guffawing. She laughed so hard her face turned bright red, and Netta began to worry for her health.

Netta poured the woman another cup of tea and pressed it into her hands. "Are you all right?" She should have controlled her tongue. But she was finding it more difficult each day to maintain her act. She missed being just Netta. She felt like herself when she was with John, but she still had a pretense to uphold. Still had lies to tell.

She buried her face in her own cup. But they were small

lies with John. Small, and false, details about her history. But her true self—her thoughts, her feelings, her desires— she readily revealed.

She tapped her finger against her cup. They *were* small lies. Microscopic really. So why didn't she feel better about them?

Lady Mary held up a hand. "I'm fine," she said and wiped her eyes.

Mrs. Brennan's chin wobbled. "I don't think such talk is appropriate in my parlor."

"Don't get your curls in a knot." Lady Mary slurped her tea. "We have discussions such as this at the club all the time. I don't see why your sitting room should be sacrosanct."

Mrs. Brennan flushed. "It's different at The Minerva. There we have a space to indulge in a little bad behavior. But this is the real world."

Lady Mary sighed. "Which is why I don't like making calls." She stood. "The real world, as you call it, is dull beyond belief. I'll see you at the club tomorrow night?"

Mrs. Brennan nodded. "It's lawn darts night. I'll be there."

Netta put her cup down on the table and sketched a hasty curtsy. "Thank you for the tea."

Mrs. Brennan nodded. "It was..." She pursed her lips as she struggled for the right word. "...interesting to meet you, my dear." She walked Netta and Lady Mary to the front door. "You look so familiar to me, Miss Courtney. Are you certain you weren't at Victorino's ball last season?"

"I'm certain." The tea in her stomach slid uneasily about. But her mother may have attended, and there was some similarity of appearance between the two. Perhaps a false name wasn't enough to protect her.

Lady Mary prodded her forward with her walking stick. "Can't be late for our next appointment. Have a good day," she called over her shoulder.

Netta let the footman hand her into John's landau and

waited until Lady Mary was settled beside her and they had rolled several feet from Mrs. Brennan's house. "Well, that didn't go well. I hope I didn't embarrass you with your friend."

"Are you in earnest?" Lady Mary arranged the cushion behind her back. "That was just the rattle-about Caroline needed. I'd forgotten how insufferable she can be. At my club, she's a different person. Open-minded and with a wicked sense of humor."

"I still should have played my part better. I was supposed to be your demure companion."

"You were supposed to practice your elocution and manners. And make an impression." Lady Mary pushed up her spectacles and peered at Netta, her eyes owlish. "I'd say John's real-world test was a success. Perhaps too much of one."

Netta rolled the fabric of her gown between her fingers. "What do you mean?"

"You do look familiar, as Caroline said. Yet John says you come from the East End of London."

She said it as if the East End were one of Dante's circles of hell, and in some places, Netta supposed it was. She didn't live there, and was glad for it, but it had seemed a convenient location to tell John. There was no way an earl would enter such a neighborhood. It gave her a level of protection against his curiosity.

Netta cocked an elbow on the backseat of the landau and tipped her face into the sun. "Wot? You've never visited? Afraid of getting your slippers dirty?"

Lady Mary pressed her lips flat. "Afraid of having my slippers stolen."

Netta's lips twitched. The woman wasn't wrong. And she was nobody's fool, a trait Netta admired. She dropped the street accent. "Very wise of you. I suppose I just have one of those faces that look familiar to everyone."

Lady Mary tapped the end of her walking stick against the coach's floor. "No, you don't. Your face is far from common."

Netta chewed her lip. This conversation was heading nowhere good. She cleared her throat. "So, what sort of club do you have?"

Lady Mary arched an eyebrow but allowed the change in subject. "A gentlewoman's club."

Netta pursed her lips. "I've never heard of such a thing."

"No one has. It's the first of its kind." Lady Mary angled the head of her walking stick so the jewels on the nob caught the sun. If Netta wasn't too much mistaken, she wasn't the only one who liked to engage in a bit of larceny. That walking stick had been in John's home not long ago.

"It's like a gentleman's club," Lady Mary said. "But without the rules. And for women. It's all the crack. You should visit."

"I'm not a gentlewoman."

Lady Mary waved a hand. "Tosh. We accept all kinds."

"In that case, I will." A chance to see such an oddity was too good to pass. From the pocket of her pelisse, she slid out her handkerchief-wrapped bundle and pulled back the edges of the cloth. She held the pile of comfits up to Lady Mary. "Would you like another? I really must find out where these are made."

Lady Mary huffed as she picked one from the pile. "Why? So you can steal direct from the source?" But she didn't sound disapproving. A touch of grudging respect might have even been laced in her words.

Netta merely grinned. The warm sun on her face. A pocketful of sweets. And satin sheets to lay in tonight, hopefully not alone. The day was good.

"This plot you have with Johnnie."

"What about it?" Netta popped another of her sweetly-gotten gains into her mouth.

"I don't want to know the details—"

"Good, because I don't have any." Netta frowned. A fact that was becoming more irritating each day.

Lady Mary held up her hand, palm out. "That's between

you and Johnnie. But...I have concerns."

"John knows what he's doing." If anyone could take the measure of his cleverness, it should be the older woman. "I wouldn't worry overmuch."

"It's not him I'm concerned about." Lady Mary shifted on the seat to more fully face Netta. "Now, I love Johnnie very much. He's always been sweet to me. It was only with his assistance that I was able to open my club. But he's not a man whose attention is ever engaged overlong." She dipped her chin to her chest and peered over her spectacles. "If you take my meaning."

Netta paused, mid-suck. All her good humor vanished. She did take Lady Mary's meaning. It would be a kind warning to a different type of woman, but unnecessary for Netta. She had no illusions about a relationship of any length with the earl.

A small ache bloomed behind her breast, and she rubbed at it. She swallowed the comfit, the morsel not tasting as good as before. "I assure you no such warning is necessary. I'm not the sort to become attached. Or have romantic illusions." Even had John been a different type of man, it still could never be. A ship to America had her and her sister's name on it.

"Good." Lady Mary rested back on her seat. "I thought you were a sensible sort of girl, but wanted to make sure. Because as good as Johnnie is to have as a friend, he's not the sort to make a dependable lover. I'd hate to see you ill-used."

Netta forced a smile. "As you say, I'm a sensible sort. And I don't allow myself to be taken advantage of." She was the one to take advantage, and then flee before the consequences could catch up to her. It was a pattern that had served her well. One that had protected not only her body but her heart. She knew just how attached she could let herself become before she had to move on.

She and John had yet to be intimate, not truly. There was no need to worry. There were weeks yet for them to enjoy each other.

Her stomach cramped. So why was she worried?

Chapter Thirteen

She pushed her concerns aside as soon as she returned home. Lady Mary waved her off, after pocketing four more of the comfits, and Netta hopped up the steps to John's townhouse.

The footman greeted her with a polite nod and handed her a note.

It read: *Find me.*

Her pulse ticked up. He was up to something. Something delightful and wicked. He made it all too difficult to keep a care. How could she be worried when there were games afoot?

She refolded the note and hurried to his study. Dark and empty of his scent.

The library was similarly deserted.

She tapped the note against her lips. His bedroom? Hers? Those options seemed rather lacking in imagination, but she climbed the steps and made a thorough search. Neither hair nor hide of him did she find, not even when she checked under the beds. "Well, drat." He wouldn't be in the servants' quarters, and she couldn't imagine John ever stepping foot into the kitchens.

The dying rays of the sun illuminated the window, the hazy London sky burnished brick orange. She walked to the casement and pressed her palms against the warm glass, watching the last sliver of the sun dip below the earth.

A flicker of brightly colored fabric disappeared into the garden gazebo.

"Checkmate." She spun, her skirts whirling, and darted

from the room and down the stairs. She found the door onto the back gardens and pressed it open.

Even in the center of London, the high walls covered in thick vines created a quiet oasis. A lark called to its mate; crickets greeted each other. And the soft tapping of a heeled boot on a wooden floor met her ear.

She ignored the winding gravel path and crossed over the lawn, hopping over a low hedge to drive her quarry to ground. His face was hidden in shadow, but the crossed legs clad in cream-colored pantaloons identified the man well enough.

"I found you." Her voice sounded breathless with excitement. She tried to rally indifference back into her words. "If this was to be a game, it wasn't difficult. And I won," she felt the need to point out.

He chuckled, the sound low and rich. It sent shivers skittering down her spine. "Finding me within the confines of one townhouse was not the game." He uncurled into standing. "I needed you in the proper location to begin the fun." Reaching forward, he stroked her cheek with the knuckle of his index finger. "And you won't win. I'll make sure of it."

"Such arrogance shows you haven't played with the right partner." She lifted her chin.

"I haven't played with anyone like you, of that I'm certain." He circled behind her. "Are you sure you want to dance, poppet? You have the option of going upstairs, changing for dinner, and ignoring the attraction between us."

"Sounds dull. Second option?"

He pulled the pins from her hair, flicking them to the gazebo floor one by one. "Second option involves you naked and moaning. Interested?"

Her nipples tingled. "What's the catch?"

"No catch. The degree of your pleasure only depends on your brazenness."

She turned and planted her palms on his chest. She ran

them up and down his waistcoat. "Then there's no limit at all."

His lips curled. "I love your assurance. It makes things that much easier for me." He ran his knuckle over her breast, making the tingles gathered there shoot down to her core. "Take off your clothes."

Netta's breath caught. "Here?"

He shifted his hand, running his finger along the edge of her bodice, his bare skin finally touching hers. "Why not? You've shown a decided lack of concern in letting the servants see you in a state of dishabille. Besides, night is falling and this garden is private. Who's to see?"

Netta bit the inside of her cheek. She was bold, but this might exceed even her audacity. Tall rose bushes circled the gazebo, providing a modicum of privacy, but there were definite gaps.

John dipped his finger into her décolletage, sliding it up and down.

Netta swallowed. On the other hand, it was a warm evening and she wouldn't get many more opportunities to be tupped in a garden by a man who was becoming more enthralling by the moment. She gave him her back. "Unbutton me."

He chuckled and leaned in close. "I knew you wouldn't disappoint," he whispered in her ear. He made quick work of her gown and within moments Netta was pulling it free from her legs. With a deep breath, she untied the laces of her stays and slid it off her body.

John's gaze locked on her bosom. She smiled to herself as she reached down and hooked her fingers under the hem of her chemise. She inched it up, the fabric dragging over her hips, catching on her breasts before sliding up and over her head. She stood before him in only her stockings and slippers.

A breeze caressed her bare skin, hardening her nipples to aching points. Or maybe it was John's expression that affected her so. His eyes had gone hooded, his nostrils flaring. He looked at her like she was the best thing he'd ever seen.

That kind of appreciation had an effect on a woman.

She raised bent arms, her palms to the sky. "Now what?"

"Now we play." He reached forwards, his destination obvious, and she brushed his hand away before he could touch her breast.

She wagged her finger. "Terms first. Then touching." Much, much touching, she hoped. Never before had she been without clothes out-of-doors, and her skin thrilled from the freedom. It loved every brush of air against it and wanted more. Wanted John's hands caressing every inch.

He crossed his arms over his chest. "Of course. I propose another game of kissing. The first person to touch the other with anything other than his or her lips, loses."

"That's it?"

He rocked his weight onto the balls of his feet. "I prefer simple contests."

She flicked a glance down to his falls. "And we are kissing each other..."

"On the mouth, you filthy wanton." He advanced a step.

"Then why am I naked?"

He grinned. "It will save time after you lose."

"I won't lose." She shifted, her thighs rubbing together. Wetness gathered at her lower lips and she didn't think a few kisses would alleviate her need. "What will my prize be?"

"If I touch you first and you win, which you won't," he quickly added. "I give you an orgasm. If I win—"

"I give you one?" She had to win. There was no way she was leaving this gazebo without satisfaction.

He swung his head side to side. "You still get your climax. Only when I win, it happens when I'm buried deep inside of you."

Her mouth went dry. Now this was a dilemma. She loved winning.

But she wanted to lose very badly.

"Deal?" he asked.

She stepped toe-to-toe with him. "Deal." She lifted her face.

He would have to kiss her first. Without the use of her hands, she couldn't yank him down to her as she'd like.

He made the most of his power. Slowly, agonizingly slowly, he lowered his head. He paused, his breath fluttering over her lips, his eyes glittering as bright as sapphires in the light from the gas lamp by the side door.

"Confound it." She stamped her foot. She should have stamped his foot. "Stop dawdling and—"

He covered her mouth with his, cutting off her demand.

His kiss was dark, dirty, and impressive considering it was without the use of his hands. Even with just his lips, his tongue, he controlled her movements. With just the slightest pressure, she knew when to angle her head. When to widen her mouth and allow him full access.

Her skin heated and her head went light. The slick glide of his tongue over hers made her whimper. The scrape of his teeth made her moan. And when finally he lifted his head, she couldn't hold back her breathy sigh.

She had never been kissed so well.

He brought his head low again, and she rolled up on her toes, eager for the next one.

He held back. "You lose," he said.

Netta drew her eyebrows together. "What?"

He ran his fingers up her arms until they reached her hands. Which were gripping his shoulders like he was the last pound cake in the bakeshop.

"Oh." She didn't remember raising her hands, but now that they were there she smoothed them along the firm muscles of his chest. "How did that happen?"

"It's a mystery." Grabbing her hips, John spun her around and placed her palms on the gazebo railing. He nudged her feet wide with his boot then curled his body over her back. "I told you I'd win. When it comes to getting what I want, I won't play for seconds."

She was wedged between two hard places. The edge of the wood railing bit into her skin from the front and John's rigid length pressed into her lower back. It was a perfect predicament to be in. Her heart beat a rough tattoo in her chest.

"Never let it be said that I can't accept defeat without grace." She arched her back, pressing more firmly against him.

He chuckled, the husky sound making her muscles go weak. "You have many fine traits, poppet, but being easy in your losses I fear is not one of them." Trailing his fingers around her hip, he skimmed over her thatch of curls and found her clit.

Her body jerked as his thumb swept a slow circle around the nub. She should argue the point. She was certain she was a fine loser. She just didn't have much experience at it. But his hand was doing unspeakable things to her body and the desire to debate the point melted into a different type of longing.

"I've dreamed of this moment for a long time." He sucked her earlobe into his mouth and tugged. "Sliding inside of you. Feeling all of your curves pressed up tight against me. Do you want that, too?"

"Yesss."

"Are you wet and ready for me?" His touch was butterfly-soft as he drew his finger down her cleft and eased it inside her channel. He groaned. "Fuck me, you are ready." He plunged in and out until she wanted to scream. It felt so good, he felt so good, but it wasn't nearly enough.

He grabbed her hair with his other hand and pulled her head back. "Say it. Say you're ready. Say you want me."

Was that even in doubt? "I want you. Now. Immediately." If that wasn't clear enough, she reached back to grip his neck, to pull him as close as possible.

He pushed her hand back to the railing.

"You're going to need to hold on, darling. This is going

to be a wild ride." His hands fumbled against her backside, and the fabric of his falls brushed against her. Gripping her hips, he tugged her back an inch until she felt the smooth head of him against her entrance.

Her toes curled in her slippers as she waited. One second. Two.

He drove into her, and she cried out. The pressure was intense, the feeling of fullness overwhelming. "Oh God. I can't...It won't..."

John cupped her breast with one hand as he bit her shoulder. He stroked her clit with his other until her body turned to soft clay. "You can. It will." And so saying, he thrust hard, taking those last inches and the last rational thought from her mind.

* * *

Netta shuddered beneath him. Around him. And he'd never felt anything so good as this woman's sex clutching tight about his cock.

He stood pressed against her arse, unmoving, reveling in the luxuriousness of the sensation. And to think, the game had only just begun.

He flexed his hips, withdrawing a couple of inches before his body demanded he press back home. His kept his thrusts shallow, leisurely, setting a pace just this side of frustrating.

Netta didn't agree with his assessment. "Faster," she demanded.

"No." He slid his hands up her waist to cup her breasts. Jesus, her breasts could make a grown man weep. They overflowed his hands, their warm weight soft against his palms. He flicked his thumbs over her nipples and groaned when her core quavered.

She pushed back against him, using the rail as leverage. "Harder."

Wrapping an arm around her waist, he held her still. He buried his nose in her hair, inhaling deeply. "Quiet. Tonight I set the pace. Besides," he said, and traced the curve of her neck with his tongue, "you should keep your voice down. You never know who might wander past."

She glared at him over her shoulder. "As you said, this is a private garden." She gave her body a delightful little shimmy. "Now no more excuses. You did promise me a climax. Get to work."

John threw his head back and laughed, the sound surprising even himself. Buried ballocks deep in a woman wasn't a time for humor. Except, with Netta, apparently it was.

He glanced at the closed side door. "As you wish." He gripped her hips, slid back until just his crown remained inside her, then hammered deep.

She moaned, the sound loud in the deepening night.

He skimmed his hand down her spine and thrust again. "What would happen if someone did see us like this? You naked, bent before me, arse pressing back, desperate for my cock." He watched as his Thomas eased from her cunny, glistening and dark in the low light. He palmed said arse and pressed his thumb between her cheeks, his touch whispering over her tight rosette.

"Oh God!"

"Shhh." He rocked back into her, every nerve ending on his length lighting up like fireworks over Vauxhall Gardens. "We wouldn't want anyone to hear."

She dropped her head. "I don't care."

Thank all that was holy, the sound he'd been waiting for met his ears. No more need for restraint. He plunged into her, watching her arse shake with each hard thrust. "You don't care if everyone knows what a little wanton you are? If they hear how you beg for it?"

Her sex tightened about him like a vise. "No," she breathed out. "Please."

She was close. The base of his spine tingled. So was he.

He pulled her upright, pounding into her through the change in angle. He gripped her jaw and turned her head. "I'm glad to hear it since we have an audience."

An audience was an exaggeration. The elderly woman shuffling beside the house had her gaze fixed on the garden path. But Netta still stiffened in his arms. "Oh God," she whispered.

He pressed his hand to her mons, grinding the heel against her clit. "Do you want me to stop?"

"No," she whispered. "Please." She reached back and dug her fingers into his hair.

"Then beg." He pinched her nipple, slowly rolling the bud with increasing pressure. "Let her know who's cock you're desperate for."

She moaned. "I"—she panted—"can't."

"Then I should stop." He slowed but had no intention of ending this.

She tugged his hair until his scalp burned. "Don't you dare."

His ballocks ached, the need to release overwhelming. "Then beg. Tell me to fuck you so hard you won't be able to walk tomorrow. Tell me, and no whispering it."

If she didn't break, he would. Sweat rolled down his spine. The planks of the gazebo creaked. He wasn't going to make it. She wasn't going to crack. She—

"Fuck me! Fuck me so hard I can't walk tomorrow." Her neck arched. She looked back at him, her eyes wild. Need warred with fear, confusion with titillation. He could read each and every beautiful emotion as they crossed her face. "Just don't stop, John."

He slammed into her, holding nothing back. Cupping her cheek, he took her mouth with his own. He swallowed her moans as he fucked her, increasing the pressure against her sensitive nub.

Her body jerked. She bit his lower lip. And with a muffled scream, she spasmed around him.

Her channel drew him deeper, milking his length, begging for his release. With every ounce of discipline he possessed, he pulled from her body. His hand had just clenched about his cock when his seed spurted against her lower back.

He ground himself against her bum, dragging out each shudder of pleasure until his muscles went limp. He dropped his forehead to her shoulder and sucked down shallow breaths.

Netta sagged against him. "Who was that?" she whispered. "Oh God, did she hear?"

John looked up, but the servant was gone. "My washerwoman. She cuts through the garden on her way home each night."

Netta spun and planted her hands on her hips. The outraged expression on her face didn't have the same effect when set over a naked body.

Without thought, John reached for her breast. She slapped his hand away.

"You had me remove all my clothes and bent me over a railing knowing someone was going to come along?" Her voice rose with each word until John worried that she *would* rouse the household. "What if she'd heard us?"

"That would have been a miracle." He wrapped his hand in her hair and tugged her close. She stood stiffly in his arms but she didn't push him away. "Mrs. Wapner hasn't heard anything for the past ten years. She's deaf." And half-blind. The perfect person to cause Netta alarm without any true threat of discovery.

She slapped his chest. "You tricked me!"

He caught her hand and brought it to his mouth. Gently, he kissed each of her fingers. "Of course. It's what I do." And how sweet it had been. The cleverer a woman was, the more satisfying a successful illusion.

He pressed a soft kiss to her lips. Toying with Netta was going to be very, very satisfying.

She curled her body against his and clasped her hands behind his neck. "I will grant you that your ruse was moderately adept."

"Moderately?" He arched an eyebrow. "I seem to remember you saying you could accept defeat with grace."

She smiled but it wasn't friendly. Her teeth looked predatory as she lowered his head to hers.

Against all common sense, John's flagging cock twitched with interest.

"I'm glad your memory is in good health." She flicked her tongue against his lower lip before staggering him with a devastating kiss. "Remember this, John Chaucer. The pleasure you give me is sweet."

She nipped his jaw. "But revenge is sweeter."

Chapter Fourteen

"Not the jonquil, I think." John squinted, but the color of the gown against Netta's body still offended his sight. "She has pink undertones to her skin and the yellows just won't do."

Netta held out an arm and examined the sleeve. "I like yellow."

"I'm sure you do, poppet." He crooked his finger at the modiste, and she scurried to bring over another gown. "But yellow doesn't feel the same about you."

They stood in one of his favorite shop's in London. Pile after pile of gowns were strewn over all available surfaces as Netta was measured, fussed over, and trussed up in every fabric and style. Usually John shopped for his mistresses, and his choices were more provocative. Dressing a woman from morning gowns to ball gowns and everything in between was a novel experience.

One that would have been more diverting had Netta appreciated his and the modiste's efforts instead of scowling at every rejected gown.

"Turn to face the window, will you?"

"It's not going to look any different facing north," Netta said, but she did as he asked.

"That window faces west, but you're right. Full sun doesn't improve the picture." He turned to the modiste. "Let's stick with the blue fabrics for the walking gowns. We'll take the four pelisses we discussed, the eight gowns over on that settee, and we really must talk about slippers."

The owner of the shop muttered something to the

seamstress next to her, who scribbled notes furiously. A portable wooden desk was wedged to her side with one arm, the contraption not looking nearly large enough to hold the list of purchases that were accruing. The girl dipped her quill into the inkwell on the corner of the desk, nodded to the modiste, and wrote some more.

This bill was going to make his banker wince.

The modiste turned her attention back to John. "I also have some lovely Belgium lace just in. It will make the most charming of chemises, or perhaps a seductive night rail or two."

Netta's cheeks flushed a delightful rosy hue. After last night, he hadn't thought she would suffer from embarrassment. He knew every inch of her body, knew how she sounded, felt, when she was brought to completion. Yet discussions of undergarments still made her blush.

He rocked onto the balls of his feet, his limbs feeling light. Netta acted as though she were a gently-born woman. He'd worried over this idea of his, wondered if she could pull off her part, but the answer was clear. She could charm any gentleman she chose.

He should know. She had charmed him.

"Include them in my order." He looked about for the gown Netta had worn into the shop. "I'll assist Miss Courtney in dressing while you prepare the bill."

The seamstress plucked Netta's gown from the top of one of the piles and bustled forwards, handing it to John. Her feet tangled in the skirt and she tripped.

John reached for her elbow. He should have reached for the desk. It flew from the chit's hands, the inkwell tumbling end over end and splashing against his jacket.

His pale peach jacket of Lustring silk with seed pearls and topaz stones embroidered into the collar and lapels.

The girl's face crumbled. "My deepest apologies," she said, addressing her employer instead of her victim. "I didn't mean to ruin another garment."

The modiste flapped her hands. "Never mind that! Get a cloth and wash basin. Monsieur, if you will give me your jacket I will see to it at once."

Netta winced. "I don't think soap and water will save it. No ink fell on my gown, did it?"

John shrugged out of the stained garment and examined the damage. "Your concern for my apparel is overwhelming," he said dryly. He looked down. "Your gown is fine. Not that it matters since it's my property, as well."

"Yes, but you can walk about without your jacket. I can't do the same without a gown."

John arched an eyebrow.

Netta planted her hands on her hips. "No."

No, even John wouldn't push the boundaries of decency that far. He handed his jacket to the modiste. "I'm afraid Miss Courtney is right. Forget the soap. Do you have any pure alcohol and vinegar?"

"I can get some." A line creased the woman's forehead. "But what will I do with it?"

"Mix a solution of equal parts of the liquids and apply it to the ink. Let it rest for several minutes, then pour salt over the stain."

"Salt?" both Netta and the modiste asked.

"Yes. That white granular mineral that preserves food and improves its flavor." John sighed. The stain was setting on his lovely jacket as they spoke and the women wanted to question his every directive. "Allow it to rest for another ten minutes and then scrub the stain with a soft brush and rinse with hot water. The ink should dissolve."

The modiste looked from him to the jacket. She shrugged. "It will do no harm to try." She turned to her assistant. "Fetch the items the earl mentioned and meet me in the back room. Monsieur," she said to John, "if this doesn't work, I will..." She swallowed. "I will of course compensate you."

He waved his hand. "We'll worry about that later.

Attempt the alcohol and vinegar solution first."

The woman nodded and hurried from the room, her seamstress two steps behind.

Netta stepped out of the yellow dress and picked her own gown off the floor. She lifted it over her head. "Alcohol and vinegar to clean ink stains?" Her question was muted through the fabric until her head popped free. "Wherever did you learn such a thing?"

He stepped behind her and worked on the buttons down her back. If his fingers lingered over their task, it could be forgiven. It went against their nature to assist a woman in covering up. "At King's College, Cambridge. I studied chemistry there."

She looked up at him over her shoulder, her mouth a tantalizing circle. "Truly? Such an education is hardly necessary for an earl, is it? Or were you that determined to never lose an article of clothing to ink accidents? I realize fashion is of utmost importance to you, but that is what valets are for."

He smacked her rump. "You are not nearly as droll as you think you are, woman."

She smirked. "I found it amusing and that is all that matters." Peering at her reflection, she adjusted her bodice. "But truly, why chemistry? What could have been the use?"

"The use?" He cocked his hip against a low bureau, tracking her movements as she slid her gloves onto her hands. "My knowledge of chemical science saved my earldom. I'd say it was of immense use."

She lifted her hands, palms up. "And? You can't start a story like that and then stop. What did your family need to be saved from? And how did chemistry save it?"

One side of his mouth edged up. "Why Netta, if I didn't know any better, I'd think you cared."

She slid her arms into a blush-colored redingote. "But you do know me better. And even though I find you arrogant and infuriating, I also think you are—"

"Preternaturally comely and uncommonly virile?"

She tied the strings of the overdress with more force than necessary. "Moderately interesting. I want to know your history." She dipped her chin and raised her eyebrows. "I also think it is time you tell me about this scheme of yours. I believe you've worked out the details and I'd like to know what my part is."

Yes, he supposed it was time. Netta needed to know what her performance would be. But something made him hesitate. If he told her and she objected, if she left.... He rubbed his chest. Well, that would put him in a poor position to reclaim his property. That could be the only reason for his reticence.

But it was one he needed to overcome. He scratched at a spot on the bureau. "My mother died giving birth to my youngest brother when I was but six. I only mention it because it has a bearing on my family's fortunes. My father, you see, used the loss as an excuse to gamble and whore his way through London. Within two years, the family was bankrupt."

He heard her gown shift as she moved closer, but he didn't raise his head. "Ever since a boy, when I mixed black pepper with gunpowder to see if I could cause a bigger bang, I was interested in chemistry. I made enough money as an apprentice to a couple men of science to pay my way through college, then I took what I learned and restored the Summerset name."

The toes of her slippers came into his line of view. Then her hand holding a small sack.

He sniffed. Licorice. That explained why she smelled of it.

She opened the sack wide and held it up to him. "I always find it easier to speak of disagreeable things when there is something sweet in my mouth. Pomfret cake?"

John huffed and raised his eyes. There was no pity or condemnation in her gaze over his fallen circumstances. Only interest. And kindness. He plucked out one of the shiny black confections and popped it in his mouth. Spicy and sweet. Just like Netta.

"Where was I? Oh yes. How I made my fortune." He swung his foot back and forth, much more comfortable relaying this section of his history. "Although pepper does nothing productive for gunpowder, I found several minerals that did. I brought my family out of debt selling my new, more stable brand to the British government." He shrugged. "Of course, now that the wars have ended, that income stream has virtually dried up. Which leads me to why I want you."

She looked down at her bosom and back up at him. "I know why you want me."

John turned to sit more fully on the bureau. He looped his finger in the closure of her redingote and pulled her between his legs. "You are more than an impressive pair of breasts, poppet. Don't undervalue yourself."

"That has never been a problem." She rested her hands on his shoulders. "Now, to my part in your scheme."

He traced his finger along the edge of her gown. "After my marvelous gunpowder invention, I branched out to steel production. My grandparents had property rich with chromite ore. I tested chromium's effects on steel and received letters patent on a new production process. My smelts are responsible for growing my family's wealth fifty times over since I became Summerset." He puffed his chest out. It had grown nearer one hundred times larger since the jumble his father had left them in. But it wouldn't do to boast.

"And how did it go wrong?" She leaned against his thigh, the fabric of her gown brushing against his falls. The light from the window illuminated her pale blond hair like a halo. With her entrancing eyes and sweet pout, she looked like an angel.

Luckily for him, she was of the fallen variety. They were much more fun.

He leaned forwards and pressed a kiss to the rounded top of one breast, then the other.

She shuddered.

"My brother went wrong. He owns the land the ore mines are on. And he lost them on a game of hazard." His stomach churned and he sat up straight. "The man who holds the deed refuses to sell. So I intend to win it back." He watched her expression as he laid it out before her. "And you, my dear, are the stakes I intend to play with."

She didn't blink. Her face held no expression at all.

"I won't lose," he was quick to reassure her. "I'll make sure of it. I wouldn't let another man touch you. You are merely necessary to get him to the table."

She tapped her thumb against his shoulder. "For four thousand pounds you want me to flirt and beguile a man so as he'll risk a deed worth tens of thousands?"

"In essence, yes."

More thumb-tapping against his shirt. "I don't just want the essence. What are the particulars?"

John exhaled slowly. "This man. He wouldn't be playing for a night of simple tupping. He likes inflicting pain. Humiliation. And I think the opportunity to inflict such on an innocent, gently-born woman, or someone he believes is such, would be too tempting to resist." He swallowed. "The fact that I will make it appear you have value to me will also rouse his interest. He seems to enjoy taking what's mine."

He held his breath. Would she be horrified? John was used to such things. To people who only liked to give pain, never pleasure. This was the point where Netta might flee, and she would be wise to do so. He knew he would keep her from harm, but how was she to trust him?

But Netta didn't run. "Surely you won't lose everything without those ores," she asked.

"They are the only known chromite ores in England," he said. "The cost to import the mineral would dramatically cut into my profits."

"Well, what about a new venture to make up for the old?" she asked. "What are you currently developing?"

John's shoulders hardened. "Nothing."

Her eyebrows knitted together. "Nothing? But you spoke of your love for science. Why not—"

"My days in the laboratory are over." His voice emerged harsher than he wanted. He didn't like the concern that it brought to her expression. Or the curiosity. Why he left his laboratory wasn't a topic he was willing to discuss.

He cleared his throat and forced his customary indifference back into his words. "Which is why I intend to win it back. Why you have been hired. Do you think you can do it?" he asked, infusing the question with a challenge.

She cocked her head. "Oh, I can do it. But I want something for it. All the gowns and slippers and fripperies you're dressing me in for the role. I want to take them with me when I leave, in addition to my four thousand pounds."

John ignored the little lurch to his heart at the word 'leave.' "Do you think you're in a position to renegotiate our terms?"

"That depends on how badly you want your deed."

He grinned. She truly was spectacular. "You are a mercenary little minx."

"A girl in my position has to be." She leaned into him, pressing her breasts against his chest. "Now, about those gowns..."

His groin tightened. He traced the outer rim of her lips. "We already made our agreement and the terms stand. But...I'll play you for the new wardrobe."

"A game?" Her eyes flared.

He nodded.

"Here." She spread her arms out wide, indicating the shop. "Now? You must be mad." But she pressed closer, her belly nestling against his cock.

They had at least ten minutes until the modiste was finished with his jacket. "Right here. Right now. If you win, you get all the gowns you want."

"And slippers."

He huffed. "And slippers. And if I win, I get..."

"Whatever you wish."

All the blood in his body flowed south. "That covers a lot of territory, poppet."

"I'm not concerned." She brushed a curl from her cheek. "Because I don't lose." He raised his eyebrows, and she sniffed. "Well, hardly ever. Now, what's the game?"

* * *

"*Da grey frwx fund hisself a bit o' fun 'n 'ardly had a heppyr time in 'is life.*"

John laughed, the vibration from his throaty chuckle traveling all the way to his ballocks.

And Netta should knew. That part of his anatomy was currently in her mouth.

She knelt on the thick sheepskin rug next to his bed, his length in her hand as she suckled his testicles. This was his prize for winning the game at the modiste's. Confounded man, she didn't understand how he was the victor once again. Although her losses were never hardships. She'd wanted to spend the night in his bedroom and that was exactly where she was.

Using the tip of her tongue, she traced the indentation between his testes, smiling when he sagged back against his bed and gripped the coverlet. She did that to him. She weakened his knees. And the rush of power was intoxicating.

"Fuck me!" He cupped her cheek, breathing heavily.

She had no worries that anyone would hear them this night. His bedchambers took up a full half of the second floor of his townhouse and there were heavy drapes over every window and doorway. The walls were white with thick gold filigree scrollwork winding up the sides like vines to a large medallion on the ceiling.

From the medallion, a huge chandelier dripped twisted ropes of crystals and several smaller chandeliers illuminated the corners of the room. Everything, even the bed, settee, and chairs were white and gold, and it felt as though she'd stepped into a fairy forest when he'd pulled her inside.

She grasped the bed frame for balance as she changed the angle of her head. The bedpost was cool beneath her hand and even though it looked and felt like gold, she couldn't believe the man had a solid gold bed. Not even the Earl of Summerset would possess such a thing. The frame was massive. Each corner post was actually two columns with delicately-wrought gold vines winding between them. The posters led up to a domed cage of the same metal, and the headboard was a lattice pattern that allowed enough space for a person to thread her fingers through and brace herself if the need arose.

She shifted her thighs together. She desperately hoped the need arose that night.

She rolled the velvety sac over her tongue. The scent of bergamot and musk rose from every inch of his skin, and he smelled and tasted delicious everywhere. She could happily spend the rest of her days in his home, just for the soap alone.

John ran his fingers through her hair. "Do you want to try that again? I don't think Herodotus would approve of your enunciation."

She tugged at him gently with her mouth, breathing him in. Loving the weight of him. Loving the groan she drew from him as though he were on the boundary of pain and pleasure and she was the master of his destiny. She gave one last lick before drawing back. "You understood well enough to know what I was saying. I'd say my lessons have borne fruit."

"Yes." Tilting his head, he ran his thumb along her bottom lip. "Amazingly well. I'm a more capable instructor than even I could have imagined."

Her stomach went tight. Was that suspicion in his voice? She nipped the tip of his thumb and considered her performance. Had she dropped her street accent too easily? Had her natural manners broken through into her role?

She should just tell him the truth. John wouldn't hold this latest pocket-sized lie against her, she didn't think. But would he involve her in his scheme if he knew she was the daughter of a viscount? He might deem her participation too risky and cut her out of her role.

And her fee.

She swallowed. That wouldn't do. "Wot? I can polish yer nob talking like a right guttersnipe if that's what 'oists your sails."

He shuddered. "Not necessary. I quite like that you no longer sound like a dying cat when you speak." He nudged her head towards his bobbing cock. "And I liked it even better when you weren't speaking at all. Come, come, deliver on my win."

Happily, Netta widened her lips and reapplied herself. A man with a woman's mouth about his cock was a man who wasn't pondering suspicious accents.

She took him deep, luxuriating in the feel of him against her tongue. The tickle when he caressed the roof of her mouth.

As far as a loser's duties went, this one wasn't half-bad. She slid her fingers under the hem of her chemise and lightly circled her clit. Her body shuddered. Not bad at all.

He gently rocked his hips back and forth. "Damn but you know how to use that mouth for more than sauce."

"'nnk ooo."

He held her head, his grip light, not pressing farther than she was comfortable, but directing her movements. He took what he wanted, and his transparent delight spurred her on to give him more. Draw on him harder. Go deeper.

He dug his fingers into her scalp. "Fuck me, yes, yessss..."

Liquid heat jetted into her mouth. She swallowed, milking out his release as long as possible.

John dropped to the bed, his chest heaving. He cupped her cheek as she pulled from his length. "That was bloody marvelous. I can't wait until you lose again."

She curled her legs beneath her and rested her head against his knee, trying to catch her own breath. "That won't happen."

He finger-combed her hair, and her eyes slid closed. With the fire crackling behind her, the soft rug cushioning her from below, and John's masculine heat all around her, she felt as cossetted as an adored child.

"Netta?"

"Hmm?"

"After this job, what will you do?" His fingers never ceased their soothing caress, but her back tensed nonetheless.

"Why?"

"I've seen many a person squander a large quantity of blunt, leaving them more destitute than they were before they'd received it." He drew his finger over the shell of her ear. "I don't want to see that happen to you."

"You don't have to worry about me." She squinted at him, trying to take his measure. "Your concern isn't a way to go back on our deal, is it? Because I'll expect payment for time served, even if you decide not to use me for your plot. And if you think to renege on—"

"Calm yourself." He blew out a breath. "I intend no such thing. I do want to ensure that once our business is concluded that you will be all right. I've become quite fond of you, poppet."

The muscles in her shoulders eased. "With four thousand pounds, I'll be as fine as a fiddle. You need have no concerns about my wasting all my money. Such foolishness must surely belong only to men." Imagine spending such an amount. It beggared belief.

But John's brother and father had apparently done so.

And her father had surely squandered such a fortune many times over. What else could account for him attempting to sell his daughters to the highest bidder.

Her insides twisted. She wasn't like them. She had plans for that money. She would know how each and every farthing would be spent. It was her and her sister's ticket to freedom.

"What street do you live on?" He wound a strand of her hair around his finger. "With four thousand pounds I'm certain we can find something more suitable, and safer."

Yes. She would find suitable and safe accommodations for her and Eleanor.

On the other side of the Atlantic Ocean.

She blinked. "My home suits me fine." Pressing her hands to his thighs, she pushed to her feet, her legs wobbly from remaining in one position for so long.

John rested his hands at her waist, steadying her. "Yes, but I'm sure it could be improved. If you'd like any assistance investing your money, you will let me know. You'll let me know if you require any assistance at all."

For once, his angelic features matched the expression in his eyes. He was truly concerned over her, Netta Pickle, the street urchin.

Her heart twinged. Dear, lovely man. Not an ounce of prejudice in his body.

And she was lying to him.

She shook her head, knocking that irritating thought right out. She did what she had to in order to survive. No one would begrudge her that, least of all John.

She laced her fingers together behind his neck and pressed closer, forcing his legs to widen. "Do you truly wish to discuss the future when our present is much more interesting?" Bending, she fluttered feather-light kisses over the corners of his mouth. "I did...lose." She forced the ugly word through gritted teeth, making him grin. "And I owe the winner several hours of debauchery, as I understand it."

John tightened his grip, turned, and tossed her on the bed.

She landed on her back, bouncing with a startled gasp.

He crawled over her, dragging his nose along her skin as he went. When he reached her neck, he nipped. "Haven't you yet learned?" He settled between her legs, his burgeoning erection pressing against her belly and sending delicious shivers through her body.

"In my games, we both come out as winners."

Chapter Fifteen

John shifted on the hard bench. The Burns Theatre was a far cry from Covent Garden. A splinter dug into his arse, and he frowned. The patrons here should demand recompense for the torture of sitting on these damned benches instead of paying for the benefit. He tossed one leg over the other, rolling onto his hip, away from the bit of wood poking into him. Christ, if—

The threadbare curtains parted, and John forgot his discomfort. Because there, standing on stage left, was Netta.

Even with the carbuncles covering her face and the obscenely large false nose, he knew it was her. The saucy uptilt to her pointed chin. The way she stood with her shoulders thrust just so.

A slow smile stretched across his face. All the nights she'd disappeared from his house. When she'd slipped from his bed last night. She had come here.

He heaved a deep breath. He needn't worry about her after she left. She had a career to go back to, sad and tawdry as this theatre might be. He would introduce her to the manager of the Drury. Ensure that she had secure work, if she wanted it. With four thousand pounds, she might decide to retire, though he didn't think it likely. She liked playacting too much. After all, how many roles had she performed for him?

Had she lived on the streets and worked her way up to the stage? Or was she the daughter of a tidy little merchant somewhere and everything had been an act?

He settled back. He would learn the truth after the

performance.

Wilberforce slid into a seat at the end of the row, resting his elbows on his knees. He didn't seem surprised when Netta came center stage to deliver her lines. Only smiled faintly at the poor joke, then tipped his head to John.

John grumbled. The bloody, sneaking bastard. He'd known all along what Netta was, where she was going. Mother hen that he was, he would have followed after Netta the first time she'd left his house. "You couldn't have told me?" he muttered at Wil down the empty row.

"Shhh!" a patron hissed behind him.

John blew out his cheeks. *The Merry Wives of Windsor* was one of the Bard's worst plays. It surely did not deserve a shushing. But he settled in to watch. Quietly. And became more entranced with every line Netta delivered as Bardolph.

She was spectacular. Her talent was wasted on such a minor character. When she was on the stage, he scarce noticed anyone else.

His concerns over her acting ability melted away. She had more than enough talent to wrap anyone, including Sudworth, around her little finger. Talent and enough moral flexibility to be the perfect woman for the job.

She *was* perfect. So why did a soupçon of unease whisper down his spine to settle in his gut? He tapped his thumb against his thigh. He had a plan. He had capable players to fill each role of said plan. He should have felt the confidence he did every time before a mission.

Yet the unease wouldn't go away.

What was he missing?

The curtains fell. John rose and rubbed at the ache in his arse.

Wilberforce wove down the aisle to join him. "A good performance, wouldn't you say?"

"A surprising one." John sniffed. "I would have liked to have known where Netta was disappearing to. If only I had a loyal servant to inform me of her whereabouts."

Wil circled his hat in his hands, his lips twitching. "You never asked me to verify her whereabouts. Sir."

John closed his eyes. He would not snap at his friend. His shoulders rounded. Especially when said friend had shown more care for Netta than John had.

He should have learned where she went each night before this. He'd thought to give Netta her privacy. Respect her boundaries. But he should have determined that she was safe.

John rubbed a knuckle into his chest. While she lived under his roof, he was responsible for the woman, after all. It could only be a sense of duty that made him feel such. "Well, let's go see what she has to say for herself. Another amusing deceit, I'm sure."

"You mean to go backstage to confront her?" Wil's gaze darted to the now-deserted stage, his eyes flickering with interest. "I believe she shares a dressing room with...with another woman."

John turned and strode to the aisle. "I'll knock. I don't suppose you drove the carriage here?"

Wil shook his head.

No, when following one's employer, a noisy carriage wouldn't do. "Well, we'll have to see if, among her many other talents, Miss Netta Pickle can sit atop a horse for her ride back home."

* * *

Netta peeled off the wax nose and warts and tossed them onto her dressing table.

"Is something the matter?" Cerise asked. She belted her silk wrapper about her trim waist and sat next to Netta at a matching dressing table.

Netta slathered face cream over her skin and wiped her face paint off with a small cloth. "No. Why do you ask?" Brown streaks remained on her cheek and she scrubbed at them.

"Because you throw your costume at the floor like it is on fire." Cerise bobbed her chin at Netta's dressing table.

"You toss your wax bits at the mirror in disgust. You"— Cerise jabbed her index finger at Netta—"are in a fine temper."

Netta stared at her reflection. She'd removed the jacket and padding from her costume and sat slumped in her chair in her breeches and chemisette. Her bare shoulders were tense blocks, her lips a twisted scowl.

Her friend had a point.

She flipped the chair sideways to face Cerise and straddled it, hooking her elbows over the back. "Do you ever feel discontent, even when life has finally dealt you a good hand?"

Cerise leaned towards the mirror and wiped the kohl from her eyes. "That is not enough information for me to respond to. Tell me what zis 'good hand' is and then I will tell you whether you should feel happy or not."

Netta sighed. There her friend went, always wanting a full accounting of facts before making any decisions. Her logic could be quite annoying at times.

"There's a man I've agreed to help recover some of his property." She pondered how much she should reveal. She trusted Cerise, but had learned to keep information closely guarded. "I'm to act as a lure, attracting another man to place that property up as a stake for a game."

Cerise pursed her full lips. "With you as the other stake?"

Netta nodded. "Somehow I am supposed to intrigue this man enough to gamble away thousands of pounds." She'd never played the seductress before. She enjoyed teasing John, but turning her wiles on another man could prove challenging. She dropped her chin to her crossed arms and sighed.

"And if you lose? Will you let zis man claim you as his prize?"

"Of course not. And my employer has the annoying habit of never losing. But..."

"But what?"

Netta scratched the toe of her boot along the seam of a floorboard. "The man I'm working for. I'm growing rather fond of him. I wonder if I should tell him who I truly am. Stop with the lies." Well, some of them. Others would have to remain.

Cerise stood and leaned against her dressing table. "Do you intend to have a relationship with zis man where honesty would be important?"

The backs of Netta's eyes burned. "No. We have no future."

"Then why tell him?" A wrinkle creased Cerise's forehead. "We are trained in deception here. And façades provide protection to us women. Do not go making trouble for yourself where none is needed."

"Of course, you're right." Netta chewed on her bottom lip. She gave her friend a half-hearted smile and repeated back one of Cerise's favorite sayings. "Men are but useful instruments; they are never our friends."

"Truly, that wounds me."

Netta whipped her head around, her heart clogging her throat at the sight of John filling the doorway.

He pressed a hand dramatically to his chest. "Such a bloodless sentiment about men is enough to give me the wrong impression of the fairer sex."

Cerise unfolded from her chair. "And you are?" She stood so half of her body blocked Netta from John.

Netta grabbed the belt of her friend's wrapper and tugged her back. "It's all right. He's...a friend."

John slowly arched an eyebrow, and every dirty thing they'd done together flashed through her mind.

She flushed. Truly, she was an experienced woman. She should be past such embarrassments. She cleared her throat. "Cerise, this is John, Earl of Summerset. Summerset, this is Miss Cerise DuBois." She cocked her head. "Did Wilberforce finally betray me?"

There was a sharp inhale of air from the hall.

John pushed the door wider, revealing a flinty-eyed

Wilberforce.

He sniffed. "I am not in the habit of revealing confidences, miss."

"I followed you on my own initiative," John said. He shrugged. "I was curious about your nightly liaisons." He strolled about the small room, picking up a discarded costume here, poking at her jars of face paint there. He cocked a hip against the edge of her dressing table, his very closeness making the fine hairs on her body stand on end. "And my curiosity was well rewarded. You are quite the surprise, poppet."

She scraped her teeth over her bottom lip. "You're not angry?"

"What? That you're not only not Ned Pickle, but now you aren't even Netta Pickle, the downtrodden woman I plucked from the streets?" He tutted. "Not hardly. Please tell me your name isn't truly Pickle."

She bit back her smile. "You're in luck. My name is Antoinette LeBlanc." The false name slipped easily from between her lips. She'd been that person for so many years it felt like the truth. "Netta still to my friends."

He ran his finger down the ridge of her nose then rubbed his fingers together, swirling a patch of face paint between them. "A much more suitable name, although not, I think, the one you were born with."

Netta's lungs stalled. She hadn't even told Cerise her true name. It remained better left unsaid. "It's the only one I answer to now. Well," she conceded, "except Pickle."

"And Mrs. Hardcourt and Colonel Burnwick and Miss Austin." Cerise retreated to her chair, keeping a wary eye on the man in the doorway as she spoke. "Netta does love to immerse herself in new characters to prepare for a role. It is one of the things we love about her. She has many friends here, monsieur. Many friends who won't let her come to any harm."

John ignored the implied warning. "A Colonel Burnwick?"

Netta shrugged. "I played a soldier last summer."

He examined her bare arms, dropped his gaze to her breeches. "Were you wearing a uniform?"

"Of course."

He grinned. "I do wish I could have seen that."

Netta stood and rested one knee on the seat of the chair. "Now that you've discovered me, has anything changed? Do I still have the job?" Her heart thumped in her chest. He didn't appear upset, but no man liked to be deceived. To acknowledge he'd been played for a fool.

But John was no ordinary man. "The only thing that has changed is my increased regard for your skill level and my confidence in your abilities." He crossed his arms over his chest. "I know now I needn't worry about your security. You can handle yourself."

Wilberforce huffed. Loudly.

John shot him a narrow-eyed glare.

Netta gripped the back of the chair, her muscles going weak. He wasn't taking the four thousand pounds away from her. She could still rescue her sister.

"Now, poppet, perhaps we might discuss— gah!" John kicked his foot, and a small furry animal flew across the room and hit the wall. He flicked his wrist, and a blade slid from his sleeve into his palm. He bent his arm back to take aim.

Netta stilled his hand. "Cerise and I would prefer not to have blood in our dressing rooms."

His nostrils flared, his gaze remaining sharp on the intruder. "Better a bit of blood than that disgusting creature."

She snorted. "Is the mighty Earl of Summerset afraid of a little mouse?"

Wilberforce stepped to the creature and nudged it out the door with his boot.

"The Burns Theatre doesn't have the funds to keep the rats out." Cerise ran the end of her belt through her fingers. When Wilberforce limped back into the room, she took a corresponding step away from him. "Netta and I have learned how to manage all kinds of vermin."

Wilberforce clenched and relaxed his hands, a gesture so quick it was easily missed. "If I'm near, that is a job you'll no longer have to perform yourself."

Cerise crossed her arms.

Wilberforce mirrored her stance.

Netta frowned at her friend. "Um, perhaps whatever it was you wanted to discuss is best done in private," she said to John. Cerise wasn't overly fond of strange men, but her reaction to Wilberforce was still perplexing. Usually she buttered her words to strangers as heavily as Netta did her morning roll. "Cerise, would you mind waiting next door?"

Wilberforce frowned. "She's in naught but a wrapper. Whatever talking needs to be done can wait until you're both properly dressed."

"I'm an actress, *cherie.*" The endearment came out as sharp as John's blade. "I've walked around backstage in much less than zis."

Wilberforce's face turned a dull red.

"It can wait until we reach home." John tucked the dagger back up his sleeve. "Or better yet, since I now know that you're ready, perhaps we can start upon the job tonight. I'd like to show you around some gaming hells. Rouse interest in my suggestive yet shy and retiring new companion. My quarry should be in one of them. Men who gamble to the extent he does can't stay away."

"You want me to go into gaming hells?" Her stomach sank to her boots.

"Yes." John ran a hand up the back of his head, rumpling his hair. "That is where one typically finds games, and gamblers."

"Yes. Right." She concentrated on keeping her breathing steady, her hands still by her sides. When he'd spoken of the game, she'd envisioned it at John's home. Somewhere private. Safe. How many of her father's contemporaries went to these hells? And more importantly, would they recognize the woman she was now?

She searched about for an excuse and came up with a plum one. "I have nothing to wear. I came to the theatre in my trousers."

John frowned. "We'll stop at home, of course. Mags will have you dressed in your new costume in no time at all. And bring your face paint. I want you to look as young as possible."

"I don't have face paint. I'll have to purchase some tomorrow."

He looked pointedly at the small jars on her table.

"I don't have the *right* face paint." She worried the hem of her chemisette. "If you want me to shed a couple of years, I will need to go shopping."

A divot appeared in Cerise's forehead, and she opened her mouth.

Netta gave a brief shake to her head, and her friend took the hint and remained quiet.

John took a step towards her. "Is there some reason you don't wish to accompany me?"

Her mind went blank. If she told him there were men she must avoid, her use to him would become nonexistent. There would go her four thousand pounds. If she were to do a thorough job of disguising herself, she would need more time to prepare.

More time to steel her nerve.

"I..." Her mouth went dry.

John looked at Wilberforce and jerked his chin at the door.

His man held out his arm. "Miss?" he said to Cerise. "I'll escort you to the neighboring room. If you'll come with me?"

Cerise looked from John to Wilberforce to Netta.

Netta nodded, and Cerise swept from the room, the ends of her wrapper swirling about her legs.

Wilberforce jerked his gaze up and blew out a breath as he followed, closing the door softly behind him.

"Now," John said, planting his hands on his lean hips, "what is the problem?"

She couldn't think of a believable excuse. One that would keep her in his employ yet avoid threat of detection. She, devious, scheming Netta, was drawing a blank.

"I've started my monthly courses," she blurted out. "I feel unwell."

His face blanched, and she sent a prayer heavenward. The magical words to end all inquiries. She should have thought of it sooner.

"Yes." He rubbed the back of his neck. "Certainly you must stay home. When we arrive, I'll ask Margaret to draw you a warm bath, shall I?"

Her throat went thick. He truly was a dear man. So much more considerate and sweeter than he liked to admit.

And she'd lied to him. Again. A small one to be sure, but they were adding up. How many lies would he allow before his forgiveness ran dry?

"Thank you." She turned her back and crossed to the small wardrobe. "I'll dress and be right out."

"Of course."

It hardly mattered. If all went as planned, he would never know of her guilt. She would remain a fond memory of his, the actress he once knew who helped him in his time of need.

And she would be across the ocean clinging to the memory of the surprising earl who'd made her laugh long after she'd thought such fancy was lost to her.

He paused behind her and pressed his lips to the curve where her neck met her shoulder. "There is an Italian opera at Drury Lane four nights hence. I'd very much like it if you'd accompany me there."

She tilted her head, giving him better access. "To rouse the interest of the men of your acquaintance?"

"Yes. In part." He ran the tip of his tongue up her neck to behind her ear.

She shuddered.

"I also intend to enjoy your company to the fullest extent while I have you," he murmured. He scraped his teeth over her earlobe. "Now hurry up and dress." He patted her bottom before moving to the hallway, taking his warmth and intoxicating scent with him. "I'll be waiting."

He closed the door behind him, and she shut her eyes. They'd both be waiting. Her excuse to avoid the hells didn't seem so clever anymore. Her deception had just removed her from his bed for the next few days.

She dropped her head to her chest.

Hoisted by her own lying petard. It was going to be a long couple of nights.

Chapter Sixteen

Netta arranged the velvet hood over her head and sucked in a deep breath. Time to start the show.

She took John's hand and stepped from his carriage. The gas lights of the Drury dazzled her eyes and she inched closer to John. As a child, she had longed to come here, to see a show so badly she could have burst from the wanting. Now, the theatre held a different sort of appeal. What would it be like to tread upon the boards of such an acclaimed stage? To hear the applause from thousands of spectators?

The crowds had thinned, the first act already begun. John had agreed with her assessment that a late arrival would only increase her allure. With the subtle shading of face paint, a slight powder to her hair, and a cloak hiding her features, she strode through the front doors with the nariest of qualms.

"Have you ever seen *The Barber of Seville?*" John nodded to a couple in the lobby but kept his stride even as they made for his box.

"No." She'd never seen any opera. Her wages didn't allow for such extravagance.

John drew back the curtain to his personal box and ushered her inside. "Good. We haven't missed overmuch," he whispered. "If you have any questions, let me know."

She nodded, her gaze transfixed. No warped and discolored wooden boards made up the stage here. The thick, red velvet curtains were held back by ornate brass hooks, and what they revealed....

"Oh!" She sank to her seat and leaned forwards, resting her elbows on the box ledge. "Look at those costumes."

John settled next to her and pressed a pair of opera glasses into her hand. "Not as charming as wax noses and warts to my mind."

She shot him an exasperated look before turning her full attention back to the stage. The lead female, Rosina, was beautiful and tragic. The Count desperate in his longing for her. Netta sighed in delight and blocked out the rest of the world.

The curtains fell on the first act, and she blinked as the house lights came on.

"I take it you find the evening's entertainment agreeable." John's voice held laughter, and when she turned to look at him, it was matched by the crinkles around his eyes.

"Very much so." She leaned back in her seat. "It's more than I ever imagined."

"Do you sing?"

"Not well. Watching a musical production is as close as I will ever get to such a performance." She shook her head. "I can never thank..." She trailed off as John's entire body went stiff. His gaze was fixed over her left shoulder, his nostrils flaring.

"What is it?" she asked, craning her neck but seeing nothing of account. Realizing her hood had slipped down her shoulders during the performance, she hastily pulled it back over her head.

"No one of account." John sat back. He took the opera glasses from her hand and slapped them against his palm. "Only my grandmother."

"Your grandmother?" She searched the boxes opposite in earnest, looking for a distinctive pair of cobalt eyes or set of high cheekbones. It was no use. Not from such a distance. She turned to reclaim the glasses, but John had already put them to use, peering through their lenses, his jaw clenched.

"Do you want to pay your compliments?" Netta followed the direction of the glasses. A woman with a fringe of snowy white hair beneath a red turban stared intently back in their direction. "I'm happy to wait here while you do."

"That won't be necessary," John said, his words clipped. "We no longer speak."

"But she's your grandmother." Unless the woman had tried to sell her grandson in marriage to a monster, Netta couldn't understand how such a close family member could be ignored.

"Your point?" He tucked the opera glasses into his coat pocket.

She pursed her lips. "My point is that she's your grandmother." This shouldn't be hard to comprehend. "You are a product of her loins. Doesn't that deserve a greeting upon meeting in public?"

"Perhaps you should refrain from speaking on matters of which you have no knowledge."

Her spine snapped straight. "And perhaps you could give me such knowledge so I can speak with more authority."

They glared at each other.

"Is this a bad time?"

Netta started. A man with a startlingly bushy beard held back the curtains to John's box. The woman next to him had thick auburn hair and curious eyes. The top of her head just reached the man's shoulder.

John stood. "No, I welcome any interruption."

Netta huffed but rolled to her feet, as well.

"Netta, may I introduce you to Maximillian Atwood, Baron of Sutton, and his charming wife, Colleen, the baroness." John waved his hand at Netta. "Max, Colleen, this is Miss Antoinette LeBlanc. Netta to those she delights in bedeviling."

Netta dropped a curtsy and smiled tightly. "I can assure you that only the earl finds me such. I am a positive delight to those who are worthy of my good graces."

John looked heavenward.

The baroness laughed. "I can readily disbelieve his description of you as he has so misconstrued my own character. No one has ever called me charming before."

"I think you're charming," her husband protested.

She patted his arm. "As you are legally obligated to do since we wed."

Sutton grumbled. "I always thought it."

John pressed his fists into his lower back and stretched. "How are you enjoying the show? I believe Miss Luciano is having a particularly superior performance tonight."

Sutton tugged on his beard. "I didn't come here to talk nonsense about performances. Step out with me. I'd like a moment of your time." The words seemed more demand than request. Having delivered them, Sutton lumbered outside, letting the curtains fall shut.

John pressed his lips together. "If you ladies will excuse us. I'll return with refreshments, after knocking some civility into my friend." He picked up Colleen's hand and kissed the back. "Never doubt it, my dear. Compared to your husband, you embody all the charm in the world."

Colleen watched the curtain drop closed and crossed her arms. "That man knows how to give a double-edged compliment like nobody else." She turned. "But I'm certain you are already aware of that."

Netta gestured to the chairs and both women took a seat. "Have you known him long?"

"Summerset?" Colleen shook out her russet skirts. Her gown was simple, but of a fine chiffon and expertly made. "Not nearly long enough to understand him. I met him shortly after I met my husband. He helped us out of a difficult situation." Her face softened. "He is a good friend, to the both of us."

Netta leaned on her armrest. "Yes, of course." John would be someone his friends could depend upon. He certainly took his role as his brother's protector seriously.

"But do you *know* him? What happened to his brother? Why did he stop studying chemistry? And what is the dispute between him and his grandmother?"

Colleen blinked. "Well." She blinked some more. "Now I feel that I don't know him at all. He has always been a bit of an enigma beneath his mask of indifference. I didn't know he studied chemistry, much less that he had a grandmother." She tilted her head. "Well, I'd assume he had a grandmother. Everyone does somewhere. But not one with whom he had a fraught relationship."

Netta slumped back into her chair. This had seemed a golden opportunity to do some of her own poking about. Perhaps she should try to corner Lord Sutton. He would be better informed.

"I do know that he has taken his separation from his service to the Crown most ill," Colleen said. "All of the men in their group worry about him."

"His service to the Crown?"

Colleen slapped her hand over her mouth, her eyes as wide as a doe's before a hunter.

"It's no use covering your mouth now." Netta leaned towards her. "I will know what you mean."

Colleen dropped her hand and blew out her cheeks. "It is not a story I can tell. If you are close to Summerset, and wish to become closer, you must ask him." She winced. "Just, perhaps don't tell him who let the information slip."

Netta tapped her foot. What could it have been? He was still a member of the House of Lords. How many services did an earl perform for the government? And one that would be enveloped in secrecy?

"But what about you?' Colleen cleared her throat. "How did you and Summerset meet?"

"I foisted his billfold." Could he have taken a cabinet position he was embarrassed about? Become an aide to the prince regent?

"What?" Colleen's jaw dropped.

Hell and damnation. Her mouth was a constant source

of aggravation. She gave the woman her most winning smile and pushed the brim of her cloak further back her head to reveal more of her eyes. Her honest and sincere eyes. "I'm an actress. Summerset befriended me and is now my sponsor. It's our little joke, my taking him for his money."

"Ah." Colleen crossed one leg over the other, letting her foot swing. "Sponsor. Is that what it's called nowadays?"

The woman's voice held amusement instead of censure, but Netta's face heated just the same.

"The services I provide for sponsorship are all respectable." If seducing a man into gambling for her favors could be called respectable. "Not all actresses also work as Paphions."

Netta pressed her lips together. It infuriated her that such an implication lingered, but it was the reason why John hadn't wanted her to let her profession be widely known. This man she was to bring to the table preferred innocent misses and an actress just didn't qualify.

Colleen squeezed her arm. "I apologize if I offended you, but Summerset must not have told you about me and Sutton if you think I would judge any honest choice a woman makes. And I do believe prostitution is an honest transaction."

Now Netta was the one to gape like a fish.

Colleen shrugged. "My husband owns a Venus club that caters to unusual tastes. I am the manager of The Black Rose. If you are interested, you should ask Summerset to bring you one night."

Netta moved her lips but no words emerged. If the baroness had said she liked to dance naked in the moonlight, Netta couldn't have been more shocked.

"Where should I take her?" John shouldered through the curtain, a glass of wine in each hand.

"To one of the new burletta shows." Colleen winked at her. "If your friend enjoys opera, I believe she will also like the musical theatre productions."

"If she wishes it." John handed her a glass then was

jostled aside by Sutton, who handed his wife a steaming cup of coffee.

Colleen pressed a hand to her abdomen and pushed the cup away. "No, thank you."

"But you love coffee."

"Not tonight."

"Before this devolves into unpleasant marital bickering, I do believe the second act is about to begin." John gave his friend a pointed look. "Don't you have your own box to haunt?"

Colleen rose and gave Netta her hand. "It was lovely to meet you, Miss LeBlanc."

"Netta, please."

"And you must call me Colleen."

John guided Colleen around the chair to her husband's side. "Yes, yes. We're all great friends. Now leave us be."

Sutton rested his hand on his wife's lower back. "We will finish this conversation," he said as he held the curtain open.

John fluttered his fingers in dismissal. He sank into his seat with a sigh. "Alone again at last."

"Alone? We are surrounded by hundreds of other patrons." She rested her elbow on her chairback and turned towards him. A faint line creased his forehead, and she longed to rub away his worry. After his conversation with his friend, his shoulders seemed to sit a little lower, as though weighted. She wished they were alone, where she could do something to improve his state of mind.

She wished she knew a way to make him happy outside of bed sport. For as compelling as he was in bed, she was finding him even more so out of it.

The house lights dimmed and the orchestra played the opening notes.

He shifted onto one hip and rested his palm on her knee. "The lights are down. Everyone's attention is on the stage. We might as well be alone."

She saw his hand on her knee, and raised him her palm

on his thigh. High on his thigh. "Have I ever told you, Lord Summerset, how much I appreciate the manner in which your mind works? You are never dull." He was thrilling, provocative, and provoking, in the best way possible. With so little time given to them, she needed to enjoy as much of him as she could before she set sail.

He leaned closer, his breath hot on her cheek. "And you, my dear, are...blast!" He rocked back into his chair.

"What is the matter? Is there a mouse you'd like me to take care of?"

He did not look amused. "We are not alone. I had forgotten my grandmother is here, even now peering at us through her opera glasses."

Netta turned to look. Sure enough, the older woman held a pair of onyx glasses to her eyes. She raised a gloved hand in a greeting John ignored.

John tugged on the hem of his jacket. "Even I am not so perverse as to perform lewd acts in front of my grandmother."

"What is the disagreement between you and her?" Netta raised her own hand, but the woman had turned her attention back to the stage.

"None of your concern."

A small muscle pulsed in his jaw and the dim light shadowed his eyes.

Her throat went thick. She rested her hand over his and squeezed. "No. And my visits to The Burns Theatre at night weren't yours. Yet you wanted to know, and so do I."

He sniffed. "You are living under my roof. I do have some responsibility for your safety."

"And my safety was your only reason for following me?" She nudged him with her shoulder. "Curiosity had nothing to do with it?"

His shoulders unbunched. "Perhaps a very little. But," he said when she opened her mouth, "I still do not want to discuss my grandmother."

"Not even if we make it a game?" She slid her hand

under his cravat to feel the beat of his heart against her palm. "For every detail you tell me about the problem between you and her, I will give you something to help you forget it."

He clasped her hand, keeping it pressed to his chest and running his thumb along her skin. "Really," he drawled, "that sounds more like a quid pro quo than a game, but I am intrigued nonetheless. All right, poppet. You win. A little background."

Her heart leapt at the word win. She so did love to win. She settled into her seat and tuned out the music and drama happening below.

"You know that the House of Summerset hasn't always been as wealthy as it is now." He stared at the curtains hanging above the stage. "My father's gambling had ruined us."

"And your grandmother disowned her irresponsible son." Netta could see the story play out in her head. The fights. The recriminations. The door slowing closing in the previous earl's face.

Yes, she might be overly dramatic in her imaginings. But it was her job to tell stories. It was what she did.

John dipped his chin. "Good guess, but wrong. My grandmother is my mother's mother. She is the Dowager Marchioness of Mallen. From an honorable family. One much too good to include a wastrel and gambler, even if he was an earl."

The bitterness in his voice stunned her. All the fanciful stories in her head disappeared. This was real life. John's life. And it hadn't always been easy. "I'm sorry."

He bit out a laugh. "Little Netta LeBlanc is sorry for me? A sad day for the House of Summerset indeed."

The back of her throat burned. She made to lower her hand, but he held it tight.

"After my mother died and my father had spent not only the Summerset fortunes but his wife's dowry, he decided to humble himself to her parents." His Adam's apple bobbed up and down. "I don't think he would have suffered that humiliation if he hadn't had three sons to care for." He huffed. "And it was all for naught. We presented ourselves before the marquess and marchioness, dressed as neatly as we were able in our used clothes, and received nothing but derision."

She couldn't stand the stark look on his face a moment longer. It was as though he were facing a firing squad, with no hope of preventing the inevitable outcome. She lowered her head to his shoulder.

"I will never forget," he said softly, "standing on her marble floors, looking up at the marchioness in her silks and laces, and thinking she was the most beautiful thing I'd ever seen. Until she looked at my brothers and me with contempt. I felt our shabbiness to our very bones."

"You weren't the one who was shabby in that situation."

He patted her hand. "Thank you, poppet." He inhaled deeply. "Anyhow, that is the story of the breach between myself and my grandmother. We haven't spoken since."

She jerked upright. "But that's been..."

"Almost thirty years."

Good Lord. When the man set his mind to holding a grudge, he did it with everything he had. She glared across the theatre to the Mallen box. What a despicable woman. Regardless of the sins of the son-in-law, she should have cared for her daughter's children.

John chuckled. "You look angry enough on my behalf to confront her and cause a scene."

"I have half a mind to do so!"

"Entertaining as that would be," he said, "I do believe you owe me several favors for my dramatic soliloquy. I intend to collect."

She gave one last pointed glare at the marchioness then erased her from her thoughts. John was at her side and in need of some diversion.

"And I intend to deliver. Has your mysterious companion put on enough of a show for the night?"

Taking her hands, he stood, pulling her up behind him. "More than enough. For the rest of the evening, I only want you to put on a show for me."

* * *

"This wasn't what I had in mind for my reward." John tugged at the curtain cords binding his wrists to the headboard of his bed. The blindfold around his eyes itched like the dickens and the fire beside his bed wasn't enough to keep his naked body warm.

That was where Netta was supposed to come in, but she was doing a damned fine job of rousing his interest then leaving him wanting. She'd undressed him, trussed him to the bed, then disappeared for a solid ten minutes for "supplies" before returning in a breathless rush.

And still cool air pressed upon him instead of her lush body.

He twisted his wrist. "I do think I should have been the one to choose the form of my reward after baring my soul to you." Something he might yet regret. He'd never told anyone that story. Marcus knew some of it, and Wil probably suspected. But the rest of his friends he'd met after he'd restocked the Summerset coffers.

Which probably explained why Sutton expressed such concern over his plan. He wanted John to consult Liverpool since the security of the state might be at risk. And he damn sure didn't want John stealing from the Dutch embassy without preauthorization from the government.

Sutton couldn't understand how important the ore mines were to John, how the thought of losing them, losing everything he'd worked for, twisted his gut and stole his breath. Once the problem was in Liverpool's hands, recovering the deed to Robert's property would become of secondary importance.

"Stop your whining." The mattress shifted beside him. "And stop turning your hand about. You'll chafe the skin right off your wrist."

He snorted. All sweetness and concern his Netta was not. When she had children and one of them fell, she would be the mother telling her child to get back on his feet rather than coo and kiss the sting away.

Something pinched behind his breastbone. Did she want to be a mother? After she left him, would she find some poor sot to marry and start a family? Or would she focus on her career? He wanted her to be happy, of course, but the idea of some other man on the receiving end of her rebukes, saucy remarks, and eyerolls made him want to punch right through his wall.

A trickle of oil drizzled onto his chest, followed by her hands smoothing the substance down his abdomen.

He relaxed into the bed. This was more like it. "If you could go a bit lower, I'd be most grateful."

"Patience." She changed directions, gliding her hands up his arms and earning her an exasperated sigh.

"You know I'll make you feel good." She brushed her lips over his.

He raised his head to increase the pressure and she pulled back. The teasing minx.

"Besides. We have all night." She traced a circle around each of his nipples and followed the caress with her tongue.

John's cock went full hard. A pulse throbbed in it, and he shifted his hips, needing it to touch any part of her.

She took pity and cupped him, squeezing lightly. "I do quite enjoy having you at my mercy. Defenseless." She swiped her tongue over his crown, and he groaned. "In fact— eep!" Her hand disappeared and the bed bounced.

John pulled at his wrists, but she'd done too good a job with the knots. "What? What's wrong?"

"You don't want to know."

"Netta." He injected as much iron into his voice as he was able. Blindfolded and tied to a bed didn't put him in a position of authority.

"Truly, it is nothing dangerous. Merely...something you would find distasteful." The bed shifted, raised as she clambered off of it. "I'll just go get a broom to get rid of it. I'll be right back. Don't move."

"Don't move?" Was she a humorist now?

His bedroom door swished across his carpet as it opened then closed.

Leaving him alone.

With something distasteful.

Perfect.

"Netta!" he bellowed.

No response.

He strung together a row of curses, their inventiveness rather impressing even himself.

And then he heard it.

The soft skittering of tiny feet.

"Bloody hell." He pulled at his restraints with all his might. Not in his home. His housekeeper and butler would be fired if they allowed vermin to roam freely. He levered himself up the bed and set his teeth to the knot at his right wrist. The whole bloody staff would be looking for new positions on the morrow.

Something soft brushed his foot.

John froze, blood thundering in his ears. Probably just the sheet twisting about him.

The sensation crawled past his ankle.

Not a sheet. He thrashed his foot about. Not a bloody sheet!

Netta's peals of laughter cut through his panic.

"Get it off!" He pulled his legs up. "Kill it with the broom!"

She laughed harder. And his brain finally started to work.

He banged his head against the headboard, a metal rosette in the lattice framework digging into his skull. "You, my dear poppet, are going to pay."

Netta tugged down his blindfold. She twirled the feather she held in the air, flourishing it like a sword. "When it comes to toying with a person's mind, I'd say I won that round spectacularly. I owed you one."

His heart slowed from its fright, but then picked up its pace for an entirely different reason.

Netta wore nothing but the delight of her victory and a proud smile. The thrusting and parrying she was doing with the feather made her full breasts bounce and her arse wiggle.

His mouth went dry.

He'd never known anyone so full of life. After all the horrors he'd seen as a spy, in the wars, borne witness to all the atrocities people could inflict, Netta was the closest thing to pure he'd ever known.

"Are you going to release me?" His voice was rough. Predatory. The need to touch her unalloyed brilliance was overwhelming.

When he was with her, he felt unsullied as well.

She ran the tip of the feather down between her breasts. "That depends. Are you going to use your freedom to carry out a revenge?"

He showed her all his teeth. "Only in the best way possible."

"In that case...." She tossed the feather on the bed and bent over him to work on his knots.

Her breasts swung above his face. He couldn't not lift his head and suck one of her pebbled nipples into his mouth. He swirled his tongue around the hard bud, inhaling her scent, enjoying her breathy sigh.

As soon as his hands were free, he gripped her about the waist and rolled her to her back, following her over. He reached for the drawer to his bedside table and pulled out a condom. He tied it around his aching cock, swiped some oil from his chest, and rubbed it over the lambskin. Resting on his elbows, he gripped her head between his hands and pushed into heaven.

He burrowed into her in one slow glide. When he bottomed out, the connection he felt with her was absolute.

And unsettling. Netta was a lovely woman, but he wasn't

a man subject to soft feelings and foolish sentimentality.

So he reared back onto his knees and did what he did best. Fucked. Hard.

Netta closed her eyes, her mouth open in a perfect 'o' as he pounded into her tight cunny. A rosy flush pinkened her skin all over, and she raised her arms to lace her fingers through the headboard, pushing into each of his thrusts.

"I've never felt anything so good," she said, chest heaving.

Neither had he. She was the sweetest fuck he'd ever had. He could screw her for—

No. He slammed the door on that thought. Hooking his arm under her leg, he lifted her calf to his shoulder and pounded into her harder. Faster.

Sweat beaded on his brow. He had one thing to offer women, and he was going to give Netta his best. She might be a brazen, devious, adorable wench, but not even that could entice him into something more lasting.

The nerve endings along his cock screamed for relief. A tickle bloomed low on his spine and his whole body tensed.

"Are you close, poppet?" He scored her calf with his teeth. "Tell me that you're close."

"Mmm." She bit her lower lip. "Almost." Much too slowly for John's liking, she trailed her finger tips over her abdomen and into her nest of curls. With one finger, she circled her clit, her body shuddering.

He joined her finger with his own. There was a time for leisure, but this wasn't it. He rubbed her pouting nub, holding back his own pleasure with all of his might. He almost wept when her inner walls pulsed around him.

"John!" She threw her head back, her face a mask of agonized pleasure.

He fell forwards, planting his hands on either side of her head and hammered into her as his balls drew up tight and ecstasy exploded out of him.

He groaned, the sound torn from deep within. His hips kept rocking into her on their own volition, eking out every ounce of pleasure they could.

The heat of her body was an invitation. He wanted to sink into her, wrap his arms around her, and not let go until sleep took them both.

Instead, he pulled out and flopped to his back, trying to catch his breath.

She patted his chest. "That was fun," she said. Her breath was as short as his at the exertion. "I should bring out the feather more often."

He swiveled his head to look at her. "I'm burning that feather."

She laughed, turning on her side. She rested her head on her hands and rubbed her toe against his calf. "You play with me; I play with you." She yawned. "Why do you add games to your bed sport?"

"Don't you enjoy them?"

She arched an eyebrow. "Obviously I do. Especially tonight's. But it is a little unusual. When you made me believe we were about to be caught, I found it..." She chewed her lip.

"Thrilling? Arousing?"

"I was going to say panic-inducing, but I'll accept your characterization."

He bent his arm, bringing his hand beneath his head. "It's called predicament play. I enjoy putting women in situations that confuse the mind. That push her boundaries, or where she feels like there is no way to win."

"Why?"

"I find the thrill can act on a woman as a drug." He shrugged. "Wasn't your crisis more fulfilling when you felt close to being caught in the gazebo?"

"All my climaxes are fulfilling." She tangled her foot in his own. "But why do you do it? It can't purely be for the woman's benefit."

"Does everything need a reason?" he asked. "It's fun. I enjoy controlling a woman's responses." When he directed a woman's emotions, her passions, it was easier to keep their relationship casual. To keep her from becoming too attached.

To keep her from looking too deeply at the man in her bed.

"Well, I thank you for introducing me to it." She nudged his leg. "You've certainly put the sport in bed sport."

He hated himself for saying it, but it was best to put her on notice. "Perhaps you can train your future husband. Make sure he keeps you entertained in the same manner."

She huffed out a laugh. "You needn't worry, John. I am harboring no illusions about our affair developing into something more."

His chest burned. Damn, but she saw right through him.

"Besides, I have no intention of marrying." She rolled onto her back and stretched. "I enjoy my liberty too much to ever subjugate myself to a husband. England's laws are not in a woman's favor when it comes to the institution. Once I have my four thousand pounds, I'd be an absolute fool to hand it over to a husband."

He stared at the delicate gold tester of his bed. "Indeed." He didn't have to worry about Netta trying to entrap him. He should be happy. She was only here for her fee, enjoying a bit of sport on the side. She was his ideal bed mate.

He turned on his side, away from Netta. Her breathing evened out, easing into slumber, while his shoulders remained hard blocks. Sleep was a long time coming. And when it did, it was disturbed by a dream he hadn't suffered in years.

His grandmother sat on a throne above him. Saying nothing. Barely looking at him. And when she did, all the loathing and shame in the world was encompassed in her expression.

John fell to his hands and knees, her disgusted gaze landing like a blow. And when he managed to lift his head, the woman sitting in judgment above him was no longer his grandmother.

Netta appeared as regal as a queen, her face hard as ice. When she opened her mouth to condemn him, he jerked awake, his body covered in sweat.

He rolled up to sitting, his head falling forwards.

Netta puffed out small breaths behind him, enjoying the sleep of the innocent.

And why shouldn't she? Netta wasn't the one who allowed a shrew to define her self-worth.

He climbed out of bed, gathered his clothes, and quietly left the room.

Chapter Seventeen

Netta poked through the offerings on the tray on the side table. Ever since the first day she'd been in residence, the platters had stopped being removed after breakfast, allowing her to nibble on the breads and cakes all day. A glass jar in John's study was now always filled with her favorite Pomfret cakes. If she stayed much longer, she wouldn't be able to fit into her lovely new dresses.

She picked up a puffy roll and had just taken a bite when loud voices sounded down the hall, growing in intensity.

The door to the breakfast room crashed open, bouncing off the wall. A head crowned in rich auburn hair pulled back into a low queue popped in through the open door. "Oy, he's not in here." His eyes lit on her and he stepped into the room more fully. "Mmm. Breakfast."

Netta's eyes widened. The man was immense, as broad across as an ox, and he was headed straight for her.

She swallowed her bite and side-stepped out of his path.

"Excuse me, miss," he said, a hint of a Scottish burr warming his words. He nodded and plucked up his own roll. "I've been riding all night and with naught but a wee bite when I changed horses."

"I told you he wouldn't be in the breakfast room at this hour." The Baron of Sutton clomped into the room after him. "You just wanted to look for crumbs."

"And I found a big one." The russet-headed fellow lifted his snack. "But who is this wee morsel?" He cocked his head, examining her from her walking boots to the roots of her hair as he took a large bite.

"I'm Miss Antoinette LeBlanc." A man who appreciated a good breakfast roll as well as she did was no one to be intimidated by. "And you are?"

"An utter boor," came another voice. Two more men entered the room. The parlor was large but these four men seemed to fill it to capacity. One of the newcomers had close-cropped blond hair a couple shades darker than John's, and Hessian boots buffed to such a shine Netta swore she could see her reflection. The other was just as handsome, his bronzed skin and nutmeg hair making him look as warm as an evening fire. He slapped his glove against his thigh and continued, "You left mud all over my carriage, Dunkeld."

The huge man swallowed the last bite of his roll and wiped his hands on his trousers. "Boots get muddy riding down from Scotland."

"Yes, but that doesn't explain how the mud came to be on the wall of the carriage, up near the ceiling."

Sutton stepped into the middle of the fray. "Gentleman. Perhaps instead of skirmishing in front of Summerset's friend, you should introduce yourselves and act like we have some manners."

The blond man stepped a shiny boot forward and opened his mouth.

Sutton cut him off. "This," he said, pointing at the man with the muddy carriage, "is Julius Blackwell, Earl of Rothchild. Julius, meet Miss Antoinette LeBlanc."

The man nodded and Netta sketched a hasty curtsy.

"And the one glowering at me," Sutton said, pointing at the blond man, "is Marcus Hawkridge, Duke of Montague."

Netta's pulse bounded through her veins like a hare. A duke. She made her curtsy a bit deeper this time.

Sutton rubbed his chin, his fingers disappearing into his bushy, black beard. "They managed to marry sisters, Elizabeth and Amanda, who I'm certain you'll meet if you remain under this roof too much longer. And lastly, the one with dirty boots and country manners is, unbelievably, a marquess. Sinclair Archer, Marquess of Dunkeld to be exact. His wife came down from Scotland with him but was sensible enough to want to rest at Rothchild's after the journey."

Sutton glanced over at the breakfast tray and picked out a lemon tart. "And you met me and Colleen, of course."

"Of course." Her thighs burned from all the curtsies. John was an earl. Of course he'd have high-ranking friends. She should have expected it. Thankfully not one was a name she recognized as being among her father's intimates.

But seeing John's friends all standing in a loose row sent a decided shiver down her spine, and it wasn't from fear of being recognized. These men were formidable enough to constitute a small army and each handsome enough to make a woman's head go soft. All grouped together as they were...well, Netta could forgive herself the tiny flutters in her stomach.

"Not five minutes arrived and eating me out of house and home already." John strode into the room, and her flutters multiplied into a thousand butterfly wings flapping in tandem. The room brightened just with his presence, as though he were the sun bringing life and energy to everyone around him.

Heat kindled low in her belly. She wasn't sure how she felt about losing her role as the star in the room, but she couldn't deny any longer the power he held over her.

He nodded to Netta, as though she were nothing more than a casual acquaintance, before greeting each of his friends with hearty backslaps and rude jests.

She turned, hoping to hide her hurt. She'd thought he'd felt free to show her affection in front of his friends. Nothing amiss had occurred between them since the time he'd slipped from his bed that morn to break his fast at parts unknown and now. No disputes that could have turned his feelings from fondness to disfavor.

She didn't demand a declaration of love before allowing men into her bed, but she did need mutual respect and affection. Had she been fooling herself believing the Earl of Summerset held her in the same esteem she did him? Was he embarrassed to acknowledge to his friends that his dalliance was with a woman not of their station?

She turned back around, lifting her chin. Or perhaps she was reading too much into a cool greeting. First and foremost, they had a business arrangement. She needed to remember that.

John strolled to the sideboard and poured himself a cup of coffee from the silver urn. "Now, to what do I owe this invasion?" He took a sip, peering at his friends over the rim.

"You know why." The Duke of Montague widened his stance and crossed his arms over his chest.

Rothchild bobbed his head in her direction. "Perhaps we should move our discussion to your library. We've already incommoded Miss LeBlanc long enough."

John chuckled and came to stand beside her. He stood beside her, but still the few inches between them remained cold. "Netta is quite familiar with the particulars of what you've come to discuss. In fact, she is integral to my plan's implementation."

A wedge of the Scotsman's second roll broke off and tumbled to the floor. "You've made that wee lass a part of your plan?"

John stiffened. "Her size is not an indication of her talents."

Netta rested one hand on her hip. Indeed it was not. And if any of these gentlemen thought to cut her out of the plot, and her four thousand pounds, they had another think coming.

"Not all talents are useful for what you have in mind." Dunkeld kicked the bit of bread towards the fireplace. "I'm sure she's...charming, but I could knock her over with a heavy breath."

Netta clenched her hands. She might be short, but she was sturdy enough. And she'd been in enough scraps to know the best way to win a fight was to avoid it altogether.

That money was so close she could almost taste it. "You don't need to concern yourself with my safety. I can assure you that I am quite capable of taking care of myself."

The look the large Scotsman gave her bordered on pity, raising her hackles even farther.

John, however, found fault with his friend's words for a different reason. "Apologize to Netta this instant," he bit out through clenched teeth.

The energy in the room shifted. The remaining men stepped closer, legs tense, as though preparing to separate the two. Dunkeld merely looked up from the crumbs he was brushing from his cravat and blinked. "What?"

John prowled forwards, looking as deadly as a large cat stalking its prey. He must have practiced walking with a book on his head for hours as a child. Except for his legs drawing him inexorably forward, the rest of his body remained still as the grave.

The effect was frightening.

She leapt forwards and grabbed his arm. "John, he didn't mean it in that manner."

"Mean what?" Dunkeld swung his head from John to Montague, Rothchild, and Sutton. "What did I say?"

"You intimated that Netta was a whore. Insulted a friend of mine. A woman under my protection." John shook himself free from her grip.

It wasn't difficult. Her hands had gone lax. "Under your protection?" she asked, outraged. "Are we back to that again?"

John ignored her and took another step forward.

Sutton stepped between the men and held up his hand. He nodded to Netta. "Please excuse Dunkeld, Miss LeBlanc. He never was taught how to speak properly. Scottish, you know."

Dunkeld scowled.

"And you"—Sutton flipped his hand down to point at John—"should know better than to allow emotions to get the better of you when there is a job to be done. Nor should you doubt the good intentions of a friend."

The moment stretched until John's shoulders lowered and he nodded.

Dunkeld turned to Rothchild and Montague. "I didnae mean to insult her," he said, his accent thickening with his indignation.

"We know." The duke patted the Scotsman on the back. "It was just your usual charm with women."

Netta planted her hands on her hips. "I have not been under any man's protection since I ran— since I left my father's house. Such nonsense wasn't a part of our deal." John couldn't think of her as an obligation. He mustn't. She'd worked hard to make an independent woman of herself. She paid her own rent, purchased her own treats, and bestowed her charms willingly on those she deemed worthy.

She did so for pleasure, for a sense of connection. Not to incur obligations.

John brushed his hand over her shoulder and came up with a stray hair. He blew it away. "In point of fact, everyone who stays under my roof is under my protection. Don't worry, poppet." He inhaled sharply. "Any such constraint you feel imposed by my duty will end when you leave. Your job will be finished, and so will any obligations."

She poked him in the chest. "I am not a duty. Nor is my companionship an act of commerce." Her father had only seen her as a commodity. Something to be traded. Sold. "I agreed to this job and will earn my wages, but everything else I give freely."

He captured her finger. With a glance over his shoulder, he raised her hand and kissed it, his back blocking the action from his friends. "Perhaps what I give, I give freely, too."

Netta's breathing slowed. If he didn't see her as an

obligation, or her favors as a commodity, well, then, his streak of protectiveness might not be all to the bad. She bit the inside of her cheek. Perhaps it was even sweet.

He also wasn't giving her a cool reception any longer. Whatever indifference he had affected upon entering the room hadn't survived the appearance of an insult against her. She very much wanted to thank Dunkeld for his clumsy words.

"Now, no more arguments," John said. "I believe you are expected at The Minerva Club."

Montague swiveled his head. "My aunt's club? Has it opened?"

"Last month." John sauntered to the wall and pulled the bell ring. "I'm surprised you didn't know. After all, Elizabeth and Amanda were founding members."

Rothchild gripped the back of his neck. "I miss the time when my wife was too afraid to leave the house. I always knew where she was."

"No, you don't," John said, his tone unusually serious.

Rothchild nodded, the edges of his lips tipping upwards. "No. I don't."

A footman stepped through, and John nodded to him. "Have a carriage brought around for Miss LeBlanc."

"Yes, my lord." The man bowed and disappeared.

Netta shifted her weight. She did want to see the women's club, but hated missing the action here. John's friends hadn't come for a boring cup of tea. Discussions would be had. Plots hatched.

She adored a good plot-hatching.

But she'd promised Lady Mary and didn't want to disappoint that woman.

"I'll be on my way then." She took one last glance at her appearance in the mirror beside the door, running her finger over her right eyebrow.

"Tell my aunt I expect to see her while I'm in town," Montague said.

"And us." Sutton took the last of the tarts from the tray.

"We all want to see Lady Mary."

"I'll tell her." With one last wistful gaze at the men, Netta turned and made for the carriage with a sigh.

Nothing The Minerva had to offer could compare to the thrill that group of men instilled. Of that she was certain.

* * *

She was certain of nothing. Not even of which direction was up.

The mirrors at the far end of the room distorted the reflection of the black-and-white striped walls into eye-straining waves. Netta's reflection, and those of every other woman in The Minerva Club's ballroom, were distorted and reverse, making it appear as though they walked on the ceiling.

Lady Mary shook her head. "This is what happens when you succumb to the compliments of an Italian glass maker. At least his skills in other areas surpassed his workmanship with mirrors. They will have to be replaced, of course."

"Of course." Netta rubbed her forehead, an ache forming.

"Look out!"

Netta ducked, dragging Lady Mary down to the floor with her as a pall-mall ball flew overhead and crashed into one of the mirrors. A shower of broken glass exploded from the impact, sending the women standing near it fleeing.

"Hmm." Lady Mary cocked her head. "Perhaps I should have all the women take aim. It will be much easier to sweep out the mistake than have the heavy panes removed."

Netta pressed her palms to the dark stone floor and dropped her head. She thought she pushed boundaries, but ever since stepping inside The Minerva Club, she realized she was but an amateur. These women were experts.

At least she now knew which direction was down. She patted the nice, solid floor before standing. "Shall we continue the tour?"

"Of course." Lady Mary flicked her skirts and marched ahead. "This, as I said, was to be our hall of mirrors. An homage to Versailles. You must come back and see it when I've remodeled."

Netta nodded and skirted around a tumble of fencing swords on the floor, one of the uncapped points tugging at her gown. If she survived this visit.

"And this is our tavern." Lady Mary swept her hand to indicate the room decorated in pearl grey and lavender. A long oak bar ran the length of the far wall, and a man in a powdered wig and cheeks stood behind it serving drinks. "We had to hire a new bartender. The last one never refused service and some of these women"—she leaned towards Netta and cupped her mouth with her hand—"don't know when to say no. It's almost as though they never snuck their husbands' whisky before."

Netta bit back her smile. "How positively unimaginative of them."

"Exactly."

A cheer rose from the corner where a table had been set up with a chess board. A woman in a jade-green caftan held up her black queen in victory.

"Your club is an amusement parlor then?" She trailed after Lady Mary through a room with a thick carpet and a game of lawn darts in play.

"In large part." She finger-waved a man in full livery over and whispered something into his ear. He nodded and glided away. Lady Mary resumed her march. "Women need to learn how to have fun. Life can be deadly serious at times; we women need a place to relieve the pressure. But we also have a library and a conversation parlor where many a debate have been held."

She threw open a wide set of double doors and circled the new room to raise the flames of the gas lamps. "We also have this stage where we hope to invite lecturers to come speak."

Netta stepped inside, and her heart leapt. She clapped her hands together. It was small, a mere eight by ten feet, but there along the back wall was the most darling stage she had yet seen. She wanted to fold it up, put it in her pocket, and take it about with her everywhere.

Lady Mary's eyes crinkled. "And of course, the odd performance would be lovely, as well."

Netta had told the woman she was an actress. After John discovered it, Netta hadn't wanted to keep that truth from Lady Mary. And now she was pleased she hadn't.

She skipped to the raised platform. It was made of solid teak, the edges carved with elaborate scroll-work. Cherubs peeked out at each corner. She hurried to the stairs and hopped up the three steps to stand upon it. The stage was sturdy beneath her feet, the grain of the wood giving its surface a sultry luster. She pushed open the hunter green curtains behind it.

"There's another room!" Netta hooked the rope on the wall around the curtain, holding it open. "With enough space for small sets."

Lady Mary joined her. "And that hallway there not only leads to the kitchens and an outdoor exit, it also contains several chambers that could be used as dressing rooms. Now if only I knew any actresses who'd care to put on a small performance for our motley group."

"It's absolutely charming." Netta stepped to center-stage and twirled. "I'd be honored to perform here any time. And I'm certain my friend, Cerise, would too."

"Good." Lady Mary pushed her spectacles up her nose and turned for the steps, Netta trailing slowly behind. "And now that you've seen the place, what say you to becoming a member?"

Netta gave one last look at the small stage before following her out the door. "I would love to but I'm afraid it's not within my resources to join a club."

"I think we can come to some arrangement. Not everything is about money."

No. Netta's throat tightened. But for the past six years her life had revolved around it. How much she could earn, how much she could save, all for the end game of taking her sister to America.

That country had once seemed her savior. Now it just seemed lonely. She would know no one but her sister. There would be no one there to make her laugh. No one to tease and inflame.

There would be no John Chaucer.

"Would you like a drink, my dear?" Lady Mary asked when they reached the tavern.

"Yes." Netta swallowed, her mouth gone dry. "Yes, I quite think I would."

Lady Mary waggled another finger, and the barkeep put two drinks on a tray and headed their way. She picked up a cut-crystal tumbler and took a sip. "Ah. The Marie Antoinette. It must be Thursday."

Netta took her own glass and lifted it to her mouth. The alcohol fumes wafting off of it made her eyes burn, but she took a small sip. And coughed. "Lovely."

"I think so." Lady Mary raised her glass. "Catherine! I didn't expect to see you today. Come join us."

Netta glanced over her shoulder, and everything in her stilled. The Dowager Marchioness of Mallen, otherwise known as John's grandmother, toddled towards them. She leaned heavily on a cane, her pale peach lace train dragging slowly behind her gown. Her chin was tipped up, the feather in her turban dipping backwards, making the slow march seem regal.

Now Netta knew where John had inherited his sense of style.

Fortunately, he hadn't inherited the woman's stone-cold heart.

The woman inclined her head when she reached them. "Lady Mary. I am all amazement each time I visit. Your eccentricities have finally found a home."

Netta narrowed her eyes. "I think The Minerva Club is

lovely. Just like Lady Mary."

The dowager turned faded blue eyes her way. "Isn't that what I said?"

"Now no more of that 'lady' business." Lady Mary waggled that powerful finger again, and another drink appeared for John's grandmother. "In this club we don't tolerate all those titles. I'm just Mary. Or May, if the spirit takes you." One edge of her lips lifted. "And I always take 'eccentric' as a compliment, dear. No need to defend me."

Netta inclined her head. Of course, Lady Mary would be welcoming of all. It did her credit.

But that didn't mean Netta had to be gracious. "I am surprised to learn you are a member of The Minerva, *Catherine*. From what I've heard of you, I would have thought the barest whisper of impropriety would have kept you far away."

The dowager raised an eyebrow, her haughtiness so reminiscent of John's it stole Netta's breath. "And you are?"

"This is Miss Netta Courtney," Mary said. "She is also a particular friend of your grandson's. The earl," she clarified.

"Were you the woman with him at the theatre?" Catherine lifted a quizzing glass that hung on a gold chain around her neck and peered through it. "I would blame my failing eyesight, but you did quite a good job of hiding your face on your own."

"Thank you." Mary wasn't the only one who could take odd compliments.

They all studied their drinks for an awkward moment.

Catherine finally cleared her throat. "And how is my grandson? In good health, I hope."

"I would say as fine as ever, but we only recently became acquainted." Netta drummed her fingers on her glass. "And as you haven't seen him since he was a boy, you won't be able to give me any frame of reference. It seems there was a large portion of his early life where Summerset's health and welfare were sorely neglected."

The dowager flushed and looked to Mary, who

shrugged. "You've started this path of redemption, Catherine, and I'm afraid it is one you must walk alone. But as much as my curiosity matches Netta's, there are only three people you need answer to, and none of them are Netta or myself."

"Redemption?" Netta huffed. She didn't think she believed in it, at least not for someone who could turn her back on three hungry children.

The woman's eyes went watery.

Netta squeezed her glass, the crystal digging into her palm. She would not feel badly for the woman. She would not.

Besides, it must be a ploy. A woman who could deny her grandchildren didn't have the capacity to cry. It was all a trick to engage her sympathies.

Catherine sniffed and turned her face, but not before a single tear coursed down her wrinkled cheek.

"I'm so sorry! I take it all back." Netta's words tripped over each other. Confound it, she'd made an old woman cry. "From what John said, I didn't think my words could upset you. Please pay me no mind," she implored. If the dowager started crying then Netta would start, and she didn't cry pretty.

"Whatever my grandson has said about me I deserve." Catherine dabbed at her eyes with a lavender-scented handkerchief. "It's no excuse, but you can't know how much I hated their father. And how much I missed my daughter. Looking at those boys was like a knife to the heart."

"Now, now." Mary patted the woman's hand. "There's no blubbering in my club. It does no good, and I won't have it."

Netta stepped forwards. "Yes, please do stop. It was horrible of me to bring the subject up. I promise not to do so again. Except—" She bit her lip.

Catherine took a deep breath. "Except what?"

"Well..." She rubbed her thumb along the rim of her

glass. "It does seem a shame that you and Summerset live in the same city but never see one another. If your attitude has changed and you wish to reconcile—"

"It has and I do." Catherine tapped the end of her walking stick onto the floor for emphasis.

"Then perhaps there is something we should do about it." John would be changing her life for the better, transforming it with the money he would give her. He would never know how much he'd saved her.

And she wanted to leave him better off, too. Yes, getting his ore mine back would help him financially, but it wouldn't transform his life.

Forgiving his grandmother, reestablishing a relationship, however, could be life-altering.

Damned if she knew how to accomplish it though.

She sipped her drink.

"What were you thinking?" Mary asked.

"Nothing yet." The task would require plotting. Cunning. Luckily, she had that in spades. "But give me a minute and I'll come up with something good."

Chapter Eighteen

John stared at the ceiling of his library, one foot propped on the armrest of the settee he lay upon, the other dangling off the seat, swinging in a gentle circle. "I don't want to do it so I'm not going to do it. You can harass me until the stars go dark, and I won't change my mind."

"Lovely," Montague said. "We've come to the point of the conversation where Summerset acts the child. He even lounges about on the furniture, just as my son would. My three-year-old son," he added pointedly.

Well, that was rich coming from the man sitting in John's chair with his own feet propped up on his desk.

"I didn't realize one of the misfortunes of age was the inability to sit comfortably." He already suffered from a knee that was wont to crackle as he climbed stairs and a decreased tolerance for spirits. Now he couldn't lounge? John scowled. He hated growing older. But he rolled into a seated position.

Rothchild ran a hand through his hair. "You must see reason. This is a matter of state security. Liverpool will provide assistance, and he has a right to know about any plot against England. I realize you're sulky since he released you from service, but that doesn't excuse playing light with our national security."

Fire churned in John's gut. "I'm not playing light. I'm playing to win."

Sutton straightened from the wall. "As do we all. But Liverpool has contacts we do not. He can provide information we don't have access to. Why do you resist seeing him?"

"His priorities do not mirror my own." John leaned forwards and braced his forearms on his thighs. "In addition to discovering Sudworth's plot, I must have the deed back to my brother's home. Without those ore deposits, my holdings will take a hit. One from which they cannot recover."

He tapped his heel against the floor. His houses in Bath and Ramsgate would have to be sold. Not to mention his villas in Tuscany and Barbados.

The amounts he paid monthly for his wardrobe alone supported four entire families of tailors. Without that steel operation, he would be forced to wear simple clothes. Sell off his jewels one by one. He would be plain. Diminished. He would be...nothing.

The disgust in his grandmother's eyes haunted him. Hunted him. Swamping his memories.

His heartbeat thrashed in his ears. He jerked on the knot of his cravat, needing more air. No, he wouldn't allow it. He wouldn't let an arsewipe like Sudworth reduce him to insignificance. He'd worked too damn hard. He would never be poor again.

"Is that one smelt so important?" Montague dropped a boot to the floor with a thud. "You still have various other enterprises. Your gunpowder mill for example."

"Due to our government's appalling dearth of wars currently, it has come to a near standstill." A circumstance he could never complain about. He'd seen too many good men die on the battlefields to want his profit to come at peace's expense.

Rothchild pulled a cheroot from his pocket and lit it from a lump of coal from the fireplace. He inhaled deeply, staring at John through the smoke. "You could always go back into your laboratory," he said quietly. "You created one new alloy; you could create another. One using a different source of ore."

John's chest tightened. "That isn't an option." Wil

harangued him about it, then Netta, and now Rothchild took up the task. It was a damned conspiracy.

His friends all gave each other looks. One that John didn't appreciate.

"You know why," he ground out.

"It was an accident." Montague ran his hand through his hair. "How long will you punish yourself?"

"I'm not the one who was punished." John stood and stalked across the room. He'd entertained this conversation long enough.

Sutton took his arm as he passed. "This woman of yours—"

"Yes?" John didn't want to hear talk of Netta. His mind was already a confused morass with thoughts of her; he didn't need his friends complicating the issue with their insinuations and veiled remarks.

He should distance himself from her, stay out of her bed. That would be the smart thing to do to keep his head clear and succeed with his mission.

He didn't want to.

"She may be smart and capable, but the plan you propose is not without danger." Sutton scrubbed his face with his large paw. "If you do lose and don't turn her over to Sudworth, he may take that very poorly. Is she truly prepared? Are you?"

"I won't lose." He'd already ordered something that would ensure his victory. "And I'll make damned certain nothing untoward happens to her."

"No matter how good a plan, there are always unforeseen circumstances." Rothchild tossed the cheroot in the fireplace. "Our past histories are proof enough of that."

"Are you volunteering to assist?" John asked.

Rothchild dipped his chin and gave him a reproachful look. "I'll be there. We'll all be there. You know we will. But it would be better, safer, if Liverpool's men were in on it, too."

John's shoulders sagged. Rothchild was right. John

should have known his friends would have his back. But a small part of him had worried they'd become too content in their retirement to pick up arms again. That they would consider his problem of a lost ore mine unworthy of their time.

Not that he *needed* their help.

But it wouldn't hurt.

He blew out his cheeks. He'd been an idiot. Of course his friends would volunteer. If the issue was important to John, it was important to all of them. That's how their friendship worked.

It also wouldn't hurt to speak with Liverpool. The prime minister's priorities might be different but that didn't mean they weren't compatible.

And if their priorities diverged, well, John wasn't one of the prime minister's spies. He didn't have to do as the man wanted.

"All right." He nodded to Sutton. "Let's go pay a visit to our former employer."

The ride to Liverpool's residence was tense, not least because they'd insisted on all jamming into Rothchild's carriage. Almost as if his friends were afraid he'd change his mind if they let him out of their sight.

"Will you move your fat arse?" John pressed his elbow into Dunkeld's side and levered out from between the Scotsman and Sutton. "I feel like the meat in a bloody ruffian sandwich."

Dunkeld sniffed. "My arse is in perfect proportion to the rest of my body. It's hardly my fault you're slender enough to snap like a twig." But he shifted, giving John an inch more breathing space.

"Gentlemen, can we stop with the gratuitous insults?" Montague asked. He leaned into the corner of the carriage and stretched his arm along the back rest. With just him and Rothchild on the seat opposite, he could spread his body and take up as much room as he liked.

John glared. "Why would we want to do that?"

"Because we've arrived." He nodded to the window, and the three-story townhouse coming into view. "I don't want the prime minister to know the sad maturity level of the men he entrusted state secrets to."

"He already knows." Rothchild pushed open the door. "Why do you think he dismissed the lot of us?" he muttered as he jumped down.

"I wasn't dismissed," Montague protested. He climbed out. "I retired."

John squeezed past Sutton before he could exit, earning a shove to the back. "An early retirement Liverpool was only too eager to accommodate." He glared up at the townhouse. How many times had he met with Liverpool here or at his club? How many tasks had he undertaken for no recompense, only from duty to his country?

And amusement. Being a spy was bloody fun, but Liverpool didn't know that. He'd traded on John's and the others' patriotism and in return had given them the boot the first instant they'd become inconvenient.

He followed his friends up the front steps. Politicians. He huffed. They were all alike.

The butler who answered their knock asked them to wait in a small sitting room by the front entrance. John stared at the portrait of Liverpool on the far wall. The grey hair was combed neatly in the picture when it usually wasn't in real life, but the bushy eyebrows were true enough. John's fingers twitched, itching to pluck the blade he'd placed in his boot that morning and throw it smack dab into that pompous face.

"Gentlemen." The man himself stepped into the room and shut the door behind him. "To what do I owe the pleasure of this visit?"

His friends looked at John, waiting for him to take the lead.

John rested his arse on a windowsill and crossed his arms and legs. "I've been asked to steal a document from the Dutch embassy."

Liverpool's eyes went sharp. "By whom?"

"Harlow Sudworth. He's a capitalist, with fingers in everything from trade to industry to agriculture." His research into the man had shown a diversity of endeavors that had impressed even John. Perhaps if he had branched out from more than just steel and gunpowder, he would have been able to weather the loss of his ore mine.

"I know who he is," Liverpool said. "A man doesn't become as wealthy as he without us taking notice."

"Well, he seems to think I'll be amenable to treason in return for some property I've lost." John gripped the window sill. "I, of course, let him believe there might be some truth to that."

Liverpool raised a thick eyebrow. "Sporting of you." He circled his desk and sat behind it. "What does he want you to steal?"

"I'm not certain," John said. "Only that it is a document signed by King William with a map attached."

Liverpool frowned. "Well, what do you think his game is?"

Sutton rocked back on his heels. "I've discovered the majority of his trading routes originate or traverse Dutch holdings. He could be trying to gain leverage over the king for plum trading agreements."

"That doesn't explain Raffles, though." Montague rubbed his chin. "Although the colony he is attempting to establish in Bencoolen used to be in Dutch territory."

"What are we doing in Bencoolen?" Sutton asked.

"The usual." Montague shrugged. "Trying to end slavery and create an outpost to challenge Dutch hegemony in the area."

"Raffles?" Liverpool interrupted.

Montague shot John an apologetic look.

John couldn't blame the slip. They weren't in the habit of keeping information from the prime minister. "The first job Sudworth had me do was add a letter to Sir Stamford Raffles's file in the Home Office. I believe he wants it to discredit the man."

"And you did this?" Liverpool's voice was deceptively pleasant, but John wasn't fooled. He knew he was treading a fine line.

"I did, but not with the letter Sudworth gave me." John crossed his arms over his chest. "I forged a new letter so if any inquiries proceed, a close examination will show the letter to be false and no harm will come to the man's reputation."

Liverpool laced his fingers over his round belly and twirled his thumbs around each other. "You boys have been busy. How long has it been since Sudworth approached you?"

John forced his gaze to remain even with the prime minister's. He wouldn't act like a contrite school boy caught stealing a pudding. "A couple of weeks."

His thumbs stilled. "And you're just coming to me now?"

"We wanted to gather as much information as we could first." Montague dropped into the chair across from the prime minister and crossed one leg over the other. "After all, that's what we've been trained to do." The smile he gave the older man was bland.

Liverpool pressed his palms to his desk and leaned forwards. "You thought you should make that decision on your own?" he asked, his voice rising.

John pushed off the sill and stood behind Montague. He placed his hand on the duke's shoulder. "I only recently informed my friends." Except for Sutton. Sutton had known almost since the first, but he didn't feel it necessary to point that out. "I thought, and still do think, that I can handle Sudworth on my own. They advised me to consult with you."

"And I thank them for it." Liverpool's words were clipped, his thumb beating a restless tattoo on the desk. A sure sign of his ire. "Why would you wish to go this alone?"

John brushed at a bit of dirt on his sleeve. "You've

shown no interest in using my talents of late. Have circumstances changed? Do you now wish to employ my services once more?"

"John." Sutton's voice was a warning, but John didn't care. The one thing he had enjoyed, the one thing he remained competent at, Liverpool had taken. He'd been bored and miserable, until...well, until Netta and this issue with his brother had arisen.

Netta. He swallowed. He would keep her safe. But the idea of gambling her like she was nothing but chattel, even if he intended a double-deal, turned his stomach.

Liverpool blew out a breath and put his joined hands behind his head. He stared at the ceiling for a long moment. "You're invested in this mission. Why?"

"Sudworth has the deed to my brother's property with my ore mines on it. I want it back." John clenched his hand, pressing it into his thigh. "I need it back. And along the way I'll find out what the man's up to."

"A man should never let anything become so important that it becomes an obsession." Liverpool cocked his head. "This feels too personal for you to be objective. Perhaps I should handle it myself."

"You'll have a hell of a lot of interference from me. I won't sit back and do nothing."

"Nor will I," Montague said.

"We're all in on this." Rothchild opened a small wooden box on Liverpool's desk and drifted his fingers over the cigars laying within. Liverpool snapped the lid shut, Rothchild's fingers just escaping. He arched an eyebrow. "It would be better to work with us than have us underfoot."

"Yes." Liverpool's pursed his lips. He looked John up and down and sighed. "It has been an honor working with the five of you. I do hope I won't have to set my men against you boys. The security of England is of ultimate importance."

His men. That phrase coming from Liverpool's mouth used to include John. And now it was used as a warning.

He was well and truly out of the spy business. No more fooling himself that after a couple of months the prime minster would change his mind. There would be no more adventures. No more intrigues.

John's shoulder blades eased down his back. And that knowledge wasn't as devastating as it used to be. As his brother had so ably shown, there was trouble enough to battle without need of his country to provide diversions. And Netta—

John blinked. Netta entertained him better than any mission ever had.

He would be fine. He'd lost his career as a chemist, now as a spy, yet he still had hope life could throw interesting challenges in his path. And interesting people.

"I understand." And he did. The prime minister's only concern was the security of the nation. But John didn't make compromises. He would uncover Sudworth's plot, stop it, and recover his brother's deed. He could have it all.

And perhaps that applied to his personal life, as well. If he and Netta were enjoying each other's company, why limit it? They could go on as they were after this mission ended. He would attend her plays, then take her to the apartments he would set her up in and put on private plays of their own.

Yes, a diverting relationship that they would both enjoy until it ran its natural course. He'd never had a long-term mistress before. Never liked a woman well enough to give her *carte blanche*.

To see her eyes light up, John would give Netta anything she wanted.

Liverpool scrubbed his hand across his jowls. "All right. Let's hear this plan of yours."

Chapter Nineteen

John pinched his forehead between his thumb and forefinger. A low throb pulsed beneath the skin. He folded the missive and slid it into his pocket.

It had been unrealistic to think Hampson's tests on iron and carbon would yield any results, even with the assistance of Robert. While both men had shown an aptitude in assisting in the laboratory, it hadn't extended to conducting their own experiments. Neither man had studied chemistry to the extent John had. Hampson could manage the smelt, but he wouldn't be developing anything to replace their current production.

He removed a small key from the top drawer of his desk and crossed his study. He unlocked the door next to the bookcase and pushed it open.

Dust motes drifted in the light which streamed from the large window. The cloth-draped lumps on the long workbench made his chest ache. How long had it been since he'd last been in this laboratory? Two years? Three? Surely it hadn't been that long since he'd made a clouding gas for one of his missions.

He ran his finger over the small burner, knowing every inch of its shape even hidden under the linen. The small potions he made to assist him and his friends for their work were nothing but a tease. Like a small bite of food when a man was starving, it only served to increase his hunger.

Robert had assisted Hampson with the experiments, that much had been clear in his manager's letter. His brother had faced whatever trepidations he might have had after the accident and re-entered the laboratory.

Of course, it was easier for him. He hadn't made the mistake.

Only suffered its consequences.

He pulled the letter from his pocket and lifted it to the light. He peered at the third paragraph. Had Hampson written that they'd raised the temperature of the alloy to 1,250 or 1,280 Celsius? Even such a small difference could affect the results. Pulling his lorgnette from his waistcoat pocket, he raised them to his eyes and brought the paper closer. Perhaps if he—

"What are you reading?" Netta poked her head through the door. Her gaze swept the laboratory, and she stepped fully inside. Her lime-green gown seeming to brighten the room, or perhaps it was the woman wearing it. "And what is this place?"

He shoved the glasses back in his pocket. "A letter from the manager of my smelt. He's informed me of the development of a new alloy he's playing with. Or the lack of developments." He crossed his arms. "And you're in what is left of my laboratory."

She wandered to a tall glass-fronted case and reached for the door. "And all these little jars—"

John leapt forwards and drew her hand back. "Highly dangerous chemicals. Don't touch."

She clasped her hands behind her back and strolled to his work bench. She found the one object not covered by a linen, his worn leather book of notes, and blew at the dust covering the page.

She sneezed.

A lead ball weighted his stomach. There was no experiment in progress. No open flames. Yet the image of Netta bent over his workbench filled him with unease. The scene was too reminiscent of the last person he'd seen bent over his work bench.

He took her elbow and drew her out of the room, locking it behind them. "The letter is further evidence that I need my chromite mines returned. It is time for you to meet our mark." He tossed the letter on his desk and dropped into the chair. If all went well, he could kill two birds with one stone. Tonight was the perfect opportunity to infiltrate the Dutch embassy, and, he hoped, flaunt Netta in front of Sudworth at the same time.

Netta leaned against his side. She combed her fingers through his hair, and the fine muscles in his face went slack. "Are you certain there is nothing of promise in the letter?" she asked. "Perhaps if you read it more closely with your spectacles on."

He removed her lovely, petting hand and glared up at her. "I do not wear spectacles."

Her gaze dropped to his waistcoat pocket and she arched a dark eyebrow.

John sniffed. "Those are purely for affectation." Until now. Bloody thirty-five-year-old eyes. "No matter. What are you up to today? Another visit to May's club?"

"I hadn't planned on it." She sucked her bottom lip into her mouth and gave him a look he couldn't interpret. "But if you'd like to accompany me, I think a visit to The Minerva would be time well spent."

"Me? At a women's club?" He patted her hip. "A bit like inviting the fox into the henhouse. I don't think Auntie May would approve." He pushed the edge of the letter with his finger. Perhaps if Hampson heated the furnace even further the alloy would—

No. He'd learned his lesson. His time of fiddling about with corrosive chemicals was over.

His head jerked forward. "What?!" He rubbed the small sting on his scalp and scowled. "Did you just slap the back of my head?"

"You weren't listening to me." Netta turned and leaned back against his desk, facing him. She crossed her arms. "I don't like being ignored."

John stared at the ceiling, fighting his grin. It wouldn't do to encourage such behavior. But she was irrepressible. "You now have my undivided attention."

"And now I don't want it. I don't think you're ready for what I had to say in any case." She tugged the letter from under her arse and scanned its contents. "This laboratory up at your estate, it is much larger than the one here, I suppose?"

"Yes. At least five times its size." It was a lovely space. One he'd designed himself. He was glad Hampson was finding some use for it, even if his experiments came to naught. He tangled his fingers in Netta's skirts and pulled her between his spread legs. He rested his cheek against her bosom as he lazily traced a circle on her lower back.

This was nice. Having someone he could talk to about his day. Someone sweet and understanding.

"And is that laboratory similarly abandoned?"

John's hand stilled. Depending on the direction of her next words, he might have relaxed too soon. "Well, Hampson putters about in it from time to time."

"But you don't?" Her bosom heaved with her sigh. "Why did you stop working in science?"

And there it was. He set her away from him. The question he didn't want to hear. "The 'why' isn't important. That part of my life is over."

She moved back into his space. Raising her skirts, she swung her leg over his thighs and settled on his lap, lacing her hands behind his neck. "Because of what happened with your brother?"

His muscles tensed. "What do you know of it?"

"Only what you've told me." She planted her nose against his, her enchanting eyes filling his field of vision. The violet at the edge of her irises seemed to glow, a bright lure that drew him deeper into her thrall. "And that is nothing. But I saw his scars. I see the guilt you bear. I am not without powers of discernment."

He wanted to be irritated. Wanted to gather his guilt about him and wallow in a self-loathing silence. He didn't speak of the accident with his friends. Not even with his brother. It hung over them like a pall.

But Netta was warm on his lap with no judgment in her gaze. It wasn't as hard as he thought to open his mouth and tell her the story.

"I set up my first laboratory in an outbuilding at Marcus's townhouse in London. I stayed with him during breaks from Cambridge." He dug his fingers into her hips. "I didn't have much of a home to return to."

She nodded. "You have good friends."

"That I do." He inhaled deeply, his chest expanding. "I had minor successes developing a more stable gunpowder and built a larger workshop at Stonesworth House. The discoveries came faster, small improvements on smelting techniques that improved the durability of metals. My confidence grew along with the Summerset coffers. Then I began working with chromium to create a new formula for steel."

The back of his throat burned. There was no way to convey the thrill he'd experienced at that discovery. The feeling that he could touch the moon, set it spinning, if he put his mind to it.

Cupping his face, she ran her thumb along his cheekbone. For once, his opinionated Netta remained quiet. A silent support.

He rubbed his cheek against her palm and sighed. "By then, I was earl. I'd expanded the laboratory to make work spaces for my brothers, although Kevin was still too young to assist. But Robert did. He had no interest in science, but he was eager to help."

Too eager. A small part of John wondered if that had led Robert to be impatient, to become careless mixing the chemicals.

John pressed his lips tight. Which was the coward's way out, to try to shift blame to his brother. He wouldn't hide behind that excuse.

Arranging his features into its familiar insouciant mask, he finished the story. "I became over-confident. Thought the formula was simple enough to duplicate and told my brother to run the next experiment and note the results. I gave him the materials. Told him the proportion of the chemicals to use." He shrugged. "I must have made a mistake in my calculations. There was an explosion, leaving him as he is now."

"Sullen and resentful?"

John frowned. "Scarred." Though the other two characteristics definitely applied.

"Does that matter overmuch?" She wrinkled her nose. "His capabilities haven't been diminished in any way, have they?" Her eyes shot wide. "Oh, did the explosion injure other parts of him? Parts of him that...uh, men find most important?"

"No!" John ran his hand up the back of his head. "All Chaucer men are quite competent in that arena. Some might say exceedingly so."

She didn't jump to agree with that sentiment, and John narrowed his eyes.

"All right," she said. "Then why does he behave such? The few times I've met him, all he does is glower and grumble. Not one smile for me. And as we both know, I'm delightful."

John did her the service she hadn't shown him and agreed. "Yes, you are." Settling his hands at her bum, he tugged her an inch closer so her heat was nestled over his groin. "But his face is disfigured. He feels a monster. And his chances for a good match have greatly diminished. No woman wants to wake up to that every morn. Would you?"

"Yes." She nodded stoutly. "In a heartbeat, if he was of the right character. A pretty face can hold much evil; why can't a scarred one hold an equal quantity of goodness?"

John's stomach fluttered. "No reason." Her mouth was right there in front of his, so he leaned forward and kissed her slowly, leisurely. "No reason at all." He squeezed her arse. "Netta, are you saying if I were of good character—"

"Which we both know you are not," she teased.

"Quite. And if I wasn't so devastatingly good-looking—"

She sighed. "Which we both know you are."

His lips twitched. "Quite. But if I were both those things, ill-favored but morally upright, that you would still have agreed to help me? Still have found yourself in my bed?"

She tilted her head, a smile dancing about her lips. "You offered me four thousand pounds. I would have agreed to help Shakespeare's monster, Caliban, for four thousand pounds."

He slowly raised one eyebrow. He didn't like how much truth might be in that statement.

"As to landing in your bed..." She wiggled her hips. "You could be poor, ill-favored, and the dissolute reprobate you are and you'd still have to drag me from it." She placed a soft kiss on his jaw, the corner of his mouth. "The Chaucer men are just that good."

He breathed deeply. That was more like it. "Netta, is there another actor who can take your place at the theatre tonight?"

She pulled back. "Why? Are we going to a gaming hell?" A flicker of concern passed across her features.

"No. Can you find a replacement?"

"There is always an extra villager who is eager to take on a speaking role." She tugged on his cravat. "Tell me where you wish to take me?"

So impatient, his Netta. So demanding. But with her love of dramatics, he knew she would approve of that night's entertainment.

"We, my dear poppet, are attending a masquerade ball."

* * *

Netta twirled, her face lifted to the ceiling, the glittering lights of the Dutch embassy's chandeliers making her dizzy.

She didn't care. She'd never danced in a ballroom in the embrace of a dashing gentleman before. One of the many things she'd missed by leaving home before coming out. Of course, she'd saved herself years of misery so the trade-off was well worth it, but she couldn't deny her joy at having a taste now of what she'd lost.

"You appear to be having a marvelous time." John took her hand and guided her in an intricate pattern down the floor, weaving between other couples. "I feel like I ought to be offended." He leaned down to whisper. "That look should only belong to me. In my bed."

She pushed off of him and skipped around the man opposite before returning to John's side. "Either way you've put the look on my face. But if you want to see a superior one in bed, work harder."

"Trust me, poppet." He placed his gloved palm on the small of her back and guided her in a figure eight. "I will be very hard for you tonight."

The music ended, and Netta dipped into a low curtsy, her gaze never leaving John. In a room teeming with black-and-white dominos, he had dressed as Oberon, king of the fairies, his costume a vivid display of rose pink and Paris green. The mask he wore was of the same emerald shade, the eyeholes embroidered with silver thread and faux diamonds.

At least, she thought they were fake. But with John, one never knew.

His gaze was hooded by the mask, but she couldn't miss the hunger as she exposed her décolletage with her low dip. She was Titania, and the gown John had chosen was of the same rose color as his costume. She hadn't thought the color would suit the flowing, red wig she wore, but John had been right. Again. Instead of letting his superior fashion sense irritate her, she'd decided to reap its benefits.

She straightened and flicked open her fan. "My lord, one would almost think you find something in this gown improper." She pressed her hand to her bosom, and the large emerald pendant nestled between her breasts. John had draped the jewel around her neck before they'd left for the evening.

She fingered the sharp rectangular edges. John didn't

know it, but it too was going to be added to her fee. He couldn't wear it, after all. "Perhaps the modiste you hired isn't quite at the level she ought to be if your focus is so diverted."

"That modiste should be given a medal of honor." John took her hand and led her to the side of the ballroom floor. "Your gown has all the trappings of modesty – not too low cut, no sheer fabrics wetted to conform to your body – but is just tight enough across the bodice to let a man know what lies underneath. If I had my way, you would wear that dress morning, noon, and night."

"Even the nights?"

His full lips curled under the edges of his mask. "Even then. At least until I could peel it from your body, slowly revealing every luscious inch of flesh below."

She snapped open her fan again and attempted to cool her face. Hidden so beneath her own mask, the swirling air did little to alleviate her heated skin.

A man in a pirate's mask and headscarf approached and made a sweeping bow. "Might I have the pleasure of the next dance?"

John never removed his gaze from her face. "No, you may not." He took her hand and led her back to the dance floor.

"John, that was insufferably rude." But delight burbled through her veins as she swung back into his arms. "And if your intent is to have me attract men, shouldn't I spend some time in their company?"

"Not men. Man. One who has not yet arrived." He grunted. "But mayhap a dance or two with someone else wouldn't go amiss. Besides, I must leave you for a short while. Don't get into too much trouble while I'm gone."

Netta stumbled over the train of her gown. "You're leaving me? Where are you going?"

"Not far." He looked over his shoulder.

Netta followed his gaze and saw a man with nutmeg hair in a black mask nod at him. "Is that—"

"There's a group of wallflowers over there you can join."
He turned her and gave her a small shove.

Netta gritted her teeth. If she wasn't very much mistaken
it was his friend Rothchild waiting for him. John was off for
some bit of skullduggery and she was supposed to drink
punch and converse about the weather?

Purely to irritate him, Netta slipped from his grip and
looked over her prospects. "I'd rather dance. Take your
time with your mystery task. I'll be quite well occupied
here." She caught the eye of a portly man in black-and-
white and smiled broadly.

He started and looked behind him.

John crossed his arms, his satin jacket pulling snug
across his wide shoulders. "All right. One dance."

"Or two. You said two before."

He harrumphed. "I do not always like the games you
play, poppet."

"Liar."

"Miss?" The domino she'd smiled at stood before her.
He bowed deeply. "Dance, ja?"

"I'd love to." She gave the Dutchman her hand. "Ta,"
she said to John. "Find me when you're done."

John scowled, but with a warning look at her partner, he
turned on his heel and threaded his way across the
ballroom.

She stepped on her partner's foot. "My apologies," she
said before finding John in the crowd again. Rothchild had
disappeared, but John was aiming for the doors he had
stood next to.

Her mask concealed her identity and she was in a well-
guarded embassy. There was nothing for her to fear, yet still
her lungs squeezed when John disappeared from sight. If
she told him her history, her fears of being recognized,
perhaps he wouldn't have left her.

If John knew her parentage, how would he react?
Would they go on as before? Or would he feel his duty
towards her had changed because she was a gentlewoman?

The Dutchman drew her into his arms for a waltz, his cheeks pink beneath his mask. "You enjoy ball?"

"Very much so." She firmed her arms to put an inch more space between them. She had teased John about wanting to dance, but truly if he wasn't her partner there wasn't much joy in it.

The Dutchman hummed the melody as he twirled her about, seemingly happy to let conversation languish. His obvious joy in dancing with her raised her own spirits. John would be back shortly. She was dressed in a fine gown and dancing to a lovely orchestra. She began to hum along, as well.

Her partner pressed his hand to her back and spun her out in time with the music.

She laughed as he pulled her back in.

"Good, ja?" He grinned down at her.

"Very good."

He spun her out again amid a wave of her giggles. Out and back until her sides hurt from laughing.

"We dance good together," he said.

The music came to a crescendo, and he spun her out one last time.

Her hand slipped from his and she stumbled into the man next to her. He caught her by her elbows.

"Easy," he said, his deep voice chilling her to the core.

Netta froze, her mouth open, her pulse racing. Her mind screamed to wrench herself from his hands, to flee, but all she could do was stare into his jade green eyes.

He wore a white mask and a jacket in the same matching silk. His cravat was knotted high on his throat. His thin lips curved.

She knew those lips. That smile. They haunted her dreams.

"How fortunate for me." Harlow Sudworth, the man who'd changed the course of her life, stood before her. "I've been wanting to speak with you all evening, and here you've landed right in my arms."

Chapter Twenty

Netta shook her head, but a monster still filled her vision. Her throat swelled shut; no words could escape.

Not that she had any to say. For once in her life, she was stunned into silence.

The Dutchman bowed to her as the music ended, but she and Sudworth paid him no notice.

"Will you give me your name, or must I wait for a proper introduction?" His voice was serpent-smooth, teasing, and the memory of how charming this man could be chilled her blood. Charming, until he didn't get his way. Then the fangs popped out.

Her body trembled, and she jerked herself back, away from the threat, and Sudworth narrowed his eyes.

A mistake. She couldn't help but make them around the man her father had sold her to. He never responded as a civilized person ought, and the best way to avoid such a predator was to remain as invisible as possible. Never attract his notice.

And most definitely never speak one's mind. She'd learned that one the hard way.

She rubbed the bump in her wrist, sucking down choppy breaths. *Smile,* she told herself. Smile and lower her gaze like a demure little miss.

She tried. Her limbs shook with the effort. Or was it from fear? No matter, the result was the same. She couldn't pretend the man was nothing but a new acquaintance. Her legs tensed, prepared to take flight.

She scented him before she saw him. His spicy citrus

aroma wrapped around her like a cocoon, a barrier of protection she could trust. John came to her side, gently cupping her elbow, his solid presence releasing the vise on her lungs. She took her first full breath since stumbling into Sudworth's arms.

"Sudworth." John gave the barest of nods. "I didn't know you were here."

Sudworth tutted. "How easily you discern my identity, Summerset. I will have to speak to my valet about concocting a more mystifying costume."

"It appears I am likewise easy to distinguish."

Sudworth flicked his gaze up and down John's brightly-colored body. "Yes, that proved no difficulty at all. But tell me," he said. "Who is your charming companion?"

"Miss Courtney." John banded an arm around Netta's waist. "She is the daughter of a friend. I've agreed to escort her about London, an arrangement for which I am much obliged." He squeezed her hip. "Her society is most charming."

Sudworth stared at John's hand on her gown, pursing his lips. "So I see." He inclined his head to Netta. "I do hope her charms haven't distracted you from your other obligations. I've been waiting for you to call upon me."

Netta clenched her hand in her gown. John knew Sudworth. By his manner, it was apparent they weren't friends, but what was their connection? Surely it was nothing but a casual acquaintance. Surely life could not be so cruel as to have Sudworth be—

"My time has been fully occupied." John twirled a strand of her fake hair around his finger. "Don't get your smallclothes in a bunch. I will see to all my obligations in my own time."

Netta loosed a strangled gasp. What freedom there was to be a man, to be an earl. John could say whatever he wished without fear. By God, he was outrageous. And wonderful.

A smidgeon more of her tension eased.

"As you are at this embassy," Sudworth said, "I hope the time to fulfill your duty is now." He smiled. "But let us speak on more pleasant matters. Are you enjoying the masquerade, Miss Courtney?" His gaze hovered on her bosom. The tip of his tongue darted out and he licked his lower lip.

Netta shuddered, her skin crawling. She flicked her fan open and cooled her face, the feathers making up the fan hiding her breasts from his vision.

Sudworth inclined his head. "Pardon me. I can't help but be impressed by your large...pendant. That's a beautiful emerald."

"Of course." John pressed even closer into her side. "I have good taste. In everything."

"In your choice of companion that is obviously true." Sudworth inclined his head again, all politeness.

She wanted to stab him through the eye with her fan.

"So are you enjoying the masquerade, Miss Courtney?"

Netta swallowed, trying to bring moisture back to her mouth. She deepened her voice, slowed her speech. "Indeed. The earl has been most solicitous in showing me the best diversions London has to offer." She truly was an outstanding actress. She didn't at all sound as though she wanted to cripple the man.

"And yet this is the first time we have met." Sudworth stepped aside as another dance began. "Where have you been keeping this lovely creature, Summerset?"

Netta and John followed him to the side of the room. "A couple of calls. A ride through the park" John spread his hands. "My Net—"

"I'm afraid I'm a bit dull for Lord Summerset." She dug her nails into her palm. She couldn't let Sudworth hear her nickname. She'd always been called Netta. He might add two plus two and come to the right damned answer. "I enjoy more sedate pursuits, but the earl has been kind enough to indulge me. In fact..." She laid her hand upon his arm and prayed he would follow her lead. "We had discussed leaving after this dance."

"Yes." John patted her hand. "The Dutch can provide decent entertainment but their food is abominable. If you will excuse us." Without waiting for a response, John led her away, saving her the necessity of curtsying to her enemy.

They waited in the spacious entry for the footmen to bring their coats. "You were marvelous," John whispered in her ear. "Just the right amount of innocence and backbone. And ending the conversation early, leaving him wanting more was inspired. How did you know Sudworth was our man?" He took her coat from the servant and helped her into it. "I must have mentioned his name before, I suppose."

Netta's head went light and she swayed. "Yes," she said, the word sounding distant.

Sudworth was John's target. She could almost laugh at the horrible coincidence. The person who'd forced her to abandon her family was now threatening John's. The reach of this one man was almost impressive.

"Netta?" John cupped her shoulders and squeezed. "Netta?"

A cold wave of despair slid through her body, and she shook. "Yes?"

He studied her face. "You're ill. We do need to get you home."

"I'm fine." But she let him bustle her into the carriage. She snuggled into his side as he draped a blanket around her body. Gave him her hands to warm between his own.

Another tremor shook her body. She was cold, ice-deep in her center, and she wasn't sure she'd ever feel warm again.

Sudworth was their target.

And there was no way she could assist John in his scheme.

No way for her to earn that four thousand pounds. It would take years at the theatre before she would have the funds to take her and her sister out of England. Years her sister might not have.

She could ask John for financial help. To provide her a small nest egg for her future. He would most likely agree. But what nobleman would assist in the kidnapping of a child? And that's what it would be under the eyes of the law. Her father wouldn't hesitate to prosecute Netta, his own daughter, if he caught her spiriting Eleanor away.

What would he do to John?

He wrapped his arm around her shoulder and pulled her closer.

She rested her cheek on his chest and inhaled deeply.

Her plans were destroyed. And she didn't have a clue what to do next.

Images of her past life, of that night, flashed through her mind, too fast to pin down, making her head ache. She needed to concentrate, find a solution, but her brain did nothing but spin in place.

She wasn't going to get what she needed, not until she'd calmed her senses enough to think straight.

So she might as well have what she wanted.

And she wanted to forget.

They pulled up to John's townhouse, and he handed her down. He drew off her mask and passed it with his to a footman. "Shall I have Mags bring you a tisane? Some willow bark tea?"

"No." She preceded him into the house and headed for the stairs, knowing he would follow. "There is nothing Margaret could bring me that I need."

"Then what—"

She took his hand and walked backwards down the hall to his bedroom. "I only need you. Tonight I don't want games or tricks." She felt bone tired, and even though she loved playing with John, the games took more energy than she had. Were a merriment she didn't feel. She opened his door and pulled him through. "I only need you between my thighs, kissing my lips, to make me feel better. Is that agreeable to you?"

He pulled her to a standstill in the middle of the chamber. He threaded his fingers under her wig and slid it off, kneading her skull as he went. "Any time spent between your thighs is more than agreeable. But are you certain you wouldn't be better with a back rub and a full-night's sleep?"

"Positive." She ran her hands over his costume, looking for the ties.

He assisted and drew the draped shirt over his head in one fluid motion.

Netta bit her lip and pressed her fingers to his hot skin. The more she knew him, the more beautiful he became. She traced the raised ridge of muscles on his chest, his light dusting of hair soft under her fingers. She drew a circle around his nipple and smiled when he sucked in a sharp breath.

Yes, a night losing herself in John's arms was just what she needed. She lowered her head and followed the path of her finger with her tongue. Tasting him, feeling him, finding oblivion in his bed.

Her problems didn't exist when she and John were together. Their heat formed a bubble, isolating them from the outside world.

John raised her hand to his mouth, nipping the end of one of her fingers before turning her around and undoing the buttons of her gown. He pushed it over her hips and down her legs. His breath tickled the inside of her thighs, and she inched her feet apart.

John chuckled. He dipped his hand under the edge of her chemise, skimming his fingers along the crease of her thigh, dancing over her outer lips, but withholding the pressure she needed. "How badly do you want me, poppet? If I press my finger in your body"—he paused, a gossamer's touch over her opening—"will I find you wet for me?"

"Getting there." She waggled her bum. "If you'd stop teasing I'd become so faster."

He bit her arse, his arm about her waist the only thing keeping her from falling forwards from the delicious shock of it. He removed his teeth, but a tingle remained on her flesh, his mark lingering.

"John..." Her fingers tangled in the strings to her stays. She was desperate to be bare before him. Aching to allow him access to every inch of her body.

He brushed her hands away and removed the garment. Even her thin chemise felt too tight, and quickly that was gone, as well. He smoothed his hands up over the backs of her thighs, over her bottom and around her hips as he stood.

He pressed against her, the silk of his pantaloons cool against her flushed skin.

His erection hard against her softness.

Running his palms up her belly, he cupped her heavy breasts, pulling her back closer to his front. He dropped his head and nibbled on the curve of her neck.

"What you do to me." John plumped her breasts up, squeezing. "I can't decide which bit of you I like best. Your bosom is most definitely in contention for that honor."

Netta bit the inside of her cheek. Even at a moment like this he still could make her laugh. Even when there were no games to play, he brought her joy.

"Most men prefer my bum." She arched her back, pushing back against his length.

He pinched her nipple and growled. "I am not by nature a jealous man, but now is not the time to speak of other men to me. Besides," he said, skimming one hand over her abdomen to cup her mons, "there is another part that surpasses both your breasts and arse." He slid his middle finger between her crease and dipped into her channel.

She shivered. "Yes, I'm quite fond of that part of my body, too." Especially when it was in his hands. No man had ever made her feel as much as John. And she was beginning to worry that no other man ever would.

He sucked her earlobe into his mouth, and her head dropped back on his shoulder. "I meant your mind, Netta. Your devious, determined, sweet little brain." He added another finger and continued slowly fucking her with his hand. "That's my favorite bit of all."

Pulling from her, he lifted her in his arms and carried her to his bed. He peeled her slippers and stockings off, then removed his own pants and boots faster than any mid-scene costume change Netta had ever witnessed. He pulled a condom from his bed side table, tossed it on the bed, and crawled over her.

His knees bracketed her hips, his palms digging into the coverlet on either side of her head. He lowered until his chest brushed her own and dragged his nose along her clavicle. He inhaled deeply, like she was the finest rose in the garden.

"How did a man ever get so fortunate in the thief who stole his blunt?" He slid one of his knees between her legs, then the other, and knelt before her. With his hands at the back of her thighs, he held her open and stared down at her sex.

He sucked his bottom lip into his mouth. "So damn lucky."

Netta's breath caught in her lungs as he scooted down and lowered his head. With his thumbs, he spread her outer lips and feasted upon her.

Netta gripped the metal lattice headboard and held on for dear life. If she combined every amazing sensation she'd ever felt it still did not equal the miracle of John's mouth on her quim.

The liquid sounds were obscene, and she reveled in them, opening her legs wider. Her hips rocked into his face, sweat beading over her skin. John used his lips, teeth, and tongue until she was but a mewling, shaking wreck.

He pulled away.

"What? No!" Netta glared at him.

He tied the condom over his straining length then placed one of her legs over his shoulder. "I am a selfish man. When you climax, I want to be buried inside of you, feel it squeezing my cock. I don't want to wait a moment more."

"Yet you weren't so impatient as to forego the linen." But Netta couldn't be vexed. Not when John was gliding inside of her, stretching her walls inch by heavenly inch. With one last flex of his hips, he filled her fully, and she felt a pinch deep inside her womb.

His eyes had deepened, glittering so darkly Netta couldn't look away. Whatever this relationship was between her and John, it had to be more than a casual bit of bed sport. He couldn't look at her such without feeling the bone-deep longing that held her captive.

John stroked back, dragging against her nerve endings, and plunged back in. "The more I'm inside you, the harder I find it to pull out before I spend." He leaned forwards, pressing her leg higher.

She moaned, and he captured the sound with his mouth. "Christ, how I dream about spilling my seed deep inside of you, feeling your silky channel milk my naked flesh dry."

The hair on his chest scraped against her nipples, the sensation so sublime it almost hurt.

He tugged her hands from the headrest and pressed them into the bed above her head, lacing his fingers through hers. "How I'd love to fuck you without consequence, the only concern we'd have was how many times I can bring you to your crisis before we both lose consciousness."

She turned her head to the side, unable to look upon him a moment more. She might no longer have the ability to leave the country, but that didn't mean this relationship of theirs stood a chance of lasting. She still had a sister to rescue through less than legal means. He was still an earl, bound by an aristocrat's sense of honor.

Unless...

He increased his tempo, driving into her hard, making the bed shake.

"Look at me," he demanded.

She obeyed. Her breath grew short at the ferocity of his

expression. The determined glint in his eye. John might call himself selfish in his desires, but he was making absolutely certain they both went up in flames.

He devoured her with his gaze. He drank in every gasp as he pounded into her, every arch of her neck as he took her higher. Closer. His eyes dropped to her breasts, bouncing from the force of his assault.

He closed his eyes and groaned. "Tell me you're close, sweetheart. I need you to be close."

"So...close..." She dug her nails into his hands, spiraling tighter, tighter, until she could hold it in no more.

She burst into a million tiny shards of pleasure. White spots danced in her vision. Ripples of ecstasy splintered out from her core, shooting to every nerve ending her body contained. She clutched at him, holding his rigid length snug, and let her mind go blank, luxuriating in the bliss.

"Netta..." John threw his head back and cursed. He jerked within her, his body shuddering until finally he collapsed.

He lay limp and heavy on her, his heat and weight a welcome comfort. Netta rubbed small circles into his back, letting her mind wander to pleasant fancies that could never be.

Unless...

John didn't behave as she expected. After all, when did he ever do what was customary for an earl? He might help her smuggle her sister from her home. Her belly fluttered. And Netta had lived concealed within London for years; why couldn't her sister?

John heaved a sigh, his breath tickling her ear. He rolled to his side, taking her with him so they lay facing each other.

"Feeling better?"

She traced a circle on his chest. "Oh, was that all for my benefit? I thank you, yes."

He grinned. "I might have received some reward from it, too." He picked up her hand and kissed the bent bone at her wrist. "How did this happen?"

"Sudden contact with the floor." Her voice wobbled. "Some men don't like to hear the word 'no'."

John stilled. "Who was it?"

She opened her mouth to tell him everything, but the words clogged in her throat. There were too many what-ifs. What if he contacted her father? What if he went after Sudworth and was hurt himself?

What if he gave her the four thousand pounds and she never saw him again?

The fluttering in her stomach hardened to cramps.

What if his concern disappeared once he learned she could no longer help him recover his deed?

Before she could fully trust him, she needed to know that he also trusted her judgment. Understood that she knew what was best for her and Eleanor.

"The name is of no importance." She snuggled closer. "Aside from my wrist, I wasn't hurt that night. I got away." Sudworth had let her get away. He had been happy to wait until the marriage bed to force himself on her. She'd seen the thrill of that power, of owning a woman, excite his every feature.

His poor wife. The last four years of her life must have been horrible living under that man's thumb.

And now he wanted that power over Eleanor.

A small tremor shook her body. She'd kill him before she let him touch her sister.

"A broken wrist is enough for the man to taste my blade," John said, eyes narrowed.

She smiled wryly and kissed his shoulder. "Your sense of proportion is sadly lacking. A broken bone isn't a capital offense. That is the least of what a man can do to hurt a woman."

His eyes narrowed even further, turning into slits. "Who hurt you? I will make him pay, and enjoy doing it."

"Yes, I'm sure you'd devise an intricate plot, making it a game." She rolled onto her back and stared at a gold vine wrapping about the tester.

He trapped her chin and turned her head to face him. "There are some things I don't play around with. Seeking vengeance on someone who harmed you would be one of them."

Something must be very wrong with her. A man vowing to spill blood on her behalf shouldn't turn her heart to jelly.

But it did.

She squeezed his hand. "Aside from the wrist, no one has hurt me. I have lived a very quiet, peaceful life these last six years."

His muscles relaxed a little. "I don't believe it. You and quiet don't belong together in the same sentence."

She shrugged. "Peaceful then."

He rubbed his thumb back and forth on her collarbone. "And have you been lonely in this peaceful life?"

She raised her eyebrows. "John Chaucer, are you asking me about past lovers?"

He dragged his finger between her breasts. "I don't have a right to know but tell me just the same." He swallowed, looking like the answer meant something more than satisfying idle curiosity.

"There have been three men," she said. She took a deep breath, unused to raw honesty. "But when I look at you, I can't remember any of their faces."

His finger paused before resuming its journey. "Four lovers and not yet four and twenty." He shook his head, looking as sad as a hound dog. "I don't know what is happening to women nowadays."

She poked his stomach. "We're taking what we want." She poked again. "And you're a fine one to talk. Colleen told me about the Venus club you belong to. How many women have you led from the path of righteousness at that particular den of iniquity?" And what would she have to do to get an invitation to the place?

He rolled on top of her. "Too many to count, I'm certain." He kissed her eyes, her nose. "But for the life of me I can't remember any of their faces, either."

He settled so naturally into the cradle of her thighs it was like he was meant to be there. "John?" she asked between kisses. "Colleen also mentioned some work you do? For the government?" He would tell her about that mystery, and she would know. Know that he trusted her, even with his secrets.

And that she could trust him with hers.

"Hmm?" He licked up her neck. "She must mean my work in Parliament." He skimmed a hand down her abdomen and zeroed in on her clit.

Her body responded even as her mind recognized it for the distraction tactic it was.

She didn't know to what Colleen was referring, but it wasn't to his duties in the House of Lords. The back of her throat burned. He still wanted walls between them? Didn't want complete honesty? So be it. She would be more than happy to accommodate his wishes. She would find a way out of the box she was in all on her own. She'd save herself, the way she'd always done.

If she could only figure out how.

"I am an earl, you know." John nipped at her bottom lip. "And I don't think I've once heard you address me as 'my lord.'" He tsked. "I propose a new game."

"What's that?" She infused her voice with a levity she didn't feel. If all John had to offer was his body, she'd take it. She had nowhere else to be that night and no idea what she would do on the morrow. She had become an expert at living in the moment.

He flipped her to her stomach. "It's a little one I like to call Master and Servant." He rested his large palm on her arse. "And I do believe my servant has been a very naughty girl."

Chapter Twenty-One

Netta took the waxed bag from the clerk, thanking him. She strode outside the confectionary shop, adjusting the brim of her bonnet to shade her face from the morning sun, and popped one of the Pomfret cakes into her mouth.

It's tang of spicy goodness did little to lift her mood. She sighed. It was a sad day when her favorite treats didn't make her happy.

"Why don't we cut across the park?" John strolled up beside her, ignoring her start. He tipped the brim of his top hat up with the silver nob of his walking stick. "It will shorten our journey and get us away from the clatter of carriages."

"You followed me again." She shouldn't be surprised. After his discovery of her acting career, he'd either accompanied her, followed her, or had Wilberforce do so each night she went to work. But today was Sunday and the show was an early one. She'd thought she'd slid out of his home unnoticed.

John rooted through the small bag in her hand and came out with a plump licorice button. "Did you take my pouch of coin again?"

"Did you leave it behind the stack of chemistry books on your desk for me to find again?" Dear, sweet, infuriating man. Giving her that small thrill of pilfering, even though they both knew he left it for her intentionally. Why couldn't he also give her his trust?

She swallowed past the burn in the back of her throat. Damnation. If she couldn't go forward with his scheme, and she didn't tell him the truth about herself, she was going to have to leave. Her options were disappearing faster than the confections from her bag.

She chewed another, her jaws aching with how hard she ground them together. She was going to miss the man. How had she let that happen?

"You were very quiet at breakfast." He took her arm and guided her around a trio of slobbering dogs, tugging at their leads. "Do you still feel indisposed from last night?"

The concern in his voice almost undid her. He might not trust her, but he did care. Would it be so unwise to tell him everything? Lay all her fears and worry bare? He would be a fool to help her remove her sister from home, but she couldn't imagine he'd actually impede her actions. She sucked on her bottom lip. Probably.

"I'm fine." She walked closer to him, enjoying the feel of his sleeve brushing against her shoulder. Even that small connection was enough to settle her nerves. Last night she'd let emotion get in the way of common sense. John wasn't required to bare his own soul in order for her to do the same. Some things weren't on a quid pro quo basis.

But it would have been nice.

Her heart beat double time. So, she'd decided. She would tell John the truth about herself. Cerise would warn her to think through the implications more thoroughly, chew on it from every conceivable angle, but the decision felt right.

The dingy sign for The Burns Theatre came into view.

Tonight. After the show, she'd sit John down and tell him all. And pray there was some way to both save her sister and remain in London. With John.

Perhaps she could get her sister a role at the theatre, as well. Hide in plain sight, as it were. It had worked for Netta.

She tightened her grip on his arm. John would come to their shows and afterwards treat them to a chocolate and pastry. Then she'd take Eleanor back to their apartments, tuck her in...and let John tuck Netta in after Eleanor had gone to sleep.

She sucked in a deep breath, ignoring the slight hitch in her lungs. It could work. It would work. She'd make certain of it.

He opened the backstage door for her and guided her in, his palm drifting lower on her back than proper.

Perhaps she'd *lay* him down and tell him the truth. Men were better listeners when on a bed. More motivated to give her the answer she wanted to hear. She smiled. That plan was much more logical. Even Cerise would approve.

"LeBlanc!" Mr. Jarvis, the stage manager, raised a hand and lumbered towards them down the hall. "I'm glad you're here. I wanted to speak to you." He ran a hand through his greying hair. "Who's your friend?"

Netta made the introductions. "Is there something the matter, Jarvis?"

"Only the casting for *Henry V.*" He blew out his cheeks and looked at John. "We start rehearsals in three weeks and start selling tickets in six."

"You don't want me for Bardolph any longer?" Her heart sank. Without this job, where would she and Eleanor go?

Jarvis snorted. "Don't be an idiot."

John straightened, his muscles tensing, but the stage manager paid him no heed.

"I want you for Henry." Jarvis folded his arms across his barrel chest and winked. "And I'm prepared to negotiate. I know how you enjoy that." He elbowed John playfully. "Discussing her salary has become like a game between us, one I always lose. But I don't mind. My mam always said I was too soft for business."

John looked at the spot where the stage manager had nudged him. He arched an eyebrow. "Yes. Miss LeBlanc is quite fond of games."

Netta's heart flopped about inside her chest. The lead. Henry. It wasn't unheard of for women to play leading men, not in the smaller theatres. But she hadn't thought she'd have a chance to star in a show. "What about Cerise?" The wax paper bag crinkled between her fingers as she twisted it. "She's the preeminent actress at The Burns. People come to see her."

"Found another theatre." Jarvis grunted. "Leaving us after this run."

Netta gaped. "Leaving?" Her friend had never mentioned another theatre. Hadn't even said she'd been auditioning. But, of course, an actress of her talent would be looking for better opportunities. She should be aiming higher.

But it hurt that Cerise had never mentioned it. They were supposed to be friends.

Like you've told her about your future plans?

Her shoulders rounded. She had always kept a wall between herself and Cerise, between herself and everyone, and this was the consequence. She never allowed herself to get close enough to truly know a person, inside and out.

She shot a look at John. What would it be like to have that with him? No secrets. No artifice. Just...them.

"That's marvelous." John took her elbow and squeezed. "You'll make a wonderful Henry."

Yes, she would. She could already envision how she'd play him. The tenor of her voice. The swagger when he walked. She held that vision for a moment, then, with a sigh, packed it away. "I can't."

John frowned. "What?"

"I can't take the part." She wagged her finger at Jarvis and forced a cheer she didn't feel. "You know I don't take leading roles. We went over this when you wanted me to play Juliet."

The stage manager rubbed his jaw. "Yes, but you never explained why. There will be more money."

Not nearly enough to make the risk worth it. Cerise's salary barely topped Netta's own modest one, not when she added in the wages she earned from helping to sew the costumes. And if she was going to strut upon a stage in

London, even one as working class as The Burns, it had to be in a role where her identity was concealed.

"I'm not ready for a leading role." She tucked her bag of sweets into her reticule. "I am content with the minor parts."

Jarvis leaned forwards and took her hand. "I know you're afraid, but you needn't be. It won't be any harder than what you already do. Besides," he said, looking her up and down, "you're too pretty to keep hidden behind disguises. If you let me help you, I'll be able to make you a star."

John peeled the man's fingers from her and tucked her hand into the crook of his arm. "Miss LeBlanc must get ready for *this* show. If you will excuse us." And without waiting for a response, he marched her down the hall, forcing Jarvis to leap aside or get knocked over.

"That was rude." She craned her head to give the manager a wan smile over her shoulder. "And I have twenty minutes yet. Plenty of time."

"Plenty of time for Mr. Jarvis to flirt with you," he grumbled.

Netta paused at her dressing room door. "What? There's nothing between me and Jarvis."

"Not from any lack of interest on his part." He pushed open the door, then caught it as it bounced off the wall and swung back towards them. He glowered back down the hall. "But at least he recognizes talent. Why don't you want the lead role?"

She pushed past him into the empty room. Cerise must already be dressed and backstage. Too bad. She would have been useful to avoid this conversation. "I never cared for Henry. He always struck me as overly pompous." She sat at her dressing table chair and removed her bonnet.

His eyebrows shot up. "Pompous? It's a lead role. You don't have to like him."

She twisted her hair up and slid the dark wig over her head. "*I* do." She tucked a stray blond lock out of sight.

"Haven't you heard actresses are temperamental?"

He stood behind her and crossed his arms, meeting her gaze in the mirror. "Every actress I've met wants the biggest role possible. What's going on, poppet?"

She pulled a pot of face paint in front of her. Her stomach pulled tight. "It's only...." She stirred the paint with her finger, focusing on the swirling brown colors. *Tell him.* The odds were better that John would help rather than hinder her plans. So why were her palms sweating and her heart racing?

"It's the theatre, isn't it?' He widened his stance and nodded. "It is shabby, I agree. Wilberforce has my pantaloons cleaned twice after I sit on the seats here. Of course I can get you a job at a higher-class theatre. All you needed to do was ask."

"Pardon?" She twisted in her chair. "You think you can just hand me a role?"

"Of course." He bent over her and adjusted his cravat in the mirror. "The manager of Drury Lane has been most eager to be a guest at The Black Rose. He'll give you a role for a night at that club."

"Just like that. No audition?" Her skin prickled, her face going hot. Yes, she had been prepared to ask him for his assistance in protecting Eleanor. But this was different. This was business. Her business.

She was a professional actress, damn it. She would earn her own parts, not be rewarded with them because she'd spread her legs for a man.

"It is good timing that this play ends in a couple of weeks." He smirked. "I'm sure it will be a great loss for Jarvis, but he'll survive without you."

"What, exactly, are you implying?"

John lifted one shoulder, all casual elegance. "Merely that your manager has developed a tendre for you. I suppose it is inevitable, considering that you work together every day."

She'd never heard anything so absurd. Jarvis was near

old enough to be her father. Not that he wasn't handsome in his own way, but they had never been anything but professional with each other. "And is proximity the only reason for a man and woman to come together? Is it merely because I reside under your roof that we have developed a relationship?"

He pursed his lips. "It didn't hurt."

Netta pushed to her feet. "I need to change into my costume. I think you should leave."

A line creased his brow. "Leave? It's not as though I haven't seen your body before."

She growled. Had she thought to trust this man with her most dangerous secret? This controlling popinjay who only seemed to like her because she was at hand?

"I hope you have a good memory. You won't be seeing it again for a long while." She pointed to the door. "Leave."

He looked adorably confused, but she didn't let it soothe her ire. Anger made it easier to keep her mouth shut. To delay the inevitable. To postpone learning how he would react to knowing who she truly was.

Her heart twisted painfully. If she was nothing but a convenient bed-warmer, he would have no reason to keep her once he understood she couldn't help him in his plot.

"But—"

"Out."

He rubbed the back of his neck. "We'll speak later when you've calmed yourself."

She pinched her lips tight. She didn't trust her voice, not when he was provoking her into wanting to scream with frustration. She stabbed her finger at the door.

"Fine." He stomped away from her, his famous glide nowhere in sight. He turned in the entry. "Good luck on your performance tonight, although we both know you don't need it. You're an excellent actress. And make no mistake." He tapped the doorjamb with the heel of his palm. "I will learn why you refuse lead roles. I will learn everything there is to know about you."

And with that dramatic exclamation, he whirled and disappeared from sight.

Netta sagged into her chair. Truly, with his penchant for drama, he should have been the actor.

She planted her elbow on her table and dropped her chin into her upraised palm.

She hadn't let anyone know everything about her in...forever. John Chaucer, Earl of Summerset was a risky person to be the first.

For Eleanor's sake, she prayed he was a gamble worth taking.

Chapter Twenty-Two

John bent at the waist and blew on the glass pipettes arranged in a neat row in their wood holder. A cloud of dust billowed up, and he jerked his head back.

Judith pawed his face, and he tucked her more securely under his arm. He scratched her behind her torn ear.

Wilberforce stepped into the small laboratory. "Shall I call for a maid, sir? It will be nice to see this room put to use again."

John started. "What are you—" He blew out his cheeks. "Why have you been following me about all day? You are as irksome as this cat, constantly underfoot." Judith started purring, apparently unbothered at the insult.

"This is only the second time we've spoken this morn," Wil said mildly. "Hardly underfoot."

"It isn't the speaking but the lurking I complain about." John picked up a pair of frayed leather goggles. They were similar to what his brother had worn that day, and probably the only thing that had saved his left eye.

He replaced them on the wide table. "Why have you been following me about the house?"

Wil didn't answer that question, not directly, of course. "I noticed that you and Miss Netta were very silent at breakfast this morning. Has something gone amiss between you two?"

"No. Everything is fine." If you could consider a child-like silent treatment from the blasted woman fine. It was better than a yelling match, he supposed. But if she wasn't talking, it was damned difficult to know why she was upset.

"Have you perhaps reconsidered her role in your scheme?"

"You'd like that, wouldn't you?" John leaned back against his worktable. "You don't want Netta to be part of it."

Wil firmed his jaw. "It isn't right to involve a woman. It could be dangerous."

John shook his head. "That woman can handle her own. She'll have Sudworth wrapped right around her little finger." Netta might be the most competent woman he knew. He wouldn't have asked her to take part in his plan if he didn't believe her capable, or that he could protect her.

But he couldn't deny he also didn't like the idea of Netta involved. A sliver of unease pricked his breast. What if something did happen to her? It would have been unconscionable if she had been merely an agent working under his command and ill befell her. Now that he knew her, liked her, the idea of harm coming to her stole his breath.

His fingers dug into Judith's side and she hissed, twisting from his grip and trotting from the room.

He wouldn't let anything happen, not to Netta. Not to any of his friends.

Wil sniffed, looking as disgruntled as an old woman. "You must do as you see fit, of course."

"Thank you for that gracious acknowledgement." John pushed off the table.

"Shall I have a maid come clean?"

"What for?" John pushed past his friend and headed for his study. "I'm finished playing about with my chemicals."

Wil followed him into the next room and stood at attention in front of the desk while John dropped into his chair. "For someone who is finished with that part of his life, you seem to be poking your head in there quite a bit lately."

John ground his teeth. He picked up his chair and turned it to face the window. There. Much better view of the gardens than his annoying friend's face. "You are mistaken. I only wandered in there because I was distracted."

"About?"

Throwing his legs up on the windowsill, John grumbled. "Has anyone ever told you that you show an awful amount of impertinence for a servant."

"Yes. You. Many times." Wil circled the desk and stood beside John's legs, his gaze also out the window, his hands clasped behind his back.

A sparrow flitted under the overhang of the gazebo in the yard, adding a bit of dried grass to a nest she hurried to build before darkness fell. John followed her path as she hunted for more material to make her home.

Perhaps he should take up bird-watching. Several other gentlemen of his acquaintance were amateur ornithologists. Yes, instead of missions saving the Crown from disaster, instead of trying to get in the head of one devilishly obdurate woman, he could watch birds. A sound plan.

"Christ." He scrubbed his hand across his jaw. "The woman's gone barmy. Up and decided to give me the silent treatment last night, for no reason."

The one eyebrow that John could see on Wil's face raised in a slow arch.

"It's true," John insisted. "We were having a perfectly pleasant conversation about her future prospects, and she went and got all huffy. Women." He slapped his thigh. "When you want peace, all they do is jabber; when you want to know what the problem is, they close up tighter than a nun's knees."

"I've never heard Miss Netta jabber."

"Hmpf." John slouched lower in his seat. That may be true, but it only made it more frustrating. If Netta told him what the problem was, he could fix it.

She'd seemed to get particularly ill-tempered when he'd discussed that manager of hers. John had only spoken the truth. Touching her hand. Giving her calf eyes. A fool could see the man wouldn't say no to having an affair with her.

And who could blame him? They both worked in the same industry. She was beautiful and cunning. Jarvis was a bit old for Netta, probably ten years John's senior, but some women seemed to like that. Who knew? After she and John parted ways, why wouldn't she turn to the manager?

His stomach clenched.

She could turn to any number of men. And John wouldn't have any say about it.

He dropped his feet to the floor and stood. "I'm going to get her to talk."

"She went to Lady Mary's club." Wil turned to face him, a suspicious twinkle in his eye. "When you do speak with her, a bit of advice?"

John plucked an onyx-headed walking stick from the stand and gave it a twirl. "Your track record with women isn't such that anyone should take advice from you."

"I know enough," Wil said. "And one thing I've learned is not to tell a woman that you take no blame in a disagreement. And truly, how likely was that in any case?"

John turned his back on the man's smirk and strode to the front door. He called for his carriage and hopped in when it arrived, telling the driver to make haste.

And make haste he did. Not ten minutes later they rolled up to the front steps of the building May had rented for her endeavor.

A burly footman was just lighting the lamps bracketing the front doors. He stepped in front of John, blocking his path. "Apologies, but this club is for members only."

"I'm a member," he gritted out.

The man looked him up and down and twisted his lips. "It's a women's club. You might dress as fine as one, but that doesn't make you a member of the fairer sex."

John gaped, outraged. "Does Lady Mary know the insolence of her staff? I'll have you know my investment paid for your services, and I can make sure they are terminated just as fast."

The door swung inward, and Auntie May stood framed in the entrance. "Johnnie. We did agree that you'd have no control over the management of my club. I'll have you know I hired him because of his delightful insolence. But," she said, turning to the footman, "this man is always welcome." She pressed her lips together and squinted at the sky. "Well, almost always welcome. The Venus and Bacchus nights he should be denied entrance. Our female members might be uncomfortable otherwise." She waved her hand in welcome and John stepped through, knocking the footman with his shoulder as he passed.

"I can't say that I approve of your choice of servants." He looked around the entry that led to a wide drawing room. But the improvements May had made to the space were a different story. The place looked a wonder. The walls were painted a cheerful jonquil and adorned with paintings in eye-catching hues of reds and oranges. Faux roman statues of naked men guarded the entrances of every doorway, and John couldn't help but raise an eyebrow about the proportions on some of the statues. The style was fun, eclectic, but retained a sense of luxury.

May gathered up her long skirts and marched down the hall. "Yes, but my members find him delightfully shocking. A pleasant change from the overly polite lives they are forced to lead. Why are you here?"

"To find my wayward stray." He sidled past two women swilling champagne as they sat in a wide wicker swing hung from the ceiling. One of them pushed off against the wall, setting the swing in a dizzying circle.

He cleared his throat. "Any idea where Netta might be in this madhouse?"

"She's playing pall-mall. But John—" May stopped suddenly, and John stumbled to avoid her. "I don't think you should go to her right now. I can tell her you wish to talk."

His mouth went dry, and he swallowed. "She doesn't want to see me? She told you this?"

May flapped her hand. "Much to your consternation, I'm sure, but women do not spend all day talking of men. And it's not Netta you shouldn't see; it's the woman she's playing with."

He narrowed his eyes. "And who would that be?"

"Your grandmother."

He clenched his hands. Bloody hell, what was that woman doing here? And talking to Netta? The shrew would flay little Netta LeBlanc alive with her viperous tongue. "Where are they?"

May sighed, but turned and led the way. The room they entered was long, with high-ceilings. The bottom half of the walls were lined with padded leather. The reason for which became readily apparent.

Netta stood in the center of the room, a mallet cocked over her shoulder, her tongue poking out of her mouth as she took aim. She swung the mallet down and smacked the red ball with more force than it was designed to see. It bounded over the carpet, knocked against the leg of a side table, bounced off the wall, and rolled to a spot not far from a small arch made of stacked books.

"Well-played, dear," said an older woman who absolutely could not be his grandmother. Her praise had sounded sincere and her smile looked warm. "If you knock it through, I believe that will be the fifth game you've won in a row."

Netta stalked to her ball and tapped it through the make-shift arch. "Sixth." Her smile dimmed when she caught sight of John and May in the doorway. She darted a look between John and his grandmother, worrying her lower lip between her teeth.

The Dowager Marchioness of Mallen clasped her mallet between fingers bent with age. "Summerset." She dipped her head. "You look well."

He looked rich was what she meant. Her acknowledgement of his wealth should have pleased him. After all, he'd made a success of himself in large part to show her up. But it only made his gut churn. "What are you doing here?" Without waiting for a response, he turned on May. "What is she doing here? She can't be a member."

May pushed her spectacles back up her nose. "Might I remind you that I also control all aspects of membership for this club. Truly, Johnnie, if you are going to be this controlling I might have to give you your money back."

"I didn't mean that you couldn't allow her to be a member." He gripped his hands by his sides. "I meant someone like her couldn't possibly want to be a member of such a club."

May spread her hands in the air. "And yet here she is. Perhaps you have something to learn of your grandmother."

"I think not." His stomach rolled, like a bucket of eels. He'd learned everything he'd ever need to know about the woman the day she'd turned him and his brothers away. He stretched out his arm towards Netta. "Come. Let's away."

Netta rested her mallet on her shoulder and came to his side. "John, I think we should all go have a drink together. Your grandmother might surprise you."

Now she decided to talk? After a day of silence? "Is this a conspiracy? Why are you even talking to her? Playing with her?"

Netta pressed her lips together and turned towards his grandmother. The head of the mallet swung under his nose, barely missing it. "She's not what you think. Not anymore. Catherine," she called. "How about a nice cup of tea and a chat?" She shot a look at John. "With a healthy shot of whisky in it."

John snagged the mallet from her hand. "You are so intimate as to be on a first name basis with her?" The betrayal of that act dug under his skin. He'd told her what sort of woman his grandmother was, what a cold-hearted bitch he descended from, and she became close friends with the woman?

"Everyone is on a first name basis in this club," May said.

His grandmother toddled forward, using her mallet as a cane. "I wouldn't mind a cup of tea." She gave him a quavering smile, making John seethe.

He didn't know what her game was, but he wasn't fool enough to play along. "I thought you didn't break bread, or tea as the case may be, with, how did you put it? 'Filthy mongrels?'" He watched her face drain of color with some pleasure. "I can assure you, grandmother, nothing about me has changed except my clothes."

His heart turned over in his chest, thudding dully. He used to dream of giving this woman the cut direct. Making her feel the shame she had burdened him with. But now he merely wanted away from her presence.

Breathing heavily, he turned to face Netta, letting her purity wipe away the filth he felt being near his grandmother. "Can we go? Are you ready?" He detested the plea he heard in his own voice.

Her face creased in sympathy. "Yes. We can go." She nodded farewell to the other two women and tucked her hand around his elbow. Her breast pressed against his arm as they walked from the building. Full dark had descended, and he wrapped his arm about her waist to protect against any chill.

"I was hoping," Netta began, "to bring about a reconciliation between you and your grandmother, but I see now that it isn't my place. You and she must make amends in your own time."

He handed her into the carriage and followed her up. "There is no reconciliation to be had."

She sighed. "You Chaucer men sure do hold grudges." He glared at her, and she quickly added, "Not that this one wasn't earned, of course. But people do change."

"Are you friends now? With that woman?" Outrage dripped from his voice. Netta had thrown him many a turn, but truly, this was too much.

She shifted to sit beside him on the opposite bench. Laying her palm on his knee, she squeezed. "My relationship to her was purely mercenary, to facilitate an accord between you two. I think it would do you good." She leaned into him. "You were my only concern."

Slightly mollified, he brushed a smudge of dirt off his sleeve. "Let's keep it that way."

She rested her head on his shoulder. "As you wish."

Since she was being so accommodating, he asked, "About last night—"

The carriage hit a bump, shifted, and a loud curse emanated from the driver's seat, followed closely by a bellow.

"Nigel?" Or was it Michael driving them tonight? He'd been in such a rush to see Netta he'd barely spared his driver a glance. "Anything the matter?"

The crack of a whip was his only reply, and the carriage lurched forwards, tossing John back into his seat. "What the hell?" He yanked the window down. A faint yell drew his attention back the way they'd come. Nigel ran after them, yelling and waving his arms, his limping steps falling farther and farther behind from the racing carriage.

"What's happening?" Netta yanked on his sleeve, demanding his attention.

"I believe we're being kidnapped." The absolute brass of the villain. John wasn't involved in any mission for the Crown. He'd sent Sudworth a note saying he had the document from the Dutch embassy, so that man should be happy. Who could possibly be on his carriage?

"What?!" Netta's eyes went wide.

John peeled out of his jacket. "Stay here. I'll sort it out." Pulling his knife from his boot, he slid it into his waistband and opened the door.

Netta grabbed his hand, her grip as hard as steel. "You can't climb out of a moving carriage."

"Better than allowing the man to take us to his destination." He pressed a hard kiss to her mouth. "Don't worry. I've had practice at this." And peeling her fingers from his own, he stood from the door and grabbed the rail on the top of the carriage.

The dark form holding the reins presented him with no identification. With a shiver of excitement, John wedged the toe of his boot at the window and slid his body to the roof. It had been too long since he'd seen this kind of action. He almost wanted to thank the poor bounder. Of course, he was attempting to kidnap Netta, too, and for that he must be put in some pain.

It wasn't hard to remain unheard as he crawled forward. The pounding of the horses' hooves on cobblestone, the creak of the wheels as they were pushed to their limits, all worked to drown out his approach.

He balanced on the board above the driver's seat and pressed his blade to the man's throat. "Stop."

The kidnapper did as he said, a little too well. He yanked back on the reins, the horses' hooves skittering as they slammed to a stop, and John toppled over the man's shoulder landing at his feet.

The man's face was clear in the street lights as he pulled a pistol from his pocket and leveled it at John. With an insolent grin, he slapped the horses back into motion and their wild careen down the streets of London began again.

John cursed. What a pathetic performance. Perhaps Liverpool was right to put him out to pasture. The carriage turned, rising up onto two wheels. The streets became narrower, less populated, and John recognized the direction they were headed.

The docks.

Where he or Netta could be spirited away with no one the wiser.

Enough of this nonsense. He rolled to his side. into the driver, presenting a smaller target. He whipped his blade around and slashed the back of the man's ankle, pressing hard to cut through the thin leather of his boot.

An unholy shriek told him that he'd managed to strike his target. The blackguard dropped both pistol and reins to clutch at his wound.

John lunged for the reins, but they slipped between the horses, dragging on the road.

Unfettered, the horses picked up speed. The sound of a wheel cracking sliced through the air, and the rough bounce of the ride became even harder. The horses turned, narrowly missing a sailor who shouted obscenities after them.

John ignored him, focusing on the slight glimmer ahead. "Fuck!" Bracing his palm on the seat, he kicked the driver off the carriage, eliminating one distraction. He needed to stop the carriage. Now. That instant. He leapt forward, landing hard on one of the horse's backs. Sliding sideways, he grabbed for a harness and hauled himself upright. "Whoa!" He pulled on the mane in front of him with one hand while scrabbling for the reins with the other. "Whoa!"

It was too late. The glimmer grew brighter, the moon a clear reflection off the water in the canal. As the horses leapt over the low wall, John swung his leg over the back of his mount and jumped into space.

Chapter Twenty-Three

He hit the water hard, his breath forced from his lungs, but he dove deeper, away from the carriage that would be following.

With Netta inside.

The force of the carriage hitting the water pushed him aside, twisting his limbs. He scissored to the surface, gasping as he broke free. The sounds of splintering wood and groaning metal surrounded him, echoing off the canal walls.

"Netta!"

The door was half-submerged, the carriage tilting to one side. "Netta!" Using his boot against the wall as leverage, he tugged the door open. Relief flooded his veins when Netta looked up at him.

"Are you all right?" they both asked at the same time.

John's heart slowed from a gallop to a canter, and a shaky chuckle slipped from his lips. "Thank God." He stretched out a hand. "Come on."

She shook her head, her hair tumbling about her shoulders. The ends floated on the water that was much too close to her face. "My ankle is stuck." She tugged at her right leg to show him.

The opposite side of the carriage had split, and large panels of wood pinned her foot in place.

"Perfect." The door bumped into his side, and he pushed it back. "Are you in pain?"

She smiled. "Only a very little. Nothing to worry over."

His heart clenched. Netta had just been in a terrifying accident, was trapped in cold, filthy water, and she was trying to make him feel better? She was unlike anyone he'd ever known.

A dreadful squeal raised the hair on the back of John's neck. He and Netta locked gazes.

"The horses," she whispered.

"Let's get you out first then I'll see to the horses."

Another squeal. The carriage shifted as one of the beasts thrashed in the water.

"Go!" She shooed him away with her free hand. "I'm fine. Don't let them drown."

John ground his jaw. Shit and damnation, neither of his options were good. But he turned and swam to the closest animal. Its nose was barely above water. He'd lost his good knife in the accident, but he still had the dagger up his sleeve. He sliced at the harness, the wet leather fighting his efforts. Finally, the animal was free.

John slapped its rump. "Ha! Get out of here." He felt his way to the next animal. The horse wasn't moving except for a slight rise and fall of its shoulders. He cut away its bindings. "Go on, you mangy cur." Tugging at the bridle, he ignored the wide-eyed panic in the horse's gaze. "There's a jetty right over there. Follow your friend." After a minute of pushing and prodding, the horse moved.

And the nose of the carriage sank farther into the canal.

Netta's shriek thundered in his ears. He kicked for the carriage door, nearly ripping it from its hinges when it swayed in the current, blocking his way.

His heart stopped as he saw only bubbles in the murky water. Then Netta's head broke the surface, gasping for air before sinking back down.

John lunged forward, cradling the back of her head and lifting it. Her face was only inches above the water, her nose nearly grazing the carriage's ceiling.

She gave a shaky laugh. "Now I think my being stuck is a larger problem than before."

He kissed her temple. "I'll get you out. Can you brace yourself, stay above the water?"

He pulled his hand back an inch, and she sank back down. He brought her back up, spluttering.

"My neck aches when you hold me above the water." She scraped her fingers along the ceiling, looking, and not finding, a finger hold. "My legs are twisted under me. I don't have the leverage to hold myself up."

"All right, sweetheart." He kissed her again. "I've got you."

A shudder wracked her body.

He had her, but he was damned if he knew what to do with her. With his foot, he felt along her leg until he reached the wood that trapped her. "I'm going to try to kick a larger hole."

She nodded.

John thanked the larger heel on his boots and struck down with all his might. The water pushed against him, lessened his power, yet Netta still cried out.

"What?"

She closed her eyes. "Just a splinter. No matter. Keep going."

Bile rose up John's throat. With how fierce his Netta was, that 'splinter' could be large enough to saw her leg in two. "New plan. How long can you hold your breath?"

Her eye swiveled in his direction. "That's not something I've ever tested."

"You're going to test it now." He slowed his breathing, thinking through each of his next steps. "On three, I'm going to let you go and try to pull the wood away with my hands. I'll come up after ten seconds. You can hold your breath for ten seconds. Everyone can."

"All right." Her teeth chattered. "One..."

"Two..." John said.

"Three." They both sucked in air and John disappeared beneath the surface. He counted the seconds in his head as he grabbed the wood around her ankle. The edges sliced into his hands but he barely felt it. He pulled with all his might, trying to tug her ankle free. Out of time, he popped back to the surface, finding the back of her head and pulling her up.

She gasped. "Are you certain...that was only...ten seconds?"

"Yes." Ten wasted seconds of fumbling around and accomplishing nothing. He needed more time.

"At least the horses are free," she said.

"Bugger the horses." His hand trembled, and he clenched it to his stomach. "We're going to go again. On three."

"John." Her voice wavered. "I'm...I'm frightened."

Her words flayed his heart. His brave, sweet Netta was never scared. When he found out who had done this to them, he would tear him apart, limb from limb. As soon as he got Netta free and safe.

"Don't be. I'll get you out." He pressed his forehead against her temple. "On three."

She gripped his wrist. "I don't want you to die, too. Perhaps—"

"No." He cleared the gravel from his voice. "No need to panic, darling." It was a perfect time to panic. "Take a deep breath."

He watched her chest fill, counted to three, and dove down. He ignored the cuts to his hands, the wicked burn of a torn fingernail and pulled harder. And still, at the end of ten seconds, her foot remained trapped.

She kept her eyes closed, her breathing labored. "Don't let me go again. Just kick the damn thing."

He panted. "But it hurts you."

"I don't think my pain is of paramount importance any longer." The carriage shifted, and she whimpered. "I don't want to die."

"You're not going to die," he said fiercely. He couldn't imagine a world without her in it. Wouldn't want to live in it. And he always got what he wanted. "You'll be fine. Tomorrow we will laugh over this, you'll see."

She huffed through the chattering of her teeth. "I don't

think I believe you."

He widened his eyes. "Would I lie?"

"Yes, with no compunction."

Damn it, she knew him too well.

"Just pull my damn leg out of there." Netta pressed her palms against the ceiling. "I don't need my foot."

"I'm sorry." He took her hand, clasped it tight. "This is going to hurt."

"Summerset!"

Something splashed into the water near the carriage.

John's shoulders sagged. Finally. Something had gone right. "Wil! Get your arse in here."

Wil's dark shape maneuvered through the door.

John grabbed his shoulder and hauled him to Netta. "Hold her head above water." And knowing his friend would take care of her, he dove down again without waiting for a response.

It took longer than he wanted. But after the third dive he was able to slide Netta's foot free from her boot and out of the hole.

Wil swam from the carriage to the dock, pulling Netta with him.

John pulled himself up then reached down for her.

She wrapped her arms around his neck like she'd never let go. "You certainly know how to show a girl an exciting time."

He held her close, hoping through sheer force of will to warm her body with his own. As they were both shaking, it likely wasn't working. "Stick with me and you'll never have a dull night."

Her lips curved against his throat.

Wil helped him to rise with Netta in his arms.

"How did you find us?" John asked.

"I thought to escort you and Miss Netta to the theatre." Wil picked his way to the canal ledge and retrieved a pistol. His limp was more pronounced from the cold. Although it would be nothing to the limp the bastard who'd done this would sport from his ruined ankle.

"Following me still?"

Wil stared at his boots. "There are other attractions at the theatre besides your ugly face."

Wil shoved the pistol in the back of his trousers. "When I arrived at the club, I saw Nigel hollering to raise the dead. Following the carriage wasn't difficult. It left a fair bit of destruction in its wake." He walked to one of the horses that was standing huddled by a building. The other horse was further down on the jetty, half in and half out of the water, wheezing. Both of his forelegs were bent at unnatural angles. "I only wish I had found you in time," he said quietly.

"There's a man. He couldn't have gotten far." The cut to the Achille's tendon wouldn't lose enough blood to be dangerous, but it would keep him from running.

"I saw him." Wil approached the injured horse softly, running his hand along the animal's nose. "Paid a sailor to watch him for us. He didn't get away."

John nodded. He pressed Netta's face into his chest, cupping her ear, but she still jerked when the gunshot sounded.

A life wasted. Wil gave the dead horse one last stroke then walked to them, his face grim. "I do hope you'll let me in on the interview with the man who took your carriage."

John nodded. "I'll be back as soon as I see Netta home and get her a doctor. Don't start the fun until I return."

Wil pulled his shirt from his trousers and gave the ends a twist. "Bring me another change of clothes, will you?"

"Of course." They turned down the street, keeping an eye out for a hackney. Three blocks over they found one.

Wil held the door and helped John in with Netta. He pounded on the side and turned, retracing their steps.

Netta curled closer to John. She undid the knot of his cravat and pulled it off, dropping the soaked cloth to the floor.

John raised an eyebrow.

She notched her head on his shoulder and rubbed her hand over his chest. "You did say to stick with you, though I dare say this isn't what you had in mind."

He adjusted his grip, bundling her closer. "This is exactly what I meant." And it was. His heart tripped beneath her palm. He wanted her next to him any way he could have her. And the knowledge of that was thrilling. Comforting.

Terrifying.

He wanted Netta. He wanted her for the long term.

He wanted her forever.

He waited for something to happen. A lightning bolt to hit the hackney. For God to strike him down senseless. After all the times he'd sworn to never want anything long-lasting with a woman, he was sure a chastisement was in order for his change of heart.

This feeling of longing wasn't natural, not for him. But he was never one to deny himself what he wanted. And he wanted Netta.

Perhaps it only made sense to make their relationship more permanent.

He tucked his chin on top of her head.

After all, with the trouble she got into, he'd need to be around to keep her safe.

Chapter Twenty-Four

Netta hobbled to John's study door and raised her hand to knock. She paused, willed her hand to strike the wood, then lowered it. Her shoulders rounded. Good Gad, when did she become a coward?

The back of her throat burned. He was going to be disappointed. Angry, perhaps. His plan relied on her enticing Sudworth into a bet. He wanted that deed back so badly, and she'd wanted to help him, but it couldn't be. She'd taken the days of recuperation, telling herself it was best to wait until she was fully healed before telling John the truth.

In case he decided to throw her out, she needed to be able to walk.

That had been her excuse in any case. John wouldn't toss her into the streets. He wasn't that type of man. She just didn't want to see the reproach in his eyes. The betrayal that she'd lied to him about who she was, yet again.

She dropped her forehead to the cool wood. She couldn't lose him. It would hurt too much.

The door swung inward, and she stumbled into John's waiting arms.

"What are you doing out here, poppet? Trying to eavesdrop again?" He brushed a strand of hair off her forehead. "I told you I'd take care of it."

It being the man who'd seized control of their carriage. She frowned. That first night of the accident the doctor had given her laudanum as he'd cleaned and bandaged her ankle. It wasn't broken, but had swollen to a grotesque size.

She hadn't known when John had left or what he'd learned, and hadn't cared.

The next day, however, he had thwarted every attempt on her part to learn what his interview of the blackguard had revealed. And the blasted man had remained steadfastly silent. It was enough to make a woman scream with frustration.

"I shouldn't have to eavesdrop." She planted her hands on her hips. "I was kidnapped, too. You should tell me what you learned from the man you caught."

He stepped close and placed a soft kiss on the corner of her mouth. "Your priority is to heal. I'll take care of everything else."

The words should have annoyed her. And made her suspicious. It was unlike John to keep information from her in a perverse attempt to protect her sensibilities. In that respect, he was very unlike the typical male. But as his soft lips nibbled at her own, as his tongue slowly pressed into her mouth, any annoyance dried up.

But she still had her pride. She pulled back. "I am almost fully healed. Stop with this nonsense and tell me."

John twisted his lips in a wry smile. "You won't let me coddle you like a normal woman, will you?"

"There are other ways I like to be coddled." His eyes lit with interest, and she held up her hand. "First, tell me what you know."

"Bloody little." He ran his hand up the back of his head. "One of the reasons I didn't want to talk is because I don't like admitting to complete and utter failure. By the time I returned to the scene, Wil was there waiting but our quarry had disappeared." He pinched his lips tight. "Apparently he had quite the sum of money on him and paid off our very bribeable sailor to release him."

"How much money?"

"Enough to make me wary," John said. "If a low-level criminal is carrying such a sum on his person, his boss must be wealthy indeed. And I let the one man who could lead me to him slip right through my fingers."

Netta cupped his cheek and kissed the corner of his frown. "From my perspective, you performed magnificently that night." He'd saved her life. Kept her calm when she'd felt the panic clawing at her insides.

She idly scratched the back of his neck. "This man who took your carriage. Is he related to your work for the Crown?" She had her suspicions about that. How many earls would climb from a moving carriage to dispatch a ruffian?

His muscles tensed against her body. "Is that what brings you to my door?"

She swallowed. If only his secrets were the only thing between them. "I..." She set her shoulders and took a deep breath. *Audentes Fortuna Iuvat.* Fortune favors the bold. "I have something to tell you."

His Adam's apple bobbed. "And I have something to tell you, too."

"Do you want to go first?" she asked hopefully.

"Not particularly."

"Nor do I."

They stared at each other, until one side of John's mouth quirked up. "I propose a game."

Netta's shoulders relaxed. This was familiar. This was fun. Depending on how John took her news, it might be the last bit of fun she had with him. "Loser talks first?"

"Of course."

"And what are the rules to this game?"

He cocked his head. "That depends on how well you are feeling. Montague is hosting a musical evening with dinner tonight. I told him I did not know if we could attend."

Her mouth went dry. "Who else will be there?"

"As his wife is barely accepted by society, I suspect all the outcasts of the ton." John pressed his lips into a slash. "I asked Montague to extend an invitation to Sudworth, as well, in hopes you'd be well enough to pique his interest further, but Montague informed me this morning he declined. Which, although disappointing, does allow us some hours of frivolity instead. What say you?" He circled around her, tracing his fingertip along the back edge of her gown. "Do you feel like being naughty tonight?"

She shouldn't. Just because Sudworth wouldn't be in attendance didn't mean someone else from her past wouldn't be. But...she *was* of age now. No one could send her back to her father's. And this might be her last night with John.

Cerise would call her impetuous. Tell her to use her head instead of her heart.

But Netta wasn't her friend.

"Besides a slight twinge, my ankle is fine. I'm in."

He smiled, his teeth gleaming in the morning light, and a delightful shiver raced down her spine. She didn't trust that look. It foretold of something wicked.

His wickedest plans were the most pleasurable.

John tapped his index finger against his pursed lips. "Wear the peach silk gown tonight. The one with the ivory lace embroidery."

Now she truly didn't trust him. She rocked up onto her toes with excitement, then muttered a curse when her ankle ached. "And you wear the navy velvet jacket, the one that brings out the blue in your eyes." If he could make demands on wardrobe, so could she. And she did adore him in that jacket. It nipped in at his waist and made his shoulders look as broad as an ox's.

A tingle started in her stomach and shivered lower. Whatever he had planned for the night, she wanted to be prepared. "I'm going to rest my ankle." She trailed her finger up his waistcoat and flipped the knot of his cravat. "I will see you later tonight."

And with a seductive sway to her hips, she sauntered out of his study and down the hall.

The ice bath for her ankle made it feel almost like new. The nap she took also helped. She was going to miss living in an earl's home. Not as much as she'd miss John. But a steady supply of Pomfret cakes, satin sheets to lay her head upon, a dressing room full of beautiful gowns...

She stared at her reflection in the mirror as Margaret put the finishing touches on her hair. It was close, but John still won out. And tonight could be their last night.

She raised her chin. So she would eke out as much enjoyment in their time left as possible. No regrets.

Her nerves crackled with anticipation the entire carriage ride to the duke's townhouse. Anticipation skittered through her veins through the introductions to the wives of John's friends. What did he have planned? And how would she win? When John touched her arm as they sat listening to music, she jumped.

He smirked. "I only wanted to tell you that I must step out. Save a seat for me at dinner. Oh"—he leaned close and brushed his lips over her ear—"and the only rule to this game is for you to not make a sound." And during the violin solo, he stood and left the room. Leaving her a fidgeting mess.

Not make a sound? He couldn't mean for her to become mute for the rest of the evening. His games didn't include rudeness to third parties, so what did he mean?

After the music ended, the two sisters, Elizabeth, Duchess of Montague, and Lady Amanda Rothchild, hurried over to her. "I don't need to know where Summerset disappeared to," the duchess said. "I am only glad he has left your side for a moment."

"Your grace?"

The woman flapped her hand. "I told you, call me Elizabeth."

Her sister turned matching chocolate eyes on Netta. Both sisters were tall and slender, with wavy, dark hair. But where the duchess sparkled with vivacity, the countess was quieter, although no less friendly.

"We have been curious to speak to you about John," Amanda said. "It is much easier to do so without him present."

Netta grinned. They wanted gossip. Women after her own heart. "What is it you wish to know?" She wouldn't spill all John's secrets, of course. But enough to discomfit him. He deserved no less, leaving her alone and desperate with curiosity.

"Colleen told us that you're assisting him to recover his property," Elizabeth said.

Netta blinked, then covered her surprise by side-stepping out of the way of guests filing from the room. She'd forgotten how close of a relationship John had with his friends, and subsequently their wives. There didn't seem to be any secrets in the group.

Unlike with her. Her stomach clenched. But that was a thought for later tonight. After the game.

"But," Amanda said, sidling closer, "his attentiveness to you all night has us wondering if there is more between you two than business."

Netta knitted her brow. "Surely you've seen John with other women on his arm? A romantic attachment cannot be such an anomaly." Not for a man as engaging as John.

"Of course not." Elizabeth nodded at a viscountess across the room. "But the other women he's introduced us to have seemed mere accessories, a pretty face and dress to match his outfit." She looked Netta up and down. "And while you are as pretty as any, you most certainly aren't a mindless adornment."

"Thank you?" While everyone liked to hear themselves distinguished, she wasn't certain how she felt about John's past lovers. Accessories? Sadly, she could well believe it. He focused so much on appearances at times, he could easily forget the humanity of his companions.

She rubbed at the pinch behind her breastbone. How capricious life was. One incident in childhood could transform an entire personality.

Netta dipped her head. "I thank you for the compliment, but whatever attachment you imagine does not exist. John and I have become good friends, but neither of us are constituted for a relationship of any length." She swallowed. "I have not domesticated him, and he certainly has not me."

The sisters shared a look. "Are you certain?" Elizabeth asked. "If ever a man looked ready to be domesticated, it was Summerset this evening."

The idea was absurd. Her belly fluttered. Someone like her and someone like John forming a lasting union? One shameless person in a relationship made it hard enough to maintain. But two was a recipe for heartache.

"Sister," Amanda chided, "you should know better than anyone that marriage and domesticity have naught to do with the other. Some marriages are very untamed indeed."

Marriage. Netta ignored the duchess's blush and focused on keeping her breathing even. Her lungs wanted to inflate like a bellows. After her one broken betrothal, she'd never, not once, considered entering into such a union. She wasn't constituted for it; John certainly wasn't.

But...to the right person, someone extraordinary enough to recompense for the loss of freedom, someone who brought her joy, challenged her, excited her, mayhap—

"My stomach tells me I am ready for dinner." She cleared her throat, hoping to rid her voice of its panicked quality. Best to put a stop to that outlandish thought before it began. "I must look for Summerset. If you'll excuse me."

She dipped a curtsy and fled from the women like they were Shakespeare's Weird Sisters instead of mild-mannered aristocrats. She searched for John, almost afraid to find him when absurd thoughts of marriage were darting through her mind, but eventually had to admit defeat and enter the large dining room alone.

She was seated next to an Italian contessa on her left, who's English was as good as Netta's Italian. No conversation was possible there. The man seated to her right was young, the son of a distant marquess, and the black sheep of the family according to his chatter. He wanted to be a poet.

"I'll never be able to thank the duke and duchess enough for their patronage of my efforts." The boy flicked out his napkin, settled it on his lap, and buried his nose in his wineglass to inhale deeply. "Without their support, I'd have been forced to enter the clergy." He shuddered. "Or become a barrister. Those were my father's only options when telling me how to live my life. But I told him—"

"Could you pass the salt, please?" She didn't mean to be rude, but his endless prattle acted like a tiny hammer tapping at her brain. Distracting her from her one burning question. Her gaze flitted to the empty chair three seats down on the opposite side of the table. It was the only chair missing a body. John's body. Where the devil was he?

The woman on the poet's other side proved a much more attentive listener, and the boy turned his conversation to her.

Netta blew out a breath as a footman removed her soup bowl and replaced it with a plate of squab, root vegetables, and a flaky roll. She was no longer hungry, but she picked up her fork in any case.

And put it back down. She frowned. There it was again. Something brushing against her leg. She moved to pull her foot back, and a large hand wrapped around her ankle.

Between the second of fright and the moment she understood it was John's hand on her body, she almost shrieked. It would have served him right if she had. She would enjoy watching him try to explain his way out of hiding under the table.

But she would enjoy whatever he was up to even more.

He skimmed his palm up her calf, the motion soothing. Sweet almost.

The tongue he used to flick against her inner knee was decidedly not.

She sucked in a sharp breath. *The only rule is to not make a sound.* So this was his game. A public seduction. Did he think she'd shy away from something so wanton?

That she wouldn't be able to control herself?

His teeth scraped above her knee, and her insides quivered. Could she control herself? This game might not be easy to win. She bit her lip and looked around the table. Two dukes sat at it, along with their duchesses. All of John's friends. Five other earls that she had been introduced to. She could be humiliated in front of nigh on thirty people.

John bit her calf, the sting disappearing quickly although his teeth did not. He seemed to wait for her to make a decision. As though even he recognized the risks of this game.

Her heart pounded so loudly she was sure others must hear it. But no one paid her any mind. Everyone was either engrossed in their meal or in nearby conversation.

She felt as isolated as an island in the middle of the sea.

On an island alone with John.

This was her last night. Her last game.

She widened her knees, and John's breath gusted across her skin. He pressed a swift kiss to her leg. The game was on.

Her chair skidded along the carpet, jerking her body flush to the table and jostling it.

The contessa shot her a curious glance.

"I just want to get closer to my plate." She gave the Italian a wide smile and picked her fork up. Her words were useless to the Italian and waving the utensil about didn't add to the explanation. But the heavy piece of silverware felt good in her hand. She might need it to stab John if he put her on the spot like that again.

Any irritation slipped away as he dragged her skirts up to her hips. The pads of his fingers danced so lightly across her skin they tickled.

She shifted in her seat and poked at the squab with her fork. She would not make a sound. She would not—

She muffled a gasp by shoving the roll in her mouth. John swept his finger up and down her crease, and the decadence of the situation clouded her head. She understood now why he'd asked her to wear the peach gown. The double layer of sheer chiffon didn't allow for any undergarments beside her stays. It was but a trifling for John to lift her skirts and have full access to her most intimate bits.

Clever man. She'd have to think of a way to make him pay for that.

He nudged at her knees, trying to prod them wider, and with a glance round the table, she obliged.

Elizabeth, bucking tradition and sitting next to her husband, smiled and raised her wine glass to Netta.

She returned the greeting, then froze as something soft and moist licked along her outer lips.

Oh dear Lord, not that. She could take a slow finger-fucking and keep a calm exterior, but if John used his tongue...

He nuzzled her clit with his nose and sucked one of her labia into his mouth.

Netta melted back into her chair. Oh, she was going to make him pay. She hooked one leg over his shoulder. She'd make him pay, and pay, and pay...

With his hands on her upper thighs, John used his thumbs to peel her open, his breath a heated contrast to the cool air.

She gulped down a breath, bracing for what was coming. She would remain still and quiet. She had control. She—

He pressed his mouth to her most intimate flesh, and her body jolted.

She was completely lacking in discipline.

The man next to her turned. "I say, this bird is uncommonly juicy." He wiped his mouth with his napkin. "Wouldn't you agree?"

She couldn't get into a discussion on squab with a poet. She would break under the pressure. "It could be juicier." She felt rather than heard John chuckle against her, the vibration making her twitch. She buried her face in her wine goblet, and the poet took the hint and turned back to the dining companion on his other side.

She'd have to think of some way to make recompense to the boy for her unbearable rudeness.

A long slide of John's tongue, from her opening to her clit, had her eyes rolling back in her head.

She'd buy his blasted tome of works. Her fingers went white around her fork. And one for John, too. Make him suffer through reading the trite musings on love and beauty that only a man too young to have real experience could write.

John scored her clit with his teeth, and Netta almost lost the game right there. The end of her fork hit the table, and the contessa shot her a worried frown.

Netta dropped the fork and tore off another bite of the roll. If she kept her mouth busy chewing, it couldn't get her into any trouble.

With his nose nudging her clit, John slowly plunged his tongue in and out of her cunny.

She panted, pressing the half-eaten roll to her lips to muffle any sound. Nothing had ever felt so good. Or so wicked. Or reckless. One last evening of abandon before the real world intruded. Before her real life, with its fears and duties and frustrations, came knocking.

Her hips rocked into his devilish mouth. She didn't want this to be her last game with John, but if it was, by God it was a masterpiece.

Her skin heated, sweat gathering at the small of her back. Her fingers clenched, crushing the poor roll.

John traced his way up to her clit, using the pressure at the tip of his tongue to flick that hard nub. Shivers shot from her core to her nipples, turning them into aching points.

"Oh God," she murmured, softly enough she didn't think John could hear.

But the poet did. "I agree. Byron's behavior has been scandalous." And he turned back to his other companion.

The tingling in her body pooled low. The rest of her felt

numb; only her sex and John's tongue existed. She was at the point where she *needed* the release. It was as critical as breathing. If John didn't play this game all the way through, she would rip his ears off before taking care of herself.

She wanted to spread herself wider, take everything John had to give, but her body didn't listen. It coiled tighter, tensing all of her muscles, drawing her legs together and trapping John's head within her thighs.

Her breath caught once. Twice. And with one last swirl of his tongue, she went over the edge.

She bit into her lip, struggling to keep silent as wave after wave of pleasure coursed through her. John kept working his tongue, drawing out every crescendo until she could take it no longer. She shoved the remainder of the roll in her mouth, pretending to moan over its buttery goodness as she reached under the table and pushed at John's head.

She might have poked him in the eye. So be it. She succeeded in disengaging him and that was all that mattered.

Her body calmed and she took her first deep breath since John had touched her.

And starting hacking as flakes of bread went down her windpipe.

The contessa reached over and gave her a sound thumping on the back.

Tears streaming, Netta gulped some wine and held up her hand. "I'm fine," she told the other guests. "He just went down the wrong way."

John shook against her thigh.

"It!" She cleared her throat. "*It* went down the wrong way."

Conversation around the table started up again, taking the focus blissfully off of Netta. She sagged back, all of her muscles succumbing to a satisfied languor. She was definitely counting that as her win. She reached beneath the tablecloth and John took her hand, squeezing it.

The poet started and looked at the table as though he could see beneath it. "I do believe something is touching me. This is the second time I've felt it." He pushed his chair back and started to reach for the tablecloth.

"It's only the family dog," Netta said. "I've been feeding him table scraps." She picked up the last of her roll and shoved it under the table.

John growled, but took the bread.

The Duke of Montague, Marcus as he'd insisted on being addressed, arched an eyebrow, shaking his head, but turned back to his wife.

Netta flushed. Her host knew there was something shifty happening at his table, and since he was good friends with John, he probably suspected its nature.

But with her body feeling as satisfied as it did, she couldn't find it in herself to care overmuch.

She sliced a bite off the squab, her appetite making an amazing recovery after her impressive show of fortitude.

John tugged on her gown.

She cut off another slice and pinched it between her two fingers. Making sure no one watched, she raised the tablecloth and held the bit of meat to John. He clasped her hand with his own and brought her fingers to his mouth, taking the bite and licking her fingers clean.

Repressing a smile, she patted his head.

A dog under the table, indeed.

* * *

Clearly, he had not thought this all the way through.

John accepted the next tidbit from Netta, but his stomach yet rumbled. And his arse was going numb. His mind had whirled at the delightful possibilities of being hidden under a table at Netta's feet, but after the game was over the reality of him being stuck under said table for the rest of the meal hadn't crossed his mind.

He rubbed Netta's bare knee. Her restraint had been magnificent. She deserved to win this one.

He blew out a breath. Which meant he had to confess his past.

He trusted Netta, but he had never told a living soul about his work as a spy. Yes, some people had heard rumors. Too many people. And his friends' wives had all learned the truth, but John had felt nothing but irritation when his friends had spouted off about their jobs with the Crown to their women.

How they would laugh at him now.

And how would Netta react? Would she recoil from a man who had spent his adult life doing unspeakable things in the name of his country? Or would she accept him as he was?

The back of his throat ached. If anyone could accept him it would be Netta. She'd already seen more of him than every other woman of his acquaintance put together.

The Italian lady crossed her legs and bobbed her toe inches from his nose.

John eased away, and brushed the trousers of the man opposite.

Sod it all to hell and back. Montague needed a larger dining table. For a duke, it was positively disgraceful to have one under five feet wide.

The man in question said something at the end of the table, his voice muffled. All the chairs but Netta's scraped backwards.

John heaved a breath. Finally. Dinner was at an end.

"I'll be right there," Netta called to someone. "There's a pebble in my slipper I wish to remove."

After a moment, she raised the tablecloth and waved him out.

"A pebble in your slipper?" he asked as he rolled out and to his feet. He stretched, a bone in his back popping.

"Better than saying a thorn in my side." She rose and planted her fists on her hips. "Really, John. At a table full of guests? What were you thinking?"

As a delightful post-orgasm flush still graced her cheeks, and a smile twitched about her lips, he didn't take her scolding seriously.

"Was that a whimper I heard when I first used my tongue?" He clucked that organ against the top of his mouth. "You disappointed me, Netta."

"You heard no such thing and I never disappoint." She patted her hair, making sure everything was still in place.

He grabbed her hips and tugged her into his body. "Of that, you are absolutely correct." He rested his chin on top of her head. He didn't want to lose this. Lose her. Would she be amenable to his offer of *carte blanche*? She should be. Their fun would go on and he was, after all, a desirable match.

But still a niggle of doubt wormed its way under his skin.

He kissed her hair. "You won. It is time for me to talk."

"Must we?" She clutched his arms and looked up at him. "Can we wait until we get home at least?"

"The words won't change depending on location."

She sighed. "I know. But everything else will change. I just want a few more minutes of...this."

John frowned. Did she know what he was to say? Did she care that much? Nevertheless, putting off unpleasant conversations was something at which he excelled. He and his brother were proof of that. That was a reckoning years in the making.

Cupping her elbow, he led her from the dining room. Montague and Sutton were standing at the doorway to the parlor, and when they saw them, peeled away to meet him at the front door.

"Leaving so soon?" Montague asked.

"And with no supper, either." Sutton looked horrified at the thought.

"Have no fear." John took his hat and coat from a footman, then turned and helped Netta into her spencer. "I ate."

Pink crept up Netta's neck, but John didn't have time to enjoy it.

"We need to talk," Montague said. He glanced at Netta. "Perhaps Miss LeBlanc could wait for you at your home."

"While I languish in boredom here waiting for your guests to depart before we talk." He shook his head. Netta's and his conversation was more important. "If you insist on this discussion"—one they had chewed over endlessly before—"come over after your party. I'll ask cook to put on a pot of coffee."

"Very well." Montague bowed over Netta's hand. "Miss LeBlanc. I hope you had an enjoyable evening."

Her flush crept higher. "Quite enjoyable indeed."

Sutton bowed over her hand next, and John frowned.

"Enough with the petting." He removed Netta's hand from his friend's and tucked it securely at his elbow. "I'll see you both later."

He handed Netta into his carriage and followed her in, sitting beside her.

"Your friends are most charming," she said.

"Is that so?"

"And quite handsome, too."

He swiveled his head to glare down at her. "I'm so pleased that you find my friends to your liking." If his tone wasn't enough to show his displeasure, he crossed to the opposite seat, dropping down heavily.

She stretched across the divide and grabbed his sleeve. He let her tug him back to sit next to her.

"You do enjoy your sulks." She rested her head against his shoulder and sighed. "And I enjoy poking at you. But let's not do that now. Not when it might be our last quiet moment together."

His stomach dropped to the floor. "Do you see our time together ending so soon?"

She was quiet a moment. "Everything has an ending. And I fear our conversation will be the beginning of our end."

They rode the rest of the way in silence. His mind churned. He didn't like endings, not unless he instigated them. Did she not wish to continue in his company unless there was a job? He blinked, the back of his eyes burning.

Did she see so little value in him except for his blunt?

He didn't want to believe it, but what other explanation was there? He'd rebuilt the Summerset fortune, he took any ballroom by storm with his sly manners and unparalled footwear, but truly, what else was there of him? He no longer assisted his country. He was too cowardly to experiment with chemicals again. And no one would accuse him of acquiring moral worth through benevolence to others.

His heart thumped, making his chest feel strangely hollow. He'd achieved what he'd set out in life to become. Wealthy. Powerful. So fashionable no one could ever look at him with disgust again.

He dug a knuckle into his breastbone. How absurd those ambitions now seemed.

They rolled to a stop in front of his home and a footman pulled the door open. John stepped out then turned to hand Netta down. The top of her head just came to his chin, and even though her spine was infused with steel, her womanly curves looked as soft and delicate as spun sugar.

Realization hit him like a hammer. Whatever her reaction to his past exploits, he couldn't involve her in his present one. She was vulnerable, and he'd rather lose everything than see her come to harm.

He almost laughed at the irony of it. In order to offer her *carte blanche*, to keep her in his life, he'd need his wealth. And in order to keep his wealth, he needed her for his scheme. Something, apparently, his newfound conscience wouldn't allow.

At the door to his study, she pressed her knuckles into her lower back, looking as threadbare as he felt.

He replaced her hand with his own and rubbed away her ache.

She leaned into him.

No. Not even to keep her by his side would he gamble with her as the stake. Taking her out of it was the right thing to do. He never should have involved her to begin with.

She dropped onto a chair across from his desk, ignoring the settee by the wall. Perhaps she was smart not to sit next to him. Best to keep this discussion business-like. Netta appreciated frankness, not mawkish sentiment and hand-holding.

He stood in front of her, leaning back against the desk. "A win in your column at last."

The smile she should have worn at a victory was absent. "Yes. So what was it you had to tell me?"

He crossed his arms and his ankles. Where to start? With the decision that affected her most, he supposed. "It's about my plan." He inhaled. Best just to spit it out.

"Netta, I'm sorry. You're out."

Chapter Twenty-Five

Ice filled her veins. Of all the things she'd thought John might say, that hadn't been one of them.

"Why?" It shouldn't matter. She'd been about to quit. But being tossed aside stung.

He shrugged. "I don't know if I can guarantee your safety. The chance isn't worth it."

Everything in her melted. "But you need a woman as a stake."

"I will tempt Sudworth with something else."

Well, that made breaking her news to him easier. She tilted her head. "That was all you had to tell me? No deep, dark secret?"

He gripped the edge of the desk. "No, that wasn't all."

A moment passed. Two.

"Well?"

"I'm getting to it." He blew out a breath. "So impatient."

"And you're delaying."

John picked up a brass paperweight and tossed it between his hands. "It's about the work I did for the government. It wasn't as a member of the House of Lords." He cleared his throat. "I am...I was..."

Netta made a circular motion with her hand. "You were...?"

"I was a spy." His Adam's apple bobbed. "I spied for the Crown."

She scooted to the edge of her chair. "Truly? How thrilling." She was never one for envy, that emotion merely a waste of time and energy. But she couldn't deny a touch of jealousy over his career. While she merely performed exciting acts on the stage, John lived them.

"You aren't appalled? I...haven't always done good things, Netta."

No. John didn't strike her as a merciful man. But he was an honorable one. With his own slightly dented code. "I assume whatever you did was necessary, and done to bad people."

His shoulders sagged. "They were as horrible as you are marvelous."

"The most miserable of scum indeed." She pursed her lips. "With your background, I can see you'd have alternatives to winning your deed back in a game."

He rubbed the back of his neck. "Yes, but nothing that would hold up under scrutiny. I don't want the mines enjoined in a legal battle. A winner-take-all game of hazard is still the direction I want to go."

"Without me." She bit the inside of her cheek. If she were a stranger to Sudworth, she would convince John to use her still. The risk seemed minimal and John's smelts were of utmost importance to him.

Leaning forwards, he tucked a strand of hair behind her ear. "Nothing need change between us. We can still enjoy each other's company as before, if you'd like. You can even remain here until we find you a more suitable apartment."

How kind of him. She gripped the armrests of her chair. How bloody magnanimous. "I didn't agree to your plan for your company. I did it for the four thousand pounds."

He winced, just a flash of one, before his features settled back into its aloof mask, one he hadn't worn around her in quite some time. "Of course, I didn't intend to renege on our terms. I had thought with my offer of *carte blanche* you could expect to prosper in many ways."

Netta shot to her feet and pressed against his legs. "Forgive me. I didn't mean it that way. Truly, your companionship far surpasses money."

A crack appeared in his composure. "But?"

She dropped her head. "But...I need that money."

Tucking his finger under her chin, he raised her face. "Why? While I admit that your situation is far beneath the station you deserve, you do not appear to be in desperate straits."

Netta pulled away and stalked about the study. "My situation is not as it appears. I am not as I appear."

A crease lined his forehead. "Explain."

She darted him a look but continued pacing. The swift back-and-forth steadied her mind. "I could not have continued in your scheme even had you not dismissed me."

"I did not dismiss you," he objected. "Merely found another use for you."

"On my back?" She raised her hand, cutting off his objection. "My apologies. I find that I become churlish when I am nervous. You are my unfortunate victim."

"Netta, stop."

She continued marching.

He stepped in front of her, taking her elbows. "Stop. Tell me what is the matter. I will fix it."

She huffed out a laugh. "You can do many things, but this cannot be fixed. It can be resolved, but I fear the resolution will not be to anyone's liking."

"For once I grow tired of games." He gave her a small shake. "Speak plainly. What is amiss?"

She stared into his eyes. The blue was so deep and dark she felt she could dive into them, find her escape. But there was no escaping this reckoning. "I am not Antoinette LeBlanc."

His nostrils flared. "Not Ned Pickle, nor Netta Pickle, and now not even LeBlanc." A tiny muscle in his jaw flicked. "Who, pray tell, have I been sharing my bed with?"

"I was born Miss Evered. Miss Agnes Evered, but my family and friends did call me Netta." It was difficult to take in full breaths; her lungs didn't seem to want to expand. "My father is Viscount Darby."

She held her breath until her head went light, yet still

John said nothing.

"Well? What have you to say to this latest deception?" She shook off his hands and crossed her arms under her chest. "Are you not grievously disappointed? Shocked beyond all measure?" The daughter of a viscount shouldn't even know the address of the theatre she worked at. Should have saved her virginity for her husband. Shouldn't have been thieving on the streets.

When she thought about what her life had become, even she was shocked. She lifted her chin. Shocked, yes. But that didn't mean she would change it. She *liked* Netta LeBlanc. Liked the freedom of being a common Cit. Of living how she wished, without the restraints of a father or husband.

What she didn't like was the carefully arranged blank expression upon John's face.

"Disappointed yes," he said. "I had thought we'd arrived at an intimacy where you'd have felt free to inform me of this before now. But shocked, no. Nothing you do surprises me anymore."

She stepped forwards, clasping her hands together to keep from reaching out and grabbing hold of him. "We have become close. I've wanted to tell you for ages, but I was scared."

His eyebrows shot up. "Of me?"

"Of how you'd react." Hurt flashed in his eyes, and she turned away, unable to see it. "I left home when I was but seventeen. I've learned hard lessons about the dangers of trusting someone. I wanted to tell you, but the part of me that's kept me alive told me to wait. Just as you didn't feel safe telling me about being a spy before now." She made her way to the study's window and pressed her palm against the cold glass.

It was as dark as pitch outside in the garden. The wavering oval reflection that represented her face was the only thing she could see.

Until another pale oval came to hover behind hers.

John rested his hands on her shoulders. "Why did you leave home?"

The tone of his voice told her he knew. Not the details, but the horror behind them. A seventeen-year-old daughter of a viscount didn't flee from her family and friends unless her circumstances had become desperate.

"It's an old story. One I'm sure you can understand." She pushed aside emotion. Spoke dully. She wouldn't allow the memories to control her. "My father spent beyond his means. He needed money."

When she paused too long, John squeezed her shoulders. "And?"

"And he wasn't clever like you. Wasn't industrious. The idea of working to earn his money never even occurred to him."

John stepped close enough that she could feel the heat from his body against her back. "That doesn't make him unusual among our kind."

"No." He was right. John was marvelously unique. What he had accomplished was nothing short of amazing. "But I would hope selling one's unwilling daughter off to a monster to marry has become somewhat out of vogue."

He stopped breathing. "You're married."

She turned to face him. "No. When entreaties to my father were dismissed, I thought to appeal to the man himself. Surely if he knew how unwilling his betrothed was, he would retract his offer. I snuck out of my house to pay a call." She closed her eyes. She should never have done that. It had been her first mistake.

But a useful one. She'd learned what sort of man her intended husband was.

John pulled her close, tucked her head against his chest, and held her tight. "Tell me."

"I'd only met him once before. I'd thought him reserved. Taciturn. But not..." A tremor shook her body, and she cursed it. This shouldn't be difficult. It had happened more than five years ago. But the memory of that night was like a living thing. Eating at her, demanding her attention.

She cleared her throat. "He refused to listen to reason. Said the fact that I was unwilling would only make our wedding night that much sweeter." John's fingers dug into her back, and she burrowed closer. "When I told him there was no power on earth that would make me say those vows, he became violent." She had learned that night that a saucy mouth could lead to far worse consequences than a scolding from her father and mother. It had taken her nigh on two years to recover her impertinence, a feat of which she was most proud.

"Who was he?" John growled.

Netta ignored the question. She needed to get her story out, tell it her way. "The bump on my wrist is due to him. I landed wrong when he threw me to the ground. I don't know if it was broken then, but it certainly was after he stomped on it." And laughed when she screamed. His laugh haunted her dreams.

She nuzzled her head against his chest, moving aside his cravat with her cheek until the rapid beat of his heart soothed her ear. She inhaled, letting his scent surround her. Wrapped up in his arms like this, truly, nothing could hurt her.

"I want a name."

Netta smiled sadly. Of course he did. Give a man a target, he would shoot it; a nail, and he would pound it. But life wasn't as simple as that.

"When I returned home, my father didn't believe me. Said I was making up stories." That had been the most painful part of the night. She had thought her father felt some affection for her. If he ever did, it was wiped clear by desperation. "The very next night I left home."

His chest rose and fell beneath her cheek in angry bursts. But his voice was gentle. "And you were seventeen?"

She nodded. "My birthday had been less than a month prior."

He pressed his lips against her temple. "I am glad you told me. I am sorry if I did anything to make you believe you couldn't trust me with it."

"If it had just been me, I would have told you the second time I bedded you."

His lips curved against her skin. "Not the first?"

"No, you still appeared a thoughtless fop, albeit a talented one." She pulled away. "I have a younger sister." Her gaze flicked between his eyes. She needed him to understand how important this was. Eleanor's safety was everything. "She is just now fourteen but I've learned that my father has betrothed her, even at that age. That's why I agreed to your job. Why I need the four thousand pounds. I've been saving up my wages, but it isn't enough. Not for what I had planned."

"What is your plan?"

"To take my sister away, start a new life with her in America." Nausea swirled through her stomach. She had been eager to make the new country her home before she'd met John. Eager for the adventure.

John seemed like the bigger adventure. But it wasn't her life she needed to secure. "I would ask that you stick to our agreement, but I cannot help you with your scheme. I know this now. So I can only beg you to lend me that four thousand pounds. Once I've settled and found employment, I will repay your loan in increments." She forced her lips into a smile. "They will be very small increments, and I would be ever so grateful if we made this an interest-free loan, but I will repay you."

He huffed. "I would give you the money, but not if you intend to flee the continent with your ill-gotten gains. There is a limit to my generosity."

She placed her hands on his lean hips. "John. I cannot stay here. Not with my sister. My father might be able to pretend that he has sent one of his daughters to the north to care for an elderly aunt"—John arched one eyebrow, and Netta nodded—"yes, that was his story. But he cannot use it for both his daughters. He will look for Eleanor. I had thought about trying to hide her in London, but it won't do. My father won't suffer the loss of another valuable piece of chattel." She swallowed down the bile in her throat.

She didn't know who she hated more: Sudworth or the man who'd created her.

"You must think me devoid of filial affection," she said. "I can assure you I once held my father in high esteem."

"I wasn't thinking that at all." John shook his head. "I was thinking how much a man's mind can contort to justify his actions when he is desperate. I cannot imagine a father doing such to his daughters. He must be mad."

Netta blinked against the burn in her eyes. John might be able to rationalize her father's actions, but she could not. With understanding came forgiveness, and that was something she was not prepared to give.

"Will you give me the money." Her heart tripped in her chest. If he refused, she didn't know what she would do.

John rubbed his jaw. "You said you know that you can no longer help me. Why is that?"

Netta narrowed her eyes. He was using her tactic back on her, answering her question with one of his own. She didn't care for it. But it was best that he knew all.

"I would no longer be of use in your scheme. Your quarry knows me." She clenched the skirt of her gown, her nails digging into her palms even through the fabric. "Sudworth is the man my father betrothed me to."

* * *

John had a new plan. Kill Sudworth. His friends would help to hide the body. Liverpool would be suspicious, but would eventually let the matter drop. Once he got the man alone, he would—

"John." Netta wrapped her arms around her middle, looking altogether more distraught than John liked. "Please help me. I need the money."

"No, you need the threats against you and your sister

271

removed. It doesn't necessarily follow that includes blunt."

"You don't wish to lend it to me." She loosed a wavering breath then nodded. "I will figure something else out."

"I don't wish for you to flee across an ocean." The thought of Netta disappearing into that uncivilized upstart nation sent a cold chill down his spine. He rubbed the back of his head. "Leaving England isn't the only way to keep you and your sister safe, nor the best way." There were two obstacles to their security. Sudworth and the father. His fingers twitched. He would enjoy making Sudworth pay for daring to touch Netta.

"But..." She frowned. "Is that possible? With my staying in London?"

"I will make sure it is so."

She looked to the ceiling and shook her head. "You are capable of many things—"

"Thank you." He prowled towards her.

"—but I fear at times your capabilities do not match your ego."

He pressed a hand to his heart. "You wound me."

"I do not, but someone else can." She grabbed the tail of his cravat and tugged him close. "You are not invincible. And not all battles can be won."

"This one can be." Slitting Sudworth's throat would be but a moment's work.

His bloodlust must have shown. Netta narrowed her eyes to slits. "You will not go about killing people. Not for me."

"Why? He deserves it."

"It's just... You can't..." She threw up her hands. "An earl doesn't behave in that manner. It wouldn't be proper."

Everyone had a different definition of proper, he supposed. He hadn't thought Netta would be squeamish when it came to the safety of her sister, but if it upset her to think on it, he wouldn't discuss the matter in front of her.

He ran his finger along the edge of her bodice. "Nothing can be done tonight. Let's talk of something more pleasant."

Her breathing sped up, the tops of her breasts heaving delightfully. "I am in earnest."

"I realize that." And when Netta was in earnest, she was a force to be reckoned with. He only needed to turn her ardor towards more pleasurable endeavors. "I can promise you there will be no blood spilled tonight. Let's not ruin the remainder of our evening."

Her tongue darted out to lick her lips. "I should leave. It would be the sanest course of action."

The back of his neck prickled. "I won't have you running away. I won't allow it."

She pursed her lips and dipped her chin, looking every inch the stern disciplinarian as she glared up at him. "Is that so?"

"'Allow' might be too bold a word." He nestled against her, loving how her lush curves notched perfectly against his body. He ran his hands up and down her waist. "But I do have some alternatives I believe we should explore."

"I am much more amenable to alternatives than orders." She pressed closer, her belly tight against his hardening cock.

Solutions to her problems would take some concentration. Removing an underage girl from her father's care was a sticky situation.

But a solution to their immediate needs was easy to come by.

He lowered his head.

The door flew open, the frame of it hissing against his carpet.

John turned and scowled at Wilberforce. "Whatever emergency you think warrants such an interruption, I can assure you..." His voice trailed off as a second figure joined Wil's in the doorway.

Netta slid from his arms. "Cerise!" She hurried over to the woman. "What has happened? Who did this to you?"

Netta's friend was wrapped in a thick cloak, one much

too warm for the weather. The skin around her right eye was swollen and a bruise darkened the skin at her jaw.

"I do not know his name," Cerise said, her accent more pronounced with her agitation. "Only zat he looked for you."

Wil stalked to the sideboard in the corner of the room and poured a liberal glass of whisky. He returned to the actress's side and pressed it into her hand. "Drink."

Cerise took a small sip, wincing. She touched her bruised lip. "In our dressing room, there was a man. Ugly. With no manners. He said I was to tell him where you were. Zat his employer wanted to speak with you."

Netta clutched her friend's hand. "Who is his employer?"

Cerise gave Netta the glass then dug through her reticule and pulled out a calling card. She exchanged it for the glass.

Netta read it, her face blanching. "Sudworth."

John strode across the room and took the card.

"He recognized me at the masquerade," Netta whispered.

"We don't know that." John's fingers itched to crumple the thick piece of cardstock, but he reined in his temper.

"He must have done." She pressed her fingers to her lips. "I have lived in London unmolested for six years, and it is only now that he's come for me." She closed her eyes. "The carriage abduction. It was him."

"Probable but not definite."

"Why would Sudworth want Miss LeBlanc." Wil's face mottled with anger. "We haven't put your plan into motion yet."

"They have a history."

Wil opened his mouth, but John shook his head. "I just learned of it tonight. It isn't relevant right now."

Wil nodded and shifted closer to Cerise, keeping a watchful eye upon the actress.

"I can never apologize enough," Netta said to Cerise. "I didn't think my past could hurt anyone but me." She gently touched Cerise's cheek. "Why did he do this? You should have told him everything you knew about my whereabouts."

"It would have made no difference." Cerise took another sip of whisky. "He believed me when I said I did not know where you were. He hit me when I refused to lay with him."

Netta gasped. "That bastard! Did he...I mean, should we send for the doctor?"

A physician was a good idea. If not for Cerise, for Wil who would break his own hand from clenching it so. John moved to ring the bell for a servant.

"There is no need," Cerise said. "I have a greater need for a modiste rather than a physician." She untied the strings of her cloak with one hand and pulled it off, handing it to Wil.

"Oh my God," Netta breathed.

John ground his jaw. The spray of blood across the bodice and large rust-colored stain at the hem were disturbing enough. But it was the bloody handprint on her abdomen that was most unsettling.

Cerise threw back the rest of the liquor. "No man strikes me without consequence. And any man who tries to take what is not his will feel the sting of my blade."

John blew out a breath. He couldn't help but be impressed. Netta had chosen her friend wisely. Tough and bloodthirsty. A lot like John himself.

Wil's nostrils flared. "This happens often, does it?"

Cerise stared into her empty glass, and John moved to fill it. Any woman who'd gone through what she had that night deserved every drop of liquor in the house.

"I am an actress at a cheap theatre." Cerise lifted one shoulder. "Men believing they can take what they want is not uncommon. Though zis is the first time I've killed because of it."

Which made John wonder if she'd killed for other reasons.

"I'm going to the theatre," Wil said. "I'll clean up things

on that end."

John nodded. If the crime hadn't already been discovered, Wil would ensure no questions were asked.

Cerise drummed her thumb against her glass, a rapid tattoo. "Dispose of the body, you mean? Already done."

John and Wil locked gazes, the same disbelief in his friend's eyes John knew must be mirrored in his own. If this woman wasn't half his size, he might have been afraid of her. Hell, he should be scared of her in any case.

Netta didn't seem to feel the same misgivings. "You're a marvel," she told her friend. "I only wish I could have been there to help you."

Oh, sure. When John spoke of killing, all he garnered was Netta's squinty-eyed disappointment. When her friend did it, she was all admiration and wonder.

John sniffed. Something about that wasn't fair.

Wil's angry breathing grew more labored, sounding like a bull in rut, and Cerise shifted subtly away from him.

Worried the man might pass out, John took him by the sleeve and pulled him to his desk. "Calm yourself. The woman is unharmed. Mostly."

Wil glowered at him.

John sighed. "We're going to be down another guest room, aren't we?"

"I already told the housekeeper to air one out."

Of course he had. Another stray. John shook his head. But if ever a woman needed a safe place to rest her head that night, it was Cerise.

The woman said something to Netta, gesticulating in that way only the French could.

John turned his back and lowered his voice. "I want men on Sudworth round the clock. I want to know where he is every minute of the day."

"There is an easy solution to this."

John ran a hand through his hair. "Yes, but then my mines will go through probate. It could take years before I can reclaim them. I want to have the deed back in my brother's hands before we strike."

Wil crossed his arms.

"Problem?"

Wil hissed out a breath. "The delay...doesn't please me. But I understand."

"Good." John clapped him on the shoulder. "Now," he said turning, "let's see to Cer...ise?"

The woman lounged on the far settee, balancing her glass on her knee and studying her surroundings.

And Netta was conspicuously absent.

"Where is Netta?" John asked.

"She left."

John's stomach clenched. She left to fetch her friend a cup of chocolate, or licorice, he was sure. She wouldn't be so fool as to—

"She said to tell you she will return later tonight and for you not to wait up for her."

John blinked, but the little black dots refused to leave his vision. He took a step forward. "Where did she go?"

"That is her business. I did not ask." Cerise swirled the amber liquid, looking wholly unconcerned.

John took another step. "Why did she leave?"

"He had a message for her, one he told me before he did this." Cerise gestured to her face. "I assume she left because of it."

John waited, the seconds ticking past, but the woman said no more. "Well? What was the bloody message?"

Wil stood next to him, his body tense.

Cerise looked at them steadily. "It was for Netta. It is her decision whether to tell you or not."

John's fingers itched to shake the woman, but common decency restrained him. That, and the knowledge that Wil would have his throat if he threatened their new stray.

Pinning Cerise with his glare, John said to Wil, "Send messages to my friends. I'm going to need their assistance to find her."

He would take whatever help he could to track the

infuriating woman down.

A bead of sweat rolled down his back. He would find her before she did anything stupid. He would find her safe.

He had to.

And when they found her, he would take great pleasure in personally, and privately, teaching her a lesson she wouldn't soon forget.

Chapter Twenty-Six

His study had been transformed into a war-room. Montague had taken over his desk, sending out missives just as quickly as he could write them. Rothchild and Sutton pored over a map of London, arguing about the best direction to approach Sudworth's house. And Dunkeld sat in the corner, cracking each knuckle in his hand, a sure sign that he was willing and ready to crack some heads.

"Are you certain she has gone to his home?" Rothchild asked. "Sudworth has other properties in London."

"Which she wouldn't know about." John paced, trying to loosen his muscles. Fights were won more easily when he was loose. Clear-headed. Indifferent.

With the way he was feeling now, he'd get his arse kicked. "She's been to his home before."

Rothchild nodded and continued his argument with Sutton.

Montague sealed another letter. "With this note, every one of my contacts will be on the streets looking for her. But as yet no one has seen her near Sudworth's house. You must consider the possibility that she just went out for a walk."

John paused to glare at him. "In the middle of the night?"

Montague leaned back in the chair. "After the behavior at my dinner table tonight, I won't presume to know what either of you might do for entertainment. A stroll about London in the moonlight seems positively tame in comparison. Your Miss Courtney is something of a free-spirit."

"Miss LeBlanc," Sutton corrected. "Courtney was the name Summerset gave her."

Rothchild shook his head. "LeBlanc isn't correct, either. He said her true name was something like Ever...Everrose? Everly?"

"Evered," John gritted out. Who the bloody hell cared about a name? They were wasting time.

Montague pinched his forehead between his thumb and forefinger. "I'm so confused."

"She's Netta." His Netta. "Just call her that." John resumed his pacing. "And you don't know her like I do. She just learned her friend had been hurt. Netta's a vengeful, devious woman. She would want to make Sudworth pay."

"Vengeful and devious?" Dunkeld leaned forward and rested his forearms on his knees. "She sounds like your perfect mate."

Sutton snickered.

John turned his back. He needed better friends. Ones who kept their absurd ideas to themselves. He looked to the door. Wil should be here. He understood the seriousness of the situation, but no, he had felt it more important to attend to their latest resident.

A thick hand landed on his shoulder. Sutton was attached to it, and John grimaced at the tight squeeze. "We'll get her back, have no fear. But I think we're all wondering just who it is we are recovering. This one seems more than your usual plaything."

John shrugged him off and straightened the knot on his cravat. "I don't know what you mean. She's a lovely woman under my protection. I want to ensure she is safe. As I would with any of your wives," he pointed out. Each one of his friends had gotten in their own fair share of trouble and John had been prepared to throw down for each and every one of their women with no questions on his part.

He sniffed. Well, perhaps a few questions. But that was only because he cared for the health and well-being of his friends. His queries had stemmed from a deep, abiding concern. That was the kind of man he was.

Unlike these interfering idiots.

Yes, he couldn't imagine his life without Netta. And yes, he would rip out the heart of any man who hurt her. But he wasn't like his friends. They had all happily settled down in marriage, seemingly content with their domesticity.

Marriage wasn't in his or Netta's future. Fortunately, he'd found the one woman more commitment-shy than he.

His friends shared a look. One that John didn't care for.

"I don't know what you're thinking," he began.

"That the last bachelor standing has been brought to his knees." Rothchild smirked. "I've waited for this day for years. There will be much mocking."

Just as he thought. Arseholes, all of them. Hearing wedding bells where none existed. He rubbed his chest. Netta would laugh at their taunts if she heard them. Where the hell was she?

"Now don't be hasty," Dunkeld said. "Perhaps she merely warms his bed better than most."

The knife at his wrist slipped to his hand without thought. He threw the blade, and satisfaction licked through him when it thumped into the wall next to Dunkeld's head. "If you can't speak of her politely," he said pleasantly, "you'd be wise not to speak of her at all."

Silence descended, with a lot of significant glances between his friends.

"Fine." John crossed his arms. "I care for her. That doesn't change anything." Except the fine thread of panic licking through him at her disappearance. That bit was different. "She's clever. And diverting. And fearless. I've never met a woman like her." And at this very moment she wasn't under his protection. Who knew what damn fool thing she was getting up to?

Montague stood and circled the desk. "We'll find her. We'll find her, and then we'll have a laugh at you. But not before, right men?" His voice said it wasn't an option.

"Aye," Dunkeld grumbled, standing. "Let's get our arses out of these chairs and on the streets. The faster we find her, the faster the mocking can begin."

"John, you and Sutton go to Sudworth's house," Montague directed. "Dunkeld and I will go to the theatre. If she's not there, we'll find out where her apartments are and head over."

"We should all go to Sudworth's." John strode to the wall and yanked his blade from the wood paneling. He cleaned it on his sleeve before sheathing it. "That's where she'll be."

Sutton dug his fingers in his beard and rubbed his chin. "You're not thinking clearly with this one. We don't have proof she went there. We need to cover as much territory as possible."

"She went there." He strode to the cannister of walking sticks tucked next to the bookshelf and chose one with a hard-edged top. He twirled it, getting a feel for its weight. Knives were all well and good, but sometimes a man wanted a real weapon, one he could bludgeon someone with.

He tossed it up and snatched it from the air. "Netta is fool enough to confront Sudworth on her own. When it comes to her friends, I fear her idiocy knows no bounds."

"I thank you for the compliment," an icy voice cut through the room.

Netta stood in the entrance, one hand on the door, the other on her wide hip. She tapped the toe of her slipper and glared at John.

A round face popped up over Netta's shoulder. The features were a softer, less-defined version of Netta.

"Look how handsome they all are." The girl grabbed Netta's shoulders and bobbed on her toes. "You were right. Staying here will be a lark."

John rested the walking stick across both shoulders, gripping the ends. He leaned his head back against it and blew out a breath. He drank in the sight of Netta, his muscles loosening with every inch of unscathed skin he saw.

She was safe. She was angry, but that made no matter now that she was back under his roof.

Netta lifted her chin. "Cerise told me that Sudworth has

negotiated the marriage contract. His servant laughed about the impending marriage, that his master wanted a taste for the fallen sister before marrying the pure one. I could wait no longer to remove her from home."

The chit ducked around Netta. "I hope you have chocolate for breakfast. I prefer the kind from Luxembourg, please."

John closed his eyes. Perfect. Another damned stray to feed.

He looked up and caught the scowl directed at him as Netta wrapped a protective arm around the girl.

And if the younger one was anything like her sister, John didn't know how he would survive.

Chapter Twenty-Seven

John's ankle turned under him, and he wind-milled his arms to keep his balance. "Sodding hell." He kicked the doll he'd stepped on to the side of the hall.

An imp poked his tousled blond head out of the breakfast room. "Ooh, Uncle John said a bad word."

John made to kick the boy, and with a delighted squeal the future Duke of Montague turned and raced back to his morning meal.

John gripped his hips. How had his home been infiltrated in only a matter of hours? It seemed as though he'd just settled Netta's sister into her room when Montague and the rest of his friends had reappeared on his front steps. Only this time, they hadn't come alone.

A thunder of footsteps sounded from the front staircase, so much so that when John turned he expected to find a horde of elephants charging at him.

It was worse.

Four sticky children, eyes wild with the thrill of destruction, pounded around the corner, coming at him as fast as their chubby legs could move. A mangy grey dog nipped at one of the girl's heels and a black and brown mutt led the pack, knocking into John as he loped past.

He raised his hands above his head, trying to side-step around the beasts that he'd sworn an oath to die protecting. He breathed a sigh of relief as the marauding children turned from the hallway to terrorize the breakfast room.

"Good Lord," he muttered. His house has been overtaken. It would need to be quarantined after all the snot-ridden disease-carriers had returned to their respective homes.

Netta's light tinkle of a laugh sounded from the breakfast room, and John straightened his cravat to join the fray. An army of mongrels wouldn't keep him from Netta, not when she had been decidedly sulky all night and morning. He had his work cut out for him charming her out of her bad mood.

Call a woman an idiot once, and she won't let a man forget it. Of course, she hadn't heard when he'd praised her cleverness and fortitude. And wouldn't listen when he'd try to point out that she'd missed the earlier part of the conversation. Infuriating woman.

She laughed again, giving her smiles to someone other than him, and John squared his shoulders. Right. He stepped towards the door, and something small and furry tangled between his feet.

"Gah!" John tripped, falling into the wall. A small orange-and-white kitten hissed at him before darting under a side table. "What in the bloody blazes is going on in here?!"

"Cotton!" A tiny female child ran forwards and peered at the kitten in its hiding place. Her starched petticoat-covered bum poked up at him, and John grabbed his hair. His home was infested. No wonder Judith had ensconced herself on John's pillow. That cat was the one sane creature left in his home. He wished that he could drag Netta away and join the feline.

The bastard responsible for three of the havoc-wreakers strolled from the breakfast room, polishing off the last bite of a roll. Montague plucked the child from the floor and plopped her over his shoulder. "This is real life, Summerset."

The child kicked her legs close to her father's face, and Montague secured them with his forearm. "And it's pretty damn marvelous. I hope you give it a chance someday."

"Ooh, papa said a bad word," the future telltale duke squealed from inside the door.

Both men ignored him.

"Your real life is my nightmare." John pushed off the wall and looked for any more obstacles that could trip him up. "One month ago everything was peaceful." Boring, but then Netta had arrived. "My home was neat and tidy." Sterile. He quite liked finding empty wax paper bags of Netta's sweets in his bedroom, one of her stockings strewn over a chair. "As soon as this is over, I deserve a return to normalcy." Assuming his new normal included Netta. If she left and he remained as he was before, without occupation, without any fire in his life, he...well, he didn't quite know what he'd do with himself.

He set his shoulders. As soon as he had his brother's deed returned and made Sudworth pay, he would have time to devise a plot to keep Netta in his life on a more permanent basis. He'd find lavish apartments for her, have jars full of Pomfret cakes on every table.

"Real life is noisy. Untidy." The child tugged on Montague's hair, and he grinned. "And it's absolutely wonderful. It's family, and you're stuck with us."

John sniffed, trying to look disapproving. But he supposed even though the children were irritating little monsters now, they might grow into interesting adults.

The child lifted her skirts, exposing her undergarments, and John stared at the ceiling. It was possible.

"In order to preserve my sanity, I want to end this tonight." John followed Montague into the breakfast room. His servants had added a second table to accommodate everyone, and John squeezed past Netta and her sister to reach his chair. Netta ignored him and leaned in further to her conversation with Dunkeld's wife, Winnifred. They had only met this morning but already seemed as thick as two thieves.

John sank into his chair and crossed one leg over the other. "I've invited Sudworth to The Black Rose, ostensibly to deliver the document from the Dutch embassy to him. I will persuade him to play for my brother's deed, giving you and the others time to implement your plans."

"I think that is the cue for the children to play outside." Colleen stood, holding an infant to her shoulder and patting his back. "And this one needs a nap."

"Eleanor, go help with the children," Netta said. "You can show them your skill at lawn bowling."

Eleanor nodded agreeably and stood.

John's boot nudged Netta's foot, and she slid it away, as though that slight contact was unpleasant.

He wasn't sure where Eleanor came by her amiability, but the trait had skipped her sister.

The children ran, skipped, and tumbled out of the room, leaving all the adults minus Sutton's wife. The noise level dropped to something bearable, and John took a deep breath.

"Right. Tonight we strike." He reached for Netta's chocolate and took a sip. "Tomorrow, everyone gets out of my house."

Netta frowned.

"Almost everyone," he amended.

"I've put out word that the club will be closed tonight for a private event. Most of the workers have been given the evening off." Sutton leaned back and draped his arm over his wife's empty chair. "I have retained the services of the girl I mentioned. With Sudworth's predilection, I'm certain he'll like her."

"Predilection?" Amanda asked.

"He likes proper young girls," Rothchild told his wife. "Enjoys watching them degraded. Broken. Sutton will offer him a show. We hope he'll agree to the game of hazard with her as the stake instead of Miss...Netta."

Amanda looked horrified. "You can't possibly mean to involve a child—"

Sutton held up a hand. "Of course not. But we have a new woman, early twenties, who can still look the part. She's agreed to a scene tonight."

Netta's knuckles went white, and John eased her fist from the table and rubbed them with his thumb. With Netta, the bastard hadn't just watched. He'd enjoyed inflicting pain himself. "He'd be a fool to gamble the ore mines for a night with a doxy. He could pay for the same for much cheaper. It's true proper misses he wants to hurt, not a simulation. But I have an alternative if he declines."

His pulse tripped at the thought of that alternative. But he wasn't planning on losing. The special order that had been delivered two days ago would ensure it.

"I wish I could be there for the fun," Dunkeld said. "But I know we all have our parts to play tonight. And I don't trust Liverpool's newest batch of men to pick up Sudworth's associates and interrogate them properly without me." He frowned. "They all seem so mealy-mouthed and... puny."

Anyone was puny next to the Scotsman, but John held his tongue. Times were changing, and the new crop of spies were a different breed than he was used to, as well.

He looked around the table at his friends and their wives. His friends now, as well. There had been many years of such talks around a table. Plotting. Scheming. Having a romping-good time.

His chest ached hollowly. He couldn't go back and revisit the past. Those times were ending. This might be the last round-table he and his brothers-in-arms were ever to have. Next time they all sat together it might be only to compare the competence of their nurses and how much Baby Annie had grown.

As eager as he was to take Sudworth apart, he couldn't deny the twinge of sorrow that this could be his last caper.

He finally had to grow up.

"I don't understand. What are the rest of you going to do while John gambles?" Netta bit her lip. "And how will it keep Sudworth away from my sister?"

"The time has come for a full frontal-attack." John twisted the ring on his thumb. "While I am winning back the deed, my friends will be dismantling Sudworth's network. We've had him watched for weeks now and have noted his henchmen, his investors. If we can't find evidence sufficient for Liverpool to move against him, we will go after his soft-underbelly."

Netta wrinkled her nose. "Which is?"

"His purse." Blunt and women, every man's weakness. "Montague will use his contacts in shipping to spike Sudworth's commerce. He will find that his clients in England will no longer use his ships."

"I've also spoken with the Carpenters and Brewers Guild, two of his largest sources of workers, and they've agreed that it is high time to press for higher wages." One edge of Montague's lips curled. "A strike might even be in order. His contracts will dry up. His suppliers will raise their rates. Without his money, he will in essence by neutralized."

"You can do that?" Netta's jaw dropped open.

John arched an eyebrow. "He may have money but he doesn't have the fortune of a good birth. Our *beau monde* bigotry will for once serve us well. Every duke, marquess, earl, and baron will band with us and lock him out of the higher echelons of society. And business."

Amanda gently cleared her throat, pushing a stray wisp of dark hair off her face. "I'm loath to ask, but are you certain your fellow peers will agree? No one here has a spotless reputation with the ton. Most look down upon us, even with the assorted titles between our families."

"They'll fall in line." Montague pressed his lips together. "I may not receive all the invitations to balls that I used to, thank God, but I am the eighth Duke of Montague, thirteenth in line to the Crown. And the five of us have enough investments spread through the country that a man would be a fool to go against us. Their fortunes wouldn't survive long."

"I wish there was more we could do to help." Elizabeth drummed her fingers on the table. "I'm not fond of the idea of us women sitting at home while you all risk life and limb."

Montague dipped his chin. "I fear it is *ennui* rather than concern that makes you eager to assist. I believe you miss the thrill of spying."

Netta turned her head and mouthed to John: *She was a spy, too?*

John nodded. Elizabeth had been an amateur in espionage when they'd met, but a talented one. He bit back a grin at the envious pinch to Netta's mouth.

"Perhaps I do feel a bit dull." Elizabeth shrugged. "I was quite good at it. I don't find it at all fair that you and the men get to have all the fun."

Montague leaned forwards and pressed a light kiss to her mouth. "Next time we have to destroy a man's livelihood and uncover his plot against the Dutch, you will be the first one pressed into service."

Amanda leaned forwards. "While I don't share my sister's sense of adventure—"

"You and Colleen each have one child for now," Elizabeth interrupted. "I remember that time when you could spend hours staring at the being you brought into existence. But wait until you have several. The desire to escape the house will become overwhelming, even for you."

Colleen swept into the room, this time unencumbered by her babe. "What's this? Has it been determined that Max and I are to have more children already?"

Sutton chuckled and drew her to sit on his lap.

"As I was saying before I was so rudely interrupted," Amanda said loudly, "although I have no desire to join in this evening's escapades, I do want to know the progress of each of your endeavors. Perhaps we could use this house as an information center. Each of you send messages here with your status?"

"That is a good idea." Montague nodded. "And if something goes wrong, having one command post to direct inquiries and requests for assistance is a sensible precaution. You ladies can be our overseers."

Netta sighed. "I love directing a show. I hate to miss it." She turned to John. "Perhaps I should send a note to Lady Mary, tell her Cerise and I can't perform this evening as we agreed. Cerise, after all, has just had a fright. It is not unreasonable to cancel."

"And Wilberforce told me this morning that your friend sounded eager to act in the small performance." John raised her hand to his lips. "He thought that it would do her good, help her take her mind off of last night."

Wil had sent Cerise and Netta's apologies to their stage manager. Effective immediately, they were no longer employed at The Burns. Both women had argued that such unprofessional behavior would harm their future employment, but had eventually understood that their safety would be harder to secure at that location.

"It will do you good, as well," he told her. "You should be performing instead of sitting about worrying when there is nothing you can do."

"I know." She slouched in her seat. "That doesn't mean I'm happy about it."

Nor was he in particular. He'd prefer Netta to stay at home with the other women and a host of servants surrounding them. But he'd spoken the truth that it would help her to perform that night. It wouldn't do for her to worry herself sick. Or to hare off and do something foolish. An unoccupied Netta was a menace.

"I would suggest you take your sister with you, but until we get her situation sorted, it's best she not show her face outside this house." The last thing he needed was a Bow Street runner at his door. After Sudworth was dealt with, John would move on to Viscount Darby. It shouldn't present a problem. The man was eager to sell off his daughters. John would pay to take the chit off his hands and place her under her sister's care.

"What of Sudworth after tonight?" Sutton rested his chin on Colleen's shoulder. "There are times when Liverpool finds it more convenient not to press charges."

All the better for John. "You don't have to worry about it. Leave him to me."

"John." Montague's voice was quiet. "Executions aren't our style."

"I think we all have blood on our hands from our past association with the Crown." John's body tensed. "And my style has always been different from yours."

"Not this different."

John's body heated. He dared any of his friends to claim he wouldn't do the same if a man had hurt their wives. Not that Netta was his wife, but still, there was a principle to uphold. The hypocrisy wouldn't be tolerated.

Netta squeezed his hand under the table. "I don't know how I feel about someone being killed on my behalf. I don't quite think I'd like it."

Her gaze was steady, without judgment, and John sighed. His job would be much easier if she were his bloodthirsty Netta today. This softer woman, showing compassion for a man who deserved none, complicated the issue.

He ran his thumb along the soft skin of her palm. "What would you have me do? Let him roam free? Go on as before?" He didn't think such an act of forgiveness was possible on his part.

"There are other ways to punish a man besides prison," Rothchild said. He didn't bother to say 'or death,' and for that, John was grateful. "We use the talents around the table. I can break into just about anywhere. Take anything of his you'd want. Or plant evidence against him, as well."

Sutton tugged on his beard. "I've seen most of his properties in London. Dry wood. Poor construction. Sadly for him, very susceptible to fire." He grinned, his eyes lighting up at the thought of arson as they always did.

"A man such as he has his self-worth wrapped up in his wealth," Elizabeth added. "When you strip that away, there will be nothing left of him. You might even be able to arrange a cell for him in debtor's prison."

"Yes." Montague buttered a roll and handed it to his wife. "The ways to destroy a man are limitless."

John's chest expanded until he found it difficult to breathe. He might lack the strong bonds of affection most men had with their brothers, but he had never lacked for family.

He looked around the table. Their plan was neat, with

alternatives and redundancies. There was no possible way for Sudworth to escape ruin. If he wasn't put away tonight, the man would wish he had been.

John rubbed his hands together. He almost wished this last adventure would present more of a challenge. A victory he could take pride in and reminisce over next to a crackling fire with Netta curled by his side.

"Oy, what about me?" Dunkeld asked, frowning. "I don't think I have any special talents that would help to destroy a man's livelihood."

John rose to his feet and stretched. "Your talent is obvious. Beat the hell out of anyone that gets in our way."

Chapter Twenty-Eight

Netta sat with one leg over the armrest of the settee, a glass of wine resting on her stomach. Members of The Minerva chattered excitedly about her, asking questions about being an actress, about performing, but Netta let Cerise respond.

She fingered the emerald pendent John had given her the night of the masquerade. It rarely left her neck these days. It made her feel closer to him to wear it.

Where was John right now? Had he left for The Black Rose? Was he even now sitting across from Sudworth, playing for his livelihood?

The thought of seeing Sudworth again made her palms sweat and stomach cramp. And she knew she couldn't assist John. But it didn't feel right her drinking wine with Mary and Cerise while he faced down the devil.

Cerise shot her elbow into Netta's ribs.

"Gah!" Netta dropped her leg to the floor and straightened, rubbing her side. "What was that for?"

"Lady Walpole just asked us a question which I feel you can answer best." Cerise's smile was all clenched teeth.

Netta recognized that look. It was one she'd learned to be wary around. Her friend was nearing the end of her patience.

"I apologize." She turned to Lady Walpole. "What was the question?"

The middle-aged woman leaned forward in her chair, the feather in her turban bobbing. "Whether it was true that actresses took a different lover each week. My sister said that they did, but I said that it would be too exhausting."

A muffled cough drew her gaze to the far wall. Wilberforce sat as sentinel in the one hard-backed chair in the room. His position hadn't changed. He'd sat in that spot through her and Cerise's performance on the small stage. He remained in that spot as they chatted after the show. The man sat and watched, and apparently tried his best not to laugh at the impertinent questions.

"Lady Walpole," she began.

"There are no ladies in The Minerva." Mary swept into the room, John's grandmother at her side. Mary arranged a pillow on the wingback chair next to Netta and helped Catherine to sit down. She took her own seat and shook out her skirts. "Titles are dropped at the door. I believe I shall have the next person who breaks that rule needlepoint it into pillows as reminders."

That horrifying threat stilled everyone's tongues for a moment.

"Now." Mary accepted the glass of port a footman brought over. "Do you want to answer questions on the sexual customs of actors or do you consider that a boorish inquiry? I, for one, would have adored having a different lover each week when I was younger. Although coordinating the liaisons with so many men would be difficult. They are such sensitive creatures."

Another snort from the far wall, but all the women had seemed by mutual agreement to ignore Wilberforce. He had been allowed into the club as their escort and then promptly forgotten.

Although Cerise's gaze had flown towards him many times that evening, Netta had noticed. Usually with scorn or disdain, but that was her friend's main manner of flirting.

"Why wait a week?" Cerise draped her arm on the seatback and gave Lady Walpole a tight smile. "I find if I don't switch up my lovers every two days I become quite dull."

Wilberforce didn't smother a laugh at that. His corner of the room remained decidedly silent.

"How did you enjoy the play?" Netta asked Catherine. A silly part of her hoped John's grandmother was impressed by her performance. John might not care what his grandmother thought, but family ties were stronger than even he could imagine, and Netta desired her approval.

"I was impressed with what just the two of you could do." Catherine gripped the nob of her walking stick with bent fingers. "And all the costume changes you made..." She shook her head. "Changing your outfits that quickly is an artform in and of itself."

Praise at changing her clothes wasn't exactly what Netta sought, but she'd take it. "I'm afraid in our haste to change costumes, Cerise and I left your backstage quite a mess, Mary. Clothing is strewn everywhere." Netta placed her wineglass down and rose. "I'd best go see to it."

At the hint of anything as dull as cleaning, most of the women stood and drifted out of the room. "I believe I'll go see if anyone is using the archery range," Lady Walpole said.

"But I want to dance," her friend said.

The crowd left before Netta heard the resolution to that disagreement. Only Cerise, Mary, Catherine, and herself remained. And Wilberforce, of course.

Cerise held out her hand and Netta pulled her to her feet. Dark shadows were emerging under her friend's eyes and her shoulders drooped.

"Go get yourself a cup of coffee and put your feet up somewhere," Netta told her. "I'll take care of the costumes."

Cerise faux-shuddered. "And face more questions about the bed sport of actresses? No, I thank you. I'll stay away from the crowds."

"I am sorry about that," Mary said. "Some people have damned fool ideas. I don't think she meant to give offense."

"And only a little was taken." Cerise pressed her hand to her lower back and stretched.

"There are places in the club that are private where you

could rest in peace." Netta turned her friend's shoulders and pushed her towards the door. "Mary, would you show her that lovely spot in the gardens by the gazebo? I believe she can rest there unmolested." She turned to Wilberforce. "But you should accompany her to be sure."

The man looked eager, uncomfortable, and nauseous all at the same time. "I'm supposed to be watching both of you."

"And I'll come find you as soon as I tidy up. Go on." She gave her friend another small push, and Cerise glared back at her over her shoulder.

Netta pursed her lips and blew her friend an air kiss.

Wilberforce stood and walked stiffly to Cerise, presenting his arm. With obvious reluctance, she took it.

"Two cups of coffee and one romantic, I mean to say private, place to rest, coming up." Mary winked at Netta and led Cerise and Wil from the room.

"Can I get you anything, Catherine?" Netta asked. "I can help you to another room first."

"No, thank you, dear." Catherine settled back and closed her eyes. "I'll just rest for a bit myself."

Netta nodded and headed for the stage. She folded the costumes and stacked them in a large chest. The silence of the room was only broken by her footsteps. The time after a performance, when the crowds were gone and the stage empty, was usually what Netta liked best. But tonight her nerves didn't calm. She handled the costumes more roughly than they deserved, her thoughts on John.

The game had surely started by now. Was he winning? Would he keep his temper and allow Sudworth to leave with only his pride harmed? And what of his friends? Was she only hours away from being free from the threat?

She blew out a breath. Waiting while others acted wasn't her style. She found she didn't care for it.

A board creaked.

Netta paused, shifting her weight, but not hearing the sound again. She looked to Catherine. The woman's face was hidden by the wingback and her dark gown almost matched the black fabric of the chair. She was almost as invisible as she was silent. The noise hadn't come from her.

Shrugging, Netta moved for the long red wig hanging off a nail, and a board creaked again.

She whirled around, and the knife the man held at waist-height pressed into her bodice.

"Who are you?"

He stepped closer, digging the tip of the blade into the fabric. "Don't ask stupid questions." He twisted his wrist, and Netta gasped at the sharp sting to her abdomen. "One of the men working here was kind enough to tell me about the exit off the stage, and that's where we're going." He jerked his head to the side door. "Move."

A pale oval peeked at them from behind the wingback, and Netta gave her head a quick shake no.

Catherine couldn't make a sound. A man like this wouldn't hesitate to hurt an old woman, not if it saved his own neck. Netta didn't know what she'd do if she were responsible for getting John's grandmother killed.

"No?" the ruffian said, mocking, mistaking her head gesture. He twisted the blade again, and Netta fell a step back with a cry.

He followed, keeping up the pressure.

"No. I mean yes. Yes, I'll go with you." She'd go with him until they were further down the hall, away from the immediate threat to Catherine. Then she'd scream and fight and hope those burly servants of the club were useful for something more than serving drinks and looking pretty.

She turned, the relief at having the knife no longer pressed into her belly quickly evaporating when she felt the point at her side. She looked around as she glided out of the backstage area, searching for anything that could be used as a weapon or a distraction.

Nothing readily presented itself.

The back hall was dim, lit only by one gas lamp by the far door. The door that exited onto a back alley. One she couldn't leave from, not if she expected to live.

"How did you find me?" Perhaps if she flung herself into

one of the rooms they passed she'd have time to lock the door before he followed.

"We've been watching you since the masquerade ball."

She pretended to stumble. "There's a pebble in my slipper." She braced a hand on the wall and made to bend down, "If I could just—"

He knocked her arm off the wall, and she stumbled in earnest. He straightened her shoulders and pushed her down the hall. "Deal with it."

"Why does Sudworth want me?" She hated the tremor in her voice. But it made no sense. "I am past the age of consent. He and my father can no longer force me to marry. What good am I to him?" Even as she said it, she knew her words were foolish. To a man such as Sudworth, a woman made helpless in his presence offered a great deal.

A broom leaned next to the exit door. She set her shoulders. When he opened the door, she would grab it and crush his bloody windpipe with the tip of the handle.

"You broke a contract of his." He prodded her with the blade again. "He doesn't take kindly to interferences in his business matters."

Netta clenched her hand. She wasn't a business matter. Her sister wasn't a business matter. And she would make him pay for thinking of them as nothing more than property.

Five steps away. Her palms tingled. She could do this.

"There's also the matter of my missing brother." The ruffian removed the blade from her back.

Netta frowned, the focus she had on the broom breaking. "What? Who's your brother?" she asked, turning to look over her shoulder.

It was too quick. He'd already started to bring his arm down. She had time only to loose a startled shriek before the thick handle of the blade struck her temple.

She crumpled to the floor, the back of her hand smacking the bristles of the broom. Her finger twitched, her fuzzy mind thinking to stick to her plan, pull the broom towards her. She fought against the blackness, but it closed tight about her, wrapping her in its senseless embrace.

Chapter Twenty-Nine

A trickle of sweat rolled from John's nape down under his collar. He rolled the dice, gritting his teeth as they tumbled over the table.

Deuce-aces. Sodding hell.

Sudworth grinned broadly. "It doesn't appear to be your night, Summerset."

Elsbeth, the charming woman they'd employed to entice Sudworth, settled on the man's lap and clapped her hands. "You win again!"

Sudworth slid his hand up her side and gave her breast a squeeze, but didn't take his eyes off John.

They were in an upper room of The Black Rose, the rest of the club empty. Three cut-throats, ostensibly Sudworth's servants, held up the back wall, one of them cleaning his nails with his knife. Sutton had brought them drinks when the game began and then disappeared.

"My luck will change." John grabbed the onyx nob of his walking stick leaning on the table and ground the tip into the carpet. "It's bound to."

"Now you sound like your brother." Sudworth plucked up a die and rolled it over his knuckles.

John gritted his teeth. The night was not going as planned. First, the man who'd partnered with Elsbeth in the humiliation scene had been late to work. Giving Sudworth much too much time to examine the altered documents John had delivered to him.

To the credit of John's forgery skills, Sudworth hadn't seemed to notice anything amiss. He also hadn't seemed overly impressed with the bait John had dangled. He'd been inattentive during Elsbeth's scene, had shown no interest in engaging with her further, and seemed eager to leave The Black Rose.

Until John had proposed a game of hazards.

And Sudworth had been beating the odds all night. John was almost afraid to propose his wager for fear of losing.

He squeezed the nob of his walking stick. Almost. Precautions had been taken.

Sudworth shoved Elsbeth off his lap, ignoring her glare. He tossed up the die and snatched it from the air. "Well, amusing as this has been, I have places to be, people to do." He scooped up the blunt John had lost.

"And here I thought you were a real gambler." John smoothed his cravat down his chest. "I still have money to waste. Why not be the fortunate beneficiary of it?"

"Do you?" Sudworth placed the dice in a wooden cup and knocked them about. "Until you earn back your deed, your finances aren't in the best of shape."

"Breaking into the Dutch embassy wasn't an end to my service?" John faked a yawn. "What a surprise."

Sudworth barked a laugh. "You do amuse me, Summerset. One more job, I think."

There was never just one more job. "And this one? Am I to steal the king's crown?"

"Nothing so dramatic." He jerked his head at one of his men. The ruffian pushed off the wall and escorted Elsbeth from the room. "All I want is for you to blow up the Dutch ambassador's residence."

John stilled. "Your definition of dramatic seems to differ from mine. What has the man done to you?"

"Nothing at all."

"And yet you want him dead." Thank heavens this charade ended tonight. There was no way to fake destroying a building.

Sudworth shrugged. "The man doesn't have to be at home."

John's mind flew. First an attempt to malign Sir Raffles's reputation. Second, a stolen document and map of apparent trading routes from the Dutch embassy. Now, an outright attack on Holland's interests.

Trading routes.... "Everything is money to you. All of this will somehow increase your profits."

Sudworth picked up his glass of Scotch whisky and took a sip. "You wound me. You don't believe I want justice against Raffles?"

John didn't even bother to respond to that absurdity. "Raffles is working on a treaty with the Dutch. Trying to stabilize the region of the West Indies. If the ambassador is attacked, relations between the two countries will be strained. The treaty might fail."

"And the British Empire might lose some of the territory it's stolen," Sudworth said.

John snorted. "Don't play that game with me. I know you care nothing about the morality of our politics." He tapped his thumb on the walking stick. "But you do care about freedom for your trade routes. And if you're worried a stronger government presence in the area will stop what you're shipping, it must not be legal."

Sudworth narrowed his eyes. "As I said, I have to leave. I don't have time for your guessing games."

"Not even for the chance to win fifty thousand pounds?" John swallowed past the lump in his throat. He would have to sell off many of his properties if he lost. He would have next to nothing. But he needed a number high enough to pique the man's interest. "I propose one more game. Winner take all."

Sudworth's eyebrows shot up. "Fifty thousand for my deed?"

"My brother's estate, while large, is in need of many repairs. It is a fair bet." He forced his shoulders to relax. "But if you are afraid of losing, I understand."

Sutton slipped through the door and gave John a nod. He shuffled to the side table and poured himself a drink. A large one. The nod told John their mission had been successful; the whisky said it hadn't been easy.

"Besides, soon that fifty thousand will be all you have to live upon." John leaned back in his chair. "I don't think you can afford not to play."

One of his ruffians pushed off the wall, not liking John's tone, but Sudworth held up a hand. "Explain."

John pretended to examine his ring. "Your scheme has been thwarted. Your associates have been taken in for questioning. Liverpool is aware of everything."

Sudworth's shoulders inched towards his ears. "I doubt he knows *everything*. Even you don't understand my motives."

"Slaves." Sutton's knuckles whitened around his glass. "The English have been trying to eliminate slavery around the world, and the effort is cutting into his profits."

"His trading ships carry slaves?" John's blood ran cold. That trade was a stain on human civilization. England's efforts reflected the best of their country. The noose was tightening, slowly but surely, on slavers. Creating chaos between nations would only make it easier for arseholes like Sudworth to evade prosecution.

Sutton nodded. "Dunkeld has learned much from the men he picked up." He turned his narrow-eyed gaze on Sudworth. "But the night is young, and there is much more your friends are eager to tell."

Sudworth slammed his glass onto the table, amber liquid sloshing over the rim.

"What?" John chuckled. "You didn't think you would get away with it, did you? That I would be so desperate for my mines that I would betray my country? You did? How droll."

Sudworth and his men tensed. Sutton tensed. Everyone in the room was as stiff as blocks of marble.

John stretched languidly. "Even now Liverpool is sending people to arrest you. Your legal fees to fight the charges will be immense. And my friends are ensuring that your other investments are soon to take a turn for the worse. You want to make this bet."

"I don't know that I believe you." Sudworth leaned back and laced his fingers behind his head. "My investments are many and varied. It will be hard to take me down. Besides, what evidence is there of any wrongdoing on my part? *You* planted a letter. *You* stole from the Dutch embassy. What have I done?"

The bastard smirked, and John's fingers itched to smack the expression off his face.

"In fact, with the information I can provide to Liverpool in service to our country, I just might earn myself a medal," Sudworth said. "I'm aware of many plots against the nation, have learned of many criminal enterprises. I think the prime minister would be happy to trade for that information."

John flapped his hand dismissively, but inside he burned. Liverpool had made such deals before. Information for liberty. The prime minister's first concern was the smooth management of the nation, and sometimes that meant letting Justice hide her eyes.

"Does that mean you no longer wish to play?" John loosed a dramatic sigh. "And here I thought you were a man after my own heart, one who relished a bit of risk-taking."

"How right you are." Sudworth waved two fingers, and one of his men sauntered over. "We are men of similar interests."

"Don't play with him, John." Robert strode into the room, and John blinked, trying to hide his surprise.

What in the bloody hell was his brother doing here?

Robert rested his hand on the back of John's chair. "The man cheats. And I finally figured out how."

"Well, of course he cheats." John pushed from the table and stood, not liking the way the hand of one of Sudworth's men drifted towards his inner pocket. He positioned himself between his brother and the rest of the room. "That doesn't mean I don't still intend to win."

He lowered his voice. "What are you doing here?"

Robert tugged at his scarf, exposing the bottom edge of

his scar. "Wil sent me a note. Said you might need me."

John clenched his fist. Damned Wilberforce. Just as interfering as Netta when it came to attempting family reconciliations.

"Is Robert joining us?" Sudworth shook the cup of dice. "Good. I enjoy beating him almost as much as I do you, Summerset."

"For the deed, I'll play." John turned, knocking his walking stick to the floor. He squatted and smoothly uncapped the nob, removing the dice he'd specially ordered and tucking them up his sleeve. He replaced the nob and stood. "I'll play, but we'll use a fresh pair of dice." He nodded to Sutton, who took a clean pair from a drawer in a bureau.

Sudworth would use the fresh pair. And if John needed it, he would use his. "You won't cheat again. Robert and Sutton will ensure it."

Sudworth chuckled. "You think you have it all worked out. That you have me in a box." He held up his hand, and his man dropped something into it. "I've survived too long to allow that. You'll play, but you won't play for the deed. That's mine. You'll play for this." He tossed the object into the middle of the table.

It landed with a small clink, the gold chain of the necklace glinting in the lamplight.

John froze. It couldn't be. She hadn't been wearing it that night. Had she?

He grasped the emerald pendant. The deep green stone warmed his palm, seeming to hold the warmth from Netta's skin within it.

Sudworth raised his hands palm up, grinning broadly. "When I said we had similar interests, I didn't mean gambling."

Chapter Thirty

The gemstone cut into John's palm. "Where did you get this?"

"Our pretty little friend gave it to me." Sudworth leaned back and hooked his thumbs under his braces. "Did you know she and I were once betrothed? She did me a favor by calling it off. She is a bit on the shelf now. I will be happier with her younger sister."

John ground his back teeth so hard his jaw ached. One small slice at the jugular. Or one tiny nick at the femoral vein and this worthless piece of shit's life would be over. John didn't usually enjoy killing, but he'd make an exception for Sudworth.

"Where. Is. She?"

Sudworth lifted one shoulder. "Girls like that, who can tell? Without the protection of a man, a woman out on the streets at night doesn't last long."

Robert stilled John's hand. He hadn't even realized he'd palmed his dagger until his brother stopped him from using it.

"My men can find her," Sudworth continued. "Whether they find her unharmed, well, that is up to you."

Sutton rested his fist on his hip, his hand a quick distance to the pistol John knew he kept at the small of his back. "Our men are exceptional at searching out lost people. We'll find her. And when we do, those that have her will be made to pay."

"That sounds like an accusation." Sudworth tutted. "Your men must already have my properties under observation, so where could she be?" He tapped his index finger against his lips. "For our last game, I propose a different set of stakes. You win, I'll tell my men to deliver little Netta when they find her. I win, you deliver her sister. Her father has already signed the contract. There's nothing you can do to stop this wedding."

A bead of sweat slid down his temple. It felt like his veins were filled with fire instead of blood. The absolute nerve of this man. He actually thought John would deliver up a small child if he lost. That John wouldn't kill him where he stood once he'd found Netta.

Sudworth must think himself invincible.

"Of course, if you'd rather play for the deed to Robert's estate instead of the woman, I'm open to that, as well." Sudworth drummed his fingers on the table. "It depends on what means more to you — recovering your wealth, or Miss Agnes Evered."

John shook his head, trying to rid his ears of the faint ringing echoing inside. It grew louder. Netta or his steel production. How bloody ironic. He'd only come to know Netta because she was helping him save his fortunes. And now he was going to lose it all because he couldn't live without her.

"New deal." His voice was raw, his words sounding like they were dragged over gravel. "I won't play games, not for Netta." Even with his loaded dice, he couldn't risk it. Risk her. "But I will trade." He swallowed, his next words sticking in his throat. "My letters patent for Netta."

Robert hissed in air. He knew as well as John that giving that away would truly be the end to the House of Summerset. At least for many, many years. Until John developed a new formula, discovered new products to rebuild their coffers.

It would hurt giving away his prized discovery. Taking his income back down to nigh on nothing. But he'd have Netta. And with her by his side, he'd rebuild, get back in the laboratory as he should have done years ago.

She had a bad licorice habit he'd need to pay for after

all.

Sudworth steepled his fingers. "Now that is an interesting proposition." He stared at John a moment. "And one I accept." He stood and stretched out his hand.

John was loath to take it. He didn't know how he'd restrain himself from yanking the man down until his nose made sharp contact with the table. But he was making a gentleman's agreement. His stomach twisted as he shook Sudworth's hand. Though there was nothing gentlemanly about it, the formalities needed to be observed.

John made to release Sudworth's hand, but the man gripped him tighter. "I didn't think you'd make such a poor choice. Don't you know that with money you can buy another woman?"

John yanked his hand free. "There isn't another woman like her." He made eye contact with Sutton and his brother, giving them small shakes of his head. They wouldn't be fighting it out in this room. Not when there was a chance Netta would be hurt. "The letters patent are in the vault at my bank. I will need until tomorrow to retrieve them."

"Of course." Sudworth took his jacket from the back of his chair and shrugged into it. "My house, tomorrow night. I'll have the girl brought there."

"Without a mark on her," John growled.

"Who can say what will have happened to a woman on the streets of London?" Sudworth's men flanked him, forming a solid wall. "She will be as unharmed as possible."

Sutton grasped one of his arms. Robert clasped his shoulder. They obviously thought they needed to hold him back.

They should have known him better. John's first objective was to retrieve Netta. That required playing nice now. His vision tunneled until he saw only Sudworth's face. But John would avenge any and every mark on her. Sudworth's screams of agony would be the music John listened to as he made him pay, cut for cut, bruise for bruise.

"I believe I'll pay a call on Liverpool." Sudworth

adjusted the cuffs of his jacket. "It's time we had a chat." He dipped his chin to look at John. "You didn't truly think I'd end up in prison, did you? Men like me never do."

John's nails bit into his palm. Sudworth should hope he ended up in jail. The other alternative was much less pleasant. He turned in place, watching as the men filed out of the room.

Sutton stepped to his side. "We'll find her, John." His words were quiet, and with as much assurance as was possible. But both Sutton and John knew. Sometimes, right didn't win. Sometimes innocents got hurt. Killed.

John pressed his hand against his thigh to hide its quiver. "Yes. We check all his properties again. Press all our informants. Netta is somewhere in London, and we need to find her."

***

"If he wants me, use me. Tell him you'll give me to him if he gives us Netta." Eleanor crossed her arms over the front of her over-large night dress and paced in front of the fireplace. It had been three hours since John had returned home, and the commotion caused by the news of Netta's disappearance had roused the whole household. Her aggravating sister included.

John fingered the necklace in his pocket. "I've already told you. If we cannot find her, I will trade my letters patent for her. You aren't getting involved."

The chit scowled. "But it will be hours before the banks open. Hours when Netta is trapped with that man." She ducked her head, her loose hair swinging to hide her face.

John gripped the back of his neck. Comforting children wasn't one of his many skills. But she was Netta's sister. The person Netta loved most in the world. He inched up to her like she was a snake that could strike at any moment and patted her shoulder. "There, there. It's all going to be fine."

She shoved her hair behind her ear and glared at him.

Montague strode into the study, Sutton a step behind. "I've never heard anyone sound less reassuring." He plucked a blanket from the back of a chair and wrapped it

310

around Eleanor's shoulders. He chucked her chin. "But it *will* be all right, dear. We'll make certain of it."

Eleanor gave him a tremulous smile. "Thank you, your grace."

Sutton chuckled. "Your scowl outdid the child's," he said to John.

John turned his back and gripped the fireplace mantel. He couldn't find Netta. He couldn't comfort her sister. What the hell good was he? "Have you learned anything?"

The pregnant silence behind him said everything.

"London is a big city." Sutton heaved a breath. "We'll keep searching, but it might come down—"

"—to me turning over my patent." He was resigned to losing his crowning achievement, but he agreed with Eleanor. There was too much time between now and the appointed exchange that evening. Too much time for Netta to be alone with the blackguards.

His knuckles went white. She was a courageous woman, but she had to be frightened. Wondering why he hadn't come for her yet. He blinked, refusing to let the tears fall.

"I can't believe you're going to give him your steel formula."

John turned. He hadn't heard Robert enter. "What would you have me do? She's worth..." *Everything.* He faced the wall once more. He felt as raw as an exposed wound. He wasn't the sort of man to show his feelings, even to his friends. Wasn't the sort of man to *feel* deep emotions.

Damn Netta. She'd done this to him. And now she'd gone and gotten herself kidnapped.

"What happened to your face?" Eleanor's question was innocent, one only a child would ask so casually.

John gripped the mantel tighter. He looked in the mirror to catch his brother's tense expression.

"Acid."

Eleanor cocked her head. "Did someone throw it on you?"

Robert locked eyes with John's reflection. "No. A miscalculation."

"Enough!" Rage exploded out of John. He spun and advanced on his brother. "You're holding onto your spite now? When a woman's life is at risk? You have a scar on your face. Who cares? It's well past time that you moved the hell on."

Robert's jaw dropped, stretching the puckered skin tight.

"While I applaud the sentiment and feel it long overdue, there are young ears in the room," Montague reminded him, with a nod to Eleanor. "Language."

John threaded his fingers in his hair and pulled until the sting helped him focus. Netta was missing and he was sure as shit that her sister wouldn't care about his foul words. Nevertheless, he blew out a breath and nodded. "Apologies. Perhaps this is a good time for you to return to bed. I'll wake you if we learn anything new."

"Which is now." Amanda hurried in, two older women following more slowly.

"Auntie May?" John ignored his grandmother. "What are you doing here at this hour?"

"It seems that everyone is here at this hour." Mary bent her finger at her nephew and raised her face. "Which means you all know about Netta."

Montague bent and kissed the offered cheek. "What do you know of it?"

"Only what Catherine has told me." Mary bobbed her head at John's grandmother. "That a man took Netta from the backstage of my club." She pressed her lips into a hard line. "I'm sorry. My security will be improved immediately."

John rushed to his grandmother. "Did he say anything? Any hints on where he was taking her?"

She gave him the look he recognized so well, the one dripping with disappointment. "Of course he wouldn't say such a thing. Not to his kidnap victim nor to any witnesses."

John's heart twisted. Of course. It had been too much to hope for.

His grandmother tapped her walking stick into the

carpet. "Which was why I had to follow them to find out."

Chapter Thirty-One

Netta breathed through her mouth but couldn't escape the stench. She had thought that time would make her grow accustomed to the smells of the dairy, but after awaking several hours ago, the foul odor persisted. The smell, combined with the pounding in her head, made her stomach turn.

She pressed her bound wrists to her abdomen. She would not cast up her accounts. The sight and stench of that would only increase her nausea and it would become an endless, horrifying cycle.

"Is there anything to drink?" she asked the two men guarding her. She shifted on her spot on the ground and leaned back against the wall. "My mouth is quite parched."

Bob, as she'd found out her kidnapper was called, held up a jug of ale with a narrow-eyed smile and pressed it to his lips. He tilted it back then pulled it away with a huff.

His friend didn't look up from the bit of wood he was whittling. "We finished the last of it an hour ago."

Bob slammed the empty jug onto the small table the men sat at. "How much longer do we have to stay here? I tell you, I can ensure she won't be getting away, with or without anyone watching over her."

"Patience." The man, whose name Netta had never heard, lifted his stick to the light and examined it.

She would call him Roger, she decided, because he and the lot of them could go roger themselves.

"Besides," Roger said. "The boss won't be happy with the damage you've already done to her. You know he likes them untouched before he plays."

Netta bit back her gorge. She would save it. She wiped at the sweat rolling down her cheek with the back of her hand. When Sudworth came to her, she would be sick on him. Perhaps that would cool his ardor.

She looked around her prison, trying to slow her racing heart. The storage shed, although large enough to hold all the equipment for the dairy, contained no windows. Just because there was only the one door past her captors was no reason to panic.

"There is an easy solution to the problem of our collective thirst." She tried to infuse her voice with unconcern. As though she were knocked senseless and held captive every other week. "We are at a dairy, surrounded by animals heavy with milk."

Roger ran his tongue along his bottom lip. "Do you know how to milk a cow?" he asked Bob.

"Do I look like a farmer?" Bob sat back in his wooden chair and crossed his arms. "I was born and raised in London. I've always got my milk the sensible way. I buy it."

Netta sighed heavily. "It isn't difficult. All you have to do is get a bucket—"

"Shut up." Bob threw the empty jug, and she flattened herself to the floor as it crashed against the wall above her. Bits of clay rained down, and she curled into a ball.

"It's not a bad idea," Roger said. He looked at a stack of buckets in the corner then looked back at Bob.

He held up his hands. "I'm not milking no damn cow. Have you seen how big those animals are?"

Netta straightened and stretched her legs out, crossing them at the ankles. "They don't bite." Lord, she hoped they would bite these men. "Nor kick. Not like horses do, and you ride horses."

The men stared at each other.

"You're not frightened, are you?" She loosed a peal of laughter, trying to imbue it with every ounce of derision she could. "Two large men like you afraid to milk a cow. I suppose we'll just go thirsty then."

Bob climbed to his feet. "I'm not going thirsty." He strode over to her and grabbed the rope at her wrists, yanking her to her feet. "If you know so much about cows, you do it."

Netta swayed, her brain clouding from the abrupt change in position. She fought against the dizziness. This was what she'd wanted. A chance to escape. She wouldn't miss it by losing consciousness now.

"Of course. All I need is a bucket and a cow." She recited a nursery rhyme she'd learned from her nurse, Dollie, as a child. There had been something about milking a cow in it. If Little Miss Muffet could milk a beast, so could she.

Wait. That wasn't the right nursery rhyme. And it was a horrid little story at that.

Bob dragged her to the stack of buckets and shoved one at her.

She put on a show of trying to grab it with her bound hands. Her nails scrabbled against the rim before she dropped it. Giving him her best wide-eyed innocent look, she held up her bound wrists. "I can't hold it when my hands are tied so tight."

Bob kicked the bucket into her shin, and she couldn't hold back her cry.

She hopped up and down on one foot as the sting eased, glaring at the bastard.

"Sodding hell." Roger rose and tromped towards them. "We were told to watch her, not abuse her. Why do you feel the need to bully?"

"She knows what happened to my brother."

Roger put his hand on Bob's shoulder. "You don't know that for certain. How many times have I told you that if you want to get ahead, you have to use your head?"

"But—"

"No buts. You are responsible for your own success." He clasped both of Bob's shoulders and looked into his eyes. "Now, repeat after me. I am the master of my own future."

Bob's shoulders curled, but he repeated the mantra.

"I am in control of my destiny."

"I am in control of my destiny," Bob repeated.

Netta stared at the men in horrified fascination. The absurdity of the situation made her want to laugh, or perhaps that was hysteria setting in. As abductions went, this one had to be one of the strangest.

"Now, do you really think this tiny thing had anything to do with your brother going missing?" Roger turned Bob to face her. "It is only through logic and reason that a man will get ahead. Not by venting his spleen."

Bob grumbled. "I suppose not." He bent and swiped up the bucket. "Loosen her ropes, will you? But not too much." He curled one side of his lips. "That wouldn't be logical."

Roger untied her binds then retied them leaving several inches of rope stretched between her wrists. It wasn't what she had hoped for, but her mobility was better than before.

She grasped the bucket. "Shall I just follow my nose to the cows?"

"Come on." Bob pushed open the door and jerked his head. "Follow me."

Netta examined the bucket as she trailed after him. The other man followed behind, leaving her little room to flee. The bucket was large and unwieldy, but she didn't think it had enough heft to do any lasting damage. Perhaps if she hit a nose it would break.

But the men never stood within arm reach. They led her to a stable lined with cattle in their stalls and told her to pick one.

"Pick a cow?" All the cow faces looked the same. Black and white and staring at the trio with mild curiosity.

"The one that looks like it has the most milk." Bob waved her forwards. "I thought you'd done this before."

"Of course." She held the bucket tight to her belly. "Many times." She peeked over several stall doors, pretending to examine the animals. She nodded at the cow in the last pen. "This one."

Roger opened the stall door and thumped a low stool next to the cow.

"Thank you." Netta gently settled herself on the stool and stared at the swollen udder swinging from the animal. This couldn't be difficult. Children performed the task in the country. Step one was to place the bucket under the cow, and that was easily done. The animal seemed not to care that three humans invaded its space. It probably wanted to get back to sleep.

Roger hooked his elbows over the gate. "I heard you're moving," he said to Bob.

"Yeah." Bob slid his fingers into the top of his trousers. He rocked up onto his toes. "Me and Sally got ourselves a bigger house."

"Jesus, don't tell the boss that," Roger said. "He'll try to fob more cats on you."

They both shuddered.

Bob looked down at her. "Where's the milk?"

"Right." Netta rubbed her hands together as best she could. "One pail of milk coming up." She stared at the udder and kept rubbing her hands.

"Get on with it." Bob nudged her shoulder. "You do know what you're doing?"

She scowled over her shoulder. "Obviously I'm warming my hands so as not to startle the poor animal when I touch her."

Roger tittered. "Too right. No female likes her udders touched with cold hands. I can attest to that."

Bob guffawed with him.

Netta chafed her hands harder. Perhaps after she filled the bucket, she could turn it over their heads. Or maybe cause the cow to charge, knock the men down.

While the men still laughed at their insipid joke, Netta flattened her hands and brought them down sharply on the cow's side.

The animal didn't even blink, much less charge.

"Oy, what was that for?" Bob asked.

"Uh, slapping their sides help stimulate the milk production."

Roger nudged Bob. "Another way in which women are

like cows. My Sally likes herself a good—"

"What a charming story."

The deep voice made the hair on the back of her neck raise. She twisted, knowing who she was going to see but still unprepared for the cold chills that swamped her when she locked eyes with Sudworth.

His gaze flicked over her body, making her feel naked even though her gown covered everything. "Miss Muffet, Miss Muffet, sat on her tuffet." He showed all his teeth with his grin.

Why did everyone think Miss Muffet milked a cow? Was there a second stanza to the rhyme she was forgetting? Or was Sudworth as poorly versed in children's literature as she?

He cocked his arm on the stall door. "I guess that makes me your spider."

She swallowed.

She really hated that nursery rhyme.

Chapter Thirty-Two

Netta stood, stumbling back until her shoulders pressed against the wall. "Why?"

She couldn't think of anything else to say. It made no sense why he'd taken her. There had never been affection for her on his part. He'd married and buried a wife in the passing years. She was no longer young enough to capture his perverse interest.

There could only be one reason for his actions. He wanted Eleanor. Netta raised her chin, keeping her expression hard. She would die before she agreed to deliver her sister to the bastard.

Sudworth flicked his fingers at her, and Bob grabbed her arm.

Netta planted her feet, but he dragged her through the straw covering the floor. He gripped the back of her neck and shoved her close to his employer.

Sudworth tugged off one glove and traced the lump on her forehead.

Netta jerked her head back, wincing at the throb of pain.

Sudworth frowned. "That wasn't supposed to happen. All punishments belong to me."

"Punishments?" She released a shuddering breath. She had the feeling that Sudworth's punishments were something best avoided at all costs.

He caressed her cheek with the back of his fingers. "You didn't think I would forget the insult, did you?" He gripped her jaw, and squeezed. "I never forget. I will take what is mine."

The first streaks of daybreak brightened the high windows of the stables. The light caught in his eyes, making them shimmer, like he was a beast from hell.

Netta tried to jerk her head from his grip, but he only tightened his fingers until she could feel them dig into her gums.

He was mad. Only an insane man could think that he could buy girls. Hurt them on his whim. That he could get away with such behavior.

He dragged his hand down her neck and squeezed her windpipe. He allowed her just enough air to stay conscious, but not enough to keep her lungs from burning.

Netta closed her eyes, gasping. He wouldn't get away with it. Whatever he did to her, he would pay. Sudworth's vengeance might have lain rotting and twisted for six years, but John's would be swift.

He loved her; this she knew. The feeling had come on so gradually it was hard to pinpoint when she knew. But she understood the look in his eyes when he gazed upon her. It mirrored her own. And when John cared for someone, he wouldn't let anything stop him from meting out justice on their behalf.

She only wished she would be alive to see it.

He pressed his cheek to hers and whispered in her ear. "After I fuck you in every hole you have, I'm going to find your sister and do the same to her."

She lashed out, swinging her arms as hard as she could.

He chuckled at the impact.

She kicked and clawed, knowing how pointless it was to struggle but doing it regardless.

He squeezed harder, blocking her air entirely.

She tried to scream, but no sound emerged. Dark spots danced in her eyes. Her ears rang. Her lungs burned. The faint popping sounds must have been the bones in her neck finally giving way.

"What the hell?" Sudworth dropped her to the ground.

She landed hard on her shoulder, but barely noticed the

pain as sweet air scraped past her raw throat into her lungs. The pungent odor of the cows didn't even smell bad to her grateful nose. She drew in another deep breath.

A new scent followed that of dung.

"Fire!" one of the men yelled. He ran past her, his legs indistinct in the smoke.

Netta pulled herself to the corner and sat up. She blinked, but the smoke only grew thicker. Only...it didn't smell of burning wood. And it didn't hurt to breathe, though it did make her eyes water like the dickens.

A figure loomed from the darkness, reaching for her. Sudworth's fingers clawed along her shoulder, and she rolled away.

He grabbed her leg, feeling his way up her body, until suddenly, he was gone.

His curses ended with a pained shriek.

Netta waved the air in front of her, trying to clear it, but she could see nothing.

But she knew instantly it was John when he slid his arms around her back and under her knees, lifting her against his chest. "I have you." She felt the words rumble from his chest. "Don't let go."

She looped her bound wrists around his neck. The tears rolling down her cheek weren't just from the smoke. Silly man. Don't let go? Didn't he know he was well and truly stuck with her? He'd found her. She was never letting go again.

An eerie silence descended as he carried her from the stables. As the smoke thinned, she saw why. Bob and Roger knelt on the dirt outside, four pistols drawn on them. Each of John's friends stood sentinel, cloth-wrapped goggles covering their eyes.

Netta blinked. The goggles were an odd accessory for the aristocrats.

Netta turned to John to ask, and a startled 'eep' slipped past her lips at his own owlish gaze.

He set her on her feet and swept off the goggles. "Something I made for my work with chemicals. To protect the eyes."

She looked from them, to the smoke drifting through the open doors. "It isn't a fire, is it?"

"No. A mixture I developed that clouds the vision." He made quick work of the rope at her wrists, gently chaffing them after tossing the bindings to the ground. "Useful when you're the only one who can see."

Steel glinted in the dawn. "Useful, but not foolproof." Sudworth stepped from the shadows and pointed his pistol at Netta's head. "You should have made sure I stayed down."

John didn't take his eyes off her face. He gave her a small, secret smile. "A circumstance that will soon be remedied."

Sudworth swiveled to aim at John.

"Don't!" Netta stepped forwards, ignoring John's raised hand. The muzzle of the gun was inches from his head. Too close to miss. "Don't hurt him. I'll...I'll go with you. Let us away and no one need be hurt."

John's gaze flicked upwards and he sighed. "Darling, do you truly–" He ducked his head and spun, slamming his shoulder into Sudworth's midsection. The gun fired, a chip of wood from the stables splintering from the bullet's impact, and Netta clapped her hands over her ringing ears.

The men hit the ground. John bent Sudworth's arm back over his head, forcing him to drop his weapon, and pressed a knife against the man's throat.

Netta leaned against the wall of the building, her legs weak. Between one breath and the next, John had ended the threat.

The Duke of Montague strolled over and leveled his own pistol at Sudworth. "I don't believe I've seen that move before. You'll have to show it to me next time we're at Gentleman Jack's."

Slowly, John rolled off of his opponent. His eyes found Netta's, a wildness she seldom saw in them fading. "–think that I would allow you to go off with him?" he finished as though an assault hadn't just take place between the first and second part of his sentence. "I'm wounded. I thought you knew me better than that."

Netta pushed off the wall and launched herself at him. Nothing had ever felt so good as his body pressed against hers. Even the jeweled cravat pin jabbing into her breast didn't lessen the pleasure of feeling wrapped safely in her arms.

"I love you," she said between kisses to his face, "more than you can ever know."

"All the women I rescue say such." But he gripped her closer.

She slapped his arm. "Do not play with me now. You could have died. *I* could have died. This whole wonderful jumble you've brought to my life could have been over."

He cupped her face between his hands, his thumbs wiping away her tears. "I wouldn't let that happen. There are still too many games in our future, poppet."

"You think you've won." Even lying on his back, Sudworth managed to look condescending. "Liverpool and I have reached an agreement. He won't try me for any crimes. You might have saved Miss Evered today, but I won't be out of your lives anytime soon. Don't get too comfortable with your whore; you won't have her around for long."

Netta shuddered.

John kissed her forehead. "I need you to go with my friends now. They'll take you home to your sister."

He stepped away and peeled out of his jacket.

She frowned. "What are you talking about? I'm not leaving you."

"You'll see me soon enough." He winked.

She crossed her arms over her chest. She didn't care how charming he was, she wasn't budging. When she let the infuriating man out of her sight, bad things tended to happen.

"Dunkeld!" John called.

The burly Scotsman lumbered towards them.

"Give the man your knife, will you? I know you carry a

great big one on your person." He flipped his own knife in his hands, the blade glinting in the early sun. "Never let it be said this wasn't a fair fight."

Realization dawned. "No. You aren't doing this. This isn't happening."

Montague slid his pistol into the front of his breeches. "I'll stay. Just in case."

"Thank you." John motioned for Sudworth to come to his feet.

Dunkeld tossed an eight-inch blade to the dirt in front of the man.

"Do you hear me, John?" Netta out-and-out stamped her foot. This was absurd. They had just barely escaped with their lives; it made no sense to risk his again. "I won't allow it."

"Dunkeld, another favor?" John pointed to her.

"Sorry, miss." Dunkeld shrugged, then placed his hands on her waist and tossed her over his shoulder.

She pounded the man's back. "Put me down!"

He hefted her higher.

Pressing her palms into his coat, she pushed up. John was facing off with Sudworth, Montague standing off to the side. Rothchild and Sutton each prodded their prisoners to their feet and followed after Netta and Dunkeld.

Leaving John to fight for his life.

"You sorry, whey-faced, unfeeling cur!" She resumed her useless beating. "Stop at once. We can't just leave him!"

Dunkeld carefully placed her inside a carriage and climbed in after her. He blocked her easily when she lunged for the door. "I'm sorry. But some things aren't fit for a woman to see."

She scrambled for the opposite door, but it stood firm against her attempts to open it. She wrenched the window down and the first full light of day fell on her face.

Dunkeld grabbed the back of her dress and pulled her back. "Please, don't make me restrain you. I would like to remain friends after today."

She gaped at him. "Friends? Isn't John your friend? How

can you let him do this?" Either John would die or he would kill. And she wasn't certain this killing could be legally justified.

The man tugged at his auburn queue before pushing it back over his shoulder. "What else can he do? Sudworth has made a direct threat against you. If he hadn't, we might have persuaded John to follow another path. But as it is..." He shrugged. "If the government won't prosecute him for his crimes, justice is only to be found in one way."

She dug her fingers into the fabric of her skirts. They still trembled. What he said made sense. Sudworth would remain a danger against her, against John. Against her sister.

Netta closed her eyes as the tremors spread to the rest of her body.

John was going to kill a man. And that was the best outcome she could hope for.

Dunkeld pounded on the ceiling. "Driver!"

Her eyes flew open. "Wait!" She grabbed his sleeve. "Please. Let us wait here. I want to know...need to know, as soon as possible, that John hasn't been..."

Dunkeld squeezed her hand, the heat from his skin doing little to warm her chilled flesh. "All right," he said quietly. "We'll wait. Stand down," he yelled to the driver.

Netta strained her ears, terrified of what she might hear, but becoming even more frightened at the silence. Had they decided not to fight? Could Sudworth have been convinced to leave them be?

Minutes passed. Netta's foot bobbed. Her hands clenched and unclenched. Her body felt ready to burst with the need to escape the carriage, fly to John.

She waited until she wanted to scream. And then she waited some more.

The door was wrenched open. John's gaze fell hungrily on her, the haunted shadows vanishing when she tumbled into his arms, her knees wrapping about his hips.

She held him tight, her breath not evening out until she was assured that the heartbeat pounding against hers was strong and steady.

She threaded her fingers into his hair, loving the silky caress of it against her skin. She yanked his head back and scowled down at him. "Mark my words. You will pay for putting me through that."

Chapter Thirty-Three

John climbed into his landau and adjusted his top hat. He kicked his boot onto the opposite seat and watched as the front door to Netta's apartments eased closed.

He sniffed. Another lovely night and even better morning. He'd worried that Eleanor's presence might interfere with his and Netta's relationship after she'd officially become Netta's ward, but the chit had turned out to be surprisingly pleasant company.

No, he and Netta could no longer play one of their games in the parlor or any other public room, but keeping their bed sport in the bedroom hadn't diminished the heat between them.

Everything was turning out the way he wanted. He crossed his arms and dropped his chin to his chest. So why did he feel more and more disgruntled each time he left her?

"Sir?" Wil turned from the driver's seat.

"What?"

"Your club?" Wil bobbed his head at the door to Simon's. "You did want to come here after Miss Evered's."

John scowled. He still hadn't become used to the sound of the name Evered. Netta LeBlanc didn't sound much better, though infinitely preferable to Pickle. "I know what I want." He kicked open the door and jumped down. The sneaking suspicion that he had no clue what he wanted only angered him more.

"Come, have a drink with me," he told Wil.

His friend set the brake and climbed down. "Don't want

to be alone with your thoughts?"

John knocked his shoulder into the man as he passed. He hated when his friends were right. He hated even more that he couldn't pinpoint why he'd been feeling so out of sorts lately. He was the man who could examine a situation from all sides. Look at a problem dispassionately, analyze all the factors.

Why couldn't he figure out what *his* problem was?

He led Wil down a carpeted hallway, past the billiards room, to the small smoking room near the rear.

He paused on the threshold. "Oh, good Lord, the whole circus is in town."

Four sets of eyes swiveled in his direction.

Montague raised his glass of whisky. "Summerset! We were just speaking of you."

Rothchild puffed on his cheroot. "Speaking of you, laughing at you, close enough."

Sutton and Dunkeld greeted Wil as John plodded to the sideboard and poured him and Wil drinks. He added another finger of liquor to his glass.

He handed Wil his drink then dropped into an armchair. He took a large swallow, enjoying the burn. "I'm glad I could provide entertainment for my friends. Might I ask the cause?"

"Your bloody blindness when it comes to your woman." Dunkeld snorted. "We thought you were supposed to be the charmer of the group."

The back of John's neck flushed hot. "I don't know what you're talking about. Everything is lovely between me and Netta. And I am always charming." He'd charmed Netta from her stays just that morning.

Rothchild pulled a folded piece of paper from his pocket. He added some more folds, concentrating on the angles. "If everything is lovely, then why have you been acting as though there were a hot poker between your arse cheeks these past weeks?" He raised his hand and made the paper sail through the air to land in John's lap.

John blinked at him.

Rothchild grinned. "Something I learned in the East."

Grumbling, John unfolded it. "You bent my deed!" He tried to smooth the creases from the paper.

"It's still legal." Rothchild blew a smoke circle into the air. "And you're welcome."

"Thanks," John grunted. He folded the paper the correct way and slid it in his pocket. It felt good having Robert's deed back in his hands. Rothchild had needed to wait until Liverpool's men had stopped watching Sudworth's home before retrieving the document, but John had known his friend would succeed. He had been the retrieval expert of their group for a reason.

With the paper in their possession and witnesses who would swear he had won it back at a game of hazards, Robert should be back in his home in no time. John had already sent a note to Hampson to direct the mines to be reopened.

"Your brother will be here shortly," Sutton said. "You can give him his property then."

"Perfect. We can have a party."

Montague sighed. "Has he been like this all morning?" he asked Wilberforce.

"All week." Wil leaned against the side table. "Every time he leaves her apartments he's as surly as a dog without his bone."

"Are her new apartments not to your liking?" Sutton asked.

"They're the height of fashion." He stared into his whisky. "I decorated them myself."

"You're not tiring of this one already, are you?" Rothchild asked.

John leveled the other earl with an iron-tipped glare.

"Why don't you tell us what the problem is." Montague crossed one leg over the other and rested his chin on his fist.

"I have no problem."

Silent seconds ticked by.

John tugged on his waistcoat. "I don't think two women

should live alone, is all. I'm concerned about Netta and her sister."

"Where else would your mistress live?" Montague asked.

"Well...with me. It worked before with Netta in my house." He blew out a deep breath as realization dawned. That was why he didn't like leaving her apartments. She should be with him. With two different residences, they were losing time travelling between, time that could be spent together.

"Wouldn't it be awkward having your mistress and her sister in your house?" Montague seemed to emphasize the word mistress in his questions, and the sound grated on John. "How will you explain their presence in your home? Will she hide away whenever a guest comes around?"

"She will receive callers with me, of course." The idea blossomed in his mind. He never should have rented those rooms for her. She should have remained with him all along. "And no one will dare question her presence."

His friends carefully looked at each other.

"What?" His voice held a bite.

"It might not be my place to say—" Wil began.

"Then don't."

"—but it sounds like what you want is a wife, not a mistress."

"A wife?" Outrage oozed from John's voice even as the word settled into his bones.

A wife.

He wasn't the marrying sort.

He told his friends that. "I don't want the legal trappings you all seem so eager to bind yourselves in. I only want to be with her every day, share her company at dinner, take her to balls, and wake up to her smile in the morning."

"Share intimate chats with her, discuss your days?" Sutton asked.

"Of course." No one could make him laugh about life's absurdities like Netta.

"Be there for her when she's sick or distraught, and have her support when you are afflicted?" Dunkeld asked.

"That goes without saying." If Netta needed him, he would let nothing prevent him from being by her side.

"What do you think marriage is, man?" Montague shook his head, exasperated. "Your preconceptions of the institution border on idiocy. It's not a trap. Nor a chain. It's about making the best life you can with the woman you love. Our prince might be able to live with his mistress, but you won't be able to do the same in our society, not without subjecting Netta to scorn and derision."

John's knuckles whitened around his glass. He couldn't let Netta face contempt, not if he could prevent it. And he did want her forever. He had no concerns of ever changing his mind about that.

Would a wife be so bad?

He took a sip of whisky. A wife. He could work with a wife, as long as it was Netta filling the position.

His muscles relaxed. The decision felt right. Comforting almost.

There would be mocking from his friends, of course. He'd besmirched the institution for so long he would deserve their ridicule. That wouldn't be a problem.

The problem was Netta. She desired marriage even less than he had.

"Of course, we must look at it from her side." Sutton picked through a bowl of nuts and popped one in his mouth. "She is an aspiring actress. A husband could get in the way of her career."

The other men nodded.

"I wouldn't interfere with her career," John objected. "Not if it's what she wants to do."

"Stage managers might worry that as a married woman she could go into confinement during a production." Rothchild rubbed his jaw.

"Confinement." John's head went light. Children. That was a frightening thought.

"And of course there is the possibility that she'll find someone she prefers better." Dunkeld snorted. "As much as our friend might pretend differently, he is not the pinnacle of desire for all womankind."

And that thought was the most frightening of all. He remembered how her former stage manager had looked at her. Men would be throwing themselves at her feet, left and right. Of course, it was up to him to keep her so happy she'd want to stay with him. But he couldn't ignore the gnawing feeling that if he wanted to keep her, and he did, he needed to make their arrangement definite. Permanent.

He examined the problem from all angles. And the best way to solve it was marriage.

"Right." He set his glass down and adjusted the knot of his cravat. "That's it then. I'm getting married."

His friends raised their glasses.

"About damn time," Montague said.

"Don't you need to ask the lady first?" Wil pointed out.

John snorted. "Ask Netta? Give her the chance to say no? How simple do you think I am?" He settled into his chair and steepled his fingers. Now that he'd made the decision, he wouldn't allow for anything less than success. With Netta, he needed to be clever. And sneaky.

Robert knocked on the open door. "Room for one more?"

John blinked at his brother, an idea forming.

Robert fell back a step. "What? What is that look?"

"You, my dear brother, are going to help me get Netta to the altar."

"Lovely." Rothchild tilted his head. "Robert, I don't suppose you are in need of some companionship. Something warm and adorable to curl up to at night?"

A line creased Robert's forehead. "What? What in the world does this have to do with my brother's wedding?"

"Nothing at all." John glared at Rothchild. "You still haven't found homes for all those cats you took from Sudworth's house?"

"Three kittens remain without a home." Rothchild pressed his lips together. "They shed most abominably." He shot Robert a hopeful glance. "Although I'm certain they'll grow out of it."

"Forget the damn cats." John stood. He removed the deed from his pocket and smacked it into his brother's abdomen. "We have a plot to hatch."

***

"Are you certain this is a good idea?" Netta peered out the carriage window, her nerves rising the closer they drew to John's house. "I had promised to stay out of John's family affairs." Not that she necessarily intended to abide by her promise. But John had been acting oddly ever since she'd moved out of his house. She'd thought to wait until things settled between them before interfering.

Robert and Catherine, Dowager Marchioness of Mallen, shared a look. "We're certain," Catherine said. "This reconciliation can only occur with your presence."

"All...right." Netta shifted on the seat. First her sister had been acting suspicious that morn, and now John's family. Was there something in the air?

The carriage pulled to a stop and the three of them climbed down. Netta's heart panged as she swept through the front door. She missed John's home. The apartments he'd let for her were sumptuous, and she lacked for nothing.

But it didn't feel like home. Not like this townhouse did.

She removed her hat and handed it to the butler. "Where is this reconciliation to take place?" And how angry would John be with the three of them showing up like an attack force?

"On the gazebo in the garden." Catherine hobbled forwards, putting her weight heavily on her walking stick.

Netta took the woman's other arm. "The garden seems an odd location."

"Not for what we have in mind." There was a hint of smugness in the woman's tone.

Netta worried her bottom lip. Just what did they have in store for John?

They made their way outside, Netta scanning the ground

for any obstacles for the older woman to avoid. A titter of laughter made her head snap up.

John's friends, her sister, and—Netta squinted—was that a vicar? stood beside the gazebo.

"What is going on?" She looked for John but didn't see him.

Eleanor rushed to her side and clasped her hands. "I'm so happy for you!" She threw her arms around Netta's neck. "The Countess of Summerset. How lovely that sounds."

Netta tugged free. "What are you going on about? I'm not..." The presence of the clergyman started to make sense. Netta fisted her hands on her hips and tilted her head to the sky. "John!"

"Yes, my love?" he said from behind her.

She spun. "Don't 'my love' me. You have some explaining to do."

"What?" He widened those beautiful blue eyes. "This? I thought you would enjoy the spontaneity of our wedding instead of a more drawn-out affair."

She grabbed his elbow and dragged him to the side. "Is this a joke? We've never spoken of marriage before." He'd led her to believe he was solidly against the idea. Before she'd met him, she hadn't been so fond of it, either.

He tucked her hand under his elbow. "We've discussed having a long-term relationship."

"Yes, but—"

"And we already spend all our nights together."

"Of course, but—"

"And everyone here would be so disappointed if there was no wedding. Our friends dressed in their Sunday best just for us." He led her to the gazebo and up the steps. "Not to mention the cost of the special license that would be lost if you refused."

She paused at the top of the stairs. Her brow knitted. It sounded as though he thought she'd refuse. That he needed to convince her to marry him. and putting her on the spot like this was his sneaky way of getting her to agree.

Yes, she'd told him she had no interest in marriage, but

that was because she'd never met the man who was her equal. Marriage to John wouldn't be a cage; he gave her wings.

There were still practicalities to be discussed, however.

"My sister—"

"Will become like my own. Schooling if she wishes it, and an obscenely large dowry, of course."

Netta pressed her lips together, striving to keep them from curling up. The devious bounder. He would have given Eleanor that in any case, they both knew it. But his flagrant attempts at manipulation did something queer to her heart.

Well, he wasn't the only one who could manipulate the situation.

"I don't know." She sighed. "It's such a big step. And *permanent*. Marriage doesn't favor women in our day and age."

John ran his hand up the back of his head. "Yes, you lose all your rights and property by marrying, but think of it logically. You have very little property to lose. And so much to gain," he argued. "You'll have a wardrobe full of new gowns and Pomfret cakes in every bowl in the house."

She tapped her finger against her lips. "True. Those are definite benefits. But the disadvantages..."

"As my mistress, you are set up in apartments several miles away."

"Very nice apartments."

He frowned. "Be that as it may, as my wife, you'll live under my roof. Have access to this body day and night."

Her lips lost their battle and twitched. "It is a fine body. But a woman in my position needs to take care."

John widened his stance and crossed his arms over his chest. His lavender jacket stretched divinely over his wide shoulders. "Name your terms, you mercenary minx."

Netta rolled onto her toes, her heartbeat racing in her chest. She was marrying the man she loved. There was nothing more she wanted.

Well...no need to be hasty.

"I might not be able to own my own property in England, but the laws aren't the same around the world." She pursed her lips. "I think I'd like my own house. A chateau perhaps, in the south of France."

"Done."

She arched her eyebrows. He gave in so easily. He must want her badly.

"And all my earnings shall go into a trust for Eleanor. A dowry is all well and good, but I want her to have independence in case she decides not to marry."

He nodded. "And I'll place matching funds in with your wages."

Her heart melted. "You are determined." She waved a hand at the flowers woven through the top of the gazebo. "You could have just asked instead of going through these games."

"Why give you the opportunity to return me an answer I don't like." He grinned. "Say you'll marry me. You know you want to."

She thought about making him suffer longer. Making a few more demands. But her excitement burbled out of her. "Yes! Yes, I'll marry you."

Her sister whooped from the lawn.

John swept her up and bent her over his arm. "You'll never regret it," he said just before crushing his mouth to hers.

She wrapped her arms around his shoulders and gave back as good as she got. She would make sure she didn't. She wouldn't wait for John to keep her happy; she would grab onto joy with both hands. She'd keep John on his toes, make sure he never went a day without smiling.

That he never went a day without making her moan.

Her parents had been poor examples for married life, but Netta knew what she wanted.

An equal partnership. Trust. Love. Fun. All elements they would have to work at to maintain, but no job would ever be so satisfying.

"There are children present," someone shouted from the

garden. She thought it was the duke.

They broke apart, each sucking down air.

"Are you certain you want this?" she asked. "Because once you say *I do*, there will be no going back. I won't accept anything less than a perfect marriage."

He tucked a lock of her hair behind her ear. "I'm certain. I love you Netta Pickle, Antoinette LeBlanc, Agnes Evered."

"You forgot Ned."

He shuddered. "And allow me to continue forgetting that particular alias."

She dug her teeth in her bottom lip. She was smiling so wide her cheeks hurt. "Consider Ned retired."

"All those days when I thought I was teaching you how to be a lady." He snorted. "And it was you teaching me the whole time."

She hooked her finger at the top button of his waistcoat and tugged him close. "What? What did I teach you?"

He cupped her cheek. "That love is the biggest game of all.

"And when it comes to games, you know I always play to win."

Epilogue

Three months later...

"Plum tart?" Netta held up a half-full platter of the pastries, crumbs dusting her lower lip.

John's groin tightened. He had licked every inch of her body just that morning, but damn if he didn't want to taste the tart right from her lips.

He glared at the party around his breakfast table. The very large party. Why the bloody blazes did all his friends insist on coming round to his townhouse for Saturday breakfast? Ever since he and Netta had returned from their bridal tour a month past, the parasites had come each week to eat him out of house and home.

A new tradition, Elizabeth had called it.

Bugger tradition.

John lifted a female urchin from the seat next to Netta and plopped her in her father's lap, taking her place. He accepted the tart. "Thank you." He squeezed his wife's thigh to emphasize the point. Then slid his palm a little higher.

Netta peeled his hand off of her. "Children present," she murmured. "Later."

John scowled and stabbed his fork into the tart. "Why do you people insist on laying siege to my home each week? Can't we have these breakfasts at someone else's house?"

Montague bucked his knee, making his daughter squeal as she held on for the ride. "No," he said. "Because then we'd never see you and Netta. You wouldn't make an appearance."

John sniffed. Sometimes it was unfortunate that his friends knew him so well.

"Were you hired for the role of Desdemona?" Colleen asked Netta. "Weren't you to try out for the role this Tuesday?"

"The manager asked me to come back for another audition next week." Netta blew out a breath. "I think he liked my performance but it was hard to tell."

"Of course, he liked it." John rested his hand on the back of her chair and toyed with the curl of hair on her back. "You are a superlative actress."

"Aww." Elizabeth gave Montague a significant look. "When was the last time you gave me such a compliment. You could learn something from your friend."

"They are newly married," Montague protested. "For the first year, men say all sorts of nonsense. Besides"—he dipped his chin and raised one eyebrow—"I show you praise in many other ways."

His wife turned pink. "That wasn't what I meant."

"And my compliment has nothing to do with its proximity to my wedding." Judith leapt onto John's lap, and he fed her a bit of ham. "Thirty years from now Netta will still be a superlative actress, and I will freely tell her so."

Netta placed her hand on his leg and leaned into him. "Thank you, husband."

Sure, she could stroke *his* leg in a crowded room without consequence. He took a sip of coffee. Perhaps tonight he could create a consequence. A naughty, wanton consequence. His lips twitched, a new game forming in his mind.

Three months into his marriage, and he couldn't be more satisfied. She gave him a reason to smile each day. She kept him on his toes. And their bed sport only got better and better.

He rubbed his thumb along her hand. Netta had been

nothing but encouraging when he'd reopened his laboratory. He had months of reading to become *au courant* on the state of chemistry today, but getting his burners lit again had felt right.

He was creating again, playing with the elements, striving for new formulas for a stronger steel. He walked into his laboratory each day with a smile on his face.

He tapped his thumb against his thigh. It was a joy practicing chemistry once more, but something was missing and he didn't know what. A slight sense of restlessness was the only stain on his happiness. He enjoyed working in his laboratory, but he didn't feel the same passion for it he once had.

Wil popped his head into the breakfast room. "I—"

A jumble of children, already finished with their meal, raced past, knocking into his legs, sending him off-balance.

He stumbled into the door jamb.

John grinned. It was amusing when it happened to somebody else. "Something I can do for you?" he asked.

Wil straightened his cravat. "I'm just going out. I might be gone for a couple of days."

John knitted his brow. "Why? Has something happened?"

"I don't rightly know." Wil hooked his thumb under one of his braces. "I met a man in a bit of trouble, and I thought I might try to help him out."

"Another stray?" At least Wil hadn't brought the poor sot home this time.

"Not according to him." Wil shook his head. "He says he was a prince of Naples, though he doesn't look the part now. Moth-eaten clothes, wild hair, but there's something about his bearing." He shrugged. "I'm curious."

"What's he doing here?" Netta asked, planting her elbows on the table and settling in.

John pressed his leg against hers. She did love a good story.

"He says he had to flee after the Congress of Vienna,

but fears foreign agents are after him." Wil blew out a breath. "His face looked to have taken a recent beating, but the dangers might all be in his head."

"Foreign agents?" Sutton looked around the table. "Should we speak with Liverpool about this?"

"The prime minister has completely cut us out of his confidence." John pressed his lips together. "I suspect he doesn't believe that we don't know where Sudworth disappeared to."

"How shocking," Montague said dryly.

"Besides, as Wil says, the man might be deranged. We can't go to Liverpool with the ravings of a lunatic." Nor did John want to. If he ever learned anything that threatened the nation, he would notify the proper authorities, of course. But other than that he no longer desired an association with the Crown. That part of his life was done.

"He says he has proof." Wil tapped the door frame and straightened. "I intend to try to convince him to show it to me."

"And if you can't convince him, perhaps we can discover the truth in other ways." John ran his hand up the back of his head. The possibilities were endless.

"Do you need a retrieval expert?" Rothchild asked. He shrugged at the questioning look Amanda gave to him. "What? My skills are available for the next few days."

Wil turned his hat about in his hands. "That's very kind of you, my lord—"

"Mine, too." Dunkeld raised his hand like a school boy. "My fists didn't get nearly enough exercise rounding up Sudworth's men. I'm available too."

"Lord Dunkeld, while I appreciate the offer—"

"Wouldn't it be nice," John said, interrupting Wil, "if we had some sort of organization to provide us with jobs we might want to take on from time to time. Something to alleviate the tedium of our conversations on what little Marcus ate for dinner and what crops are yielding the most this year?"

"I hope you are not saying you find my company dull already?" Netta asked sweetly. "Because there might be repercussions to you if that were so."

He leaned over and pressed a kiss to her soft cheek. "Of course not, darling. You could never be dull."

Elizabeth glared at him. "I am not the type of mother who talks about what her children eat each day."

John pursed his lips but remained silent. Let her believe what made her happy.

"And crop yields are immensely fascinating," Winnifred said. "Why our barley has—"

Dunkeld cupped her shoulder. "Dear, while agriculture is a topic of endless interest to me and to your scientific mind, not all feel such. Especially not these simple-minded louts."

"I take Summerset's point." Montague drummed his fingers on the table. "I do miss feeling of service to a country in need. Perhaps...we could turn our skills to individuals who need assistance."

"A private agency?" Sutton raised his eyebrows. "For what? Spying? Detecting?"

"Either." John's blood pulsed through his veins. A private agency. A place to exercise their talents, indulge their lust for adventures without any restraints from Liverpool. And to help people, of course. "Both. Whatever we want to make of it."

Rothchild stood. "I propose Wil's friend be our first client. I'll accompany him and speak to the man. See what sort of assistance we can provide."

Wil rubbed the back of his neck. "Truly, it isn't necessary. And the man isn't a friend, just someone I noticed who—"

"This agency will need more people than just us." John twirled a lock of Netta's hair around his finger. "We don't want to do the drudge work, after all. I say we put Wil in charge of hiring more men. He's good at getting people to do as he wants."

His friend narrowed his eyes.

"Come, come," John chided him. "It won't be difficult. We still have many contacts from our time working for the Crown. I'm sure for the right amount of blunt they'd be happy to go private."

"The difficulty of the task wasn't what I objected to. Sir."

John merely grinned at him. The idea was marvelous. Why hadn't any of them thought of it before. Yes, they all had wives and families now and didn't have the time to make it a full-time occupation, but a little intrigue on the side?

Now that was damn near perfect.

Elizabeth clapped her hands together. "This sounds wonderful. I can't wait to start my first assignment."

Montague's face blanched. "Well..."

"I'd be happy to manage the books for this endeavor," Colleen said. "And if any clandestine meetings need to occur, The Black Rose will be available for such assignations."

Sutton swallowed. "You're a fine bookkeeper, and on that we can have no objection. But I would like to keep threats to our club, and to you, at a minimum."

Winnifred ran her finger down Dunkeld's chest. "I do hope," she said, her voice silky, "you gentlemen aren't planning on keeping this agency all to yourselves. When you gave us your vows, there was an implied promise to share your lives with us."

"And it isn't as though any of us are unaccustomed to a little danger," Amanda said firmly. "We want in."

Rothchild grasped the back of her chair and leaned over his wife's shoulder. "*Et tu, Brute?*"

She patted his hand and bit her lip to keep from smiling.

John turned to Netta as she placed another plum tart on her plate. "You have remained suspiciously quiet. I hope that means you have no interest in this venture."

She licked a spot of sugar off her thumb. "Not at all. It means that I have no worries about carrying my point. You will need someone as multi-talented as I, someone who can play any role, take any part." The smile she gave him was all smug assurance, and it stole his breath as it always did. "I and the rest of us ladies will be involved in this agency." She leaned close and whispered in his ear, "And you will love every minute of it."

Her breath fluttering past his skin made his groin pull tight. Yes, when she wasn't turning his hair grey from worry, Netta would undoubtably give him much to savor.

The little minx would be a benefit to the agency, as would all the women. They all had skills to bring to the table, and a lick of excitement hummed in John's chest at the idea of working side-by-side with the intoxicating woman next to him.

He caught the eyes of the men around the table. His friends. His family.

To a man, each of them found it difficult to say no to their women...especially when their wives were right to demand their share in life. Their share in excitement and intrigue.

They would ensure their safety, of course. Keep them away from the largest dangers.

Netta popped another bite of tart in her mouth, her lips curving mischievously as she chewed, her eyes glowing with humor. She bobbed her eyebrows and winked.

John's stomach spiraled to the floor.

He didn't know who he felt worse for. Himself for thinking he could control any bit of this woman, or the unlucky bounders she was about to be unleashed upon.

God have mercy on them all.

* * * *

About the Author

Like almost one-third of all romance writers, Alyson Chase is a former attorney. (Seriously, what is with all of us disillusioned lawyers?) She happily ditched those suits and now works in her pajamas writing about men's briefs instead of legal briefs. When she's not writing, she's probably engaged in one of her favorite hobbies: napping, eating, or martial arts. (That last one almost makes up for the first two, right?) She also writes humorous, small-town, contemporary romance novels under the name Allyson Charles

Connect with Alyson at:

www.alysonchase.com
www.facebook.com/AlysonChaseAuthor
Twitter: @1alysonchase
Email: alysonchaseauthor@gmail.com